HEAT SHOCK

BY ROBERT GREER

Isolation and Other Stories

Limited Time

The Devil's Backbone

The Devil's Red Nickel

The Devil's Hatband

HEAT SHOCK

ROBERT GREER

PRESS

Published by Warner Books

An AOL Time Warner Company

AUTHOR'S NOTE

The characters, events, and places that are depicted in *Heat Shock* are spawned from the author's imagination. Certain Western locales are used fictitiously, and any resemblance between the novel's fictional inhabitants and actual persons, living or dead, is purely coincidental.

Copyright © 2003 by Robert O. Greer

Mysterious Press Books are published by Warner Books, Inc., 1271 Avenue of the Americas, New York, NY 10020.

Visit our Web site at www.twbookmark.com.

Ⓦ An AOL Time Warner Company

The Mysterious Press name and logo are registered trademarks of Warner Books, Inc.

Printed in the United States of America

First Printing: October 2003

10 9 8 7 6 5 4 3 2 1

Library of Congress Cataloging-in-Publication Data

Greer, Robert O.
    Heat shock / Robert Greer.
        p. cm.
    ISBN 0-89296-753-6
    1. Vietnamese American women—Fiction. 2. Uranium mines and mining—Fiction. 3. Emergency physicians—Fiction. 4. Cancer—Patients—Fiction. 5. Women physicians—Fiction. 6. Game fowl—Fiction. 7. Colorado—Fiction. I. Title.

PS3557.R3997H43 2003
813'.54—dc21   2003046306

For my darling wife, Phyllis.
Departed now,
but always and forever
the light and love of my life.

ACKNOWLEDGMENTS

I owe an extreme debt of gratitude to my overburdened secretary, Kathleen Hoernig, who helped me run a literary magazine and a busy surgical pathology practice while the manuscript of *Heat Shock* was being completed. Her support in typing the manuscript and readying it for my editor was yeomanly. Finally, I would like to thank Connie Oehring for her keen literary and copy editor's eye, and Scot and Mercedes Ross, and the crew at Red Hill Motorcycle Werx for sharing their knowledge and mechanical insights.

HEAT SHOCK

Evolution is a messy business.

—STEPHEN JAY GOULD

CHAPTER

1

Luke Redstone had experienced every imaginable form of pain during his sixty-nine years, but nothing approached the deep, visceral, knife-edged agony that had him doubled over, grasping his knees in anguish in a patch of high-mountain slough grass a few yards from the back door of his ramshackle cabin. He'd suffered the pain of bone-numbing, subzero frostbite at Chosen, as a twenty-year-old marine during the Korean War. He'd battled through the pain of foot rot, the result of five years spent mucking yellow-cake uranium ore in the dank mines that dotted Colorado's Western Plateau. But neither could begin to match what he was experiencing now.

Rising on one elbow, he eyed the orange glow of the noonday sun and realized that he had less than eight hours of daylight to complete the task ahead of him. "Man's gotta protect what's his," he mumbled, nearly to his knees before a new knot of pain doubled him over. He grimaced and tumbled headfirst into the boggy grass as his thoughts drifted back to his years in the mines. Suddenly he began shaking, comparing the current pain with those from long ago, recounting the time he'd lost his footing in the Big Rondo Mine, near Moab, and plummeted down a fifty-foot shaft. Only his quick reflexes as he grabbed frantically at the protruding rocks along the shaft's jagged walls had broken his fall and saved him from certain death. He'd broken his spine in the fall and was plagued with back pain and recurring muscle spasms ever since.

Defying a new spike of pain, he forced a resilient smile—the kind of smile his Cherokee grandmother always claimed every good Indian needed in order to confuse the white devil and hold pain and tragedy at bay. His grandmother had been right. His near-tragic mine-shaft fall had changed his life. Within months of the accident he'd left the uranium mines to begin breeding his birds.

The pain erupted again, exploding deep inside him the same way it had for the past several months. Bracing himself for a new wave of the inevitable, he closed his eyes and tightened the muscles in his stomach as another surge corkscrewed through his body, ending in a crush of agony in the hollow of his chest.

When a final bolus of pain ripped through his rib cage, spinning him sideways, Redstone turned giddy. "Beat you again! Yes, yes, yes. Yes siree!" He was home free now, and he knew it. Recognizing the rib cage pain as the final event in what had become a predictable cycle, he broke into a grin, aware that for the next five hours he'd be virtually pain-free. "Gonna make it now; gonna make it now for sure," he muttered. "Won't need no doctors or no grave diggers today."

Struggling to remain on his feet, he focused his attention on the rows of gamecock cages that lined the rear wall of his cabin. Moving unsteadily toward the cages, he wet his lips, puckered, and desperately tried to whistle, hoping to enlist another of his lifelong remedies for pain. The resulting sound was less a whistle than a hiss, but the thinness of the effort failed to slow him down. Closing in on the cages, he forced a smile, aware that as long as he could smile and whistle, he'd be up to the grueling task ahead.

CHAPTER

2

It was just past dusk when Roland Septian began his belly crawl through slough grass and willows toward Luke Redstone's cabin. Chilled to the marrow after hours of dodging lightning strikes and shivering through a series of late-afternoon Colorado high-country rain showers, Septian adjusted his slicker and again found himself questioning why he was breaking one of three lifelong cardinal rules.

He'd broken scores of rules in his thirty-eight years—trashed most of them, in fact. But during ten years in the military, a stint as a mercenary, and even his ten tumultuous months as a post–Gulf War black marketeer, he'd never once wavered from the three Holy Grail survival imperatives he'd lived by for years: *(1) Never sleep with the same woman more than twice; (2) never give an adversary the slightest goddamn whiff of an even chance; and (3) never, ever do a rich man's bidding.*

He dodged a couple of fresh cow pies and pondered whether the fifty thousand dollars Jack Kimbrough had given him to "close the books on Luke Redstone and his gamecocks once and for all" was really worth breaking rule number three. Assuring himself once more that it was, he shook a puddle from the collar of his slicker, shivering as a rivulet of cold water rolled down his neck, and continued crawling.

With an Igloo cooler filled with dry ice, and a machete dragging at his side, he inched his way toward Redstone's split-log cabin in the foothills outside Grand Junction. By now his legs and lower torso were caked with mud. Several yards behind him, a two-ton Angus bull snorted, forlornly pawing at the muddy creek bed just beyond its snotty nose. Intermittently the bull stopped pawing to sniff a dead companion a few feet away. The now lifeless bull had been blocking Septian's path to the cabin, refusing to move even after he'd slammed a hefty fence post across its flank. In the seconds it had taken Septian to unsheath his machete, the bull had stared at him menacingly, as if to communicate that he was trespassing. The upswing of the blade had slit its throat with surgical precision, and the bull had dropped to its knees as if praying before rolling over on its side and expelling a loud last gurgle. For good measure, Septian had cut the animal from testicles to ribs, releasing a gush of fetid air. After wiping the bloody machete in the grass and resheathing it, he had proceeded, unfazed, toward his objective.

Septian had been shadowing Redstone for over a week, learning the aging cockfighter's routines and mentally recording his idiosyncrasies. He knew that each day the man known simply as Stone rose early for a breakfast of eggs and beef jerky, and that although the cabin had a well, Stone preferred to take his water directly from a nearby creek. He also knew that until very recently Stone had been spry and wiry. But what he knew best was everything there was to know about the lay of the land, including the exact location of every one of Stone's dozen prize gamecocks.

Septian had committed every square inch of Redstone's isolated creekside plot to memory. He'd taken the time to sketch the pyramidlike arrangement of gamecock cages propped on stilts just beyond the cabin's back door. He even knew the heights and shapes of the four gooseberry trees that shaded the back entry.

As he moved toward the three-strand electric fence that secured the cabin's perimeter, Septian slowed his pace, aware that the briefest contact with a single wire would mean a serious jolt. He'd thought about crashing the fence with an ATV or even a Humvee but had decided against it for fear of losing the element of surprise and bringing a well-armed Redstone out of the cabin, shotgun blazing.

He paused for a moment to size up his final approach just as a light flashed on in one of the cabin's windows. Tossing his cooler over the fence, he unsheathed the machete and began scraping out a hollow beneath the bottom strand of wire. Why, until now, had there been no sign of Stone all day?

The old codger had disappeared on him before, only to resurface in the mountain mist of daybreak or the blackness of night. But this time things seemed different, oddly out of sync, eerily punctuated by the silence of the gamecocks. Normally they clucked and pecked and scratched all day long. But during the past three hours, he'd barely heard a sound. Reassuring himself that he only needed to snatch a bird or two, and that if push came to shove he'd gladly dispense with Redstone, he continued digging. Having dug enough of a hollow, he shoved the machete beneath the bottom wire and gingerly wriggled after it. Then, after quickly reattaching his gear, he was back on his belly and crawling toward the cages.

The gamecocks he needed were housed separately from the rest of Redstone's birds, a half-dozen superstar cocks quartered all by themselves. Hugging the ground and keeping an eye out for Stone, Septian slipped across a patch of gravel and thatch, half expecting the old man to come charging from the cabin. But the only evidence of life remained his own steady breathing and the rustling of cottonwoods and aspens in the distance.

He was within ten feet of the cages when a second light flashed on inside the cabin. Startled, he rolled behind a skunkberry bush, unsheathed his nickel-plated Detonics .45 from the leg holster, hunkered down, and watched for movement inside. A sudden gust kicked up, swirling an oily newspaper spackled with gamecock droppings across his face. Unfazed, he tossed the paper aside and waited, gun at the ready. As quickly as it had come up, the wind died down, restoring the unnatural quiet.

Septian let out a weak sigh. He'd come too far, planned too long, and spent too much time on surveillance to alter his plan. Convinced now that Stone wasn't going to charge him, he reholstered the gun and moved on until the doors to the cages he sought came into view and the birds in the adjacent cages began raising a ruckus. Telling himself that in a pinch one bird might have to do, he rose to a squat and, with the cooler thumping at his side, duck-walked his way toward the cages, the tip of the machete's sheath dragging in the dirt.

A few feet from the cages, he stood, realizing only then that several of the doors hung partially open. When a coyote howled in the distance, he wondered if one of Mother Nature's scavenger dogs had gotten there first and derailed his plan. Hesitantly he swung back a cage door, then another, and another before finally banging the door to the last empty cage shut and shouting, "Shit, shit, shit!" Gritting his teeth until his temples throbbed, he crouched back down and worked his way over to a second group of Stone's superstar cages, only to find that each cage housed not a feisty gamecock but a run-of-the-mill white leghorn hen.

Frustrated and seething, realizing now that Stone had pulled a switch, he drew the gun. Racing toward the cabin, he kicked in the back door almost without stopping and fired two quick rounds, knocking out the two lights inside. Pivoting in a circle, the .45 aimed chest high, he squeezed off a third round, shattering a water pitcher on a nearby table.

"Goddamn sly old motherfucker!" he screamed. "Sly fucking bird-switching, cocksucking old coot!" he bellowed, tripping over something in the semidarkness. Kneeling down to see what it was, he shook his head in disbelief as he lifted a knot of extension cords off the floor. Grabbing the cords in one hand, he followed them back to a shopworn light timer jutting from a greasy electrical outlet. Slamming a fist to the floor, he snatched the timer from its socket and tossed it aside. "Damn it. The slick-assed goddamn son of a bitch." The old man had tricked him using a half-dozen worthless chickens and a beat-to-shit light timer. Amazed at Redstone's resourcefulness, Septian began to snicker. The high-pitched nasal sound soon escalated to a wheeze and, finally, a booming, unrestrained laugh as Septian began firing indiscriminately around the room.

CHAPTER

3

Walker Rios stood chest deep in fifty-degree water, fly-fishing just a few yards from a treacherous thirty-foot drop-off in the western Colorado White River National Forest. Over the course of fifteen minutes, he had slowly worked his way from the safety of the White River's grassy opposite shore; now the fly at the end of his leader could drift down a riffle and bob its way into the mouth of a promising still-water pool.

That morning he'd driven his road-weary pickup from his base camp, two miles down a rutted Forest Service road and past an isolated one-person ranger station before finding the overgrown Jeep trail that had put him within walking distance of what the sad-faced ranger had guaranteed him was the finest unspoiled stretch of gold-medal trout fishing in the state. He'd parked a quarter mile from the river, in a clearing bordered by stunted sagebrush and dead chokecherry trees, then hiked to the river through a tinderbox of underbrush and fallen pine.

Eyes still glued to the water, he watched the nose of an inquisitive trout surface, bump his fly, refuse it, and quickly disappear. Excited at the prospect of having stumbled across a trout "honey hole," he sidestepped his way a few feet closer to the perilous drop-off before glancing downstream. Seeing the series of small rapids, he felt an instant tightening in his gut as he thought about the other reason he was here.

He looped out a new cast and watched his leader curl out onto the water as he tried not to think about the midsummer accident that still gnawed at his subconscious, killing him slowly inside.

Two months earlier, on a sun-drenched morning, during a routine float trip through Glenwood Canyon, he had lost a boy from the ten-person river raft he'd steered and commanded for more than a decade. The boy, a gangly, soft-spoken, eager ten-year-old, had fallen overboard during a white-water run, slipped beneath the surface of the cold, murky water, drifted into a whirlpool vortex, and disappeared. Rios had immediately tossed out a lifeline and jumped into the water in a valiant attempt to save the child. After forty-five minutes of diving in search of the boy, he had to be pulled from the river by forest rangers who'd feared he'd be the second casualty of the day.

The Colorado River had severed a nerve in Walker Rios that morning, leaving a normally self-assured outdoorsman forever emotionally scarred. Until the accident, Rios, a seventh-generation offspring of Spanish land-grant immigrants, had spent most of his life stepping just out of harm's way. Until then he had navigated every major white-water river in the United States without a single injury to his passengers or himself. Until then he had undertaken first descents of rivers in Alaska, Sumatra, and New Guinea and never suffered any injury worse than a few cuts, bruises, and ligament strains.

After returning from a tour as a marine intelligence officer during the Persian Gulf War, he had built his river-running company on what he liked to call Latino guts and hard work, and in the ten years that followed, Wild River Descents had garnered a sterling reputation as one of only two rafting outfits in the West to boast a five-star Forest Service rating. Now everything had changed.

Turning away from the rapids, Rios worked his way midstream, hoping that a little fishing luck would signal better times ahead. He was in the midst of a back cast and on the verge of accepting the idea that if nothing else, the trip had been mildly conscience-soothing, when he spotted a fish rising several yards away. Interrupting his cast, he waited for it to rise again. When it finally nosed cautiously above the water, he realized he was out of casting range. Working his way slowly toward the rise, he eyed the widening surface ring, watching it fade only inches from the rocky slip of shoreline that marked the drop-off.

He gazed at the water, waiting for a rise again, recognizing now that he'd encountered a lunker. Steadying himself on a boulder, he looped out a cast that landed delicately on the water. Seconds later the end of his fly rod jackknifed underwater. Adjusting a controlling finger on the screaming line, he shouted, "Son of a bitch!" as he stepped off the slippery boulder into the waist-high midstream current, desperately trying to maintain control of the huge rainbow. Twenty feet away it rose again, corkscrewing three feet into the air and taking five additional feet of line before nosediving in a defiant splash near the water's edge.

Realizing that his line was into the reel backing, and convinced the monster rainbow could easily win their tug-of-war and snap him off, Rios gave a little slack and began working his way downstream, trying to control the fish in the powerful midriver current. When he tugged back gently on his rod tip to make sure the fish was still on, the big trout responded with a run that bent the fly rod in half, plunging the tip a foot beneath water before finally snapping the line.

Dumbfounded, Rios shook his head and smiled in wonderment. "Not today," he whispered.

Still in awe, he began reeling in line, oblivious to the telephone-pole-sized tree trunk moving downstream toward him. He was busy estimating the girth of the lost rainbow when the gnarled old snag crashed into the backs of his knees, sending him tumbling backward over it and slamming his head on a jutting boulder. Both ears began ringing, and blood gushed from one nostril as the current grabbed him, dragging him downstream. Semiconscious and gulping water, he fought to regain his footing. As he struggled to stand, his thoughts flashed to a drowning ten-year-old, to *the accident*.

Disoriented, with his head bobbing in and out of the water, he managed to make out a shoreline in the distance. Fighting to keep his head above water, he stumbled and clawed his way toward safety, losing the fly rod and most of his gear. He was seconds away from blacking out and finally going under when the current suddenly began nudging him toward shore. With each new wave the water became shallower, until he found himself overwhelmed with relief. Barely conscious, he patted his way onto land, inching his way to safety on his belly. He was still blindly crawling along the rocky spit of land when he began his tumble toward the jagged rocks below.

CHAPTER
4

After two weeks of dry mid-nineties heat, the moist afternoon air rushing past Carmen Nguyen's face felt uncommonly refreshing. Glancing toward the mountains, she noticed thunderheads building to the west. Thinking, *Finally, some relief,* she throttled back and felt the weight of her motorcycle shift beneath her as she eased down an I-70 off-ramp toward the heart of Grand Junction. Street traffic was surprisingly light, and within minutes she was negotiating her six-hundred-pound, immaculately restored 1947 Indian Chief around the first of the four bright yellow speed bumps and into the staff parking lot of St. Mary's Hospital. The gate and speed bumps suddenly had her thinking about other barriers.

One of the thousands of throwaway love children from America's longest and least popular war, she had spent a lifetime confronting barriers and navigating the cultural minefield inhabited by all Amerasians. In a sense, speed bumps were nothing new.

The product of a Vietnamese mother and a black GI, she would always be *my den,* a black half-breed, whether in America or Vietnam. The name Carmen, given to her by the father she had never known, in honor of the tragically beautiful, free-spirited temptress and heroine of the all-black-cast 1954 film *Carmen Jones,* only served to emphasize that all too often in America, she didn't fit in. For most of her life, comments like *"How'd you get a name like Carmen if you're Vietnamese?"* . . . *"You're black?"* . . . and *"Nguyen? Don't sound like no sistah's name to me"* had reiterated the point nearly every day.

As a child she had cleaned houses, collected garbage, driven a cyclo—the Vietnamese pedicab equivalent of a taxi—and begged on the streets of Ho Chi Minh City. But unlike most of her Amerasian compatriots, who all too often ended up wallowing in the muck of discrimination in their homeland, she had been lucky. She'd had the privilege of an education and the advantage of a strict upbringing by a loving, caring aunt. By the age of ten she was a math whiz and fluent in English, French, and Vietnamese.

She and her aunt left Vietnam as part of a flotilla of boat people in the late fall of 1979. They landed, half starved and petrified with fear, in their new homeland on the Northern California coast. There Carmen, then only fifteen, began manufacturing her own luck, first in California and then as a National Merit Scholar from the small town of Palisades, Colorado, where she had ultimately settled, just outside Grand Junction. Twelve years and a lifetime of sacrifices later, she had sat at a graduation ceremony, basking in the warm June sun, waiting to receive a University of Colorado medical degree.

Despite her successes in her adopted homeland, haunting voids remained in her life. She knew nothing of her father except that, by her aunt's account, he and her mother, who died when Carmen was only four, had been star-crossed lovers. Aside from confirming her parents' passion for each other and that yes, her father had been black, her aunt never spoke about either parent, no matter how hard Carmen pressed the issue.

And there were other demons in her past. Horrific war-linked memories of a place called My Lai still triggered night sweats and bouts of terror. And more recently, a career-crushing stumbling block had come close to ending her near-perfect American dream. She'd been forced to leave a promising position as a University of Utah cancer research scientist and stellar medical oncologist after blowing the whistle on a group of top-level administrators who were skimming money from university research grants. The whistle-blowing incident had tarnished her reputation, cost her her job, and forced her to leave Salt Lake City and return home to Colorado in a face-saving compromise. Blackballed in oncology circles and too devastated to return to the world of science, she'd taken a job in the St. Mary's ER.

Carmen felt the motorcycle's front tire thump over the final speed bump, flexing the chrome spring below the handlebar. Coasting into a parking slot, she unstrapped her helmet, looped it over the handlebar, and ran her hands through her short jet-black hair. Glancing down at the word RESERVED spelled out across a spider web of cracks in the asphalt, she stepped to the rear of the bike and opened the well-worn leather saddlebags containing her work clothes and the bevy of medical journals she'd pored over until two A.M. last night. Peeved at allowing her thoughts to drift off into what she thought of as "apocalypse land," Carmen shook her head to clear the cobwebs and set off across the parking lot toward the hospital's north entrance. A few steps from the door, she stole a look back at the Indian, glistening yellow-gold in the sun. Smiling and recalling the twelve long months she'd spent restoring it, she continued into the hospital, the heels of her roper boots clunking down the corridor of gray institutional tile.

Halfway down the corridor, a security guard with an empty coffee thermos swinging from his thumb greeted her with an enthusiastic wave. "Evening." The man broke into a toothy grin.

Carmen returned the smile. "Evening to you, Jim."

"Riding your beast today?" said the man, his tone almost reverent.

"You know I am," said Carmen. Months earlier she had successfully treated the man's twelve-year-old daughter for a recurring bladder infection that had plagued her for years.

"Gonna get me an Indian one of these days."

"Time's a-wasting."

"Think I'll have a look at yours on the way out, if you don't mind."

"Take your time."

"Count on it, Dr. Nguyen. No reason my mouth shouldn't water a bit before I head home."

Flashing the man a quick smile, she said, "I've been there myself," before continuing down the hallway.

The chunky guard watched her walk away. Her lean runner's physique and long, quick strides triggered thoughts of his once-trim youth. "Sunset," the name she'd given her bike, was something else, he told himself as he turned to leave. "Yep," he murmured to himself, Dr. Nguyen and her motorcycle were two of a kind—as unique and perfect a pair of exotic beauties as he had ever seen.

The churning, wind-whipping noise of helicopter rotors had Rios convinced he was back on the battlefields of Desert Storm. He wanted desperately to speak, to say something to prove he was alive, but it took every ounce of energy he could muster just to breathe. He heard someone shout, "Head for the clearing; we'll load him in the chopper." Then came a voice he thought he recognized: a high-pitched voice that seemed out of place in a battlefield. "Hang in there, buddy," the voice said seconds before Rios lost consciousness.

Bearing the head of Rios's stretcher, the sad-faced, squeaky-voiced forest ranger whom Rios had encountered earlier that morning stumbled awkwardly as he worked his way up the hillside and toward a small clearing. "Is he going to make it?" asked the man struggling with the opposite end of the stretcher. The ranger tripped over a rock and crashed to one knee. His companion, clad in fishing gear and managing Rios's IV, reached out and steadied him as the IV line jiggled in sync with the ranger's answer: "Don't know. He's just damn lucky you found him at the bottom of that ravine. Luckier still that you had the sense to come get me. No way he'd a had a snowball's chance without these fluids we're pushin'!" The ranger looped a kink out of the IV line as he maneuvered the stretcher toward the clearing. "I see the chopper. Let's move it!" he shouted as they zigzagged their way around boulders and sage thickets toward the idling helicopter.

Concentrating on keeping the stretcher level, and unaware that he'd nearly reached the chopper, the man who'd found Rios suddenly dropped his end. Rios let out a moan and then a throaty rasp as the stretcher thumped to the ground.

"I've got it," said a black-clad paramedic, appearing as if out of nowhere from the chopper's doorway. Laying the IV bag on Rios's belly, he reached down, grabbed the fallen end of the stretcher, and helped the ranger shove patient and stretcher into the helicopter's belly.

Rios momentarily regained consciousness. Jerking his arm skyward, he dislodged the IV.

"He's popped his IV," the ranger shouted, leaping into the chopper and grabbing Rios's arm.

"I'll start a new one," said the paramedic, brushing the ranger aside, giving their pilot the thumbs-up sign, and checking Rios's vitals.

Rios felt a pinch in his arm as the rumble of the chopper's engines rose toward power takeoff. He tried to say something, but all that came out was a lengthy groan. When he tried to speak again, a stream of urine trickled down his leg.

The chopper lifted off in an unstable wobble before boring its way through low-hanging clouds and climbing in a burst of power into the ice-blue sky. The muscles in Rios's body tightened at the roar. "Incoming," he mumbled—his first intelligible word since losing consciousness.

"It's okay," said the paramedic, now down on one knee at Rios's side. "It's okay, buddy."

Another strange voice, Rios told himself—one that also didn't fit. A voice that shouldn't be here with him in Iraq. "Who are you?" he wanted to ask. "Why are you here?" But it was all he could do to breathe. *No matter,* he told himself as he drifted back into unconsciousness. The strange voices and the incoming artillery fire would soon disappear. And after that, he could take a much-needed break from the war.

CHAPTER
5

The helicopter carrying Rios landed in a brisk twenty-mile-per-hour wind, pitching and yawing its way to touchdown. Just beyond the landing pad, Carmen Nguyen stood anxiously waiting to meet it. The sound of a chopper, even muffled and distant, always gave her chills, melding into gunfire and the distant screams of war.

Accompanied by a third-year surgery resident and a baby-faced trauma nurse, Carmen charged the helicopter as the paramedic attending Rios slid back the chopper's door.

"Ruptured brachial artery and possible spinal trauma," the paramedic screamed above the high-pitched engine whine and the whipping thumps of the rotor blades.

"Got you," said Carmen, leaping up into the chopper's belly and sliding on bended knees up next to Rios.

"He's bleeding like a stuck pig," said the paramedic. "His BP's seventy-five over fifty and dropping. Keeps mumbling, 'Incoming.' He's been in and out of it all the way here."

"And the rest of his vitals?" asked Carmen, ripping back Rios's shirt, snapping the buttons.

"He's breathing on his own, but his pulse is real thready."

Carmen walked her fingers along Rios's neck. "He's got a pulse—not much of one, but it's there. Let's get ready to move him. I don't think we have much time."

"Think he'll make it?"

"We'll know in a bit." Turning back toward the doorway and the nurse, Carmen said, "Sarah, give me a hand here. We need to pump more fluids or we're looking at irreversible shock." In seconds the nurse was beside her, starting a second IV.

"Need any more help in there?" the resident, feeling left out, called up to Carmen.

"Nope. We've got three hands on deck in here; that should do it. Why don't you run back and tell the ER that we've got an unstable bleed-out on the way. Be ready for cut-downs. I'll need five—no, make that six units of blood. I'll have a catheter in by the time we arrive. And, Frank, we'll need blood gases and a chest film too. Notify the OR he'll be coming straight up to them."

"Got ya," said the resident, taking off in a sprint.

Slipping a catheter from a soft pack at her feet, Carmen glanced over at the paramedic, then up at Rios's drawn, ashen face. "What's his name?" she asked, looping out the catheter.

"Walker Rios, according to his fishing license."

"What happened?"

"Took a dive off a thirty-foot cliff into a puddle."

"Damn." Carmen shook her head as she finished ripping Rios's shirt down to his belt buckle. Watching his chest rise ever so slightly, she said, "Okay, boys and girls, time to rock and roll."

As the last rays of the setting sun crept past his window, Luke Redstone sat up in his hospital bed and slammed an empty coffee cup down on the nightstand next to him, shattering the cup and sending porcelain fragments skittering across the floor. "You, there. You, there in the white. You better let me outta here!" he barked at a nearby nurse. "You hear me? I want outta here now."

The young nurse attending Stone didn't flinch. A day of Stone's bizarre antics had taught her new lessons in tolerance. "As soon as I see a discharge order, Mr. Redstone. And believe me, when I do, you'll be the first to know." Stooping and shaking her head, she scooped up the remnants of the coffee cup and tossed them in the trash can at the foot of Stone's bed.

"Discharge order, my achin' ass! You're holdin' me against my will. That's a federal offense." Stone slammed a fist down onto the nightstand, hunching himself up farther in bed. His badly sun-damaged skin, craggy face, and thinning hair mirrored every one of his sixty-nine years, but his eyes, light hazel and full of sparkle, still gave testimony to the boundless energy he'd always had.

After spending most of the previous afternoon moving his gamecocks from their cages at his cabin to a safe haven in the foothills some forty miles away, he'd considered dropping behind a big rock to die, but he hadn't, and by the time he'd recaged all his birds, the pain racking his body had been so intense he'd barely been able to see.

The only thing that had kept him going was imagining the look on the face of whoever was stalking him, hoping to steal his birds, when they realized that the prize birds he'd left behind weren't fighting cocks at all but plump Colonel Sanders grade A frying hens.

He'd made it back to Grand Junction and almost to the shabby motel where he planned to keep a low profile for the next few nights, when he was hit by pain so excruciating that he thought he was back in Korea, where enemy bugles were once again blaring, sounding the charge for hordes of Chinese Communist soldiers to descend out of the mountains onto his position. When the mirage of Chosen reservoir appeared in the distance, he'd pointed his pickup away from the hotel and in the direction of St. Mary's Hospital.

He'd strolled into the ER, announced to a receptionist that he was feeling a little tired, and slumped to the floor. Within seconds Carmen Nguyen, who had been standing a few feet away jotting notes in a burn victim's chart, was at his side. When Stone didn't respond as she shook him by the shoulders and asked if he was okay, Carmen shouted for a crash cart, checked his pulse, then his airway, and prepared to begin CPR. Before she could place her mouth over his, Stone opened his eyes, blinked Carmen's delicately proportioned, exotic features into focus, and said distinctly, to her dismay, "Shit, this must be heaven." From that moment she'd taken an unusual interest in Luke Redstone's puzzling medical problem, a problem that had kept her poring through medical journals much of last night.

Stone raised his fist for another gavel-pounding of the night-stand, but the nurse gave him a look that said, *Don't you dare,* and he stopped his arm in mid-descent. "Get me Dr. Nguyen. She knows all about my case. She'll let me out."

The nurse frowned, her eyebrows pinching together in disgust. "Dr. Nguyen's not your doctor, Mr. Redstone. I've told you that before. She's simply an ER doc who happened to be on duty when you came in. Dr. Williams is in charge of your care."

"Hell if she ain't. She's the one who put me here. She's also the one who had 'em pokin' me, stealin' my blood, and makin' me pee into a cup half the night and all this mornin'. At least I ain't hurtin' no more, 'cause a her treatment, so she's damn sure figured out somethin' about my problem." Stone wagged an arthritic index finger at the nurse. "She's my doctor, all right; don't care what you say."

"I understand, Mr. Redstone. I understand very well," said the nurse, recording a note concerning Stone's pain medication in his medical chart before rushing from the room.

"Well, good-bye to you, too," said Stone, lurching forward in his bed. Exasperated, he began fluffing two pancaked pillows. "Hard as rocks," he muttered, thumping the top pillow with his fist just as Carmen and the reticent, stoop-shouldered Dr. Williams entered the room.

"How are we doing today, Luke?" Williams said tentatively, expecting the response of a lion.

"Don't know about you, Doc, but I'm doin' just fine. Not a pain in my bones," said Stone, catching the doctor by surprise. "You folks dispense real good medicine." Smiling at Carmen, he rested his head back on the freshly fluffed pillows. "Got my release papers in order?"

"Not quite yet," said Carmen, shaking her head.

"You promised," said Stone.

Dr. Williams stepped between Stone and Carmen. "We've

found, Mr. Redstone, that you have an unusual, quite serious problem. You won't be going home today."

Stone's eyes widened, locking on Carmen's as she punctuated Dr. Williams's comments with a nod. Suddenly Stone felt as helpless as he had four decades earlier during his free fall in the Big Rondo Mine. "What is it?" he said, his words halting and tentative.

"It's a disease I rarely see, but fortunately Dr. Nguyen had experience with it when she worked at the University of Utah."

Stone's eyes never wavered from Carmen's. "This disease you're stickin' me with—got a name for it?" he asked, bracing himself for the answer.

"Yes." Williams cleared his throat. "I'm afraid you have hairy cell leukemia."

Stone took a deep breath and considered what would become of his birds if something happened to him. The first two words of the strange-sounding diagnosis meant nothing to him, but he understood the word *leukemia* very well. It was, after all, a disease that had killed at least half a dozen other people who had once mucked yellow-cake uranium ore alongside him.

"You're sure about what I got?" said Stone, elbowing his pillows, directing the question to Carmen.

Reluctantly Carmen said, "Yes."

"Well, ain't that a hoot. Here I am more than forty years down the road from muckin' uranium, and the damn yellow-cake's still chasin' me. Whatta you think about that?"

"There could be other causes for your illness. We can't prove it's directly related to your days in the mines," said Williams.

"Tell that to some stupido, Doc. I got more sense." Stone winked and flashed Carmen a look. "What's your take, Dr. Nguyen? You seen this kind of sickness before. Don't you agree it's the yellow-cake still on my tail?"

Carmen didn't answer. Stone's question hit too close to home—she knew all too well what it was like to be chased forever by the past. Suddenly she found herself thinking about Vietnam and the massacre that had cost her her mother.

CHAPTER

6

Roland Septian paced his stifling tent's nine-by-nine-foot plywood floor, cell phone to his ear, still seething over his failed raid on Luke Redstone's cabin. "The old coot made me—don't ask me how," Septian barked into the phone. "I swear he never caught a glimpse of me the whole time I was doggin' his ass."

On the other end of the line, Jack Kimbrough's response was garbled. "I can barely hear you."

Frustrated with the reception, Septian stomped the floor panel and adjusted the phone to his ear. "Damn it, Kimbrough, you're breaking up!"

"Did you sleep while you were tailing him?" shouted Kimbrough, his mouth now pressed to the phone's mouthpiece as he sat back in a wing-backed leather chair and surveyed the starkness of his downtown Denver office.

"Of course! I was glued to his ass for a week."

Kimbrough's laugh tailed off in a snort. "Then that's when he pegged you. Count on it. While you were sleeping. And that's when he moved his birds."

Septian shook his head in disbelief. "I would have heard something. Noise from inside the cabin. A vehicle, horses—an ATV, for Christ's sake. Shit, the son of a bitch had to move a dozen or so of those goddamn chickens!"

"Gamecocks, Lieutenant. There's a difference."

"Gamecocks, then," said Septian, frowning at being corrected, and incensed at being called "Lieutenant," a rank he'd earned during Desert Storm at the risk of his life and had later been stripped of for endangering the lives of a platoon of candy-assed reservists. "The point is, he's disappeared, and so have his birds."

"Only briefly," said Kimbrough. Imagining the look on Septian's face, he took a sip of the martini he'd been savoring. "Redstone's an old man. Trust me, he won't stray too far from home. Forget about him for the moment. Right now you need to deal with that Navajo recruiter of ours, Narine."

Wiping his brow, Septian stepped outside his tent to eye the towering sandstone arches and the burnt-orange cliffs of Utah's slick-rock desert. He was in the middle of nowhere, past Cisco and Moab—miles and miles beyond the canyon lands of the development arch. And once again, much to his consternation, he found himself babysitting a platoon of candy-asses. But this time he and his former Desert Storm commander, retired Army Colonel Emerson Walls, had twelve worthless Indians in tow instead of a platoon of scared-as-shit reservists. "I can handle Narine. Redstone's our problem. Son of a bitch has the whole Western Slope of Colorado and most of eastern Utah to get lost in."

"Not with what I hear's ailing him. Word on the cockfighting circuit is, our friend Redstone's real sick." Kimbrough took another sip of his drink and smiled. "An old adversary of his, a cocker named Jimmy Turner, swears to it. He'll be calling you with a line on where Redstone's stashed his birds. Claims they're somewhere out there in the desert close by. He told me he can take you right to them anytime, day or night."

"How soon?" asked Septian, wondering how Kimbrough always seemed to be one up on him when it came to scrounging up the inside dope.

"Soon enough."

Kimbrough rose from his chair, walked to the front of his desk, and glanced around the sparsely furnished white-walled room. His office reflected his minimalist philosophy of never working, spending, eating, playing, or even screwing to excess. "And, Septian, this time take DeVille with you. I don't want you to come up empty-handed again."

"Sure you want DeVille to know that much?"

"I don't have much choice. Just cover your ass. Tell him you're scouting the terrain, that you're a nature lover, that you're into fighting cocks—who cares? And give him a couple of thousand to keep his mouth shut. I've had him checked out; he knows who Redstone is anyway. Turns out DeVille's father was a cock-fighter too."

"That's strange," said Septian, gritting his teeth, angered by the fact that once again Kimbrough was only telling him half a story.

"That it is," said Kimbrough, not used to having his orders questioned. "And by the way, have you been clocking in regularly with Colonel Walls?"

"Every day," said Septian, peeved at having to answer to anyone.

"Good. I wouldn't want Walls to get his shorts in a knot. He needs to know you're there for him, that he's got some inside help."

"He's covered," said Septian, his tone almost boastful. Pausing momentarily, he said, "Got a question of my own. What's the real reason I'm baby-sitting DeVille? Fucker's a wimp. Why the hell do I need to keep tabs on him?"

"Because I said so. Good enough?"

Livid at being reprimanded a second time, Septian stepped back inside his tent and retrieved a rolled-up topo map from the top of an army footlocker. Slipping off the rubber band, he dropped to one knee and unrolled it.

"What are you doing?" asked Kimbrough, aggravated by the interruption and confused by the new background noises.

Without answering, Septian pulled a yellowing photograph of Luke Redstone and one of his gamecocks from beneath a paper clip. Someone had scribbled the name *Thunderhead* across the photo just to the left of the gamecock's beak. Smiling at the thought of making Kimbrough wait, Septian finally said, "Double-checking all my objectives." He took a lighter from his pocket and sent the image up in flames.

"Your objective right now is to handle Narine and then hook up with DeVille," said Kimbrough. "Forget about everything else."

"Sure thing," said Septian, watching the photo curl into a thin gray film and thinking, *Screw you, you pompous fucking asshole,* as he flipped up the mouthpiece on his cell phone, ending the conversation.

A thousand bucks was a thousand bucks, but six months of monthly needle sticks were starting to get to Ariel Roundtree. And the trips from the middle of the Utah desert back and forth to Denver were pure-dee bullshit.

"Are you ready for your blood draw, Mr. Roundtree?" The tall, dark-haired woman posing the question uncapped the syringe she was holding and smiled.

"Yeah," said Roundtree in a low-pitched drone. He hated the woman's preachiness. She always sounded as if she were talking to a kid, and it rubbed him the wrong way.

The woman's smile broadened. "You've been an excellent patient over the months—you and all of your Navajo friends."

"We try," said Roundtree sarcastically, counting the seconds until he'd be out the door. Big cities like Denver bothered him. They'd given him the willies ever since he was a kid. On top of that, it was a big city that had once turned him into a druggie and stolen most of his youth. He was the kind of man who needed the wide-open spaces of the barren Navajo reservation or the Colorado Western Slope.

Flinching as the thick needle pushed into his arm, he looked up and eyed the woman, wondering if she actually did work for his friend Larry Narine, as Narine continued to swear. He doubted it. She was too clean, too white, too crisp. And on top of that, she had a worldly kind of look that was light-years beyond the grasp of a loser and loner like Narine. Telling himself that he'd ask her who she really worked for when she finished his blood draw, Roundtree fixed his gaze on the wall and sat back in his chair.

Withdrawing the needle from his arm, the woman covered

the wound with a piece of cotton. "Six months, six good draws. Can't beat that," she said, applying a flesh-colored strip of tape.

Sensing an opening, Roundtree blurted out, "You work for Larry Narine?"

"Who?"

"Larry Narine."

The woman shook her head without answering.

"Walls, then?" said Roundtree. If it wasn't Narine the woman worked for, then it had to be Emerson Walls, Roundtree's old colonel—the man who'd had him and eleven other Navajos bivouacked in the scorching Utah desert for the past eight weeks, learning to be firefighters.

The woman smiled. "You're done for today, Mr. Roundtree. See you in a month." She dropped the needle into a large red Hazmat container that reminded him of the janitorial bucket he'd only recently stopped pushing around, and handed him an envelope.

Roundtree fingered the envelope before jamming it into his pocket. "In a month," he said, rising from his chair, his thoughts once again turning to Larry Narine. Aware that over the past six months Narine had had his blood drawn the same number of times, Roundtree found himself wondering whether Narine, too, had received ten hundred-dollar bills for his pains. He was sure that he hadn't. After all, Narine was a recruiter, a snake-oil salesman who had persuaded ten down-on-their-luck Navajos to follow him into the Utah desert, supposedly to learn to fight cargo container fires. And it was Narine who had convinced every one of the men to belly up to the bar once a month and part with a little of their blood. It was probably fair that Narine got paid a little more. He'd ask him about the money as soon as he got back to their base camp. It didn't really matter if Narine got more; he simply wanted to know.

Roundtree eyed the woman as she wiped down the armrest of his chair with alcohol, and wondered whether she thought he and the rest of Narine's recruits were so dirty that she had to disinfect the place each time they made a visit. She probably did, he

thought, forcing back the urge to call her a bitch, knowing he'd
see her again. Turning to leave, he eyed the woman's crisp, spot-
lessly white form-fitting uniform, wondering as he walked out
the door if her panties were just as clean.

Jack handle in hand, Larry Narine struggled with the damaged
Humvee wheel rim. He was beginning to question the wisdom
of having signed on with Roland Septian, his former first lieutenant, and their introspective Desert Storm commander, Emerson Walls. Walls had always made him nervous, largely because
he tended to ponder things too much. Septian, on the other
hand, was simply a nutcase who scared him to death.

But for twenty thousand dollars and a chance once again to
become part of an elite group of men, he had bought into their
desert firefighting scheme. Now he was marooned in the eastern
Utah desert, suffering through endless days of 105-degree heat,
drinking piss-smelling goat's milk, and wondering what he and
the eleven men he'd recruited were really here to do. He knew
for certain that with Walls and Septian in charge, mastering firefighting techniques wasn't the whole mission.

He and Septian had forged an uneasy comrades-in-arms kind
of relationship as members of a Walls's Abrams tank battalion on
the battlefields of Kuwait and Iraq. Unlike Septian, an edgy,
gung-ho, kill-'em-and-yank-their-nuts-out poor excuse for a
human being, Narine had never felt any sense of being a true
warrior during the Persian Gulf War. He had never once feared
the inept Iraqis and in fact had always considered his greatest
enemy to be American friendly fire.

Orphaned at the age of two, Narine had bounced around from
place to place until he was eighteen. Although he had a sister
and nephew to whom he was close, his only true sense of family
and self-worth had come during the war.

Three months past his thirtieth birthday he remained just as
insecure as he'd always been, and he had the feeling that two
more weeks of tinkering with vehicles and playing firefighter in
the blistering desert would truly test his sanity. Despondent and

irritable, all he really wanted to do was collect his money, go home to Grand Junction, play catch with his nephew, and watch the Cubs.

Sliding back from straddling the tire, Narine set aside his hammer and watched Septian jog toward him, shading his eyes against the sandblast of wind in his face. "What's your hurry?" Narine called out. "You not hot enough already?"

"Nah, Walls needs to see you ASAP," said Septian, out of breath and spitting sand. "Something about one of your recruits."

"What's the matter? I handpicked every man. Chose 'em just like you and that Kimbrough fellow said."

"Hell if I know. Walls just sent me to get you. Better close up shop."

Shaking his head, Narine set down the jack handle, grabbed the tire for support, and rose to his feet. "This mission's starting to stink," he said, dusting himself off.

"Ain't it, though?"

Narine took a step toward the headquarters tent and was halfway through a second stride when the two pistol rounds hit him, separating the base of his skull from his spine. His body made a hollow, swishing noise as it landed facedown in the sand.

Sheathing the World War II-vintage Luger, Septian cocked his leg and kicked Narine in the ribs. "In this business, it don't pay to be a recruiter or an orphan, my friend." Kicking the lifeless body again, he stood back and laughed as he watched Narine's forearm disappear beneath the drifting sand.

CHAPTER

7

"Our Navajo boys are just about ready," said Emerson Walls, speaking on a bulky military field telephone in the sweltering, stale air of his tent. The thermometer dangling from his pack zipper read 103 degrees.

Jack Kimbrough, four hundred miles away in his air-conditioned Denver research lab, leaned back in his chair and kicked off a custom-made Italian house slipper. Bending to massage his foot, he said, "Are you on a secure line?"

"As secure as any."

"And every one of your Navajos is ready to take the plunge?"

"All eleven—minus Narine, of course. I understand from Septian that Narine's, ah . . . moved on?"

"Good." Kimbrough, clad only in loose-fitting gym shorts, broke into a self-satisfied grin as he glanced around the semi-darkened lab. Across the room a test tube agitator droned on. "Have you got the drill perfected?"

"Down to a gnat's ass."

"And when we're set, your boys'll be prepared to battle a real blaze?"

"Guarantee it."

"They'd better be. I've spent eighteen months setting this up. For everything to work, we have to nail the temperature to within three degrees and the humidity to within six percentage points. On top of that, we have to time the burn perfectly. Even the elevation needs to be on the money. As close as possible to seventy-six hundred feet or we're looking at failure. Bottom line is, Colonel, we're not fooling around with field artillery shelling estimates here; we're dealing with real, live science."

"Like I said, we're set," said Walls, frowning at Kimbrough's backhanded insult.

"Do you have all the necessary burn permits?"

"Every one of 'em. Signed by the regional Forest Service director himself. Everything's in order."

"It better be. I had to slip that tree-hugging backwoodsman twenty grand for the okay."

"That's peanuts if everything turns out the way you claim."

"It will," said Kimbrough. He was basking in the glow of the recent financial success of his company. Boasting $250 million in annual sales, Particle Trigenics had become the largest manufacturer and distributor of air filters, gas purification units, respirators, and disaster containment gear in the United States. As the company's president and CEO, Kimbrough had seen his reputation as a financial wizard rise just as fast.

A former sharecropper's son, Kimbrough had escaped the West Texas plains on the strength of his football-catching skills and enough brain power to become the first in his family to attend college. Later, after earning a Cal Tech Ph.D. in physics, he had toiled in obscurity as a Public Health Service environmental engineer for almost a decade, struggling all the while to shake his image as a loner and country hick. He eventually fled the halls of government to begin amassing a fortune selling disaster containment gear, which he'd developed as a sideline, to fire and police departments, safety-conscious universities, major corporations, and, more recently, the Department of Defense. Now he planned to take his business to another level with a newfound niche that he expected to rake in not mere millions, but billions.

"No more security risks like Narine out your way, are there?" asked Kimbrough.

"No," said Walls, always the good soldier and a man who understood the chain of command. He was well aware that Larry Narine hadn't just walked off into the desert, as Roland

Septian had claimed. Walls listened to the howl of the wind outside his tent and questioned why, five years after his separation from the army, he was still following orders. He was also mindful that the answer was linked to the hundred thousand dollars Kimbrough was paying him to make certain that eleven Indian nobodies were adequately trained to establish a perimeter around a cargo container fire in the mountains.

"We're on a time clock now," said Kimbrough, breaking Walls's concentration. "Showtime's in less than two weeks."

"We'll be set. Count on it."

"I am. You can bet your life on it," said Kimbrough, turning his attention back to the nearby test tube agitator. "Let me know how your Navajos do in their drills this week. But remember, when it comes to the real thing, I don't expect them to actually put out the fire."

"Got you on all counts."

"Good. And, Walls, keep an eye on Roundtree, that Indian you've got leading the pack. He's smarter than he looks."

"What makes you think that?"

Kimbrough beckoned to a woman standing in the semidarkness. Clad only in black lace bikini panties, she walked across the room, her firm, tanned breasts barely jiggling.

"I have my sources," said Kimbrough, running his hand through the thick auburn hair of Rebecca Ellerby, the woman in charge of the monthly blood draws on Walls's men. Smiling, she dropped to her knees and began massaging the insides of his thighs.

"I'll keep an eye on Roundtree."

"Do that. I'll talk to you tomorrow." Kimbrough cradled the phone. Listening to the low hum of the agitator, he relaxed as the woman worked her fingers up and down his thighs.

"Who'd believe I'm taking care of *this* kind of business in a research laboratory?" she said, cupping him in one hand.

Without answering, Kimbrough smiled and slipped a finger across her lips. She was just a research associate, he told himself. There was no way she could possibly have any idea of the value of the Navajo blood she'd been drawing. She was, after all, just a cog in the wheel, like so many others. Leaning over, he slipped the panties down over her hips and felt himself harden in her hand.

CHAPTER
8

Although Walker Rios's condition was listed as stable, his psychological status remained as fragile as a rose in bloom. His own brush with death had only served to intensify his guilt over the boy he'd let drown. Deep in thought, he didn't hear the doctor enter his hospital room.

"You've had a rough go of it for the past eighteen hours, Mr. Rios," said the balding physician.

"Guess so," said Rios, his tone uncharacteristically morose.

"How are you feeling?"

"Like a pincushion with a headache."

"Strange description, but surprisingly accurate. You banged up your spine a bit, but you'll get over that. Your biggest problem is that you lost a third of your body's total blood volume."

"So that's why I feel like my motor's had all the fluids drained?"

"Probably. After all, you did crash-land off a cliff." The doctor offered a sympathetic smile. When Rios didn't respond, he said, "Mind if I check your legs? Need to make sure that when you're up to it, those babies still work." Before Rios could answer, the doctor pulled back the edge of the bedsheet.

"Fine by me," said Rios, wiggling his toes and flexing his ankles as the sheet disappeared.

Taking a rubber mallet and what looked like a six-inch pin from his coat pocket, the doctor smiled, adjusted the pin between his thumb and forefinger, and said, "Let me know exactly what you feel."

"Or if I don't feel anything?" Rios said sarcastically.

"That too," said the doctor as he began pricking the right leg from midcalf to knee.

"Pinpricks," said Rios, his response a near-shout.

"Good."

"More pinpricks," he added as the doctor moved to the other leg.

"Can you sit up in bed?"

Without answering, Rios sat up and leaned forward.

"Great," said the doctor, slipping the instrument back into his pocket.

"It's good to know that my legs are in working order, Doc. Problem is, my shoulder feels like there's a melon growing inside of it."

"That's because you severed your brachial artery and partially dislocated your left shoulder. The surgeons slipped your shoulder back in place and repaired the damaged artery."

"How far did I fall?"

"Thirty feet or so, they tell me. Could've broken your neck, but you didn't," said the doctor, lifting Rios's right leg, cradling it, and tapping his knee with the rubber mallet. "Good," he said, watching the leg snap forward.

"Guess I could've bled out," said Rios.

"Could've, if a savvy old forest ranger and Dr. Carmen Nguyen hadn't been riding shotgun on your life."

"Kept me from going over to the other side?" said Rios with an insightful nod.

"Sure did."

Rios frowned, trying his best to place the two people responsible for saving his life. "The ranger I vaguely remember. But who's Dr. Nguyen?"

"The ER doctor who got to you just before you slipped into irreversible shock." Eyeing his patient sternly, he added, "Nobody recovers from that."

"A last-second angel," said Rios.

"Well put," said the doctor, dropping the mallet back into his pocket. Recognizing that Rios needed a positive nudge, he said, "Give yourself a couple of weeks. You'll be surprised at how well you do."

"What about white-water rafting again? It's how I make my living."

The doctor hesitated before answering, "Down the road, maybe."

"How far down the road, Doc?"

"That I don't know."

"Take a guess."

"Six months, a year."

"Too long, Doc."

"I wouldn't try to shorten it," said the doctor, turning to leave. "You might end up doing more harm than good."

"Then maybe what I need is another angel or two."

"Maybe," said the doctor, leaving Rios pouting and flexing his thigh muscles against the bed.

Carmen Nguyen had never known anyone to recover from the onset of irreversible shock. Walker Rios had been a first. And, she'd never seen anyone with hairy cell leukemia and a white-blood-cell count in the hundreds of thousands walk into an emergency room on his own, the way Luke Redstone had.

Carmen was in her Aunt Ket's old barn, packing the rear brake-drum bearings on the Indian and asking herself why some people, in spite of the odds, always seemed to persevere. Probing between the hub and drum of the dismounted wheel, she located the brake-drum fitting, grabbed the grease gun from the floor, snapped the hose nozzle onto the nipple, and squeezed the lever until a cuff of grease oozed from around the fitting. She wiped away the excess grease with a shop towel, wondering as she did, *What on earth makes these two men so special?*

Perhaps it was a superior level of fitness. Rios, a six-foot-three, well-toned mass of river-rafting muscle, certainly fit the bill. But

Redstone was an altogether different story. He was a desperately ill slip of a former uranium miner who had very pointedly and quite accurately described the risks of having lived with *"decades of yellow-cake on his tail."* Why he was still alive, when the principles that governed medicine dictated that he should have succumbed to leukemia months ago, had her stumped. Stumped to the point that she'd been puzzling over not only clinical medical journals but investigative research publications as well.

As she stretched to pick up the Indian's front wheel for remounting, the door to the garage creaked open. "Thought I'd find you here," said her aunt, swinging the door back to a wash of sunlight. "Got a Federal Express delivery for you." Ket Tran eyed the bulky envelope in her hand. "It's from Utah, with a University Hospital return address," she added, her tone discernibly suspicious. "Thought you were through with them."

Appreciating her aunt's concern, Carmen said, "It's just a bunch of research papers. I had them sent here because I knew I'd be working on the bike all day."

"Didn't know you still had friends in Salt Lake."

"A few." Carmen worked the wheel into place.

"The envelope's pretty hefty."

"It's information I promised to get for an oncologist who's treating a leukemia patient at work." Carmen pushed the cotter through the rear wheel nut, bent it over, and wiped her hands on the grease rag.

"I see." Reluctantly accepting Carmen's explanation, Ket turned to leave.

"Wait, I'll walk up to the house with you." Carmen crossed the dusty floor and clasped hands with her aunt. As they moved out into the Saturday-afternoon brightness, she stopped and looked around the fruit orchard—the one place that, more than any other, had grounded her firmly in America during her adolescence. It was a forty-acre magical island that Ket had paid for by pruning trees, picking fruit, shoveling snow, and mopping floors.

"That Utah address had me worried," said Ket. "Thought for

some reason you might be headed back to Salt Lake," she added, handing the envelope to Carmen.

"No way," said Carmen, pausing to drink in the intoxicating smell of ripe peaches. "Never," she added, still wondering what it was that made people like Walker Rios, Luke Redstone, and Ket Tran so amazingly resilient.

CHAPTER
9

In its first life the windowless two-story brick building baking in the midday sun of lower downtown Denver had been a carriage house and livery stable, catering to the Queen City's wealthy and influential. On the heels of its horse-barn days, it had become an infamous brothel, serving the equally demanding needs of local politicians, cowboys, and miners. But for most of the twentieth century the building had simply been a warehouse, that often overlooked conduit and way station of American commerce. A 1920s advertising mural for Bull Durham chewing tobacco still covered most of the building's east wall, the anatomically correct bull continuing to flake away, bit by bit, over the years.

Jack Kimbrough had purchased the building on the banks of the Platte River to serve as a major storage facility for Particle Trigenics, reserving the wing that faced the Rockies for the research and development side of his business. It was an arm of the company he kept cloaked in secrecy, a unit charged with investigating issues as diverse as the molecular mechanisms of human immunity and the physics of red-blood-cell circulation.

For more than a decade, Kimbrough had been trying vainly to match his business success with a tangible R & D record that would prove to detractors that he wasn't just a West Texas bumpkin who'd made a lucky business strike, but an investigative research scientist of substance. Years earlier, at Cal Tech, he'd been laughed at and called a hayseed, a dumb jock, and a rube. During that rocky four-year tenure when he'd argued that physics and medicine should be symbiotic rather than separate sciences, he'd been uniformly scorned. Soon Jack Kimbrough would correct that injustice.

For years Kimbrough had made a habit of leaving his Seventeenth Street high-rise office during the noon hour to run over a mile to the Trigenics Platte River R & D facility. It was his way of linking himself to what he liked to think of as the true milieu of science.

Weaving his way through the Sixteenth Street Mall lunch crowd, he picked up his pace, eyeing the tobacco mural on his R & D facility in the distance.

Designed for expansion and equipped with state-of-the-art molecular biological equipment, the place had languished unproductively for years, until the recent arrival of Dr. Felix Tangay. Tangay, a timid, nervous Filipino, was a cutting-edge molecular biologist who had signed on eighteen months earlier as the division's lead scientist. In the space of a year his research team had developed an artificial skin barrier for burn victims that was so effective at curtailing infections that Trigenics could barely keep the product in stock. Giddy with Tangay's success, Kimbrough had agreed to fund a five-year investigation of Tangay's pet interest, radical protective genes. To celebrate the collaboration, he'd traveled with Tangay to the Philippines.

Early during the two-week trip, Kimbrough had attended a cockfight in Manila, where the life-and-death, winner-take-all atmosphere struck a West Texas chord. He spent two additional weeks in the Philippines, traveling from large *topados* in the cities to trembling bamboo shacks in tiny villages, drinking in the history of cockfighting and feasting on the nightly performances of blood and death. Returning home addicted to the sport, he spent much of his time during the next two years traveling to cockfights throughout the Western United States.

Until he caught Luke Redstone's act in a makeshift cockpit inside a dilapidated barn near Grand Junction, he had remained content to be a spectator. But after weeks of watching Stone's cocks destroy the competition, his scientific curiosity got the better of him, and he began to question why those birds were always such clear winners. He followed Stone to cockfights across Colorado, New Mexico, and Utah, watching him win routinely, but his attempts to investigate the lineage of the birds always resulted in dead ends. When, out of frustration, he eventually tried to purchase a set of Stone's breeding stock for ten thousand dollars, he was told by Stone, in words that continued to haunt him, "I don't sell my birds."

Perspiring and winded from the run, Kimbrough now stood talking to Felix Tangay in a three-thousand-square-foot research laboratory, one of six that represented the R & D backbone of Particle Trigenics.

"Everything points to the development of a radical protective trait in the old cockfighter's birds," said Tangay, handing Kimbrough a folder bulging with papers. "It's all there, summarized down to the last protein—eight months of work. And all gleaned, I might add, from the carcass of a rotting domestic fowl." Tangay beamed as he surveyed the lab's battery of state-of-the-art scientific hardware and gene splicing equipment. "Hard to believe what a little grave-robbing, a few stray chicken bones, and DNA sequencing can do."

"I'd say we've got our answer, then." Kimbrough patted the folder and smiled.

"I wouldn't be so quick to say."

Kimbrough opened the folder and flipped through the papers. "Always the skeptic, aren't you, Felix? How much more proof do we need? We've got gamecock tissue samples that all show inactivated heat shock protein, and six months' worth of blood samples from a bunch of Navajos that show the very same thing. Seems like a match to me."

Tangay shook his head. "You're a scientist, Jack. You know very well that what we've got here is only half an answer. In vitro studies are fine, but unfortunately they're just extrapolated test-tube science. So a few blood samples from your Navajos show inactivated heat shock protein. Big deal. From what you've told me, not one of your Indians shows the slightest sign of a single physical radical developmental trait. Physically, every one of them is as normal as you and me. Same holds for that old geezer Redstone's birds, at least from the samples. So all we've really got here are a few gamecock tissue samples that lack heat shock protein. Somewhere along the line we're going to have to find a freak of nature out there with totally depleted levels of heat shock protein. That's the ticket we need to prove that depleted heat shock protein levels lead to activation of radical protective genes and, ultimately, to a cadre of invincibles."

Kimbrough nibbled on his lip in frustration. "Suppose you had a chance to sample tissue from one of Redstone's live birds? Would that help tie up the loose ends?"

"It would be a hell of a start."

Kimbrough's voice boomed. "I'll have one for you, or something just as close, within a week."

"You've been saying that for months and I'm still waiting. You should know better than most, delays can be costly when it comes to science."

Kimbrough bristled and checked his watch. "You'll get your delivery, Felix. Right here, and within the next two days," he said, turning to leave. When he reached the explosion-proof double-doored exit, he turned back to Tangay and flashed a cold, hard frown. "And, Felix, since we're being so candid here, try not to make the mistake of criticizing me again. It might soothe your ego, but it's not healthy for you or your science." Pushing through the doors, he left Tangay staring nervously at the floor.

Jogging down the hallway and back out into the sun-drenched summer day, Kimbrough wondered just how far he could trust a man like Tangay. He was a foreigner, after all, who had the reputation of being a scientific rogue. Pleased that he'd never shared certain things about his platoon of bivouacked Navajos with Tangay, Kimbrough picked up his pace. Only he and Rebecca Ellerby, his research tech, current source of sexual contentment, and plant inside Tangay's lab, were aware of exactly why his Navajos were the perfect recruits for the exercise he'd so meticulously planned.

The child of a poor man, Kimbrough had learned never to share everything he knew. There was a piece of the heat shock protein puzzle that Felix Tangay didn't have—a piece worth billions in the long run. A fragment to the puzzle that could only be fully evaluated by putting his Navajo recruits' feet to the proverbial—and literal—fire.

CHAPTER
10

Never liked Stone. Never cared a shit for his birds either,"
grumbled Jimmy Turner, a grizzled fire plug of a man who
looked much closer to fifty than his true age of sixty-five.
"Fuckin' squat-assed, thick-legged freaks," said Turner, squinting into the midmorning sun. "Every one of 'em. His clarets, his
butchers, his fuckin' Arkansas travelers, even the goddamn
grays he raised. Droopy, double-eye-lidded birds with feathers
puffed up that always seemed to be reflectin' somethin' off of
'em, day or night. Sissified birds, if you can believe that. Birds
that liked to lift up on their toes before a match like they was
either gay or Indian fancy-dancin'. Carnival birds, if you get my
drift, most of 'em straight-out freaks. . . . No use for Stone or his
birds, no sirree. But I got plenty o' use for the fifteen hundred
you anted up. Plenty of use for that," said Turner, glancing back
toward Roland Septian and Brandon DeVille and focusing on
the 30.06 rifle slung over Septian's right shoulder.

Since leaving their desert base camp, Septian and DeVille had
been trailing behind Turner, listening to him ramble on nonstop
for close to an hour. They were carrying insulated plastic coolers
filled with a mixture of dry ice and isopentane, an arctic slurry
that maintained the temperature inside the coolers at minus 144
degrees Fahrenheit. "How much further to the birds?" asked
DeVille, breathless and sweaty from following Turner up and
down hills, through chokecherry thickets, and now across a
football-field-sized island of knife-edged bedrock.

"Far enough to keep a pussy like you from findin' 'em. You

wanna find gold, you gotta work at it, my man. And I ain't never known you to do much of that," Turner added to the gasping DeVille. "One thing for sure: When he hid his stock, Stone was countin' on a soft-serve like you doin' the lookin'. But ain't no way in hell he'd ever be able to hide that circus full of cock mutants of his from me. I know that uranium-muckin' bastard's half-breed ways. Should—for twenty years we both been makin' a livin' at the very same game."

Angered by Turner's sermon and incensed at being called a gold brick, DeVille stopped and spit between Turner's feet. "Screw you, old man."

Turner laughed and picked up his pace.

"No chance you could've made a mistake?" said Septian, barely catching up with Turner before slipping on a tilted slab of rock and nearly losing his balance.

"Watch yourself on that shale," said Turner, maintaining his pace. "The stuff gets a little wet from dew and it's slicker'n eel snot. Lose your footing on a hillside like this, and on the way down you'll cut your ass to ribbons."

"Can the geology lesson, Turner. It's time to deliver the goods," said Septian, regaining his balance.

Turner snorted back a laugh and pointed toward a hilltop just ahead. "It's just over the rise. They'll be there, just like I said." Pausing on a level slab of fractured shale, he waited for DeVille to catch up. When DeVille reached the spot, puffing like a steam locomotive, Turner smiled and stroked his chin. "Mind answerin' somethin' for me, DeVille? I know your old man mucked with Redstone in the mines and that he even seconded for him when the old man started out breedin' cocks. What's your angle in this? You plannin' on takin' over Stone's breedin' stock?"

"I'm planning on whipping your ass, old man, if you don't shut the fuck up."

"Just try me, son. Guarantee ya', it wouldn't be much of a fight." Turner shot DeVille a broad, toothless grin. As they moved toward each other, Septian pulled the Luger from his waistband holster and fired into the dirt. "I'll shoot you both.

Right here and now. Leave you for the fuckin' buzzards. Believe me, it would make my day." Then, motioning up the hill with the Luger, he said, "Move your two sorry asses—now."

Scrabbling uphill in silence, Turner and DeVille darted icy stares at each other until they reached the top. Down below, protected by a clump of aspen barely visible from the summit, a line of galvanized cages glistened in the morning sun. "There's your Emerald City," said Turner. "Stone spent a pretty penny settin' this up. Got close to twenty birds housed down here. Automated water and food dispensers, flow-through ventilation, even tree-lined shade. Everything he needs to keep those cocks of his happy and fat. Shit, the way he's got it laid out, he can leave and forget about the hummers for the better part of a week."

"How'd you find them?" asked Septian, relieved that he'd finally found the birds Kimbrough had sent him after.

"Let's just say it's my business to know the competition," said Turner as they worked their way down the other side of the hill.

"We only need one or two birds," said DeVille, stumbling in the dirt, eager to get the raid over. "This should be pretty easy. In and right back out."

Turner shook his head. "One bird, two, ten, or fifty—Stone'll know somebody's been here. You can count on that."

Septian smiled. "Could've been dogs or coyotes that got 'em."

"You don't know Stone real well, do you? Trust me; he'll know," Turner countered.

"Then let's get what we need and get out of here," said DeVille.

"You're on the money for once," said Turner, sidestepping his way down the hillside, barely displacing the unstable rock as Septian and DeVille stumbled along beside him. "We'll wanna approach the birds slowly; otherwise there'll be one hell of a racket."

"Who the shit cares?" said Septian, closing in rapidly on the cages.

"It's your eardrums," said Turner, with a shrug.

Suddenly the birds were active, scraping at their flooring,

pushing against the cage wires, clucking, crowing, and raising a ruckus. Septian knelt in front of a cage and stared at the cock inside. The cock turned to face him, angling its head so that one dark, unreflecting eye peered out. The bird blinked its wrinkled eyelid. Its feathers, thinned for battle and lying tight against its body, resembled shingles on a roof, and its thick, curving beak drew to a point like the end of a fine writing instrument. But it was the cock's massive legs that held Septian's attention—muscular legs set on horny, clawed, and spurred feet. Legs that were disproportionate to the rest of the cock's body. "This one doesn't look like any chicken I've ever seen," Septian said finally.

"The others won't either," said Turner. "On the cockfightin' circuit they're known as 'Stone's travelin' freaks.'" Stepping away from Septian, Turner moved to where DeVille stood, several feet away. Grinning at DeVille, he said, "But you knew that already, didn't you? You been around Stone's gamecocks before, back when you was a kid." Turner nodded toward Septian. "Wonder if Ace down there knows about that? Maybe I should clue him in."

DeVille didn't answer. Instead he opened the door to the cage in front of him and grabbed the retreating bird firmly with both hands. "Come inject this one," he called out to Septian. "Better make it quick. I can't hold the fucker all day."

In three quick strides Septian was at his side. Reaching in his pocket, he pulled out a syringe and injected the squirming cock in the thigh. Within seconds the bird was a limp six-pound knot of muscle and feathers in DeVille's hands. Grabbing the cock by its legs, DeVille dropped to one knee and spun the top off the cooler. A frosty plume of gas rose into the air as he dropped the bird inside.

"We'll take another one," said Septian. "But this time I get to pick," he said, sounding like an excited child as he paced in front of the cages, eyeing the cocks inside one by one. Rubbing his hands together, he broke into an ear-to-ear grin. "I want another fat one with those tree-trunk legs."

"Take your pick," said DeVille, wondering why the hell they'd taken such a strange side trip from their desert base camp.

CHAPTER
11

Since leaving academic medicine for life at St. Mary's, Carmen Nguyen had lived by one hard-and-fast rule when it came to committing herself to a patient's post-emergency-room care: *She didn't.*

As a result, she was finding it difficult to rationalize why she'd become so caught up in what happened to a grizzled, out-of-sorts old cockfighter with hairy cell leukemia. It certainly hadn't been Luke Redstone's vulnerability that had attracted her to his case. She recognized that Stone was the kind of person who could take care of himself, even in the face of death. He'd told her as much when she had visited him in his hospital room a second time, and he'd emphatically told her that the most important thing in his life was not his own well-being but that of his birds.

Clearly her interest in Redstone's case hadn't been triggered by a need to salvage another life. She'd spent the past two years in the ER doing that. What had piqued her interest, stimulated her scientific curiosity, and made her ignore her rule about post-ER patient involvements was the fact that the only two cases she'd ever seen of hairy cell leukemia had been in men who, like Luke Redstone, had mined uranium along the Colorado Plateau. In the end, her scientific inquisitiveness had seduced her, just as it had for most of her medical career. Now, as she turned down the hallway that led to Stone's room, she was hoping she hadn't taken too big a bite.

"Where the hell you been? It's almost noon," said Stone, glancing into his bathroom mirror and catching sight of Carmen. "And don't mind my privacy," he added, crooking his head toward her as he massaged a two-day growth of beard. "A woman bargin' in on a man in the john don't faze me in the least."

"I'll come back later."

"No, no. Come on in," said Stone, his harsh tone softening. "See, I'm quick as a fox," he added, spinning to face Carmen. Moving heel to toe across the room, right arm flexed and index finger to his nose, he added, "And I'm steady as a rock," before plopping down, winded, on the edge of the bed.

"Glad to see it," said Carmen, prepared for what she knew was coming next.

Stone slipped into bed, stuffed two pillows behind his back, and leaned back into them. "Now, how about my birds? I'll hold this place responsible if somethin' happens to 'em. And I'll sue. You got pull, Doc. I need to get outta here now!"

"We're not through with your tests," said Carmen, sliding a chair up next to the bed and taking a seat. "Your birds will have to wait."

Pleasantly surprised, Stone said, "'We'? I thought Doc Williams was in charge of sawin' my bones."

"He's asked me to help."

Stone broke into a broad smile, surprising Carmen by responding with something other than a frown or a threat. "It'll take more than your good looks to fix what's ailin' me."

"I'll pass that on to Dr. Williams," she said, squirming in the uncomfortable metal chair. "Now, maybe we can start where we left off yesterday. You were about to tell me about working in the mines."

"Yeah." Stone nodded. "Ain't much to tell, really. I mucked uranium just like a bunch of other down-and-out folks livin' on the Colorado Plateau. Did it for close to five years after I came back from Korea."

"You were in the army?"

"Hell, no, the marines! Got a Navy Cross to prove it. Wasn't the war that got me in the shape I'm in now, though. It was them goddamn mines. I'd take war over them death traps any day," he said, watching Carmen's eyebrows arch and her eyes widen. "Sorry about cussin'. Force o' habit," he added.

"No problem." It had been Stone's comment about war, not his swearing, that had triggered Carmen's reaction. "Mind telling me where you worked?"

Recognizing that Carmen still seemed shaken, he said, "A better question's where *didn't* I work? Let's see. Worked outside Cisco, Utah, at the Big Indian Wash. Dog-holed around Moab. Mucked at Mi Vida, the Happy Jack, the Joe Jr. mill, and Dove Creek. All in all, I'd wager I pulled my share of yellow-cake outta close to a dozen or so mines."

Carmen frowned and shook her head, well aware of the names, all treacherous holes in the earth that had once dotted a five-hundred-square-mile triangle along the Colorado Plateau from Moab to Dove Creek, Cisco to Grand Junction. During her days as an oncologist, she had treated her share of former uranium miners for lung cancer, lymphoma, and even leukemia, and most of them had trodden the same high-risk path as Stone. "If I mentioned the names of a couple of patients I treated, do you think you'd recognize them?"

"Maybe, maybe not. A lot of people worked in them mines. What's with the connection 'tween them and me anyway, Doc? You plannin' on treatin' me, or are you searchin' for some kinda uranium-muckin' family tree?"

"Treating you, of course. I'm just looking for background information that might help."

"Ain't none. Sometimes the mines gobbled up people and swallowed 'em whole. Other times they didn't. It's the chance you took muckin' yellow-cake. I ain't complainin'. Pretty much took all I could from life. Only thing I'm lookin' for now is a ticket outta here so's I can get back to my birds."

Carmen was amazed at how anyone could be so stoic after mining high-grade uranium ore for years, all the while breathing its cancer-causing by-product, radon gas. Shaking her head, she said, "I hate to mention this, Mr. Redstone, but you seem more concerned about your gamecocks than your health."

Stone responded with a laugh that rumbled up from his belly before trailing off into a series of fitful coughs. "Everybody calls me Stone, like I told you yesterday, Doc. And trust me, I ain't *more* concerned. I'm just bein' honest with myself. Some of us muckin' ore back then had an inklin' about what might come. Most didn't. Sometimes we'd amuse ourselves comin' off a shift by breathin' on a radiation counter and bettin' whose breath could peg the needle the highest. No matter what you think, though, we wasn't fools. Just a bunch of unawares Indians and ignernt country loads—most of us high-country drifters and cut-loose kids. Folks that, for the most part, never cashed a six-buck-a-hour paycheck in their lives before the mines come along."

"They didn't ventilate those mines," said Carmen, her tone indignant.

"And half the time we didn't wear the damn respirators they give us," countered Stone. "Like I said, it was all about money. You ever been poor?"

Carmen didn't answer, as the turbulent years she'd spent in Utah suddenly began playing back in her head. She had championed a cause once, and it had cost her a promising career. She didn't need a second cause to celebrate. Looking at Stone sympathetically, she swallowed hard. "We'll begin your chemo-therapy as soon as your red-cell counts pick up. There'll be transfusions, of course, and nutritional supplements to take. We're serious about treating your disease, and we expect you to be the same." Her voice trailed off until it sounded hollow.

"Didn't mean to spook you, Doc. Just wanted you to know where I stood. Now that we're square with each other, let's get back to my birds."

"Yesterday you told me they'd be fine for a week."

"That was when I figured I'd be outta here today or tomorra'."

Carmen shook her head. "You're off by a week—perhaps even more."

"Then I'll walk right now. I won't let you folks do a damn thing."

"You'd be jeopardizing your life."

"Wouldn't matter a shit without my birds." Stone jumped out of bed and headed toward the closet. "Don't need nothin' but my shoes and my clothes."

Carmen rushed to block his way. "I'll make sure someone tends to them."

"Promise?" he said, winded and gasping for air.

"Promise."

"Don't lie to me," said Stone, staring directly into Carmen's eyes.

"I don't lie, Mr. Redstone. It's not in my nature," she answered defiantly.

"Good," he said, his eyes still locked on hers. " 'Cause if somethin' happens to my birds now, I'll hold you accountable."

After a trip to the hospital library and a barely edible fast-food meal, Carmen found herself back at St. Mary's and on her way to see Walker Rios, at the urgent request of his attending physician. She felt her stomach tighten as she thought about how she'd ended her visit with Stone. She'd made a bargain that now, in the early evening darkness, seemed more like a pact with the devil. In return for making sure his birds were okay, she'd asked Stone to look in on a fellow patient, Walker Rios. Stone had agreed only after she informed him that Rios was a fellow marine in need of a boost.

The psychologist counseling Rios was calling his condition post-traumatic depression, brought on by the combination of a recent tragic death he felt responsible for and his own near-fatal accident. His psychologist had requested the consult, claiming that a visit from the doctor who Rios was convinced had saved his life might help stave off a brewing depression. Carmen wasn't sure how she could help the ailing river guide, but she had reluctantly agreed to see him, largely because she understood what it was like to be chased by lingering sadness.

As a child in Vietnam she had been told by classmates, teachers, and people on the street that her American father had a tail and that *my den* women developed twelve anuses as they aged. Like all *my den* children, she'd been classified as dim-witted, incapable of understanding ideas such as truth, family, country, honor, and hard work. Until the day of her motorcycle race across the Vietnam countryside toward freedom, she'd been fearful of becoming just another *my den* whore. Then, in her new homeland, she had persevered despite a more subtle, American brand of discrimination, but she had never been able to fully close that door on the damage to her psyche. She still trembled at the thought of that dark door to the past ever swinging open again.

It was just past eight P.M. when she reached Rios's darkened room. A buzzing fluorescent bulb above the bed afforded the only light. Rios was sitting up in bed reading a copy of *Fly Fisherman*, his wavy jet-black hair shimmering in the artificial glow.

Rapping lightly on the partly open door as she entered, Carmen said, "Mr. Rios, I'm Dr. Nguyen."

"Come on in." Rios set aside his magazine and looked up at Carmen, who appeared even more exotic than she'd been described. Dressed in surgical scrubs and a freshly laundered lab coat, with a dog-eared guide to laboratory values and a stethoscope bulging from one pocket, she looked more like an over-eager intern than a seasoned physician.

"Hope I'm not disturbing you."

"No. Just reading, wondering if I'll ever be doing any fly-fishing or river rafting again."

"Shouldn't be a problem, but it'll take time. Mind if I turn on the overhead light?"

"Fine by me." Rios watched Carmen walk across the room and flip on the light switch, thinking as she did that she moved like a dancer.

"Better," said Carmen, getting her first look at Rios since she'd last seen him, struggling for life in the ER. Alert and coherent now rather than tottering on the brink, he was much larger than she remembered—rugged-looking, even—with barely a hint of gauntness. "How are you feeling?"

"Great," said Rios, his voice brimming with sarcasm.

"Things will get better with time."

"Good. So when I'm running white water in the future, I'll barely remember that I killed some poor kid."

Hoping to temper Rios's pessimistic outlook with a note of encouragement, Carmen countered, "That's probably not—"

"That's bullshit!" boomed a voice from the doorway, cutting Carmen off. "Pure bullshit, Walker, and you know it." Out of uniform and dressed in street clothes, Warren Anderson, the burly Mesa County sheriff and Rios's lifelong friend, looked less like a peace officer than an overstuffed grizzly as he lumbered across the room.

Recognizing the sheriff from TV news footage and his tireless support of the hospital's annual lung cancer benefit, Carmen watched as he strode to the foot of the bed. "Quit feeling sorry for yourself, man. The Forest Service people looked into what happened to the Miles kid, and so did my office. Anything out of the ordinary, they would've pulled your white-water permits. And friend or not, I would've been forced to slap your butt in jail. It was an accident, Walker, and not your fault. The boy stood up to search for his camera when he shouldn't have, and he only had one arm through his life vest. Lighten up on yourself or you're gonna dig a hole you can't get out of." Then, looking at Carmen with boyish innocence, he said, "Sorry about the intrusion, Doctor . . . ?"

"Nguyen."

"Pleasure," said the sheriff, extending his hand.

Rios turned away without responding as he once again found himself running the ill-fated trip through his head. He'd never had a fatality during all his years of river rafting. And he couldn't remember a single person—except his brother, who'd once been acting the fool while swamping for him—being tossed from his boat. But now rationalizations and a perfect safety record didn't matter. The boy was dead, and his death was a direct result of something that he, Walker Rios, had done wrong that day. Until he pegged exactly what it was, he knew he'd have no peace.

"I'd try listening to the sheriff," said Carmen, interrupting Rios's self-flagellation.

"It wasn't his boat," said Rios.

"And it wasn't my big burly ass that blocked for your narrow, skinny butt during four years of high school so you could get a football scholarship to CSU. Come off it, Walker. Bad shit happens to good people every day. Step back into the real world for a minute."

The sheriff's comments seemed to settle Rios momentarily. "What about the kid's parents?"

"In time they'll heal. We all do."

"And if they don't?"

The sheriff shrugged, turned to Carmen, shook his head, and took a seat. "Afraid I'm not his nursemaid or a shrink. He's all yours, Doc."

"The sheriff seems to know you pretty well," said Carmen, stepping back up to the bed.

"We started out in grade school together," said Rios, looking into her eyes.

"So that's why he can get away with being so blunt?"

"He's that way with everyone. Besides, he's a cop and we're both no-nonsense ex-marines."

Carmen looked at the sheriff, who confirmed Rios's comments with a nod and a smile. "Did anything he said make any sense?"

"To him perhaps."

"The part about not blaming yourself for the boating accident seemed to be pretty sound advice. Maybe you should take it."

"I'll mull it over."

"Do that. And while you're at it, I want you to try something else." Carmen pulled a rubber exercise ball from her coat pocket and handed it to Rios. "It's just the thing for getting your arm strength and muscle tone back. Start with a few squeezes an hour and work your way up."

"To what?"

"There's no limit," said Carmen, stepping away from the bed.

"So you're in charge of not only saving lives but physical therapy too?"

"No, that would be Dr. Whitner, but I'll be around."

"I see." Rios transferred the exercise ball from his good right hand to his weak left one.

"Keep up the reps," said Carmen, nodding a good-bye to the sheriff before striding from the room with the realization that, like it or not, she now had two new patients on her hands: a craggy old cockfighter with leukemia and an injured river guide in need of a psychological mend. Men who, like her father, had once been marines.

"I'll do that," called out Rios, squeezing the ball with a grunt. Clenching it again, then again, he was halfway into a fourth painful squeeze when the ball slipped from his hand and bounced to the floor, out of reach.

CHAPTER

12

I never lie. The three words she'd uttered in defiance to Luke Redstone rang in Carmen's ears as, sweating in the midday sun, she negotiated her bored-out two-stroke dirt bike along a bumpy cow path, weaving between stubby chokecherry trees and serviceberry bushes. She had first learned to ride on a moped, as a shy seven-year-old delivering black-market cigarettes on the streets of Saigon. By the age of ten, despite the protests of her aunt, she was working as a money changer, blistering those same streets on a Kawasaki 75. She and Aunt Ket had made their freedom run across Quang Ngai Province, down bomb-crater-riddled Highway 521 to the South China Sea, on a junkyard derelict Carmen had pieced together from the frame of a burned-out Yamaha and boxes of bartered parts.

As the high desert wind whipped through her hair, she kept asking herself the same question: Why, after her Utah experience and despite her pledge never again to become entangled in another patient's personal problems, was she here? She'd thought about sending someone she trusted to check on Stone's birds, but she hadn't, and she suspected it was because even at the age of thirty-eight, she was still trying to prove that in spite of being *my den* she fully understood the ideals of truth and honor. That regardless of being a black Amerasian half-breed, her word could be trusted.

Now, instead of enjoying two hard-earned days off, hiking the Grand Mesa as she'd planned, she was eating dust and speeding along too fast for the terrain in order to soothe her conscience and keep a promise to a dying old man. The map Stone had sketched for her on the back of a patient progress sheet had been drawn remarkably to scale. The map, frayed at the edges from her repeated references to it, detailed exactly where Stone had hidden his prize gamecocks.

The birds couldn't survive beyond the end of the week without her help, he'd told her in a fit of frustration during another of their spirited visits. Once she located his hideaway south of Dominguez Canyon, she would have to check the birds' water bottles and replenish them, restock their food jugs with pellets, and hose down the dropping pans in the bottoms of the cages. "After that you can check out their health," Stone had commanded.

Carmen rose out of the saddle and throttled back as she approached the rugged backcountry that Stone had warned would eventually turn into a sea of shale. Threading her way through pockets of sharp, loose rock, she worked her way up a hill to the ridge that Stone claimed protected his birds from "contamination by the outside world." Although Stone hadn't explained why his gamecocks were tucked away in such desolate country, and she'd never come right out and asked, she suspected the ruse was because he either owed someone money or was dodging the law.

Easing the dirt bike to a stop on the ridge, she found herself gazing down on stands of aspen that framed several acres of flat irrigated land. The cages that Stone had assured her would be there glimmered in the sun. The bare rock she'd been avoiding on her way up the hill petered out a few yards beyond the summit, giving way to a downslope blanket of wildflowers, stunted sagebrush, and willowy grass. Carmen checked her saddlebags to make certain the bottled drinking water she was carrying was secure. Then, in a rush fueled by a sense of adventure she hadn't felt in years, she gunned the bike's engine, kicking up dirt as she roared downhill.

The acreage below looked less inviting than it had from above. The trees seemed sparser, the grounds less fertile, and the confining cages rusted and dull. Weaving her way through a stand of aspen, Carmen cruised to a stop, killed the bike's engine, and walked slowly along the rows of cages that housed a menagerie of preening, pecking, scratching, forlorn-looking birds. She peered into each cage: a white-speckled pinto, a big red, a dusty-brown bird with its right eye swollen shut, and next to it a stately black, then an undersized bantam. Only now could she begin to appreciate how Stone made a living. Wondering how he could bring himself to profit from such a brutal sport, she paused at an empty cage near the middle of the cell-block-style layout and pulled back the door. A moth fluttered out. Startled, she stepped back, fanned the moth away, and continued her inspection. The next two cages were also empty.

After two more cages, housing roosters with badly sheared combs and partially detached beaks, she was almost ready to forget her promise to Stone, get on her motorcycle, and leave, when out of the corner of one eye she spotted a mammoth bird staring at her from the shadow of its cage. It was russet, with enormous legs and a disproportionately thick neck, and its comb brushed against the top of the cage. Carmen stared, amazed at the bird's size, then picked up a twig and ran it across the cage door. The big cock continued eyeing her but did not move.

The bird in the next cage, startled by the noise, began pecking furiously at its food dispenser. She checked—out of food and water. Looking around her, she spotted the funnel-shaped food pellet bin and the hundred-gallon water tank nestled in the protective shade of an aspen stand, just as Stone had described them.

She had taken two steps beyond the line of cages when a loud crack erupted from the west. A second later, she heard a whistling and then a *thwack* at her feet, followed by another crack. She knew the way of bullets, which outrun the noise of their own firing and can kill you before you even hear the shot. Dropping to the ground, she began crawling furiously back toward the motorcycle as Stone's gamecocks began banging and scraping at the sides of their cages. Several more shots slammed into the trunk of a big pine next to the dirt bike just as she reached it.

Praying that the next bullet did not rip through her or the gas tank, she launched onto the bike and kick-started the engine. Aware that she made a perfect silhouette for whoever was sniping at her from the gully, she gunned the engine, slunk down against the bike frame, and broke full bore for the stand of aspen. Thirty yards into the run, shots splintered a small boulder, sending rock chips sparking off the front spokes. Miraculously, the tire appeared to be undamaged. Weaving her way through aspens, she found the path that led back up the hillside she'd come down. She was about to charge up the hill when the past caught up and rolled over her.

The bike coasted to a stop. Across a gulf of more than thirty years, the aspen grove suddenly was a rice paddy. "Mama! Mama! I'm over here!" Carmen screamed as the racket of small-arms fire filled the air. But no one answered. She could stay here, she told herself, hidden in the rice paddy, where no soldiers would ever find her. She was about to step off the dirt bike when a bullet chirped past her ear and smacked into a tree limb, jolting her back to reality.

Screaming, "Killers! Killers! Killers!" as the rear tire fishtailed around, Carmen broke out of the aspens, taking a diagonal route up the hill. Halfway up the hillside, a shot pierced her saddlebag, sending water spouting everywhere. A final shot dinged the front yoke as she crested the hilltop. With her heart racing and sweat streaming down her neck, she glanced back, took a deep breath, and throttled up. Soon she was fireballing her way across the dry Mesa County backcountry, thanking God she was alive as she streaked for Grand Junction and home.

Brandon DeVille stepped from the gully he'd been hiding in and strolled toward Stone's cages, his scope-mounted semiautomatic rifle slung over his shoulder. Laughing, impressed at what a hell of a shot he was, he couldn't stop gloating over having made one of Redstone's flunkies piss her pants. He slung the binoculars over his other shoulder and broke into a trot as he pondered how easily he could have knocked the woman off the dirt bike anytime he'd wanted.

He had to give her credit, though: She could flat-out ride a fucking motorcycle. And although he'd never seen her before, she'd be easy to trace. Colorado *ABD100*—that should be an easy enough plate number to remember.

CHAPTER

13

Felix Tangay was fuming because, as usual, Jack Kimbrough was late for their appointment. He was already angry over the temperature in the lab, which for some unexplained reason had crept from its preprogrammed setting of seventy-two to a blistering seventy-eight degrees. Well aware that in the precise world of molecular biology, a six-degree temperature swing could prove catastrophic, Tangay walked over to the room's thermostat and hastily reprogrammed it. He relaxed as the air conditioner clicked on and he felt the rush of cool air. Satisfied that no harm had been done, he stepped to a nearby refrigerator. A sign taped to the door read, *For Non-Research Purposes Only*. He opened the door, took out a sandwich and an overripe banana, and walked over to his desk to have a late lunch.

Two years earlier no one had taken his research seriously: not the college he taught at, the National Institutes of Health, or a single one of the hundreds of dot-com pharmaceutical start-ups that he'd been pestering to dump money into his investigation of radical protective genes. Aware that most of his colleagues considered him just another bespectacled, fidgety, job-usurping foreigner with bad teeth, middle-age acne, and crackpot ideas, he'd been forced to muddle along as a cellular and structural biology professor at a backwater Midwestern college. His job with Trigenics had come as the result of a chance meeting with Jack Kimbrough at a research workshop in Boston. Kimbrough, always trolling for ideas that had possible commercial applications, had hired him on the spot after hearing of Tangay's research involving developmental anomalies in fruit flies.

Tangay had been convinced that certain fruit fly anomalies he was seeing in his research were precipitated by the altered function of a common animal amino-acid complex known as "heat shock protein 90," and when Kimbrough offered him twice his annual college salary and a state-of-the-art laboratory to work in, he had jumped ship.

The concept he'd shared with Kimbrough during the Boston meeting involved the alterations in HSP90 that occurred when his fruit flies were exposed to extreme changes in temperature. The resulting developmental defects ranged from deformed eyes and legs to elongated thoraxes and bizarre mutations in wing thickness, size, and shape.

What intrigued Kimbrough the most, though, and what sealed the deal for Tangay's employment, were two facts about heat shock protein that flew directly in the face of accepted science: The abnormalities Tangay had documented occurred rapidly after the insects' exposure to extreme heat or cold, not incrementally over time as one would expect; and, also contrary to popular scientific dogma, the bizarre anomalies were rarely life-threatening.

Tangay called what he was seeing in the laboratory "rapidly adaptive protective development," or RAPD for short. Unfortunately, his RAPD theory flew in the face of long-accepted Darwinian doctrine, which held that evolutionary changes in all living things are a glacially slow and gradual succession of minute adaptations—never a one-time developmental rocket blast, as Tangay claimed.

At Trigenics he had tried unsuccessfully for nearly a year to move his experiments from fruit flies to other species until, doubting himself and ready to call it quits, he had gotten from Jack Kimbrough a dead, maggot-infested gamecock for study.

Tangay had seen Kimbrough's zeal for cockfighting firsthand, and he hadn't needed to ask where the bird came from. He'd spent six months evaluating tissue samples from the bird and running tests identical to those he'd run on his fruit flies. In the end, he'd come away with only a minor HSP/RAPD break-through. Now, however, Tangay suspected that the two new frozen gamecocks that Kimbrough's strongman, Roland Septian, had brought in just twenty-four hours ago held the ultimate RAPD key.

Nibbling his sandwich and pondering his next research move, Tangay barely looked up when Kimbrough rushed into the lab. "Sorry I'm late. Got held up in a meeting. How about bringing me up to speed?"

Tangay set the sandwich aside and rose from his seat. "I just set up an experiment to determine if tissue extracts from the deformed eyelids of the frozen gamecocks that Septian gave me show evidence of HSP90 mutant chromosomes. Want to have a look?"

"Absolutely," said Kimbrough, cautiously surveying the lab. "No one else here, is there?" he added, following Tangay to a room designed for DNA extractions.

"Just us chickens," said Tangay, taking a handful of hot-start tubes from a countertop and placing them one by one in the wells of a DNA thermocycler. Giving Kimbrough a wink, he turned the thermocycler on and said, "Here goes phase one of our genotyping."

"What do you expect you'll find?" asked Kimbrough, forcing a smile.

Tangay double-checked the number of desired DNA amplifica-tion cycles on the thermocycler. "A slice of genetic history," he said authoritatively.

"I know that." Kimbrough's response was noticeably terse. "I'm talking specifics."

"Mutant stocks, genetic variations, a myriad of chromosomal deficits—that's what I expect. In other words, I expect to find proof that HSP90 really is a chaperon protein and the bottom-line reason for the strange physical alterations we've seen in the birds."

"And if HSP90 turns out to be the reason for all these protective development mutations . . . ?"

"Then I've reproduced what I found in my fruit fly experiments, not just in a second species, but in a whole different *phylum!* That's a pretty big step toward proving my protective development theory about heat shock protein."

"Reproducibility—the gold standard of science." Kimbrough smiled and stroked his chin.

"Right. But don't book your Stockholm flight quite yet. It's only a start. This new experiment may shed light on the molecular mechanism responsible for the bizarre changes in the birds, but it won't tell us *why* they occurred. And when you come right down to it, that's the real key."

Kimbrough frowned and looked perturbed. "Felix, I think it's best that you leave the whys and wherefores of the heat shock equation to me. Your job right now is to focus on proving that your protective development theory works in more than just fruit flies."

"Fine by me. I've got enough here to keep me busy for months."

"Try a week."

"What?"

"I need some answers within the week. The day before Labor Day at the latest."

Tangay checked the calendar on his watch. "No way."

"Afraid so."

"Seven days?"

Kimbrough nodded.

"All I'll probably be able to confirm by then is whether the protective developmental traits I've recorded in the birds are truly HSP90-related. And that'll be pushing it."

Kimbrough jammed his thumbs into his pockets, rocked back on his heels, and stared into space. "Will you be able to tell if the physical changes in the two frozen birds Septian gave you are tied directly to decreased HSP90 levels?"

"Perhaps."

"I've got a lot riding on this, Felix. 'Perhaps' isn't good enough."

Tangay shrugged. "Sorry. I can't do any better than that on the basis of an experiment involving just two birds."

"I can provide you with a dozen of the damn things if that's what it takes."

"It would help."

"Consider it done. You'll have the gamecocks tomorrow."

Tangay's face turned suddenly pensive. "Let's say I determine that HSP90 is the key to all the anomalous physical changes we're seeing in the birds. What then?"

"Then, my friend, I've struck the scientific mother lode and pretty much turned Darwin's theory of gradual evolution on its head. Think of it, Felix: I'll have proof that a single protein is largely responsible for controlling evolution. I'll know with certainty that Mother Nature's children change their proverbial spots not over millions of years, as we've always believed, but thousands of times more quickly. In terms of evolution, you might as well consider it an overnight change. More importantly, I'll have a theory and data to back it up that's not only rock-solid scientifically but sexy, too." Kimbrough smiled and rubbed his hands together expectantly. "And nothing in the world, my good friend, sells like sex."

Tangay frowned, recognizing that not once in Kimbrough's description had his own name been mentioned. Realizing that the answer to a question that had been haunting him for years might soon be for sale, he said defensively, "I'm not certain you'll want to market *our* little genie quite yet."

Noting Tangay's emphasis on "our," Kimbrough's smile disappeared. "I'll take that under advisement," he said, staring blankly at Tangay. "Right now, why don't you stick to the job at hand."

Tangay nodded and squeaked out an "okay" as he watched a decidedly peeved Kimbrough turn, stroking the thermocycler as if it were the soft skin of a woman, and smile.

CHAPTER
14

Sweating in the blistering afternoon sun, Roland Septian stood outside his tent and faced down Brandon DeVille. "You're a fucking dumb-ass cretin, DeVille. You were posted at Redstone's to keep an eye out for the old coot, not to blast away at some motorcycle-riding black bitch."

DeVille shrugged, took a step back, and stared beyond the tent at the Chinook twin-rotor helicopter struggling to lift a semitrailer-sized cargo container off the desert floor. "How the hell did I know who she was? I figured she was one of Redstone's flunkies, out there to check on his birds. Thought it would be fun to scare the damn biker bitch off."

Septian shook his head, wiped his brow with his forearm, and scanned the surrounding pinnacles and sandstone outcroppings that jutted above the ruddy desert floor. As he gazed out at the sandy strata, generated by restless seas that had covered the land several times over hundreds of millions of years, he realized that he was looking at a landscape born of time. It was a concept at the very heart of the current mission, and one that he knew would be lost on a man like DeVille. "Well, now you do, jackass. She's a doctor at St. Mary's. Her name's Carmen Nguyen, and she's been treating our friend Redstone."

"What's his problem besides old age?" said DeVille, looking back toward the cargo container and the hovering chopper.

"He's got leukemia," said Septian, passing on what Jack Kimbrough had shared with him earlier in the day. "That's why there was no sign of him when we snatched his birds the other day. The old geezer's been in the hospital most of the week."

"Leukemia? I'll be damned. I always knew those fuckin' uranium mines were graveyards. Looks like Redstone's gonna end up croakin' from the same damn disease as my old man."

Ignoring DeVille's assessment, Septian said, "Think you can refrain from shooting at anyone if we go back out to Wild Horse Draw to pick up a few more of the old coot's birds?"

"Sure, if no one shoots at me first."

Septian shook his head in disgust. "Son of a bitch. You *are* as dumb as a brick. Start shooting at someone this time and I'll cut off your nuts, got it?"

DeVille nodded without answering.

Septian looked skyward as the chopper, now aloft, swooped overhead with the cargo container in tow. "We'll go back this evening, when it's not so hot."

DeVille shrugged. "Fine by me." Then, mumbling "Fuck you" under his breath, he pivoted back toward the boxy olive-drab tent where he and his Navajo team were bunking. Trudging up a sand hill, he hawked up something grainy and spit it far on the desert wind.

He'd hated the desert since childhood, which he had spent tagging along with his half-Navajo father from one dusty hole to the next. He'd seen enough high desert to last two lifetimes, but his old friend Larry Narine had offered him ten thousand dollars for just three weeks of firefighter training, and he'd taken the bait. When he'd asked Narine what the risk of getting killed on the job might be, Narine had handed him a neat bundle of hundreds and said, "Pretty damn high."

Recalling Narine's words, DeVille stepped into the tent. A dozen shirtless men, wearing underwear or soiled army fatigues, sat or sprawled on the two rows of cots lined up along an uneven plywood floor. A footlocker and a pedestal-style washbasin sat at the foot of each cot.

DeVille nodded to a few of the men, glanced suspiciously toward Larry Narine's empty cot, walked past it, and plopped down on his own cot. He sat motionless for a few moments before looking over at Ariel Roundtree.

"How did things go this morning?"

"Not bad." Roundtree leaned back on both elbows. His dog tags rattled against the Silver Star on his chest. "Not good either."

DeVille frowned and scanned the stifling tent. The gamy smell of unwashed bodies hung in the air; he could almost taste the sweat ground into everyone's clothes. "What happened?"

"Ricky had trouble again, hooking up to the chopper. The chopper never got the container off the ground in the allotted time."

"But I saw it fly off with the container in tow."

"I had to finish the hookup myself."

DeVille shook his head and looked down the line of cots to where a short, pudgy middle-aged man with bulging eyes sat reading a book. Jumping up, DeVille stormed over and grabbed Ricky Little Dove by the fraying neck of his T-shirt. "Hope you didn't chicken out again, you little maggot. 'Cause if you did, I'll make sure you don't see another penny of your fuckin' money." DeVille cocked his fist and watched Little Dove cower. But the blow stopped short as DeVille let out a surprised grunt and dropped to his knees.

"I'll snap your goddamn arm out of its socket," said Ariel Roundtree, his six-foot-five frame towering over DeVille.

DeVille squealed in pain. Without loosening his grip, Round-tree said softly, "Ricky, why don't you go get us some water." As Little Dove got up, Roundtree eyed the other men sternly. "Show's over." When they failed to move, he shouted, "I said the fuckin' show's over!" When the men who had gathered around headed back to their cots, Roundtree released DeVille's arm. "Some-times you act a lot more like a white man than a Navajo," he said. "You know Ricky's slow."

"He's a dumb shit," said DeVille, rising to his feet, his eyes locked defiantly on Roundtree's. "I don't know why Narine ever recruited him."

"Because Colonel Walls needed twelve of us, idiot."

"Don't that seem strange to you?"

"No stranger than bein' paid a thousand bucks a month for a shot of my blood."

DeVille shrugged. "You know, Roundtree, sometimes I think you're as dumb as Ricky."

"I wouldn't want to test that theory," said Roundtree. "You might find out I'm a lot smarter than you think. And as for Ricky, do you know how hard it is to hook a cable up to a chopper when you're suddenly surrounded by fire?"

"It's only hard if you're a half-wit."

"Can it," said Roundtree, watching Little Dove's approach. "Let me handle this."

"I . . ."

Roundtree shot DeVille a look that said, *Shut the fuck up.*

"Got water for you," said Little Dove, shoving a tin cup into Roundtree's hand. "Got one for me, too," he added with a grin.

"Thanks." Roundtree took a slow, deliberate swallow, watching as Little Dove did the same. The two men took turns sipping water until DeVille shrugged and sauntered away. They sat silently for a few moments before Roundtree spoke. "Now, tell me, Ricky. What seems to be the problem with the cables?"

"No problem. I just got a little scared."

"Why? Because of the fire Colonel Walls set around the cargo container?"

"No, that wasn't it. It was the helicopter. It was noisy. And there was a lot of wind. I lost my concentration."

"I see. Suppose for the next drill I'm up there on the container with you the whole time."

"That would be great." Little Dove broke into a toothless grin that quickly faded to a pleading stare. "You won't let DeVille hit me if I screw up? You'll look out for me—just like when we was kids?"

Roundtree nodded. "Sure will."

Little Dove took a gulp of water and looked around the tent for DeVille. "DeVille's gone," he said, smiling broadly.

"Good," said Roundtree, once again wondering what the real link was between his blood, Ricky Little Dove's, their missing man Larry Narine's, and Brandon DeVille's. Suddenly he found himself questioning whether twenty-five thousand dollars under the table was really worth risking the lives and health of ten other men.

CHAPTER
15

As he sat talking to Luke Redstone, enjoying the soothing late-afternoon breezes sweeping through the St. Mary's picnic grounds, Walker Rios felt himself relax for the first time in days. Earlier he had struggled to roll his wheelchair out to the peaceful refuge, relishing every second of the effort. The picnic area with its sixty-year-old cottonwoods reminded him of the backyard he'd known as a child, and its peacefulness somehow seemed to ease his lingering guilt. He'd increased his rubber-ball compressions to over a hundred, and though he hated to admit it, he couldn't wait to impress Carmen Nguyen with his improvement.

Stone took a sip of Johnny Walker from the flask in his lap. "Glad Doc Nguyen decided to hook us up," he said to Rios. "Sure you won't have a hit? Stuff's premium—Black Label."

"No, thanks."

"Suit yourself, then. But don't say I didn't ask," said Stone, breaking into a contented smile.

After orchestrating what he was calling "a clean jailbreak" from the oncology unit, Stone had been bending Rios's ear for almost an hour, seemingly oblivious of the half liter of methotrexate feeding from an IV pole down a coiled polyethylene tube and into his chest.

"Like I was saying. Back then the Second Marine Division was one hell of a unit." The IV line jiggled as Stone talked. "Baddest sons of bitches that ever served. Saw a buddy of mine cut two frozen fingers off at the knuckles during the height of the war 'cause waitin' for medical attention would've slowed down our platoon. Nipped 'em off with his Kabar, quick as a blink. Had a been his johnson, I think he would've done the same. Ever see anything like that during Desert Storm?"

"Not quite," said Rios, wondering how often Stone had regaled others with his tales of Korea.

"Guess you couldn't of. Too damn hot. Never cared for the heat. Makes things dry rot." Stone pulled his flask out, stole a look around, and took two quick swigs.

Rios shook his head, eyeing Stone's IV bag. "Are you sure you should be belting that stuff down like that?"

"Shit, if the leukemia don't kill me, the chemotherapy will. Might as well pick my own poison, don't you think?"

Rios responded with a hesitant nod.

Sensing that the conversation was about to stall, Stone said, "That Doc Nguyen's some lady, ain't she? Smart as a whip, and on top of curin' what's ailin' folks, I get the feelin' she can see what's inside their heads. Like gettin' us together, for instance. Easy to see from talkin' to you that that shoulder injury of yours ain't the only thing causin' you pain."

"That obvious?" asked Rios, surprised at Stone's insight.

"As the stink on shit. And I can tell you this, too: You better be gettin' yourself in the right frame of mind, Captain, or you'll sure enough end up losin' your war against the blues."

Rios smiled at being called "Captain." No one had called him that since he'd left the marines. "How'd you know I was a captain?"

"Doc Nguyen told me. That, and a little more than she probably should've about you. Face it, my friend: Blues or no blues, if you don't wanta sink under, you gotta get up and swim."

Rios shrugged. "So you and Dr. Nguyen think I'm a ship primed to sink?"

"Can't tell really. You never know about feelin' blue. Besides, I ain't known you but an hour. Some folks hang themselves on account of the blues. Others shake it off like cows do flies. Don't really know what kinda blues you got. Know one thing, though: You had what it took to become a marine, and that tells me you got what it takes to shake whatever's ailin' you."

Rios smiled at the straightforward logic of the pale, slump-shouldered, unshaven old man who was hooked up to a bag of poison, staring straight at death and apparently unperturbed by it. Suddenly his own problems seemed far more manageable. "Guess it's the kind of blues I better start dealing with."

Stone broke into a toothy grin. "Those are the easiest kind to whip." Glancing at his watch, he said, "Hell, I better highball it outta here before one of those shock trooper oncology nurses realizes I'm AWOL. Let's hook up again tomorrow."

"Sure thing."

Stone fumbled with the drawstring on his pajamas, deep in thought, as Rios rose and watched the clouds gathering over the mountains. Neither of them heard Carmen Nguyen's quiet approach until she stepped between them.

"Mr. Redstone, I need to speak with you," said Carmen sternly.

"Okay, Doc. But first I gotta—"

"Now!"

Stone shot Rios a bewildered look and shrugged.

"You may leave, Mr. Rios," said Carmen, her tone insistent.

"I ain't got no secrets; he can stay," Stone countered.

"This is confidential. Mr. Rios, please leave."

Rios turned his wheelchair to leave. "See you later," he said, nodding at Stone.

"If they don't string me up for breakin' hospital rules." Stone clamped his wrists together as if he were about to be handcuffed. Smiling pleadingly at Carmen, he said, "I promise. I won't break outta that oncology unit again."

"That's not what this is about," said Carmen forcefully.

"Then what's got you so spooked, Doc?"

Aware that Rios was still within earshot, Carmen whispered, "I went to check on your birds."

"One of my birds take a bite outta you? That what's got you so upset?"

Carmen glanced toward Rios and then back at Stone. "No. Someone tried to kill me." The words came out in a loud rush, stopping Rios in his tracks.

Stone shot out of his seat. His clenched fist rocketed skyward. "Goddamn son of a bitch! He's taken this too far." Eyeing Carmen sympathetically, he added, "You okay?"

"A little rattled, but I've dodged gunfire before. What I need right now is a name—one that I can take to the sheriff. You must have some idea of who was shooting at me. We can save the whys for later."

"Oh, I've got a name, all right," said Stone, watching Rios's wheelchair inch back toward them. "But you can bet that SOB wasn't doin' the shootin'. He's too slick for that. More than likely he had some flunky doin' his dirty work."

"A name, please!"

"Jack Kimbrough. He's a big-shot businessman out of Denver. Been tryin' to buy birds from me for over a year. Never done nothin' like this before, though."

"Thanks." Carmen turned to leave, nearly tripping over Rios. "Sorry."

"No harm, no foul," said Rios. "By the way, did you see who was shooting at you?"

"This isn't your concern, Mr. Rios. And no, I didn't."

"Were you hurt?"

"No."

"Mr. Kinlow's taken shots at you before, then?"

"Kimbrough," Carmen corrected. "And no!"

"Were there any witnesses to the attack?"

"Mr. Rios, you're out of line. Please leave."

"Sorry about the questions," said Rios apologetically. "I'm just trying to prepare you for Sheriff Anderson's grill. Believe me, he'll be ten times worse. I know the man."

"Do you?" said Carmen. "I wouldn't have thought so from the way you acted when he was here the other day."

"I'm better now," Rios said with a smile. "Thanks to Stone here, I'm learning to chill."

"Good. This might be a good time to start."

"Okay." Rios spun his wheelchair around, but Stone interrupted the retreat. "You should probably let him stay, especially considerin' the fact he's got an in with the sheriff."

"And why's that?" asked Carmen.

"'Cause that land you was snoopin' around on when you got shot at ain't exactly mine. Truth is, Doc, you was trespassin'."

The look on Carmen's face turned to frustration. "Whose land is it?"

"Don't rightly know. Just know it ain't mine."

The idea that she'd been trespassing had never crossed her mind. Feeling violated and confused, Carmen sat down next to Stone. She could plead ignorance when she talked to the sheriff, but she didn't want to get Stone in trouble with the law. Feeling powerless, she stared blankly into space.

Recognizing the look, Rios wheeled his chair up next to her, reached into the pocket of his hospital robe, and pulled out the exercise ball she had given him. "It helped," he said, squeezing the ball several times. "And so did he." He nodded at Stone. "I owe you one. Thanks for the support."

Carmen looked at Rios without answering, not caring who owed whom. It was all she could do to keep her emotions in check as, once again, the sound of gunfire began playing itself over and over again in her head.

A backdoor cold front and a rash of early-evening thunderstorms had dropped the temperatures along most of the Colorado Plateau into the forties, blanketing the region in low-hanging clouds and a chilly mist. Brandon DeVille and Roland Septian sat in a Jeep on a freshly paved highway shoulder, inhaling the heavy smell of new asphalt as they prepared to snatch more of Luke Redstone's gamecocks. DeVille cupped one hand to his brow and stared into the clouds, dreading the trek they were about to make across two rocky mesas.

"I never signed on with Walls to traipse around the fucking backwoods looking for chickens. I thought we were gonna fight fire," said DeVille.

Septian shot him an unsympathetic glare. "You took the two grand for this side job; now, quit your bitching. We'll be done in a couple of hours. Then you can bellyache to someone else." Septian started the Jeep and bolted off the shoulder, thumping onto a washboarded gravel road that looked as if it hadn't seen a vehicle in weeks. "Cutting south like this should save us some time," he said, shifting into second and accelerating, slamming DeVille back in his seat.

"If you don't kill us driving like a maniac or shred the tires on scab rock."

"We've got plenty of time before we have to worry about that. Sit back and relax. Dream about your extra two grand—think about that lady doctor you should've popped."

DeVille's expression turned pensive. "Believe me, I've thought about 'em both. Just like I've thought about why we're out here chasing down a bunch of roosters when we're supposed to be concentrating on something else."

"And what's your conclusion?"

"Don't have one yet, but I'm close."

"Don't rack your brain too hard—you might damage it," Septian snorted as he downshifted and turned on the Jeep's headlights.

DeVille was getting fed up with Septian's arrogance and his dumb-Indian jokes. If he was getting two grand for his part in their little chicken heist, then he could be pretty sure that Septian was getting double, maybe even triple. Not only that, but if hijacking a few roosters paid so well, there could be a windfall for the taking, once he pegged what Septian and Colonel Walls were really up to. One thing was certain: The firefighting escapades and the gamecock heist were linked, no matter how much Walls and Septian tried to pretend they weren't. They were connected just as surely as his blood-drawing trips to Denver were

connected. And there were other common threads, like the one
tying the men in his desert platoon together: They were the sons
or nephews of men who had mucked uranium on the Colorado
Plateau fifty years earlier. When you came right down to it, he
had Septian's number, and if things turned ugly in the short run,
he was prepared to deal with Septian more directly. He felt the
reassuring lump of a gun pressing against the small of his back
and smiled to himself.

They jostled along in silence for the next fifteen minutes, until
the Jeep's headlights danced off a group of sandstone outcroppings at the base of the hills that guarded Stone's backcountry
oasis.

"Scab rock coming up," said DeVille. "Better slow this puppy
down."

Septian tapped his brakes. "I'll get us as far as I can go safely.
Then we'll have to walk. You up to it?"

"Yeah," said DeVille, peering into soupy darkness.

A loud crunch echoed from beneath the front tires as Septian
stopped the Jeep.

"Bad place to stop," said DeVille.

Septian flicked the headlights to high beam. "Damn! Can't see
a thing. I better get out and check."

DeVille shook his head. "Take my word for it. Won't matter if
you look all night long. We're in a pocket of shale. Just back up
and let's skirt around it."

Ignoring DeVille, Septian stepped out and walked around to
the front of the vehicle, where he steadied himself on the bumper
and felt along the ground. "Think you're right," he called out,
flipping over several pieces of the jagged claystone. "Shit." Stepping back to the Jeep, Septian eased back into his seat.

"What did I tell you? Now will you—"

In one quick motion, Septian shoved a long wedge of razor-
sharp rock into the soft flesh just above Brandon DeVille's lar-
ynx. DeVille raised his arms defensively and let out a gurgle as
Septian swung the rock again, this time against his temple, with
a life-ending crunch. "So much for you and that fuckin' gun in

your pants, you little rodent. Think I'm some kind of blind fuckin' idiot?"

Tendrils of blood trickled down from DeVille's crushed windpipe as Septian reached over and closed his bulging eyes. After making sure that his dead companion was strapped securely in his seat, Septian backed the Jeep out of the shale pocket and continued toward Stone's hideaway.

It was a little past nine P.M., and Stone's room was dark when Rios showed up in response to the urgent call of five minutes earlier.

"You there, Stone?" said Rios, gliding his wheelchair past the foot of the bed and inching his way toward the bathroom and the overpowering smell of feces and urine.

"Stone?" said Rios, in his haste slamming one of the wheelchair's foot supports into the wall.

"I'm cleanin' up a mess," said Stone finally, his voice echoing up from the bathroom floor. "Had myself a little accident."

"I'll call a nurse."

"Hell, no, you won't. Don't want one of them vamps up here pokin' and proddin' every orifice. Besides, this ain't nothin' I can't handle myself. That poison they been shootin' me up with just gives me the runs."

"You need to ring for a nurse." Rios squinted at Stone, down on all fours and mopping the floor with paper towels, and shook his head. "If I'd known you were this sick from your chemo, I would've stayed put in my room. I'm calling a nurse."

"No! Don't! Semper fi," said Stone, struggling to stand.

"Don't start that marine shit with me, Stone. This isn't boot camp, Iwo Jima, or Chosen." Slipping out of his wheelchair, Rios looped an arm around Stone and pulled him up into the chair's seat.

"Shit, for somebody who's supposed to be a half quart low, you're stronger than a bull," said Stone.

"Can it, Stone," said Rios, nudging the wheelchair back against the bed. "I'm two seconds from calling for a nurse. Now that I've got you on my power throne, maybe you'll tell me why—besides having the runs—you put out a five-alarm call for help."

Stone gave Rios a wink. " 'Cause I'm bustin' outta here, and I need a little assistance."

"You won't get it from me; you're way past the sniffles. Walk out of here and you're signing your death warrant."

Stone grunted and pushed himself up in the seat. "I'm not stupid, Rios, and I damn sure ain't naive. Ain't a repair kit out there nowhere that can fix what I got."

"You never know. Give the chemo a chance."

"A chance to keep me kickin' an extra four months, shittin' and pissin' my pants and throwin' up all over myself? No way."

"Four months is a lot longer than the week or two you're probably looking at if you leave."

"Shit, man, I didn't call you up here for no debate. Bottom line is, I gotta do what's best for me and my birds. What I need from you is a little help."

"I won't help you kill yourself."

Stone smiled. "I'm not expectin' you to do that. What I want you to do is help Doc Nguyen take care of what's mine."

"What?"

"It's simple. Anything happens to me, she's gonna be in charge of my birds and everything I own. I just need to know she's got some backup from you."

"You're leaving everything you own to her?"

"You got it. I ain't got no kin, and she saved my bacon when it was in the fire. She checks on me twice a day, and she spent two nights readin' up on how to treat what I got. Besides, she damn near got her ass shot off lookin' after my birds. What's the problem? You think I should maybe leave everything to you?"

"No," said Rios, shaking his head for emphasis.

"Well, then it's settled."

"Fine. But I'd say right now you need a lawyer a whole lot more than a one-armed river guide."

"Trust me; she's gonna need your help. Kimbrough, the asshole that's after my birds, plays for keeps."

"Thought you said when you called that Carmen had gone to talk to the sheriff."

"She did. Told me so herself. And she's gonna talk to him again tomorrow. But the kinda law that the sheriff dispenses wasn't never intended to handle folks like Kimbrough."

"You're sure?"

"As sure as the sun's gonna rise in the east tomorrow mornin'."

Rios nodded thoughtfully. For the first time in weeks, he had the feeling he was needed. "What's Kimbrough's angle in all this?"

"I'll tell you what I think his game plan is if you'll agree to back up Doc Nguyen."

"I'll consider it. First, fill me in on Kimbrough."

"Okay, but it'll take a while."

"I've got all night," said Rios, resisting the urge to tell Stone that since their initial meeting in the picnic area, he'd spent several hours learning everything he could about Dr. Carmen Nguyen.

CHAPTER

16

Carmen's only previous ride in a police car had been as a child, after Aunt Ket slugged a man who had propositioned her on a Saigon street. Carmen couldn't recall all the details, but she did remember the man running for help with blood streaming from his mouth, and she recalled being carted off to a police station, where she sat trembling in fear on a cold metal bench while Ket was being interrogated. She remembered the police car smelling like mold, and the room with the bench being as cold as the inside of a refrigerator. What she remembered most, however, was watching Ket give her interrogator her wedding band and all the money in her pocket before they were allowed to go.

Now, instead of shivering in fear, she was speeding down Highway 50 south of Grand Junction in Warren Anderson's sheriff's cruiser, trying her best to ignore the high-pitched hair-dryer whine coming from the car's faulty air-conditioning. It was just past noon. Last night's freak cold front had moved east, and she found herself once again nervously thumbing through the sheaf of papers in her lap.

Early that morning she'd been paged from the ER to check on Walker Rios. She'd responded to the page only to learn that it had been Rios and not his doctor who paged her, and that Luke Redstone hadn't shown up for their scheduled breakfast meeting. When Stone's bed was found empty and his clothes and duffel bag gone, hospital security had mounted a search, but he was nowhere to be found.

"You're going to see the sheriff anyway," Rios had said to

Carmen after mounting his own unsuccessful twenty-minute search. "Might as well have him look for Stone while he's trying to track down whoever it was that took those shots at you." Rios had then taken a sealed business-size envelope, plump with papers, from his pocket. "Give this to the sheriff. Trust me—it'll help him out," he'd said, smiling slyly as he handed it to her.

That envelope rested on the cruiser's dusty dashboard as, for the third time now, Carmen read through six pages of Rios's meticulously handwritten notes—notes that represented a virtual chronicle of Carmen Nguyen's and Luke Redstone's lives. Turning her attention from the papers to the sheriff, she said, "How could Rios have learned so much about Stone and me in less than twenty-four hours? I'm telling you, it's scary." She frowned and nervously tapped the papers with her fingers.

Sheriff Anderson gave her the confident smile of someone with inside dope. "Not really. No more scary than the fact that he writes as well with his left hand as his right, or that he speaks three languages, has a Bronze Star, and walks around with a metal plate in his head. He probably asked every nurse, doctor, technician, and orderly at St. Mary's what they knew about you and our elusive Mr. Redstone. And knowing Rios, he probably had every one of them singing like a canary. Wouldn't surprise me if he even got a peek at Redstone's medical records or your personnel file. After all, he had almost half a day," the sheriff said with a laugh.

"There'd be no way. Those things are confidential."

The sheriff's laugh soared. "Did Rios tell you he was a former marine and that he served in that nasty little desert skirmish folks like to call the Persian Gulf War?"

"He didn't have to. I went on-line and reviewed his previous medical records." Carmen shot the sheriff a self-satisfied grin. "They confirmed not only his military history but his blood type too. Technology cuts both ways, Sheriff."

The sheriff smiled, never taking his eyes off the road. "Did your little database excursion tell you what Rios's assignment was during the war?"

"No."

"Then let me fill you in." Sheriff Anderson's expression turned serious. "He was an intelligence officer working out of Doha. Remember those smart bombs you saw exploding every night on the six o'clock news? The ones the military claimed were so accurate they could take out an outhouse on Mars?"

"Yes."

"Well, Rios was the guy picking most of the outhouses."

"Sounds serious."

"War always is," said the sheriff, his mouth a grim line. "Before that he spent three years on assignment in Washington, D.C. Never knew exactly what he did back there. But I know that when he came back from Desert Storm he was pretty much burned out. Wasn't until he left the corps and went back to white-water rafting that he seemed to get refocused. No offense, Doc, but I'd bet you a dollar to a dime that in addition to what's in those papers you've been reading, Rios also knows how old you are, what hospital you were born in, where you ranked in your high school class, and what size unmentionables you wear. He's still got real serious connections, if you know what I mean."

"That resourceful?" said Carmen, surprised at how much Rios and sixty-four-year-old Aunt Ket, who'd been an intelligence courier for the U.S. Army in Vietnam, had in common. Now she understood why Rios had been so analytical about the attempt on her life, and why his assessment had seemed so coldly matter-of-fact. She prided herself on recognizing character traits, and she was surprised she hadn't recognized such telling ones in Rios. The man was calculating, analytical, and resourceful. Now she understood why the papers in her lap were so detailed.

"I'd say. But I wouldn't knock it. With Rios on your side, you and this Redstone character you've been going on about have eyes and ears out there you never could have dreamed of."

Carmen glanced down at the sheaf of papers. "Rios claims that Stone will head back to get his gamecocks. Guess we'll find out soon enough."

"From what you've said, sounds like those birds of his are all he has. Question is, can he get to them with leukemia riding his back, and a gut-full of that chemotherapy of yours slowing him down?"

"He's a tough old man."

"Then I take it you're betting he can."

Carmen nodded.

"And what if that shooter of yours, the one you say tried to kill you, gets there first? Is he tough enough for that?"

"I don't think so."

"Me either. Unless he also rides a motorcycle the way you claim to."

Recalling her harrowing escape from the ambush at Stone's, which she'd described to the sheriff in detail yesterday evening, Carmen said, "Not many people can."

"I wouldn't be so cocky, Doc. Never know when you might be put to a second test."

Carmen smiled without responding, eased back in her seat, and let the cool breeze from the air-conditioning blow in her face as she reconsidered Rios's notes. In addition to Rios's profile of her and Stone, one full page distilled a conversation Rios and Stone had had about Jack Kimbrough, ending with the suggestion that the sheriff "question Kimbrough ASAP about the Carmen Nguyen shooting." She found it interesting that Rios had circled the word *Carmen* and underlined it three times.

The final two pages of notes had her confused. Boldly written and less meticulous than the others, they detailed what Stone had told Rios about the fighting prowess of his gamecocks. Given Rios's skills at discovery, she wondered what else he and Stone had talked about. Perhaps they'd discussed her reasons for leaving the University of Utah when she was supposedly at the top of her game. Or maybe Rios had uncovered details about Aunt Ket's employment during the Vietnam War. Whatever he and Stone had discussed, one thing seemed clear: Rios appeared to have overcome his bout with depression and replaced it with a newfound sense of purpose.

The sheriff slowed the cruiser as they approached the turnoff to a rarely used county road. Pulling to a stop, he rolled down his window. "Hmm," he said, looking down at the road. "Busy."

"How can you tell?" said Carmen, staring out the window at what looked like nothing more than a disused gravel road.

"All the tire tracks. Lots of traffic in and out of here for an old track like this." The sheriff rolled up his window and turned the air-conditioning up a notch. "Let's hope Redstone and whoever took those shots at you aren't out here playing cowboys in the woods," he said, nosing the cruiser down the badly rutted road as Carmen shaded her eyes, straining to see in the bright midday glare.

CHAPTER
17

A pair of circling turkey vultures caught Sheriff Anderson's eye long before Carmen shouted, "There's someone out there, in a red shirt and a cowboy hat—I'd swear to it."

They bumped along, closing in on a lone figure kneeling in front of a battered pickup, all but lost against a backdrop of low gray hills. Carmen rocked forward in her seat. "It has to be Stone. Who else would be out here in the middle of nowhere?"

The sheriff nodded without responding, checked the sky, and saw a single vulture, coasting downward.

When the kneeling figure stood and began waving his arms back and forth overhead, Carmen let out a sigh of relief. "It's him!" she breathed as the sheriff slowed his cruiser to a halt a few yards away from the pickup.

Stone, unshaven, draped in baggy clothes, and barely able to walk, slouched toward the car as Carmen grabbed a black crash bag from the backseat. Leaping from the car, she raced for Stone, wrapping a supporting arm around him as he slumped to one knee and mumbled, "Thanks."

"Are you okay?" she asked, checking his pupils and then his pulse as she sat him on a nearby rock.

Stone nodded, looking dazed.

"Breathe," she demanded, counting each heartbeat.

"Someone took my birds," he said, choking on the words.

"Sorry." Carmen pulled a stethoscope from the crash bag, noticing as she looped the instrument out that Sheriff Anderson was walking toward where the buzzards had come down.

Slipping the end of the stethoscope beneath Stone's shirt, she listened, then said, "Can you sing?"

"Sing what?"

"The national anthem—I don't care; just sing."

"O-oh, say can you see, by the dawn's early—"

"Great. You're getting plenty of air," she said, cutting him off and bringing the stethoscope around to his back. "Breathe deeply for me, in and out. Good," she said. "Now cough."

Stone offered up a halfhearted cough.

"Harder."

Stone obliged with three forceful coughs.

"Fine. I'm going to start an IV, and then we'll head for some shade. Over in those rocks," she said, pointing toward a clump of boulders. "After that, it's back to St. Mary's."

"My birds are gone, Doc." Stone grimaced in pain.

"We'll have to deal with that problem later." Carmen wiggled an IV line from the crash bag, then found a thermometer.

Stone eyed the thermometer. "Before you tongue-tie me with that thing, I need to tell you somethin'."

"What's that?"

"There's a dead guy, half-buried in a bunch of rocks—in that dry wash just behind us."

Swallowing hard, Carmen slipped the thermometer beneath Stone's tongue and looked around for the sheriff.

Stone took the thermometer out of his mouth. "Over there," he said, pointing just past the tailgate of his truck and glancing skyward.

Carmen stood, shaded her eyes, and gazed toward an outcropping of rocks. She could see Sheriff Anderson kneeling just in front of the outcropping. Then, following Stone's lead, she looked up into the sky toward a half-dozen rising and circling buzzards.

Jack Kimbrough stood in Felix Tangay's research lab, studying the first page of a tattered four-column spiral notebook. The first column was filled with a series of dates, the second with the names of fighting cocks and their weights; the third column contained entries of only one word: *won* or *lost.* The final column was empty. The grease-stained notebook, its pages yellowed from age, lacked a back cover. The front cover, filled with huge block letters spelling out LUKE REDSTONE, hung by a thread from the book's spine.

"Do you realize the entries in this notebook go back to the nineteen-fifties?" Kimbrough called out across the lab to where Tangay and Roland Septian were busy transferring tissue samples into a stainless steel liquid-nitrogen cylinder. "Where'd you find it?" asked Kimbrough, handling the notebook as if it were a rare, centuries-old parchment.

Septian looked up as a plume of gas swirled from the uncapped cylinder. "Believe it or not, in the bottom of one of the old coot's bird cages. In a compartment covered by a layer of tin and a couple inches of chicken shit." Septian laughed and stepped back from the cylinder. "Guess he figured nobody would ever think to look there."

Tangay transferred the last of the dozen tissue samples into a metal cassette the size of a half-dollar and lowered this into the liquid nitrogen. He said to Septian, "Better get your fingers off the lip of that cylinder if you don't want them to freeze and break off. I told you to put on gloves." Tangay removed his own bulky insulated gloves and waited until Septian finally backed away. "Everything's on ice," Tangay said, smiling as he walked back across the lab toward Kimbrough, who had been remarkably quiet throughout the tissue-transfer procedure. "We should be set."

"And you think you'll be able to tell from your examination of the tissues which birds are HSP-deficient?" asked Kimbrough.

"Basically," said Tangay.

"I'm betting on that big son of a bitch," said Septian. "He sure as hell didn't look like your everyday chicken."

"I wouldn't be so certain," said Tangay. "Size alone may not be our key. Giants occur quite frequently in nature, but it's a safe bet they don't all underexpress heat shock protein. No, there's something else at work here—something we're missing. Something besides a simple reduction in heat shock protein levels caused the eye color variations, the changes in feather density, and the alterations in bone structure we're seeing in these birds. The important thing now is that we have a road map of sorts. Now we know that the physical changes we're seeing in the gamecocks are equivalent to the changes I found in my fruit flies."

"Sounds like black magic to me," said Septian.

"Nature's magic." Tangay smiled knowingly. "More fascinating and much more complex." Glancing at Kimbrough, who was once again engrossed in Stone's tattered notebook, he said, "What's so interesting about that thing?"

"History," said Kimbrough, dropping the notebook into a briefcase on the countertop. "Sometimes it's more important than science."

Kimbrough closed the briefcase as Tangay punched in the code to the power-interruption alarm built into the cap of the liquid-nitrogen cylinder. "Just think," said Tangay, entering the last digit, "an entire set of genetic changes and their associated mutations occurred in these birds, probably in less than a half century. Who'd suspect that some old cockfighter would be out there unknowingly operating what amounted to a molecular genetics lab all that time?" He set the alarm with a final click. "In a couple of days we'll know if the heat shock protein data from *Gallus domesticus,* a.k.a. your common barnyard chicken, correlates with what I found in my fruit flies. If it does, we're in the money."

"Looks good all the way around," said Kimbrough, swinging his briefcase off the countertop, noting that Tangay had included himself in the HSP financial equation. Nodding at Septian, he said, "Ready?"

As Septian moved to leave, Tangay asked, "By the way, Roland, after all this time how'd you finally convince that old cockfighter to give up his birds?"

"We offered him the right price," said Septian, smiling at the lie.

"Must've been plenty hefty."

"Plenty," chimed in Kimbrough, waving Septian ahead of him through the doorway.

Kimbrough and Septian didn't speak again until they were speeding south on Speer Boulevard in Kimbrough's BMW convertible. "Think you can count on Tangay to do what you've asked?" said Septian.

"Yes. He's a first-rate scientist," said Kimbrough, loud enough to be heard above the wind noise.

"I'm not talking about that. I mean, can you count on him to keep his mouth shut about what he finds out about that protein?"

"That's why I pay you, my friend." Kimbrough floored the accelerator, speeding through a caution light. "To make certain the right mouths stay shut."

The Mesa County coroner was a tall, thin-lipped retired pathologist from California who had been elected to his part-time post two years earlier by promising the Mesa County voters that he would reduce the coroner's office budget by a third, cut the technical support staff in half, and, if necessary, save the taxpayers even more money by singlehandedly performing every autopsy that came down the pike. During his first year in office the number of coroner's cases were down, and he had managed to keep his promise to the electorate. But a rash of recent ranching accidents, backcountry skiing deaths, and mobile home fires now had him wishing he'd remained in California. As he baked in the sun, with a gaggle of vultures circling overhead, and stared at the naked remains lying a few feet away, he could only shake his head.

"No ID, no money, no wallet, no clothes," said Sheriff Anderson, snapping off a pair of latex gloves and slipping a small leather-bound notebook into his shirt pocket as the coroner knelt beside the body.

"John Doe, then," said the coroner.

"Not quite." The sheriff turned and pointed back toward where Stone and Carmen were sitting. "The man perched up there on the rock—with the IV in his arm and the good-looking doctor attending to him—claims that our John Doe's real name is Brandon DeVille. Says he was an out-of-work carpenter."

"A dead carpenter now—with no eyes," said the coroner, studying the faceup body.

"Yeah, buzzards got here ahead of us," said the sheriff, stuffing his gloves into a hazardous-materials bag. "What do you make of this?" He pointed to a four-inch gash running down the left calf.

"Probably sustained it struggling with his attacker."

The sheriff frowned in disagreement. "The wound edges look awfully clean, and they don't approximate. Looks like somebody cut a hunk of muscle out of his leg."

The coroner bent down for a closer look. "Could have got cut with another piece of that rock," he said, eyeing the wedge of shale poking from DeVille's throat.

"Or a knife," said the sheriff.

"Why would someone stab him in the calf?"

"Hell if I know. But it seems strange to me that it's his only other wound besides the blow to the temple."

"I've seen stranger in my time. Let me remind you, Sheriff, that it's my job to determine the cause of death, and our friend here sure as hell didn't die from the injury to his leg."

"Fine. You do that. Just give me a bottom line on everything once you're done."

"Easy enough," said the coroner. He reached into the black station wagon that doubled as a hearse, and brought out a body bag.

"Need a hand?" asked the sheriff.

"Think I can handle it by myself. Got a collapsible gurney in the wagon. Besides, I've got a few more things to do here," said the coroner, frowning and recalling his campaign promise to cut costs. "Are you finished?"

"Sure am," said the sheriff, turning to make his way uphill to where Carmen and Stone were seated. "Call me when you have a preliminary report," he called back to the coroner, who was dictating into a microcassette recorder.

Carmen and Stone were talking in near-whispers when Anderson reached them. "Hate to break up the party," he said, panting from the uphill walk, "but I need a few answers."

"Happy to oblige," Stone said in a feeble voice.

"Cut the shit, Redstone. I want to know what's so special about those gamecocks of yours that made you have to come out here in the dead of night to check on them. Your birds are responsible for Dr. Nguyen here getting caught in an ambush. And now it looks like a man's been killed because of 'em. What the hell's going on?"

"What makes you think DeVille's death has anything to do with my birds?"

The sheriff frowned. "Don't push my patience, Stone. Housing and breeding gamecocks, not to mention cockfighting itself, are illegal in this state. Sick or not, I'll lock your ass up if you don't start telling me the truth."

Stone looked briefly at Carmen before staring off into the distance. "Son of a bitch stole my birds. Every one of 'em. I should've never, ever talked to him. Knew he didn't belong the first time I met him." Stone massaged the loose skin sagging from his forearm, then looked back at Carmen. "You gonna ride back with me in that ambulance you got comin'?"

"Yes," said Carmen, her tone reassuring. "Now tell the sheriff what you told me."

"You'd think they could get an ambulance out here before a hearse," said Stone, looking down the hillside at the coroner's station wagon pulling away. Clearing his throat, he said, "It all started at a cockfight over near Vernal, Utah, about a year and a half ago. That's when I met him. I'd seen him around at fights before, but that was the first time we really talked. No way you coulda missed him, dressed the way he was. Fancy hand-tooled boots, pricey cowboy hat, three-hundred-dollar pants. Didn't fit in one damn lick. Didn't have to, though—guy he had with him was there to make sure of that. Muscle-bound, thick-necked sucker, with eyes that wasn't no more than slits. That time and every other time I ran into the two of 'em after that, the one with the muscles was packin' heat. I know the outline of a gun when I see one, even under a jacket."

"Got names for me?" The sheriff pulled a notebook and pen out of his shirt pocket.

"The city slicker's name is Jack Kimbrough. They call him J. K. for short. But I never learned the name of that snake of a body-guard of his in all the times we talked. Tell you this, though: He's the kind that would kill you in a heartbeat."

The sheriff jotted Stone's descriptions and the names *Jack Kimbrough* and *Snake* in the notebook. "Go on."

"Kimbrough won big that first night over in Vernal. Laid a ton of money down on Sweet Dream's Cousin, one of my kick-ass grays. Think he cleared seventeen-fifty that night, but it mighta been more." Wavering, Stone looked at Carmen and cleared his throat.

"Go ahead," said Carmen, checking his IV line and then his pulse.

"After that I couldn't seem to shake Kimbrough or his friend. Seems like every cockfight I was at, he and that snake of his would show up. If I tried to duck 'em, they'd run me down. If I showed up early, Kimbrough would wanta talk. SOB made hisself a royal pain in the ass, if you get my drift, and he never once let up on wantin' me to sell him a bunch of my birds."

"Sounds like he could spot a winner. Did he or that strong-arm friend of his ever threaten you?"

Stone laughed. "Threatened to buy me a new truck once. Right after he won twenty-two grand outside Slick Rock, bettin' on my best claret, Gaucho's Son. Said he'd buy me any kind of truck I wanted if I just sold him a couple of my birds. Told him cockers like me don't sell their breedin' stock. That I'd be out of business if I did. He gave me a sly smile, looked over at his friend, and told me that sometimes it's in people's best interest to sell. That's when I got the feelin' he'd just as soon kill me as not. And that's why four months ago I started makin' sure to avoid him like the plague. Been pretty successful up to now."

The sheriff finished jotting notes. "How did Brandon DeVille fit into all this?"

"Shit if I know. I found him half-buried in a rock pile twenty minutes before you showed up. Spent all night and most of the mornin' trying to figure which way Kimbrough took off with my birds. Only thing I know for sure about DeVille is that for most of his life, he was a loser. Nothin' like his old man, Charlie. Now, his old man was a gamer. Even spent a while on the cockfightin' circuit with me before he went back to the mines. Claimed that cockfightin' was too uncertain a payday when you had to support a kid."

"Why'd you call the son a loser?"

"'Cause he spent most of his life playin' Buddha to a bunch of other Navajo drunks and dopers who didn't know how to do much else 'sides piss and moan. Funny, too, since DeVille wasn't no full-blood. Lazy sucker was half French."

"What did they complain about?"

"About anything and everything. Most of 'em just wasn't raised right."

"Do you know if DeVille knew Kimbrough?"

"Don't think so, but I couldn't swear to it," said Stone, wavering from side to side between quick gulps of air.

"Better make this quick, Sheriff," said Carmen, checking Stone's pupils and pulse before staring toward the county road. "He's running on fumes."

The sheriff nodded and looked up from his notes toward a streak of dust rising in the distance. "Looks like your ambulance is on the way," he said, following the dusty contrail across the plain. "I'll want to talk to you some more about this," he added, tucking his notebook back into his shirt pocket.

"You know where to find me."

"Sure do." The sheriff looked at Carmen. "Take good care of Mr. Redstone, Dr. Nguyen. He's the closest thing we've got to a witness in a murder. I wouldn't want anything to happen to him. In the meantime, I think I'll go have one last look at the area where I found DeVille. Don't have the luxury of a crime scene team out here in the boonies—gotta do most things myself."

Carmen nodded and watched the sheriff walk away. When she was sure he was out of earshot, she turned back to Stone, looking exasperated. "Why didn't you tell him about your missing breeding records, or mention that dozens of other people besides Kimbrough think your birds are next to invincible? And why didn't you mention that you think that henchman of Kimbrough's broke into your house?"

"He'll dig most of that up on his own. And I didn't tell him some of them things for a real good reason. In case you missed it, my cockin' activities ain't exactly on the squeaky-clean side of the law. Besides, I've got some investigatin' I need to do on my own."

"Investigating! On your own! I don't think so. Unless you plan to do it from your bed in the oncology unit at St. Mary's."

"That's what I figured you'd say. And that's why I was hopin' I could count on you for some help."

"Are you serious?" Carmen's voice rose nearly an octave. "The last time I agreed to help you, someone tried to kill me. Believe it or not, I got the message."

"My birds are gone, Doc. Maybe they're even dead by now. And in case you've forgotten, you made me a promise. I'm countin' on you to help me remedy things."

"I . . ."

"Let me finish, Doc," he went on, cutting Carmen off. "You're gonna have some help this time around. The serious kind. And from a marine."

Carmen shook her head in disbelief. "You didn't con Rios? He's only half a step healthier than you."

Stone smiled and patted the cell phone peeking from the pocket of his vest. "Talked to him last night and sealed the deal early this mornin'. Said he'd help. He's gettin' discharged tomorrow. Told me five days of bein' cooped up in that hospital of yours was all he could take," added Stone, his complexion suddenly ashen.

"He's pushing it," said Carmen, pumping up the blood-pressure cuff around Stone's arm.

"Ain't we all? You gonna help or not?"

Without answering, Carmen slipped the bell of her stethoscope just below the blood pressure cuff.

"No problem," said Stone, slurring his words. "Don't need an answer this second. Just remember, though. You think long, you think wrong." Suddenly listing to his left, he slid off his rock perch, popping his IV as he crashed to the ground.

CHAPTER
18

Sugar Cane Colby, raised dirt poor in the sharecropping cotton fields of the Mississippi Delta, settled in Grand Junction after six years in the air force, with a final stint at Peterson Air Force Base, in Colorado Springs. The day after his discharge, he followed the Colorado River west, hooking up with Walker Rios by chance during a Glenwood Springs Fourth of July Colorado Riverfest. He spent that summer and the next working as a boatman for Rios, saving every dime he made. The third summer he left the whitewater world to open a now wildly successful Grand Junction car wash and diner called the Guadalajara Car and Grill. Known for its authentic adobe construction, blinding chartreuse color scheme inside and out, and spicy New Mexican food, the Guadalajara had flourished, thanks in large measure to Colby's wife, who was a native New Mexican with a hundred years' worth of family recipes, and the best deep-fried chimichangas in the state.

The morning breakfast-burrito crowd had just about cleared out when Carmen and Rios walked into the Guadalajara. Colby was busy resetting a table when he glanced up and saw them. "Well, if it ain't Walker Re." Struggling to keep from telegraphing the fact that Rios looked like hell, he added, "See you're navigating with one wing." Eyeing the sling supporting Rios's right shoulder and his badly swollen hand, Colby shook his head. "Thought you knew, man—only Superman can fly."

Rios nodded, smiling broadly, and shook Colby's outstretched hand, squeezing hard enough to let his friend know that no mat-

ter how bad he looked, he still had the hand strength of an oars-
man.

"Did you get the get-well card and Jack Daniels I sent?"

"Sure did."

Colby looked relieved. "Sorry I didn't make it by the hospital.
Had nothin' but problems here all last week," he said, casting a
disparaging glance in the direction of the car wash. "Haven't
drunk all the J. D. up yet, have you?"

"No."

"Great. Means I might still get the chance to help you turn old
Cousin Jack into an orphan." Smiling and tipping a make-
believe hat, Colby turned to Carmen. "Morning, ma'am. Steve
Colby. Most people call me Sugar Cane." With a sudden look of
recognition, he added, "Wait a second—I seen you in here
before. Let me think. Yeah, with Mrs. Tran. I'd swear by it."

Carmen shook Colby's hand and smiled. "Carmen Nguyen.
I'm her niece."

"Yeah, Mrs. Tran. Always orders her sopaipillas with half a
dozen extra packets of honey. Fine lady. You need to come in
with her more often."

"I'll make a point of it."

Colby gave Carmen a thumbs-up. "Tell her the next time she's
in, her meal's on the house." Turning his attention back to Rios,
he said, "Other than your wing and listing a little to the left,
you're lookin' pretty good, bro."

Rios glanced at Carmen. "Cane's been known to stretch the
truth."

"He's recovering," said Carmen. "Unfortunately, it's a medical
concept he doesn't seem to understand."

"Can you tell she's a doctor?" asked Rios. "Thinks I'm pushing
my apple cart too fast."

"Then you better listen to her." Colby pulled two menus from
a stack on the table next to him and offered one to Carmen.
"Breakfast is on me."

"That's not . . ."

"Consider it part of your recovery plan," Colby said, waving

Rios off. "Courtesy of Maria," he added, pointing to his wife, who was waving frantically at Rios from the kitchen. Rios waved back as he followed Colby to a table near the back of the restaurant. "Figured you'd like a quiet spot," said Colby, pulling out a chair for Carmen.

"You're way ahead of me, Cane."

"Gotta be. I'm from Mississippi, remember?" Colby winked, handed them each a menu, and walked away.

The restaurant was bustling once again when Rios washed down the last of his scrambled eggs with black coffee. Watching him drain the cup, Carmen said, "What should I do, then, go back on my word?" Her tone was pointedly defensive.

Rios eyed Carmen's plate, still piled high with home fries. "You told Stone that you'd check on his birds. You did like you promised and nearly got yourself killed. You kept your word. It's time to butt out."

"Butt out and let you handle Stone's problem, I take it? A man who weighs twelve pounds less than he did a week ago and has his hands full simply negotiating a flight of stairs?"

"In case you missed it, Doctor, your hospital released me a couple of hours ago."

"To go home and recuperate, not scour the countryside looking for stolen gamecocks."

"There's no rule against recuperating and lending a helping hand to a friend at the same time."

"Maybe Stone'll solve the problem himself."

"Good God, Carmen, open your eyes. Yesterday you hauled Stone out of the backwoods he was sharing with a dead man, and carted him back to St. Mary's barely alive. After he tells you, by the way, that some nut from Denver named Kimbrough and his gun-toting strongman stole his birds. I might still be a little woozy, but it sounds to me as if Stone's into something way over his head."

Surprised at being called by her first name, Carmen eased back in her chair and locked eyes with Rios. "Stone's dying, Walker.

Neither you, I, nor modern medicine is capable of changing that. I hope you're not planning on soothing your own psyche by trying to help Stone. Because if you are, I've got another medical tidbit for you: You're not physically up to it."

The look on Rios's face turned sullen as he tried to shake the lingering image of a small body being dragged from the Colorado River. "Call it what you will. Right now it's a way of coping. Let's leave it at that."

"And if it gets you killed?"

"It won't."

Rios's answer turned the conversation into twenty seconds of steely silence, broken only when Carmen said, "I'm the one who promised Stone that I wouldn't let anything happen to his birds."

"Sometimes promises can be hard to keep."

"I know. But I never go back on mine," she replied, staring blankly past Rios as if he suddenly weren't there. "So, any ideas about what Kimbrough is really up to?"

Rios answered reluctantly, surprised by Carmen's response. "From what Stone told you about Kimbrough's Denver operation, I'd say Kimbrough's looking for some kind of cockfighting inside straight."

"Gamecocks that are assured of winning every fight?"

"Maybe. But it probably goes much deeper. Murder usually does." Rios sat forward in his seat and rubbed his injured shoulder. "I want to check out the photocopies of the original log book Stone kept on his roosters. The originals that he told you were missing when he last checked on them. Pretty shrewd of Stone to keep a backup log."

"Sounds like a reasonable place to start. But what if the records turn out to be a dead end?"

"Then I'll make a phone call to Denver and get a heads-up on our Mr. Kimbrough from another former marine. Trust me. She'll help us get to the bottom of this," said Rios, pouring himself another cup of coffee, relaxing back in his seat, and smiling at how Carmen's eyebrows had arched the instant he'd said "she."

*   *   *

Moving his men, vehicles, and several tons of equipment out of the sun-parched Utah desert to their final objective was a piece of cake compared to moving a tank battalion, Emerson Walls kept reminding himself as he packed the last of his gear into an olive-drab Suburban. Since bivouacking in the desert weeks earlier, his original platoon of twelve Navajos had dwindled to ten. He hadn't investigated what had happened to Larry Narine or Brandon DeVille, and he didn't care. When Ariel Roundtree had asked about the two missing men, he'd told him they had deserted. After all, in the grand scheme of things, the disappearance of two Indians didn't really matter. What did matter was having his remaining men prepared to fight a certain fire on a mountaintop, proceeding with his plan to divert attention from the fire, and, of course, his money.

Slamming the Suburban's tailgate, he looked around one last time at what had been home for too long. The only evidence that anyone had bivouacked in the area were the dying desert flora in the trampled spots, two limed and filled latrines, and some scattered tire tracks.

A skinny, droopy-eyed man in army fatigues and a Denver Broncos Super Bowl cap jogged slowly up to Walls. Davy Boy Lopez nodded back toward the Humvee he'd climbed out of. "We're ready to move out, Colonel," he said, showing the broad gap between his front teeth.

"Good," said Walls. He double-checked the trailer hitch on the Suburban. "Keep in contact and stay fifteen miles apart. Any irregularities, mishaps, or breakdowns—"

"Call you," said Lopez, completing the sentence.

"Right. And if any communication problems arise?"

"We take orders from Septian."

"You got it," said Walls, smiling at the response, knowing that he'd come as close to making soldiers out of a bunch of loser Indians as anyone possibly could. Shading his eyes, he fixed his gaze on the first vehicle in the line of four. "Move 'em out."

Lopez waved his arms like semaphores, and the truck at the

front of the line choked out a plume of black smoke before lumbering off. With a self-satisfied look, Lopez turned and headed back toward his own vehicle. Watching Lopez walk away, Walls couldn't help but smile. Two months earlier Lopez had been a falling-down drunk, a broken-spirited fifty-year-old Navajo whose greatest claim to fame was that he could balance a beer bottle on his nose. Now, after eight weeks in the desert, Lopez was not only sober; he had a fat wallet, and he'd learned a skill. And to top everything off, he'd earned the right to be point man on their secondary operation—a diversion that Walls had personally mapped out.

Walls prided himself on his reclamation projects—human ones sometimes, but mostly otherwise. That was what he'd done as an officer in the army's munitions, armored, and chemical command units for more than twenty-five years: clean up the U.S. Army's junk after wars. First in Vietnam, then Desert Storm. It was, after all, what he knew how to do, and what he did best. Following the Persian Gulf War, he'd stayed behind with part of a battalion to help out with the scores of lingering oil fires and to clear away the half-dozen Abrams tank carcasses that had been accidentally hit by friendly fire.

It was his Gulf War cleanup experience that had led Jack Kimbrough to contact him. But it was Roland Septian who had convinced Walls to take on the job of turning a bunch of human cast-offs into an elite firefighting unit. Now the real test was at hand. His men would soon have the real thing to cope with instead of some flatland training fire. Walls expected his men to be up to the task. He climbed into the Suburban, popped a CD into the deck, and turned up the volume on his favorite Chopin etude.

Farther down the convoy, Davy Boy Lopez's truck lurched forward, following in the tracks of the rig in front of it. Lighting up a Camel nonfilter and turning to Ariel Roundtree, Lopez said, "I'm a little nervous about this. We've been practicin' on two-acre fires, five at the most. Think we'll be able to handle one that's a couple hundred?"

"Sure. Long as we don't get interrupted, and long as you keep everybody's attention up on Powderhorn."

Lopez swallowed hard. He'd pushed for the diversionary assignment at the Powderhorn ski area because it had taken him away from the desert and the daily monotony of the firefighting drills. When he realized the assignment required blowing up a couple of ski-lift towers, he'd had second thoughts. But by then he was in over his head. He'd accepted an extra three grand and bragged to the rest of the men about how he would pull off the mission. He didn't want to look like a coward.

"Walls got you up to speed on Powderhorn?" asked Roundtree.

"Yeah, we had three dry runs."

"Sounds like you'll do fine," he said, though he had known since their grade school days that Davy Boy didn't do well under pressure.

"Hope so," said Davy Boy. He added sheepishly, "What are you gonna do after this?"

"Don't know, really. But one thing for sure: I ain't goin' back to cleanin' out portable shitters. What about you?"

Lopez answered his boyhood friend with silence and a smile; he'd rather die than go back to being a drunk. Gunning the truck's engine, he took a drag on the Camel and closed the gap between his truck and the one ahead.

CHAPTER
19

The voice on the phone was sugary sweet. "Floyd's Bail Bonds, Flora Jean Benson speakin'."

"Keep your eyes on the target and your head down," Rios said softly into the mouthpiece of the vintage 1930s telephone. He glanced across the library of his Grand Junction home, where Carmen sat slumped in his favorite easy chair, thumbing through a copy of *Paddler* magazine.

The second bedroom of the one-story bungalow had been transformed into a library with oak paneling, a vaulted ceiling, skylights, floor-to-ceiling bookshelves, and a ladder on a trolley. Overflowing with books, including hundreds of signed first editions, and protected by a state-of-the-art security system, the library was his safe haven. A place to escape a fatherless childhood, war memories, and now the rafting tragedy that continued to dog him.

"Rios?" said the excited, high-pitched voice on the other end of the line.

"None other."

"I'll be damned, sugar. If this ain't a blast from the past. Last time I saw you, you were hitchin' up your pants, haulin' ass down an airport concourse tryin' to catch the last flight outta Denver to Grand Junction."

"I wouldn't have been running if you'd been wearing a watch, Sergeant."

Flora Jean snickered. "They make them things for officers, too, Captain. Manage to get yourself one yet?"

Rios glanced at his battered wristwatch. "Been wearing the same one since a week after coming home from Desert Storm. Funny thing about that watch: It came in the mail out of the blue. Never did find out who it was from."

Flora Jean grinned. "Good thing, too, honey—you havin' that watch, I mean. 'Cause time's money. We're operatin' in America now, sugar, not the frickin' desert."

Rios laughed and thought about the first time he'd met Flora Jean. He'd been sent from his Saudi Arabia headquarters to an outpost a hundred miles beyond Basra in southern Iraq, on a midnight intelligence mission to confirm whether an Iraqi dairy was producing munitions rather than milk. First Sergeant F. J. Benson was to be his contact. He had been surprised to find that Sergeant Benson was a six-foot-tall, plain-faced but imposingly statuesque black woman with closely cropped hair and penetrating dark-brown eyes, who looked as if she belonged in a Las Vegas chorus line rather than the marines. The first words out of her mouth after a crisp salute had been unorthodox but to the point: "Glad you're here, sugar. Now let's check out whether ol' Saddam is makin' gunpowder or buttermilk."

Flora Jean's greeting and down-home familiarity had caught him off guard, and he'd been ready to ask for someone else to provide staff support, but before he could, a shelling barrage had rocked their outpost. During the next hour, as they hunkered down, flashlights and Day-Glo yellow highlighters in hand, he and Flora Jean had sifted through aerial photos and reams of intelligence material while the building around them crashed piece by piece to the ground. Amid the chaos, he had learned that Flora Jean, too, was from Colorado, that they had both climbed more than half the state's fourteen-thousand-foot peaks, and that despite her penchant for beginning and ending every sentence with "sugar," Sergeant F. J. Benson was not only fearless—she damn well knew her shit. At his request they had worked together several more times during the war, eventually flying home together on the same troop transport. Over the years they'd exchanged Christmas cards, postcards, and occa-

sional notes and even talked about pairing up to climb a few
more Colorado mountains. But they hadn't, and the current
phone conversation was their first in over two years.

Glancing up from his watch, Rios said, "See you're still working for that same bondsman, CJ Floyd. How's the job?"

"Not bad. But it took me a while to convince CJ that I could do
more than type and answer the phone. Now I'm writin' a third
of the bonds that walk in. I've even done a little bounty huntin'
with CJ on the side. In fact, I'm runnin' the place by myself for
the next two weeks while he's fly-fishin' with a friend of his up
on the Snake River, outside of Baggs, Wyoming. Hope to heck he
catches somethin', 'cause he's hell to be around when he comes
home skunked."

Thinking back on his own recent fishing trip, Rios rubbed his
injured shoulder and glanced in Carmen's direction. She had
moved from her seat to a spot next to his burglar-alarm keypad,
where she was flipping through a book. Turning his attention
back to Flora Jean, he said, "Think you could spare a little time
to help me out with a problem?"

"You know I can, sugar. Just name it and I'm in." They broke
into synchronous laughter, the kind shared by people who have
occupied the same foxhole during wartime.

"Great. I need some dope on a guy over your way named Jack
Kimbrough."

"Hold on, sugar; let me get a pen."

"Okay," said Rios, looking back at Carmen and realizing for
the first time that without a white lab coat or the unisex drab-
ness of OR greens, she was truly striking. Showered by afternoon rays from a skylight and silhouetted against a backdrop of
books, she looked softly feminine, less the coldly efficient doctor.
When he realized that Carmen had caught him staring, he
looked down and hugged the phone to his ear.

"Got one," said Flora Jean finally. "Shoot."

Rios cleared his throat, looked up, and smiled self-consciously
at Carmen. "Kimbrough runs a company called Particle Trigenics, right there in Denver. They manufacture fire retardants,

respiratory filtering equipment, and disaster gear. PTG's their stock exchange symbol."

Flora Jean whistled. "Stock exchange? You're talkin' money now, sugar. What's your boy Kimbrough done?"

"I'm not sure, but I think he's into something illegal, and more than likely real high-tech."

"Drugs?"

"No, drugs don't seem to fit. This little piggy's into something a lot more complex, and whatever it is, it's forced either him or one of his henchmen to try and kill a doctor friend of mine over here in Grand Junction."

"He sounds real sweet."

"Compared to the strongman he keeps on a chain, he probably is. Problem is, I don't know his strongman's name. Can you profile Kimbrough for me, drop an ID on his trained seal, and give me a heads-up on his operation?"

Flora Jean laughed. "That and what time he takes his daily dump. At Floyd's Bail Bonds we aim to please."

"You're on," said Rios, quickly adding, "By the way, did your boss know you were in marine intelligence when he hired you?"

"Nope. But he does now, and believe me, a little IT background comes in real handy when you're shadowboxin' with the bottom-feeders we have to deal with every day."

"You'll need it here too, Flora Jean. Kimbrough's crafty. And he's certainly not your average street thug. I wouldn't underestimate him or that trained goon of his. They play for keeps."

"That bad?"

"Yep."

"I'll keep that in mind when I'm scoutin' around. How soon do you need the info?"

"As fast as you can get it. And, Flora Jean, like I said, be careful. One man's already dead behind this."

"I'll be sure to keep things real low-key."

"One more thing. With Floyd out of town, have you got any backup?"

"A girlfriend in the building next door."

"Come off it. You know what kind of backup I mean."

"I'm serious. She's a lawyer, and a damn good one. Used to work for Floyd herself. Name's Julie Madrid, and she knows how to use a gun."

Rios shrugged. "Whatever keeps you in your comfort zone. Just don't get yourself in a bind."

"Wouldn't think of it, sugar. By the way, if drugs ain't Kimbrough's game, what's he peddlin'?"

"Like I said, I'm not sure. But it has something to do with gamecocks."

"Fightin' chickens? You're yankin' my chain."

"No. I think he's into supercharging the damn things. What I can't figure out is why. There damn sure wouldn't be enough money in winning cockfights to keep a corporate highflier like him in a year's worth of tailor-made suits."

"You can count on one thing, sugar. If it ain't money he's after, it's power. And if it's not one of them two he's doggin', he's chasin' after fame. The checkoff list for men like him is real short, and it never seems to change."

Rios couldn't help but smile at Flora Jean's straightforward logic. "Right to the point, Dr. Benson. Now that you've psycho-analyzed Kimbrough, why don't you tell me how much your little probe's going to hit me in the wallet?"

"Who's payin'? You or that doctor friend of yours who almost got theirself killed?"

"Me."

"You?" Flora Jean's voice rose in surprise. "Then you must owe that friend of yours big-time. That or you're totin' around a boatload of guilt over 'em almost buyin' the farm."

"Let's just say for the moment that I need to keep busy and my mind needs to stay occupied."

"Shoulda told me that from the start. Two hundred bucks a day and expenses. Double that if I have to use my lawyer friend."

"Sounds good to me."

"One last thing, Rios. Tell me that friend of yours—the one you say almost got killed—isn't a woman."

Rios chuckled, aware that Flora Jean knew his penchant for linking up with problem females. Glancing at Carmen and watching the sunlight glimmer off her hair, he said, "Afraid I can't."

Flora Jean sighed and shook her head. "Figures. I'll be back in touch. In the meantime, sugar, keep your eyes on the target and your head down."

Smiling, Rios hung up and turned to Carmen. "Looks like we've got ourselves a Denver connection and a little extra backup on this thing with Stone."

"Maybe we should let the sheriff handle it," said Carmen, setting aside the book she'd been reading.

"We're in too deep now. Besides, Stone's counting on us. I figured you for being a little more game."

"And I pegged you for someone who pumps iron and takes nutritional supplements, not someone who reads books."

"Looks can be deceiving."

"They most certainly can." Carmen tossed her hair and nibbled the corner of her lip, the way she had all her life when she was nervous. "I flipped through *The Day of the Locust* while you were on the phone. I haven't thought about that book since college. There's a description of a cockfight in it, you know. Gruesome. Made my stomach knot up."

"Most fights are, whether they involve bantam roosters, wild dogs, or human beings."

"Stone claims that over the years, his birds almost never lost a fight."

"And he may be telling the truth. Think I'll reserve judgment until I take a look at the photocopies of that missing log book of his to see if they bear him out."

"Do you think they'd be worth killing for? The records, I mean?"

"I'm not certain. But I know one thing: Those log book records and Stone's birds are what's driving Jack Kimbrough's quest."

Carmen looked surprised. "*Quest?* That's a strange way to put it."

"Not really. He's on the same treasure hunt that we are, except he knows what he's looking for, and we don't."

"And you, Walker Rios—what are you looking for?" asked Carmen, recognizing that Rios suddenly seemed to be caught up in a game.

"A break in the routine. A way to help out a dying old man. And maybe a way to cleanse away some guilt. I guess when you get right down to it, I'm looking for more substance and less white water in my life."

"Seems to me like you might be heading for more rapids."

"I'll take my chances." Rios removed his arm from the sling and began slowly flexing it. "The way I see it, I can work like hell to try and get this arm of mine back to a hundred percent, or I can walk around with it in a sling and hope for the best. The first option carries a certain degree of risk. The difference be-tween the two is the level of reward at the end. Dealing with this problem of Stone's instead of sitting on my thumbs and waiting for things to take their course is pretty much the same kind of choice."

"And if you or Stone—or that Flora Jean person you were just talking to on the phone—gets injured or killed? Then what?"

"Then at least I didn't tuck tail and run, or roll over and pee on my belly. And most of all, I didn't sit around moping and end up drowning in guilt."

Rios's answer brought back memories of her bitter Utah expe-rience. She had lost her friends, her reputation, and ultimately her job because she'd stood up to an embezzling hospital admin-istrator and a department chair who would rather cut corners than properly monitor cancer patients in drug trials. "I've been burned for taking a stand. It's something you don't forget."

"Sometimes you have to lick your wounds and move on."

"Or let them heal and start over."

The look on Carmen's face told Rios that they'd moved from Stone's problem to something deeply personal. He didn't want to ask her what it was, but considering his current physical limi-tations, he needed to know whether she would continue to help. "Hate to press the issue, but it's time to call the question. Are you in or out?"

"I'm in," said Carmen hesitantly, caught between sympathy for an old cockfighter and a challenge from a stubborn river guide. As she slipped *The Day of the Locust* back onto the shelf, she had the feeling that the security blanket she had wrapped herself in since leaving Utah was about to be stripped away. Deep down, she had always known that sooner or later it would come to this.

CHAPTER
20

Julie Madrid sat at the antique barrister-style rolltop desk in her law office, sifting through papers. She'd spent all afternoon profiling Jack Kimbrough and his company, Trigenics, for Flora Jean, including an hour on the Internet, an hour of library time, and a half-hour of snooping by phone. Now, before Flora Jean's problem became hers and began eating its way into the only free time she seemed to have anymore, she glanced across the room at her friend, who was also busy flipping through papers, and said, "Gotta call it quits. I've got a sick kid to get home to, and I started this morning at six. We've got enough on Kimbrough to choke a horse." She closed the folder of papers she'd been examining and slid it across the floor.

"Time don't matter, sugar," said Flora Jean, picking up the folder. "There's always work waitin' when you're dealing with scum."

Amazed as always by Flora Jean's stamina, Julie could only shake her head. It had been three years since her friend had replaced her as CJ Floyd's right hand. In that time she'd watched Flora Jean grow from a rough-around-the-edges recruit, who'd initially rubbed CJ the wrong way, into a hard-nosed, insightful bail-bonding agent. Still, with CJ out of town and Flora Jean snooping around the treacherous edges of money and power, Julie was worried. "I'd take this one slow, Flora Jean. For what it's worth, you're batting in the big leagues."

Ignoring the warning, Flora Jean glanced down at the manila folder she'd added to the ones already in her lap. She flipped it open and stared at Julie's profile of Jack Kimbrough. "Looks like our Texas country boy's made a name for himself, sugar. He's worth seventy million at least. Question is, did he earn it on the up-and-up?"

"Seems like he has, but he's got a ruthless streak that comes out loud and clear. The last three pages in that folder you're holding pretty much spell it out."

"Ruthless? You can say that about a lot of business folks."

"Maybe, but by all accounts, Kimbrough's streak runs exceptionally deep. Check it out—the last three pages." Julie checked her watch. "Sorry, babe, I've gotta run."

Flora Jean rose from her chair and stretched. Her ebony skin and six feet of height were a marked contrast to Julie's fading summer tan and petite five-foot-four-inch frame. "Watch yourself on this one, Flora Jean," Julie said as they headed toward the door. "Remember, Kimbrough's got a goon, the one your marine buddy Rios warned you about. And from what I could piece together in one afternoon, it looks as though he does most of Kimbrough's mopping up."

"Rios called him a trained seal."

"I'm betting he's more of a shark. I couldn't dig up much on him, not even a name. Most of the Trigenics documents I latched on to simply refer to him as an associate. Nameless people always make me nervous. Maybe you should wait for CJ to get back before you tackle this."

"Don't have time. Besides, this ain't CJ's fight. It's mine."

"Then like I said, I'd watch myself. You might very well be stepping into a huge pile of it."

Flora Jean laughed as they stepped through the doorway and into the noise of the rush-hour traffic booming past the quiet enclave of converted Victorian homes that made up Denver's bail bondsmen's row. "Don't worry, sugar. I've dodged my share of shit storms before."

"I know you have," said Julie, locking the door behind her. "Problem is, this one could be a hurricane."

*   *   *

It wasn't until hours later, as she reread Julie's notes while pol-
ishing off a slice of pecan pie at Mae's Louisiana Kitchen, that
Flora Jean understood what Julie had meant about Kimbrough's
being ruthless. *Heartless*—even *savage*—might have been a better
word. According to Julie's dossier, Kimbrough had made most
of his money by worming his way into the corporate and mu-
nicipal fire-safety business. Back-room deals, end runs around
government regulations, and sabotage of competitors were his
trademarks. His company's respirators, flame retardants, and
firefighting gear had been recalled half a dozen times over the
twelve-year life of Particle Trigenics. In the wake of the recalls,
he'd paid local, state, and federal fines of hundreds of thousands
of dollars, and he'd had his license to manufacture air filtration
equipment suspended twice. Despite the slapped wrists and
recalls, the company was not only still doing business, it was
expanding and flourishing.

As far as she was concerned, scamming the government was
yesterday's news. Everyone did it. And like her mama always
said, even the corner grocer has a little larceny in his heart. But
only when she got to the last three pages of Julie's notes did
Flora Jean fully begin to understand Kimbrough. She felt a chill
as she read how two Trigenics drill press operators had been
killed in an explosion that Kimbrough claimed was the result of
their own procedural shortcuts and incompetence. A criminal
negligence trial had followed, at which the families of the dead
men had argued that safety protocols at Trigenics were next to
nonexistent. Excerpts from transcripts of the trial revealed an
arrogance in Kimbrough that Flora Jean found hard to believe.
When asked whether the two Trigenics employees, men who
had been with the company since its inception, were competent
at their jobs, Kimbrough had responded that they were as skilled
as any simpleminded layman lacking a formal education and a
background in particle physics could hope to become.

Following a plea bargain that included provisions that

exempted him from criminal prosecution, Kimbrough had shelled
out $450,000 to the plaintiffs' families and then kept a low pro-
file for a year and a half, later surfacing to tout Trigenics' R & D
breakthroughs that included the new generation of industrial
respirators, the line of fire-retardant chemicals and firefighting
gear, and the artificial-skin bandage for burn victims.

"What a prince," mumbled Flora Jean, taking a sip of coffee
and shaking her head.

"Who's that?" asked her waitress, appearing instantly with a
refill.

"One of our stellar Denver businessmen, sugar. A multimil-
lionaire."

"You know him?"

"Nope," said Flora Jean, wrapping her hand around her coffee
mug and smiling. "But I plan to get better acquainted real soon."

Felix Tangay had just started a heat shock protein extraction
procedure when he heard something in the hallway outside
his research lab. It was the third time that evening he'd been
distracted by strange noises: first a loud thump, then a faint
scratching, and now a swishing sound like pieces of fabric rubbing together. Skittish by nature and paranoid about safeguard-
ing his research data, he walked over to a file cabinet near the
door, pulled out the baseball bat he kept there, and called out,
"Who's there?" When no answer came, he stood motionless, listening intently but hearing only the agitator stirrer on the countertop next to him. Finally he set the bat aside and returned to
what he was doing.

He had been busy genotyping all day. In the process, he had
discovered a gene mutation common to every gamecock tissue
sample Septian had brought him, and he was positive that re-
duced heat shock protein levels in the gamecocks were responsible for the mutated trait. Unlike anything he'd observed in his
fruit fly experiments, there was something unique about the
amplified HSP DNA he'd isolated from the gamecock tissue. He
suspected that the unusual DNA finding was linked to the dra-

matic HSP90 reduction in the birds, which in turn had to be
responsible for the increases in leg muscle mass and the huge
increases in lung capacity he was finding.

He was about to turn down the speed on one of the two agita-
tors when a popping noise startled him, followed by the hint of a
door closing and then an unmistakable thump. Rushing back to
the file cabinet, he grabbed a nine-shot .22-caliber revolver from
the top drawer. He worked his way across the lab toward the
chemical storage room where the noise seemed to have come
from. The storage room, which separated the laboratory from his
office, had been designed so that deliveries could be made via a
ramp that opened directly onto an alley. Knowing that no one
should have been able to enter the storage room from outside
without triggering an alarm, he cautiously approached the room's
only interior door. The room echoed with a deep, hollow-
pitched thud when he swung the heavy, explosion-proof steel
door back against a half-empty drum of xylene. "Who's in
there?" he called, stepping into the storage room and switching
on the single overhead light. "Better come out." With his arms
locked out in front of him and the revolver pointed straight
ahead, he worked his way down one of the four narrow aisles
formed by rows of chemical reagent drums stacked two high.
"I've got a gun," he said in a quaking voice.

Near the end of the aisle, he pivoted back toward what
sounded like a footfall and, beside himself with fear, squeezed
off a shot that penetrated a ten-gallon plastic carboy of tissue
fixative. The nauseating smell of formalin, embalming fluid's
workaday cousin, quickly permeated the room as a second bullet cracked into the back wall. Tangay backtracked down the
aisle, shaking and praying silently. Halfway down the aisle he
heard what sounded like scratching. As the sound intensified,
he realized it was coming from above him. When he looked up
to pinpoint the source of the noise, the lights went out and a
landslide of boxes and chemical drums clattered down on him.

In a rush of adrenalin, he fired two shots at the tall figure pelt-
ing down the aisle away from him. Soaked with formalin, he

clawed his way over boxes and fifty-five-gallon drums toward a set of double doors that opened onto the alley. When he reached the wide-open doors, the intruder had disappeared. Still clutching the .22, Tangay screamed, "Shit! . . . Shit! . . . Shit!" as he descended a cargo ramp and walked up the alley into a stream of high-intensity light arcing down from a nearby telephone pole. *"Bésame el culo!"* he screamed, waving his gun defiantly overhead before finally stuffing it into his waistband and returning to the storage room.

Back inside, he turned on the lights and realized that the room's alarm wires had been cut. In a near panic, he leaped over boxes, slipping in a pool of commingled chemicals, and raced for his office. The office door was open and the lights were on. Stepping into the room, he noticed immediately that the top drawer of one of the file cabinets had been jimmied open. Shaking and mumbling obscenities in Tagalog, Spanish, and English, he walked over to the drawer and yanked it back. Several hanging files were missing. Five folders in all, he told himself, counting them off as he rummaged through the drawer, aware that each missing file had been stamped CONFIDENTIAL and sealed with a red tab.

Tangay's arms dropped limply. His skin stung from the caustic bite of formalin, and his nose burned from the fixative's pungent, vinegary smell. Cursing himself for not being a better shot and for not calling security the first time he'd heard strange noises, he reached for a nearby phone. Then he kicked the wall, livid that he'd kept hard copies of his research data in the office, and terrified because the call was going to have to be to Jack Kimbrough.

Flora Jean sped down Fourteenth Avenue in her Four-Runner, one hand cupped to her bleeding right ear, which had been nicked by the second bullet from Tangay's .22. Still a little giddy from the adrenaline, she thought back on her days in Marine Corps intelligence. She chuckled despite the searing pain as she fumbled with her cell phone and punched in Walker Rios's phone number, thinking to herself that she'd just earned a second Purple Heart.

It was close to one A.M. by the time Jack Kimbrough arrived at Tangay's lab. He spent a few moments pacing the laboratory, five minutes combing the alley and delivery ramp, and several more minutes striding through a storage room that still reeked of formalin; then he finally turned to Tangay and said, "Why the hell didn't you call security when you heard the first noise?"

Tangay shook his head. "I don't know. Guess I just didn't think much of it."

"So while you weren't thinking, someone stole your goddamned files and got away with information worth hundreds of millions." Looking at Tangay as if he were a traitor, Kimbrough said, "This whole heat shock thing is bigger than you think, Felix. Much bigger, damn it!"

Tangay hung his head, afraid to respond.

"Double-check everything. I want a list of exactly what's missing. I'll have someone clean up here and take care of our security problem."

"Anything else?" Tangay asked sheepishly.

"Yes. From now on don't keep hard data on the heat shock research in your office or your lab. And in the future I want the results of every HSP experiment you do, on a daily basis, hand-delivered to me on a disk. No E-mail, no phone calls, no letters, no carrier pigeons."

Tangay nodded.

"You may leave. I'll handle everything from here."

Tangay walked back to his office, feeling defeated. After gathering up his briefcase, he left without another word, unaware that Kimbrough was engaged in an animated telephone conversation with Roland Septian.

Septian stood naked in his bedroom, clutching a cell phone and looking at his groggy reflection in the full-length mirror. "You got me out of bed, Jack. I hope this is serious."

"Serious enough," countered Kimbrough. "Someone broke into Tangay's lab. Five heat shock files are missing."

"Bag the culprit?"

"No. But Tangay got trigger-happy and wounded whoever it was with a twenty-two. I found a few drops of blood on the delivery ramp to one of the storage rooms."

"So the little prick can shoot—who'da thunk it? Say, think it might've been that Nguyen broad again?"

"I don't know, but I'm certain she's the link."

Septian's tone turned expectant. "Do I detect an assignment?"

"Yeah. Do the half-nigger, half-gook bitch!"

Septian smiled at his reflection. "Will do," he said, aligning his body in the mirror. "It'll be a job I'll enjoy."

CHAPTER
21

Ariel Roundtree nosed the lead truck along Ward Creek's aspen-clad rim and into the 346,000-acre Grand National Forest. For the next forty minutes the trucks, groaning and belching soot, worked their way along the narrow seven-mile Crag Crest Recreational Trail, staying precisely ten minutes apart. Stopping at the trail's cul-de-sac loop, Roundtree reached for the binoculars on the console beside him, adjusted the focus, and gazed out toward the surrounding mountain ranges and emerald lakes.

"Don't see how you can start much of a fire up here," said Davy Boy Lopez, squirming in the adjacent seat. "It's greener'n Ireland."

"We're just cresting the edge of the national forest," said Roundtree. "Fire danger territory's actually the BLM land we'll be setting up on down below."

Lopez frowned. "Seems to me like Walls could've picked a better test site than this. Winds can play hell with a fire up here. Let me see those glasses."

Roundtree handed the binoculars across the seat. He didn't often agree with Davy Boy, but this time he knew his cousin was right. Under the right conditions, he and the rest of his men could end up as blowup fodder in a forest fire capable of swallowing them whole. "No different from puttin' 'em out in the desert. Did we have a problem there?" he said, hoping to calm Davy Boy's fears.

"No, but we didn't have a whole forest full of kindling out there, and we didn't have no accelerant to deal with. If you ask me, we're risking a hell of a lot just to test out a bunch of fire-retardant zoot suits and some newfangled breathers." Davy Boy glanced back toward the just arriving second truck in the convoy, the one Emerson Walls had loaded up with the accelerant they would also be testing.

"Quit worrying. We've had enough drill. We won't be doin' any more than puttin' out a superheated container and the area surrounding it, just like in the desert. By the way, you're lookin' in the wrong damn direction." Roundtree reached up and pushed the binoculars another twenty degrees west. "Our objective's on the other side of this mesa. We'll be settin' up on a private parcel and a hunk of BLM land outside the forest boundaries. It's about thirty miles from your diversion up at Powderhorn."

"Then let's head for it. Looking at all that dry timber makes me nervous."

Roundtree restarted the engine and nosed the truck toward lower ground. "Give Walls a call," he said, handing Davy Boy his cell phone. "He'll wanna know where we're at and how far we are from the objective."

Davy Boy began punching in numbers. "Yes, sir, *mon capitain*," he said sarcastically. "Almost forgot for a second that you're a fuckin' war hero and I'm just a dumb-ass res Indian."

Felix Tangay was back in his office, red-eyed and perplexed. The previous evening's break-in had kept him up most of the night, and he'd spent half the morning talking to the two nosy cops who had discovered the incapacitated alarm during a routine patrol. It had taken him the rest of the day to settle his nerves and get back to the task of genotyping the heat shock protein mutations he'd discovered in the seven frozen gamecock tissue specimens. The experiments involved straightforward DNA extractions using polymerase chain-reaction genotyping, and while six of the DNA amplifications had been routine, results on the seventh tissue sample had proved totally confounding.

That sample had shown a dramatic increase in the expression

of mutant traits at all experimental temperatures above twenty-five degrees Celsius, or seventy-seven Fahrenheit. More important, each time he introduced heat shock protein into the equation, it readily buffered the temperature sensitivity of the mutant traits, causing the mutations to be more noticeable at higher temperatures.

Uncertain why he was seeing such a dramatic heat-related variation in the seventh sample, he had decided to determine why the heat shock protein response was so impaired at high temperatures in that particular specimen. After two frustrating hours of trying to get the procedure he'd perfected in his fruit flies to work on the gamecock tissue, he'd finally succeeded.

Now he sat poring over his experiment log book, reviewing every step he'd taken in his analysis of tissue from the seventh bird—from the moment Septian had delivered the specimens to the lab until Tangay had run the very first DNA amplification procedure. Looking up from his desk, he glanced across the room toward the liquid-nitrogen carrier Septian had brought the tissue samples in, and remembered that six of the specimens had been standard frozen bullion-cube-size pieces of tissue, ready for processing, whereas the seventh, a good three times larger than the others, had needed to be trimmed to processing size by one of the technicians.

Since his lead tech had prepared all the samples for DNA isolation, Tangay had never actually seen the subsequent digestion products. Still puzzled, he walked briskly down the hallway to the lab, where two techs were busy at opposite benchtops just inside the doorway. "Rebecca, I need to speak with you a minute," Tangay called out to the slender woman in a rumpled white lab coat.

Rebecca Ellerby, looking surprised to see him, said, "I thought you were busy double-checking our results."

"I decided to take a break." Tangay walked over to the benchtop and picked up a beaker half-filled with baker's yeast. "Think you can answer a question that's been puzzling me all day?"

"I'll try."

"Those seven tissue samples I had you prepare our digestion products from—did you notice anything unusual about them?"

"Besides the fact that one of them was bigger than the others?" asked Rebecca hesitantly.

"Yes," said Tangay, watching her eyes dart nervously from side to side.

"There was a bit of a difference. The cubed ones minced up quite nicely. But that seventh one, even after I sectioned it, took almost an hour to digest."

Tangay stroked his chin. "Would you mind getting one of the remaining frozen pieces from the seventh sample so I can take a look at it?"

"No need," said Rebecca, aware now that she'd have to call Jack Kimbrough as soon as Tangay left. "It was so difficult to digest that I set up another sample from the digestion this afternoon. I'll get it for you." She walked to the end of the benchtop and returned with a piece of tissue in a clear plastic cassette. "Have a look," she said, handing the half-dollar-sized cassette to Tangay. "I was just getting ready to microdissect off a piece for a backup run in case I had problems with the tissue digestion again."

Tangay snapped back the plastic top on the cassette, extracted the tissue from inside, and rolled the dense piece of muscle between his thumb and forefinger.

"Anything wrong?" asked Rebecca, noticing a look of shock spread across his face. When he didn't answer, she repeated the question, certain now that she should have lied all along about the seventh specimen.

With befuddlement etched clearly on his face, and his voice almost squeaking, Tangay said, "Finish your digestion. I need to go see Kimbrough!"

CHAPTER
22

Wincing in pain, Flora Jean switched the receiver from her gauze-covered right ear to her left and began debriefing Rios on the break-in at Trigenics. After giving him complete details of the shoot-out, she took a bite from the steaming hot dog garnished with honey mustard, coleslaw, and hot peppers, and braced the phone against her shoulder. While eating, she flipped through the papers she'd stolen from Tangay's lab. So far, she still couldn't make heads or tails of the scientific hieroglyphics.

"Hell, Walker, all I know is that they're experimentin' on chickens, and that the research lab they're doin' it in looks like somethin' out of *The Twilight Zone*. Lucky for me, whoever was shootin' at my ass was a bad shot. I asked my lawyer friend Julie to look over the papers I lifted, but she passed. Said if she had to defend me on a breakin'-and-enterin' charge she couldn't be an accessory. You're gonna have to check these puppies out yourself."

"Can you get the papers to me by this evening?" Rios asked, squeezing the rubber ball as he talked, wondering whether the tingling in his left hand would ever disappear. "I've got someone working with me who can probably decipher what's in them."

"I can fax 'em right now."

"No. I don't want any kind of paper trail left behind."

"I can send a runner; it's better than a four-hour drive over there to Grand Junction."

"Got someone you can trust?"

Flora Jean took a bite of hot dog and thought for a moment.

"The nephew of a friend of my boss's. Name's Darryl Gentry. He's as straight as they come. College kid. Does odd jobs for us every once in a while."

"Send him."

"I need an address."

"Twelve-eighty Colorado. Tell him to pick up a Grand Junction map. It'll be easy to find."

"I'll have him there by six."

"Good. And, Flora Jean, take care of that ear."

"Don't you worry, sugar. Dr. Benson's on the job. Suffered cuts worse than this cuffin' bond skippers and perverts."

"You're a sweetheart."

"Remember that when you send my check. . . . Later." Flora Jean cradled the phone, patted the dressing on her ear, and wolfed down the last of her hot dog before dialing Darryl Gentry's number to tell him she had an express delivery to Grand Junction.

Carmen grabbed her helmet from a chair, locked up her office, and headed out the door of the ER into the late-afternoon sunshine, hoping to be able to catch Rios by cell phone and bring him up to speed on a few new insights she'd gotten from a rapidly deteriorating Luke Redstone. Her ten-hour shift had included a futile attempt to save the life of a sixteen-year-old who'd rolled his four-by-four off the nearby Book Cliffs, as well as a lengthy and enlightening heart-to-heart talk with Stone.

Stone's cancer had spread to his liver, and he now had a fungal infection in one lung. She'd checked in on him at noon to find him resting quietly in bed, thumbing through a poultry nutritional-supplement magazine. When she'd asked how he was doing, he'd said in a near groan, "I'll be back on my feet real quick." When she'd pointed out that his poultry magazine was thicker than some of her medical journals, they'd both laughed.

After that, the conversation bogged down, and it was only when she mentioned that Rios had someone in Denver checking out Jack Kimbrough that Stone had opened up, detailing his colorful life and explaining how he'd come to spend more than four decades raising his birds on the Colorado Plateau.

Late in the conversation, Stone had struggled out of bed, pulled back the mattress, and produced a photocopied set of the original gamecock breeding records that had been stolen from him. The records, laid out in meticulous detail, documented the breeding process that had enabled Stone to develop gamecocks that he claimed were superior to any others in the world. When she asked Stone how he'd managed to get the records delivered to St. Mary's, he'd smiled and said, "You ain't my only friend in the world," before launching into the story of how he'd developed his champion gamecocks.

"I bred most of my birds from a single rooster named Thunder Head," he'd confided in a nostalgic tone. Then, struggling to breathe, he pointed out the amazing results of his breeding methods to Carmen, page by photocopied page. Flipping through the final pages, he added that he'd bred his gamecocks to be "as indestructible as cockroaches and as vicious as man."

From her preliminary review of his records, Carmen could see that over the years Stone had indeed produced a strain of gamecocks that had steadily increased in strength, size, stamina, and combativeness. Nonetheless, she remained skeptical of Stone's tales about his cockfighting career and his claim of one hundred consecutive victories, until he asked her to pull out a cardboard box from beneath his bed. The box, filled with an assortment of cockfighting paraphernalia and scores of photos, also contained a photocopy of a four-thousand-dollar check signed by a man named Jimmy Turner. A handwritten note signed by Turner and substantiating Stone's claim of one hundred straight wins had been stapled to the back of the check. When Stone matter-of-factly told her that it was Turner she'd have to track down if she ever hoped to find out who'd tried to kill her and determine the whereabouts of his birds, she'd been left speechless. And when Stone pointed Turner out to her in one of the photographs from his box, grinning like a Cheshire cat as he bit the head off a losing gamecock, Carmen realized that even with Rios's help, she was in way over her head. Sensing her trepidation, Stone down-played Turner's antics, saying, "He don't do that no more."

She'd spent the rest of her time with Stone working up a pro-file of Turner, including where he lived, who his friends were, where he liked to hang out, and what he might know about the missing birds. When she asked Stone for the easiest way to find Turner, he laughed and said, "Where else? At a cockfight." He then scribbled a list of upcoming dates and times on a napkin. "There's one tonight," he added, completing the list, sounding a little wistful that he couldn't attend.

When she asked, "Should I go?" Stone had grinned like a kid. He quickly jotted down directions to the cockfight on the other side of the napkin and handed it to Carmen, adding in a restrained whisper as he adjusted the oxygen clip in his nostrils, "Be sure to take Rios with you. And be sure one of ya has a gun." Looking around the room as if to make certain no one was spy-ing on them, he added, "Trust me—you might need it, Doc. You'll be running with a whole different breed."

Felix Tangay covered the sixteen blocks from his laboratory to Trigenics' Seventeenth Street corporate offices in a near run, only to be forced to cool his heels in an anteroom filled with overpriced art, uncomfortable chairs, and flower arrangements that made him sneeze.

He was still out of sorts from the early-morning grilling he'd endured from cops who'd been more interested in why he had a gun in his lab than in the fact that a thief had broken in and stolen a year's worth of research data. Above all, he was upset because he suspected that Kimbrough had been manipulating him, keeping him in the dark about the true reasons for their research. Now, thanks to the very enlightening tissue sample number seven, he had an inkling of what Kimbrough was really up to.

Unable to decide whether to confront Kimbrough with his suspicions directly or skirt the issue for the time being, he found himself sweating and hyperventilating to the point that he had the hiccups. Fidgeting uncomfortably in his seat, he took three deep breaths and slowly exhaled. Seconds later, Kimbrough's executive secretary walked up and said, "Dr. Kimbrough can see you now." Nervously adjusting his tie, Tangay nodded, rose slowly from his chair, and went into Kimbrough's office.

Kimbrough was at his desk jotting notes on a scratch pad. "Felix. I hope you're not here about the break-in," Kimbrough said. "I've had it up to here with Denver's finest. Enough's enough." Stretching out of his chair, he walked around to the front of the desk. "I've got our security people on the problem— we'll solve it ourselves. By the way, did you know they found blood on the delivery ramp outside your lab?"

"No."

"Tiny droplets that the cops somehow missed. But our security people spotted them right off. Looks like you scored a hit on our thief," said Kimbrough, smiling broadly.

Unsure whether to take solace in the news that he'd shot someone, Tangay stared past Kimbrough and toward the wall of windows behind him. "Think they're hurt?" he asked, punctuating the query with a nervous hiccup.

"They probably barely got nicked, but I've got security checking out emergency rooms, twenty-four-hour drugstores in the area, and a dozen or so doctors' offices, just in case. Quietly, of course. We don't want to upset the police." Kimbrough patted Tangay reassuringly on the shoulder. "Knowing that our people are on the job should set your mind at ease, don't you think?"

Tangay nodded. "About the break-in, sure." His response was noticeably tentative.

"You don't sound too happy, Felix. Is there something else?"

"Well . . . yes."

"It's not your research records, is it? You can replace them, can't you?"

"Of course. No, it's not that."

"Is there a problem with the specimens?" asked Kimbrough, surprising Tangay with the question.

"In a manner of speaking . . ."

"I see." Kimbrough walked over to one of the two large leather sofas in the room, sat down, and glanced toward the floor-to-ceiling windows that looked out on the Front Range of the Rockies. Patting the cushion next to him, he looked up at Tangay. "Have a seat. This isn't Twenty Questions, Felix. Spit out what's on your mind."

Unable to dodge the issue any longer, Tangay blurted out, "One of the tissue samples Septian delivered probably isn't from a gamecock."

"It isn't?"

"No. Sample seven. Just a bit ago I had a look at it. The muscle's too dense, and I've had a hell of a time trying to digest any of the pieces Rebecca cut from it."

Kimbrough responded calmly, unperturbed by Tangay's technical problem. "What about the heat shock protein levels in that tissue sample? Could you digest enough of the specimen to determine what the levels were?"

"Yes," said Tangay, forcing back a hiccup.

"Well, were the HSP levels up or down?"

"Down."

Kimbrough stroked his chin expectantly. "And did the mutated traits increase with the application of additional heat?"

"They sure did, over twentyfold." Tangay took a deep breath. "In fact, there was a direct correlative response. As the mutated traits increased, the HSP levels in tissue sample seven decreased by a factor of a hundred. That's ten times what I found in my fruit fly experiments, or in any of the other gamecock specimens Septian delivered. The critical thing here is that the heat shock protein depletion and the subsequent tissue mutations are clearly tied to tremendous bumps in temperature. That's not what I found in my fruit flies or any of the other gamecocks. Tissue sample seven has to be from another source."

"Maybe it's a fluke," said Kimbrough, forcing back a smile.

"It's not."

"You're certain of that?"

Tangay shook his head vigorously. "I've got Rebecca running

protein sequences on it this very instant. I'll know where the tissue's from by tomorrow morning, but I'm certain it's not from a gamecock."

Kimbrough's smile faded. "Perhaps Septian made a mistake. He's the one who harvested the tissue samples and snap-froze them out in the field. We'll have to ask him about it."

"If he did, he made a big one."

"Think we can recover from the error if he did?"

"Depends."

"On what?" said Kimbrough, noting an air of smugness in Tangay's response.

"On whether or not the tissue sampling error was made on purpose."

"And if it was?"

"Then, depending on the source of the sample, someone would have a hell of a lot of explaining to do."

"I take it you mean Septian?"

"He'd be first."

"I see." Kimbrough relaxed back into the supple leather of the couch. "Well, for the moment the issue's moot. We don't really know our mysterious sample number seven's source. So, in the meantime, why don't you characterize the sample the same way as all the others. Once you've done that, perhaps we'll have a better idea of how to proceed."

Tangay swallowed hard before responding. "I'll expect to be compensated if this is a real breakthrough."

Kimbrough's smile resurfaced. "Of course, Felix, of course. But don't let your expectations get too high. This could all turn out to be a bust."

"I don't think so."

"And why not?"

Tangay thwarted a hiccup with a quick gulp of air. "Because my electrophoresis data shows that in that same tissue sample there are a bunch of stress proteins you don't find in chickens. We could be dealing with a scientific breakthrough worth millions."

Kimbrough rose from his seat and fixed an intimidating boss-to-subordinate stare on Tangay. "Maybe you should try thinking less about money and more about science, Felix. Finish your tests and call me in the morning."

"Sometimes the two go hand in hand," said Tangay, rising from his seat, surprised by his own directness. Without responding, Kimbrough accompanied him to the door.

Beads of perspiration dotted Tangay's brow as he headed for the elevators. He'd been straightforward and he'd been evasive with Kimbrough, and he wasn't sure that either strategy had worked. He'd know better after he finished sequencing the protein in tissue sample seven. After that, he and Kimbrough would have plenty of time to discuss the correlation between money and science. He was certain the stress protein sequences Rebecca Ellerby was running would speak for themselves, defining the exact source of their mysterious tissue sample seven—and setting him up for life.

CHAPTER

23

Carmen wasn't certain whether Rios's stubbornness was meant to show her that he was tough, whether he was out to prove to himself that he could come to grips with his lingering guilt, or whether he was simply manifesting further signs of post-traumatic stress disorder. But during a tension-charged cell phone conversation with him, as she sat on the Indian's saddle in the St. Mary's parking lot, Rios had assured her that he felt well enough to stand a forty-mile motorcycle ride across the high-desert country of the Uncompahgre Plateau to check out the cockfight Stone had told her about. She'd argued with him, explaining that he was only six days past surgery, insisting that if they had to go, they should at least take his truck. But Rios had stubbornly countered, "Be at my place by six—on your bike and dressed in black." Then he'd filled her in on Flora Jean's break-in at Trigenics and, without letting her get in another word, casually mentioned before hanging up that he'd have the research records Flora Jean had stolen ready for her perusal by the time she arrived.

She arrived at Rios's house a little past six, dressed in a black T-shirt and form-fitting black jeans, just in time to meet Darryl Gentry, the runner Flora Jean had sent from Denver, as he mounted the front steps. Responding to Gentry's announcement that he had a package for Rios, she said, "I think what you're delivering is actually for me." Gawking and looking star-struck, Gentry tripped his way up the rest of the steps to meet Rios at the door. After introductions, he polished off three sodas and a

quarter of a pecan pie while bringing Rios up to speed on Flora
Jean's post–Desert Storm life and devotedly eyeing Carmen as
she sifted through five folders of stolen research records.

As she reviewed the files, Carmen found herself stealing
glances at Rios, pondering why he looked as if he had her number. She couldn't quite put her finger on it, but her attraction to
him seemed to be related to his apparent fearlessness in the face
of danger. She would normally have told anyone asking her to
review stolen records to drop dead, and she made it a rule to
ignore people who had the gall to tell her what to wear and
when to ride her motorcycle. But Rios had a knack for worming
his way around her defenses, smothering her resistance. Worse
than that, he had a way of making her feel as though she needed
to be included in his plans.

She wondered if his ability to marshal her support so easily
was related to the time he'd spent as an intelligence officer, and
whether he had studied the art of manipulating people into
doing his bidding. And she found herself questioning whether
he could be as ruthless as he was stubborn, finally surprising
herself by pondering what kind of women he had been with in
his life.

Ultimately, Darryl Gentry broke her concentration as he rushed
out of the house and slammed the door in a rush to get back
to Denver. "Kids," said Rios, shaking his head.

Carmen nodded in agreement, watching as he rolled a topo
map out on his desk. After carefully highlighting their route to
the cockfight, he looked up and said, "So what do you think?
Do those research records Flora Jean lifted tell us anything new?"

"More than we knew before," said Carmen, mulling over the
fact that she and Rios were dressed almost identically. "Kimbrough's people are into some real strange science. They're
investigating the role that stress proteins play in the life cycle of
chickens."

Rios shook his head. "Thought I'd heard everything. Chickens,
proteins, and stress. Makes perfect sense," he said with a
chuckle. "Are there any particular proteins that top their list?"

"Heat shock proteins. I worked with them briefly when I was an oncologist at the University of Utah."

Rios said, "This heat shock protein must be a popular little bugger."

"It's *these* proteins. There are more than one. I'd bet a hundred or so have been identified by now. The scientists I knew who were seriously into investigating them were interested in the role they play in healing wounds—surgeons, for the most part, working with cancer patients who'd been treated with therapeutic radiation."

"What did they find?"

Carmen shrugged. "It's been three years since I left that world, Walker. I haven't kept up. But their premise was that heat shock proteins play a role in accelerating wound healing in patients who develop skin ulcers from their radiation therapy."

Rios's eyes lit up. "Wound healing . . . hmm. Suppose instead of a cancer patient you had an injured gamecock. Think one of those heat shock proteins could help you out?"

"Since wounds heal pretty much the same way in birds and mammals . . . I'd say yes."

"Anything else in those research papers jump out at you?"

"There was one other thing. Something really strange, and something you wouldn't expect to find in a scientist's daily laboratory log. A reference by Kimbrough's lab director, a guy named Felix Tangay, to the financial implications of his research—and a note about Tangay possibly striking out on his own."

Rios walked over to where Carmen was seated, noting the faintest hint of jasmine as he approached. "Can you show me?"

Carmen pulled one of the color-coded Pendaflex folders from near the bottom of her stack and removed a sheet of paper she'd tabbed. "I circled the comment," she said, pointing to a handwritten paragraph near the top of the page:

Extrapolating HSP90's protective deterrent capacity from fruit flies to other species is speculative. No hard data exists to support the concept that HSP90 can act as a protective deterrent in species other than fruit flies. But if it does function in this capacity, evolutionary science as we know it might well be turned on its ear. Financial rewards could be mind-boggling. Keep options open.

"Sounds pretty matter-of-fact," said Rios.

"That's what I thought, too, until I remembered something Stone told me about what he'd learned from a lifetime of raising gamecocks."

"What was that?"

"That his gamecocks were bred to be as indestructible as cockroaches and as vicious as man."

"The words of an overconfident breeder?"

"No. More like the words of someone who understood the significance of what he had stumbled onto. Much like Tangay. Only Tangay seems to be looking at it in terms of a possible financial payoff, while Stone's focus has always been simply to breed champions. We might find out a lot more tonight, especially if one of Stone's birds happens to show up in the wrong hands."

"Do you think one might?" asked Rios, surprised at Carmen's insightfulness.

"If an old cockfighter Stone told me about, a man named Jimmy Turner, shows up, it's very possible. I think Turner's in this whole heat shock protein thing up to his ears. I'll fill you in on him on our way to the fight."

He caught another whiff of jasmine as he sat down. "How are the shocks on your bike?" he said, rubbing his injured shoulder.

"Fine, if you're healthy," said Carmen sarcastically. "I know I've asked before, but why the bike and not your pickup?"

"Because we're going to a cockfight. When in Rome, as they say . . . Trust me, there'll be as many motorcycles there as pickups."

"None like this one."

"I'm counting on that. Besides, a little flamboyance never hurts when you're trying to pick up information—sort of gets folks to drop their guard."

"And this all-black second-story getup we're wearing—what's its purpose?"

"I'll explain on the way. Right now let's head for the fight." As Carmen rose and headed for the door, Rios's eyes followed her, the same way they had during breakfast at the Guadalajara Grill.

"Before or after they start shooting at us?" said Carmen, certain now that their outfits were meant to serve as camouflage.

"We'll both know when the shooting starts," he said as he dead-bolted the front door and set the alarm. He stood on the porch for a moment and gazed out at the setting sun. "Now, let's have a look at that bike." Watching Carmen descend the steps toward the Indian, silhouetted against the flame-bordered clouds, he found himself smiling, inhaling her fragrance and thinking it heavenly.

"Ever been on the back of a big bike?" asked Carmen.

"Lots of times."

"You're lying."

"No, I'm not. They just haven't been moving."

They both laughed as Carmen straddled the Indian and dropped her full weight onto the kick starter. The Indian roared to life, and she backed the throttle off to a low, throaty rumble before nodding for Rios to climb on behind.

"Hanging on with one arm's gonna be tough," he said, grasping her around the waist.

"I'll take it easy. Got the directions?"

"Down to the last turn," said Rios, relaxing his grip and patting the map he'd refolded and pocketed.

"How far are we going?" asked Carmen, handing him the larger of the two black helmets looped over the handlebars.

Rios ran the route through his head, slipped the helmet on one-handed and cinched the chin strap, and eased his arm back around Carmen's waist. "Twenty-five miles down Unaweep Canyon."

"Piece of cake," said Carmen, reaching down and sliding the

hand shift into first. "Let me know if your shoulder starts hurting."

"And fifteen miles on dirt roads after that," Rios added, feeling her abs tighten.

Carmen braked and clutched, shifted back to neutral, and put her foot down. "You're in no shape for that kind of ride."

"In for a penny, in for a pound," Rios called above the rumble of the bike's engine.

"But . . ."

"But nothing. Step on it before we're late."

Carmen shook her head, throttled up, and wove out into traffic.

"We wouldn't want to keep the gamecocks waiting," Rios shouted, tightly grasping Carmen's waist and breathing in the intoxicating scent of jasmine as the big bike thumped into second.

CHAPTER
24

Jack Kimbrough tapped the wooden ladle on the pot of beef broth and set it aside, turning his full attention to Rebecca Ellerby, his inside track to Felix Tangay's research world. Shaking his head, he said, "I never expected some second-rate Filipino crackpot to figure things out."

"Well, it looks like he has, and if not, he knows that that seventh tissue sample I've been so slow to assay isn't from any gamecock."

"You think he knows what it is?"

"He will soon enough." Rebecca picked up the ladle, ran an index finger along one edge, and raised the finger dripping with broth to Kimbrough's lips. He licked it off before she laughed and snatched it away.

"When will your HSP90 assays be ready?" he said, grabbing her wrist.

"Tomorrow, midmorning."

"Damn. Guess we'll have to deal with the problem." Kimbrough thought about all the time and money he'd sunk trying to make sense out of a gamecock developmental anomaly he'd accidentally stumbled onto soon after Tangay's arrival at Trigenics. His obsession with cockfighting had been the catalyst that moved him away from Trigenics' bread-and-butter business and into Tangay's research world of protective developmental genes.

It had taken him a year of following Luke Redstone around four Western states, where he'd been forced to rub shoulders with the kind of scruffy, marginal, uneducated people he'd spent his entire adult life trying to avoid, just to get a handle on what made Stone's gamecocks so invincible. He'd had to spend another six months swallowing his pride and playing backcountry hick to fully appreciate that the muscular and motor-skill superiority he was seeing in Redstone's birds might just as easily apply to human beings. He had finally figured the whole thing out one night after a cockfight, when Stone, loaded with liquor and cash, told him the story of how, fifty years earlier, he'd developed a foolproof system for training his birds on the desolate, uranium-rich Colorado Plateau.

By the end of that two-hour conversation, Kimbrough had realized that Stone, without even knowing it, had more than likely bred into his birds the protective developmental trait that made them so unbeatable. The next day Kimbrough had begun his search for a group of human equivalents.

"Can you stall any more?" asked Kimbrough, taking separate bowls of freshly sliced carrots and minced celery from the refrigerator.

"No! Besides, if I did he'd simply do the HSP extractions himself."

"Cocksucker! That little rodent's trying to worm in on what's mine. I won't let him do it." Kimbrough slammed his fist onto the cooktop.

"Calm down, Jack," Rebecca said, lightly touching his chest.

Kimbrough rolled his tongue around inside his mouth, waiting for the calm he knew would eventually come. It was close to a minute before he spoke again. "This heat shock protein business is a lot like cooking, when you really get down to it." He spooned carrots into the simmering broth.

"How's that?" said Rebecca, relieved to see his rage waning.

"Simply this," Kimbrough said. "You and I know that the human developmental process has mechanisms for correcting problems and setting them right after mutational accidents. Otherwise, with all the errors in our DNA codes that we've suffered over the centuries, we'd be wiped out." Dumping the celery into the broth, he continued, "Developmental accidents can happen for a whole host of reasons—improper coding instructions, for instance. But fortunately, most of the time, developmental errors are repaired by switching mechanisms that prevent our own DNA mistakes from playing havoc on our bodies. The problem with the system, of course, is that the repairs only mask the error—they never correct it."

"You're preaching to the choir, Jack. What's your point?"

Kimbrough gazed down into the simmering broth and began slowly stirring it. "The genetic instructions that underpin the development of cats, rats, gamecocks, and even human beings guarantee that the dominant physical structure of each of those species will change over time. And when you come right down to it, those genetic instructions are pretty much akin to the directions for making this soup."

"This better be good, Jack."

Kimbrough smiled, turned down the flame, and placed a lid on the pot. "My directions for making the soup—which, of course, we call a recipe—are critical to the soup's outcome. Proper directions like 'Simmer over a low flame in a large pot, stirring continually until the broth thickens' are absolutely mandatory. And when followed correctly, the end result is that the raw ingredients are ultimately transformed into something else: soup. But as you and I both know, errors occur during cooking, and because they do, it's prudent to have what I like to think of as a salvage protocol waiting in the wings. Think of it as culinary trouble-shooting. If you heat the soup too long, or understir the broth, or get distracted by a phone call and walk away, you'll need to institute a corrective action, such as 'If the broth becomes too thick, beat briefly for five to ten seconds with a large wire whisk,' if you expect to salvage the soup. And even then, some cooking errors can't be fixed, and the broth ends up spoiled."

"And the analogy is . . . ?" asked Rebecca, lifting the lid and inhaling the soup's spicy aroma.

Giving her a playful shove, Kimbrough said, "That the development of everything, from gamecocks to human beings to your favorite soup, can go terribly wrong."

"Unless genetic trouble-shooting mechanisms like heat shock protein kick in," Rebecca countered.

"Correct. Then if the organism, be it a gamecock or a human, runs into development problems, it may be able to protect itself against outside forms of stress. All by virtue of a simple protein's corrective action."

"And if that trouble-shooting mechanism is missing or simply not working quite right?"

"Then you get mutants. Deformed, invincible, and, sometimes, terribly profitable mutants," said Kimbrough, smiling and patting Rebecca on the bottom. "Fruit flies that grow into ten-winged monsters. Five-pound gamecocks with the leg-muscle mass of a thirty-pound dog. And humans who over time develop traits that make them indestructible."

"And the ultimate moral to this cooking fable of yours is . . . ?"

"Very simple: If you distract trouble-shooting genes like HSP90 with an effective quotient of outside stress, you may be able to dramatically alter the physical organism itself, thereby transforming skin into a protective coat of armor, or the liver into an organ that, when injured, never bleeds. In fact, I think I can manipulate the HSP90 protective development process enough to make it as valuable as Microsoft Windows, or Teflon."

"And you think Tangay understands this too?"

"I believe he understands enough about HSP90's potential to want to cut himself in on the action."

"You don't think he knows about your dealings with the Kazakhstan splinter group?"

"Of course not. But he knows that in the long run, our heat shock protein experiments are designed to produce a product that will be for sale."

Rebecca frowned. "That's a bit of a way off. You haven't finished testing your hypothesis on the Indians."

"That's the part he doesn't know—until he sees the HSP90

assays from tissue sample seven and figures things out." Kimbrough turned off the stove. "And even then, all he'll know for sure is that the heat shock data on that particular specimen came from a human being."

Rebecca looked concerned. "If I were you, I'd let those Kazakh fanatics of yours know there's a fly in the ointment. They scare me, Jack. They're not like us," she said, gently stroking Kimbrough's arm. "And they don't strike me as the kind of men who'd appreciate a partner like Tangay."

"Trust me—they don't give a rat's ass about you, me, or Tangay, or one whip about how many partners I bring in. What they're looking for is a way to keep themselves in power. Can you think of a better way to do that than to assemble half a dozen or so battalions of Supermen?"

Rebecca shook her head. "Tangay's pretty much our only problem, then?"

"Pretty much," said Kimbrough, gathering his utensils and walking toward the sink.

"What do you plan to do?"

He dropped the utensils into the sink. "Take corrective action, what else?" he said, flashing her a look that said the rest.

CHAPTER

25

Ignoring the stares of the cockfight onlookers, Rios fished the cell phone from his leather jacket and exchanged a few clipped phrases. Carmen had just negotiated the Indian past a cluster of battered pickups and parked it beneath a huge cottonwood.

"Who was that?" she asked as Rios tucked the phone away.

"None other than Warren Anderson himself."

Adjusting her eyes to the fading light, Carmen was suddenly aware of how much attention a fully restored vintage motorcycle could attract at a place like this. She looked around at the assemblage: dozens of tattooed men in bib overalls and baseball caps, and nearly equal numbers of sunburned, hard-looking women in tight jeans. "Did you tell him we just rode into a Colorado backwoods version of Hell's Kitchen?"

"Sure did. He said that if I didn't like being interrupted at the wrong time, I shouldn't give out my cell number."

"I agree," said Carmen, watching the approach of a large man wearing a red bandanna, a half-dollar-sized silver earring, and a leather vest that corseted his ample bare belly. "What did the sheriff want?" she said, nodding in the man's direction.

Rios responded with a wink. "Not much. He just wanted to let me know that Brandon DeVille, the dead man out there in the desert, died of cerebral trauma from a blow to the temple—and the transected trachea didn't help him any."

"Surprise, surprise!" said Carmen, her attention focused on the 350-pound behemoth who was now only a few feet away.

"There was something else," said Rios, stepping away from the bike. "According to the coroner, most of DeVille's organs showed some strange kind of scarring. The coroner claims the scars are a dead ringer for the kind he sees in the lungs of former uranium miners."

"Think there's a connection between the organ scarring and those heat shock protein studies Kimbrough's people are involved in?" she said, her eyes still on the man now circling the Indian.

"Could be," said Rios. "Like it?" he said matter-of-factly to their new companion.

The man grinned. "Sure do. Think maybe I should take it for a ride."

"Afraid you'll have to ask my old lady about that." Rios nodded toward Carmen, at the same time taking a quick inventory of the man's four-thousand-dollar Rolex, gold belt buckle, and hand-tooled stovepipe boots. As he handed his helmet to Carmen, he caught a strong whiff of bourbon.

Carmen squared herself to the man and said, "No joy rides at cockfights. It's a rule."

"Then I s'pose you'll just have to break it for me, sister." He shot Rios a look that said, *You best not move,* and slapped his belly as he stepped toward the Indian.

Rios waited until he swung his right leg up to mount the bike, then calmly kicked the left leg out from under him, steadying the bike as the heavy body fell like a poleaxed steer. A split second later, Rios was kneeling over him, his right knee resting on the beefy neck.

"I'd stay put if I were you."

"You goddamn—"

"Oh—did I say 'please'?" Slipping a Smith & Wesson Airweight .38 from his sling, Rios eased the barrel behind the man's left earlobe. "Little gun, big hole. Now, my old lady said it real polite: no free chariot rides tonight. Another time, another place, perhaps." Rios gave the gun barrel a quarter turn. *"Comprende?"*

Wide-eyed and sweating, the man nodded as far as Rios's knee allowed.

"Good. Now, when you get up, you're going to tell the lady you're sorry." Rios glanced up at Carmen. "She's going to say 'no problem.' And after that you're going to go on your merry way."

Trembling, the man rose, nearly tumbling back to the ground in the effort. Cutting his eyes toward the gun barrel, he said, "Sorry."

"No problem," said Carmen.

"Great seeing you." Rios palmed the .38 back into the sling just as two men in logging boots and tractor caps strolled up to admire the Indian. Nodding amiably to them, he watched the big fellow stagger away.

When she was certain that the man was out of earshot and the other two had moved along, Carmen let out an exasperated sigh. "What if he has friends, Walker? Drop-kicking him on his butt like that might not have been such a good idea."

"I don't think he'll be back. He's not the type, and neither are any of his friends. He's just a show-off drunk with too much time on his hands."

"You're sure of that?"

"As sure as four years in Marine Corps Intelligence can make you—you learn to size people up."

Carmen patted the Indian's twin teardrop gas tanks. "I hope you're right, because the three of us stick out like sore thumbs."

"Me too, because I'm counting on our well-nourished friend passing around the news that he had a run-in with us. It'll make us seem bigger than life, and out here that just might give us an edge."

"Gut feeling again?"

Rios smiled. "You can pretty much bet that someone who wears a Rolex watch and tailor-made boots and tries to muscle in on a couple of obvious outsiders at a cockfight is pretty much an outsider himself."

Carmen shook her head. "You're a complex man, Walker Rios. I hope you're right."

Rios adjusted the .38 in his sling and smiled. "That's what my old lady says all the time."

She suppressed a sudden urge to giggle and shook her head as he slipped his arm into hers. "How's your shoulder?"

"Fine. Shall we join the party?"

"Why not? It's the least one's old lady can do."

They walked downhill through a maze of low-riders, monster trucks, choppers, and pickups toward a cockpit constructed of corrugated tin and badly warped four-by-eight sheets of plywood. A series of portable lights powered by a rumbling diesel generator bathed the cockpit and the adjacent woods in light. Another hill flanked the far side of the cockpit. Halfway up the hillside stood a brick pumphouse, and beyond that the poorly lit remains of an old wooden water tower, perched precariously on three weathered legs and creaking in the breeze.

Near the cockpit's entrance several men milled around, smoking and shooting the breeze. A man puffing on a foul-smelling cigar looked up briefly at Rios and Carmen before continuing his conversation with a friend. "That claret of Raymond's has legs like a horse," he said, the words rising on a plume of smoke. "I'd put my money on him if I was you." Then, turning toward a tall man in bib overalls, he said, "You can take it to the bank."

"Son of a bitch can't peck one lick," the man countered. "And on top of that, the fucker's slow."

The man with the cigar retaliated, "Don't matter. He'll kick the livin' shit out of anythin' that gets in his way." Then, eyeing Carmen again as she walked by, he said, "Nice ass."

"And firm," said the other man. "I've told you before, there was boatloads of 'em like that over in 'Nam. Nothin' better than a little piece of half-and-half, I used to say." The man grabbed his crotch and laughed.

Carmen bristled and turned back toward the men, but Rios bumped her with his hip, knocking her off stride. "Sorry," he said, helping her regain her balance, locking her arm tightly in his and moving her along.

"Why'd you do that?" asked Carmen, looking back at the men in disgust.

"To help you recognize the difference between impostors and the honest-to-goodness thing. The nose tackle with the Rolex was a fake. Those two chimney sweeps are the real deal."

"Did you hear what they said?"

"Yeah. But playing at being my old lady requires knowing when to hold and when to fold. When you're in a war zone, you always pick your battles. And like Mr. Berra said, it ain't over till it's over."

Still incensed, Carmen held her tongue as they skirted the cockpit and made their way up the back hillside toward the pumphouse. She was learning more about Walker Rios every second. He could be mercurial, intuitive, and calculating, and he was turning out to be much more complex than she'd ever imagined.

Several hard-faced men and women stood near the pumphouse, all of them surrounded by wire cages housing gamecocks. As Carmen and Rios approached, they could hear the birds crowing and flapping against the sides of their cages. Their restlessness reminded Carmen of Stone's birds, and she thought of Redstone and why she was here.

Rios removed his arm from Carmen's and walked up to a rangy ponytailed man who had a foot propped on one of the cages. "Seen Stone around?" he asked boldly.

"Nope, ain't seen him in weeks. Heard he's been sick."

"Same here," said Rios. "What about Jimmy Turner?"

"He's here," said the man, staring at Rios, trying his best to place him. "Ain't seen him, though. Just heard he's about."

Rios glanced down at the man's bird. "I see you're working grays these days."

"Mostly," said Ponytail, stepping back from the cage. "A few Arkansas travelers, too." He shot Rios a snaggletoothed smile. "Ain't never had no sure-fire winners, though."

"Who has, 'sides Stone?" said Rios. "He sure the hell's got the knack."

"Sure the hell does," said the man, looking at Carmen, who was now squatting in front of his cage and peering inside.

"Ain't seen you or the lady 'round here before."

"We're from New Mexico. Stone's distant kin. We only make a couple of fights a year over here on the Western Slope."

The man nodded, undressing Carmen with his eyes. "How's the New Mexico circuit?"

"Not bad," said Rios, wondering how long he'd be able to run his bluff. "Never been as lucky as cousin Stone, though."

"And you never will. SOB wins eight fights outta every ten. But you know that already, don't you?" said the man, a hint of doubt in his tone.

"I know he had Thunder Head," said Rios, hoping he'd correctly recalled the name of the bird Carmen had mentioned.

The man nodded. "So I've heard. Fuckin' bird never lost. One bird like that, and shit, I'da been flush for life."

A chunky woman wearing denim overalls, a flaming red shirt, and a ship captain's hat interrupted the conversation, inserting herself between the two men. "You two paid your three bucks?" she asked.

"Paid Lucille when I came in," said the cock handler.

"And you?" she said, narrowing her gaze on Rios.

"No."

"Pay up, then, or leave."

"I've got it," said Carmen. Rising from her knees, she pulled a ten-dollar bill from her jeans pocket and handed it to the woman.

The woman looked Carmen up and down suspiciously, extracted four crumpled ones and a yellow flyer from the bib pocket of her overalls, and shoved them at her. "Read the rules, sweetie," she said, giving Carmen a wistful wish-I-was-your-size kind of look as she strolled off.

Carmen stuffed the bills into her pocket, then unrolled the flyer and scanned it.

COCKPIT RULES

1. *Weigh your birds in by 8:00.*
2. *No alcoholic beverages allowed and no guns.*
3. *It's your job to keep your bets straight.*
4. *All fights will be blind matched.*
5. *No saw, sectioned, or flat-edged gaffs.*
6. *No refunds after entry fees are paid and no withdrawals.*
7. *Band switching is disallowed.*
8. *Worthman Derby Rules apply.*
9. *Handling signal strictly enforced.*

The Management

Amazed that an illegal sporting event could be subject to rules, Carmen shook her head and handed the flyer to Rios, who slipped it inside his sling without looking at it. Turning his attention back to the cock handler, he said, "Only costs two bucks a head down in New Mexico."

The man grinned. "Inflation." Looking up the hillside into the near-darkness, he asked, "Still lookin' for Jimmy Turner?"

"Sure am."

The man pointed toward the decaying water tower. "He usually sets up all by himself up there."

"Thanks," said Rios, noting a lone, lamp-lit figure standing just to the left of one of the tower's rotting struts. "Good luck."

"Luck don't count. What counts is the heart of your bird. Any kin of Stone's should know that."

Rios nodded. Taking Carmen's hand, he headed for the water tower, barely visible in the darkness.

"Interesting conversation," said Carmen as they walked hand in hand up the narrow trail. "I didn't realize you were related to Stone."

"We're all related when you go back far enough," said Rios with a laugh.

Uphill and away from the glare of the cockpit lights, Carmen could see the arena for what it was: a clearing in the middle of a forest of towering spruce and hundred-year-old stands of aspen—and an eerie playing field for a gruesome 2,500-year-old blood sport. They were fifteen feet away from the lone figure standing beneath the water tower before Carmen realized the man was black—the man biting off the chicken's head in Stone's old photo.

"Jimmy Turner?" asked Rios, slipping out of Carmen's grasp and walking up to the man.

Caught off guard by the intrusion and visibly upset, the man said, "Yeah. Now get the hell out of here. Can't you see I'm preppin' my birds?"

An antique cherry-wood dental instrument case sat open at Turner's feet. Two rows of felt-lined drawers stairstepped up from the case's floor. The top two drawers held gaffs of all sizes and shapes, chamois squares, bill waxes, and vitamins. The middle drawers bulged with moleskin, healing tape, gaff pointers, blade polishers, and dubbing shears. The bottom drawers, difficult to see in the dim light of the battery lamp, looked as if they contained stimulant capsules, ointments, and miniature rolls of waxed dental floss.

When Turner noticed how intently Rios was examining the case's contents, he bent over, collapsed the drawers, and snapped the case shut. "Move along, son, or I'll move you. And take the woman with you."

"I'll do that. As soon as you tell me whether or not you stole Luke Redstone's birds."

Turner smiled, reached down behind his case, and grabbed a pipe wrench. "You two cops? 'Cause if you ain't, I'm gonna break some goddamned legs." Lunging forward, he swung the wrench at Rios's knees. Before he could cock his arm for a second swing, Rios toe-kicked him in the groin, and Turner collapsed to his knees, groaning in pain and gasping for air. Watching him writhe in pain, Rios bent down, picked up the wrench, and handed it to Carmen.

"Can we talk now?" he asked.

"About what?" said Turner, his voice tight.

"About Stone's birds and where they might be."

Turner cupped his groin with both hands. "Don't know where they are for certain," he said, his words sputtering out in little gasps. "But I know one thing for sure." He looked up at Rios mockingly. "The sons a bitches are damn sure dead."

CHAPTER
26

The evening's cockfight crowd had filtered in, and except for Roland Septian and several on-deck handlers, most of the spectators were now seated in the portable aluminum stands that circled the arena. After following Rios and Carmen from Grand Junction and waiting patiently for the crowd to build, Septian had made his way into the parking area among a group of five boisterous drunks with a month's pay in their pockets and enough pent-up fan zeal to make them oblivious to his presence. The men had peeled off toward the arena, leaving Septian beside the vintage motorcycle that gleamed in the moonlight.

He smiled and stroked the Indian's gas tank lovingly. He had never seen a fully restored Indian, and as a motorcycle buff he was impressed by the meticulous authenticity of the work. The leather saddle, more than fifty years old and shiny from use, had no cracks, and the smooth golden fenders were perfect. The twin teardrop fuel tanks inscribed with the cursive *Indian*, the vintage flathead engine, and the chrome springer fork all shouted "Classic!" in unison.

He'd ridden motocross as a teenager until he flipped his bike during a race and tore up his knee while trying to cut another boy off. Since then he'd found other ways to stoke his competitive nature, take out his aggressions, and navigate from point A to point B, but he'd never forgotten the toys of his youth on the harsh Nebraska plains.

Even after following Rios and Carmen for days, Septian still wasn't certain whether they were lovers, do-gooders, comrades by circumstance, or simply friends. They weren't sleeping to-gether—he'd shadowed them long enough to know that. And aside from an apparent shared interest in Luke Redstone, they seemed to be two people who should have been headed in very different directions. The fact that he didn't have a clear take on them had him worried. He didn't need Rios playing hero to some black half-breed split-tail, and above all he didn't want the Nguyen woman to have a second shot at a breakaway run on her motorcycle, like the one that had spirited her away from Brandon DeVille. He'd been waiting for a chance to deal with the pair together, and unwittingly they had picked the perfect place.

Dropping to one knee, he slipped an ice pick from the pocket sewn inside his jacket sleeve. He looked around to make certain no one was watching, then jammed the pick into the Indian's front tire and then the rear. The hiss of escaping air was barely noticeable.

Rising to his feet, he stowed the ice pick, dusted off his hands, and casually strolled toward the cockpit, thinking that later he'd kill Rios and the woman while they struggled with two flat tires and before they had a chance to ask for help or flag a ride back home. Maybe it would be a couple of close-range pops in the back of the head, or perhaps two high-powered rifle shots from concealment. It didn't really matter. He had the weapons for either scenario, and the rest of the evening to work it out.

The walk from the water tower down the hillside to the cockpit, carrying his birds, had been a struggle for Jimmy Turner. The sickening ache in his groin had subsided to the point that he now could talk without tripping over his words, but Rios's thun-dering kick still had him feeling woozy. "You FBI?" Turner asked through gritted teeth, furious that Rios and Carmen were still glued to his side. He'd decided against retaliation, because he wasn't quite certain what Rios might have stashed in his sling. But now, as they stood in the grassy on-deck handling area next to a rickety row of bleachers, he could think only of revenge.

"No," said Rios. "We're not FBI or the cops."

"Then what's your angle? And hers?" he added, eyeing Carmen.

"Think of us as good Samaritans," said Carmen, noting the look of undisguised rage.

Turner set his cages down, tapping the tops for good luck, and climbed up into the bleachers without responding. Carmen and Rios followed on his heels. The arena turned briefly quiet just seconds before the crowd began clapping and stomping as they watched the first two handlers of the evening enter the cockpit with their birds.

Turner pulled a crumpled draw sheet from his pocket and studied it, hoping he'd soon be able to shake Carmen and Rios. "Got a bad draw," he mumbled, shaking his head. "Hate goin' third. First, fifth, even last, but never third. Three strikes and you're out. There's a good reason to never ever be third."

Rios shrugged off Turner's logic and wedged his way between him and Carmen.

"I ain't gonna steal your woman," said Turner, scooting aside.

"Didn't think you would," Rios replied. "I'm more concerned about you swinging another monkey wrench her way."

"I don't usually start but one fight a night, ace. And I never look for a second. Trust me—you got bigger problems than me to worry about."

"Clue me in," said Rios.

Turner savored his next words. "Glad to. Stone's birds are already dead, like I told you up there on the hill when your woman was checkin' my birds out. And I can tell you for sure that the man who killed 'em enjoyed every second of it." Turner smiled, flashing a gold-capped eyetooth.

"Does your Mr. Kick-ass have a name?"

"Sure does. Name's Roland Septian. And to keep him outta your hair, you'll have to do more than crack him in the nuts."

"I'll remember that."

"Have you seen him here tonight?" asked Carmen.

"Nope. Besides, if he was here and lookin' for the two of you,

you damn sure wouldn't know it." Turner punctuated his response with a self-satisfied grin.

"On the off chance we hook up with Septian, how about a description?" said Rios.

"Smallish, not near as big as you. Five-ten at the most. But solid-built, with a baby face and one of them thick, football player kind of necks. Hair's black as mine, and he likes to keep it slicked back."

"How old's your friend Septian?" asked Rios, watching the two cock handlers in the center of the pit set their birds down and wait for instructions.

"He ain't my friend, and as for his age, I don't know. Thirty-five, forty, maybe somewhere in between," said Turner, watching the pit as the fight referee dropped his arm to start the action.

"Race?" asked Carmen, taking mental notes as the two cocks circled each other and closed, pecking, jumping, and kicking furiously.

Turner looked surprised. "White boy, of course! But he always looks tanned, like he spends a lot of time at the beach."

Before Rios or Carmen could ask another question, a roar erupted from the gallery, reverberating off the cockpit's rickety walls. In the center of the pit a midnight black cock with a stubbed red comb, bulging chest, and heavily scarred wings sat atop a copper-colored bird with a bright yellow neck. With surgical precision the black bird, smaller than its opponent, lifted one leg and drove the gaff lashed to his spur deep into the middle of the other bird's back. The gaffed bird ratcheted into a series of convulsions as it struggled to stand.

"Handle 'em!" shouted the referee, a goateed, balding man standing at arm's length from the birds. The handlers stepped forward and grabbed their birds. The black bird's handler smoothed its feathers, checked its neck, wiped its eyes clean, and quickly repositioned the bird to fight. The other handler desperately massaged his bird's legs and back in an attempt to get it to stand, but the injured bird kept falling onto its side. Frustrated and desperate, the handler reached under the cock's tail, inserted his little finger beneath it, and massaged the bird's testicles. The bird gave a rigid start and briefly stood erect.

"Pit your birds," the referee called out the instant he saw both birds standing.

The copper-colored bird staggered toward its smaller, reenergized opponent. Sensing a kill, the black bird rose a good eight inches from the pit floor, turned in midair, and buried a gaff through the other bird's beak and into its brain. Fragments of the copper-colored bird's beak fell as the victor rose into the air once again and thundered down on his opponent, this time gaffing its neck. Blood gushed from the wound as the bird slumped over, dead. The referee stepped forward to declare a winner as a new roar erupted from the crowd.

Carmen turned away from the action and winced. "Barbaric!"

Smiling at her distress, Jimmy Turner rose to his feet and began stomping in sync with the crowd. "Just think of it as ballet," he shouted.

"It's cruel," said Carmen, turning to Rios and burying her face against his shoulder.

"So's everything else in this world," said Turner, clapping and stomping as two new handlers entered the cockpit with their birds.

Six matches later Rios and Carmen were still sitting in the stands. The winning cocks, with wounds ranging from broken beaks to assorted bruises and punctures, had been caged by their handlers and carried off. Six of the losing cocks had been given unceremonious burials by their owners in the nearby woods. A seventh bird had been plucked, gutted, and quartered in preparation for the frying pan.

Jimmy Turner had left the stands for his fight twenty minutes earlier, buoyed by the fact that he had been able to switch his match from third to seventh. His bird, a gray named Rustoleum, pecked, stabbed, and hacked away at its opponent for fifteen minutes before surprising the other bird with a rise and spur thrust that caught it squarely in the right eye, plucking the eye cleanly and dropping the cock in the dirt like a stone. A mound of bloody flesh and feathers now rested in the center of the cockpit, its owner distraught, as Turner caged Rustoleum and moved to collect his winnings.

"Lucky seven," said an exuberant Turner to anyone within earshot as he seized a wad of moist, crumpled bills from a man wearing an Oakland Raiders cap and stuffed them into his pocket. In the rush to change the order of his fight he'd forgotten about Rios and Carmen, but as he stepped out of the cockpit, Rustoleum's cage swinging at his side, he found himself again face to face with Rios. "Son of a fuckin' bitch. You still here?"

"We both are." Rios nodded toward Carmen, several feet away and down on one knee, checking on a wounded bird for a young handler.

"What the fuck you want now?" Turner set the cage down in front of Rios and shot him a look of dismay as a rush of people brushed by looking for better seats for the final match of the evening.

"A few more answers. After that we'll be on our way. Why don't we move out of the stampede?" Turner nodded and headed back uphill to the water tower, to retrieve the last of his birds.

As he and Turner walked away, Rios heard Carmen tell the young handler, who looked to be no more than sixteen, "Your bird has a blood clot under its wing. It'll have to be drained. I'll start; you'll have to finish. Now watch." Carmen inserted a needle beneath the bird's wing; the bird fluttered and thumped as she drew off half a syringe of blood. Moving the boy's hand to the syringe, she said, "You should be able to draw off another cc. After that the lump should disappear, but watch out for bleeding."

"Thanks," said the boy, drawing the plunger slowly back.

"Sure thing," said Carmen, rising and jogging up the hill.

Looking back for Carmen, Rios stopped in a patch of wet grass and said, "Hold up a sec. Before you rushed off for your match you were about to tell me how Stone trained his birds. Care to elaborate now?"

"Then will you disappear?"

"Depends on the answer."

Turner shrugged, set Rustoleum's cage down, and let out a sigh. "Over the years Stone usually kept a couple dozen prime fightin' cocks around, along with enough breedin' records on 'em to choke a horse. When they ate, when they shit, when they pissed. Son of a bitch was always real meticulous. To the point of even leg-markin' his stock to keep his breedin' lines exact. One of his secrets—one I use myself, by the way—was to never cage his birds except for transport. If you want good fightin' cocks, you gotta let 'em roam. I can still hear him sayin' that today. Stone pretty much perfected the roamin' technique every cocker in the West uses now to train his birds.

"In the early days of his breedin', when he first left the mines, Stone had a place over near Placerville, 'bout thirty miles south of here. Back then he kept his birds outside, each one tied by one leg to a twenty-foot cord on a swivel. That way they'd have damn near a thousand square feet of exercise area to run around in durin' the day. On top of that, bein' outside and all, they got to munch on grasshoppers and millipedes and other bugs and enjoy the kind of food that was natural for 'em."

"Did his methods work?" asked Rios, again checking on Carmen.

"Damn sure did. That and raising their day roost." Turner smiled as if the idea had been his own. "What Stone did was make his cocks roost in car tires that he stacked up four feet off the ground. That way they'd have to jump up to their roosts in order to bed down. Does wonders for their legs." Turner patted his right thigh. "On top of that, he made his birds do road work just like boxers, runnin' 'em around obstacles that included a bunch of old oil drums he had spaced out around the property."

"Did he have any other tricks?"

"Nothin' special. He liked to rub down his birds' thigh muscles with a mixture of glycerin and alcohol. Said it made 'em more supple."

"Did he give them drugs?"

"No more'n anyone else. Vitamin K so they'd clot, testosterone seventy-two hours before a fight, maybe a little heart-stimulatin' digitalis every once in a while."

"And you do the same?"

"Down to the penny. Like I said, Stone's methods worked."

"Then why aren't your birds' winning percentages the same as his?"

"'Cause I never had that bird of his named Thunder Head. Son of a bitch was made of steel. Couldn't no other cock take him—damn bird won the world championship series down in Sunset, Louisiana, three years in a row. After that they made him retire."

"Was Stone raising his birds over in Placerville back then?" asked Rios, reaching back for Carmen's hand.

Turner frowned and concentrated. "Come to think of it, I don't think he was. Thunder Head was Stone's first gamecock. He was still minin' when he bought that bird, and livin' down the road from here in a old mine town—Uravan. I think he started workin' out his trainin' methods there."

"Uravan? Old uranium site?"

"Sure was. Worked there myself."

"Anything left of it?"

"Not much now. Few mill ruins, a bunch of settlin' ponds . . . and a plaque. But back when Stone was livin' there, in the fifties, it was a town of better'n four hundred. Place mined a shit pot of ore. In fact, some of it was shipped down to that lab in New Mexico where they made the first atom bomb."

"Los Alamos," Carmen chimed in.

"That's the one. Anyway, ain't nothin' in Uravan today. The whole town, includin' the houses, stores, post office, and even the schoolhouse, been long gone. Lost to one of them government environmental projects designed to clean up radioactivity."

"Uravan was a Superfund site?"

"If that's what you call 'em."

"Last question," said Rios. "How much land did Stone have in Uravan?"

"Hell if I know. Just know it was a good-size parcel. But aside from the fact he could run his birds on it, the land was pretty much worthless."

"Why's that?"

" 'Cause back then, what wasn't bein' mined wasn't worth shit."

Rios nodded understandingly, then looked at Carmen. "Did you save the boy's bird?" he asked, noticing her blood-smeared jeans.

"I hope so. What about you? Figure out why Stone's birds are all world-class?"

"No. But I've got a hunch. One I'm going to need some serious help with." To Turner he said, "Thanks for the info."

Turner responded with a dismissive grunt.

Recognizing that he'd pushed the man as far as he could, Rios hooked his arm into Carmen's. "Let's find that golden chariot of yours and call it a night."

"Let's," said Carmen, responding with a grin as they headed back down the hillside.

Turner watched them walk away. Farther down the hillside, in a glade just beyond the still brightly lit arena, he could see a familiar figure moving along the leading edge of a group of departing fans. Smiling to himself, Turner rose and gingerly touched his groin. It appeared that Roland Septian, without ever knowing it, would more than likely settle his score for him.

CHAPTER
27

Carmen could see from forty feet away that something was wrong with the Indian. Breaking out of Rios's handclasp and running toward the bike, she moaned, "The tires are flat!"

"Stay put," said Rios, jogging up behind her and shooting a quick glance back over his shoulder toward the cockpit entrance. Except for a few stragglers, most of the crowd had dispersed, and aside from the rumbling tractor-motor generator, the forest glade had turned remarkably quiet. Feeling a twinge of nervousness, Rios peered out into the surrounding darkness. Aside from two flatbed trucks parked on a slope fifteen yards away, he couldn't make out much. The water tower, the pumphouse, and the road they had come in on earlier that evening had all disappeared into the night.

"Keep an eye out for anything that moves," Rios said.

"Okay," said Carmen, her attention focused on the bike. She ran her hand along the pancaked front tire tread and then the white sidewall. "That man did it. Fat Boy—the one you dumped on his butt when we came in."

Rios didn't answer.

"Walker?"

"Stay where you are and do exactly as I say," Rios responded in a near-whisper. Moving to the back of the bike, he knelt and felt along the rear tire. "Is the gas tank full?"

"Yes, except for what we burned on the way down."

"Does this thing have enough power to get us out of here on two flat tires?"

"Easy. The motor's stroked out to eighty cubic inches from the original seventy-four, and it's got eight-inch flywheels. I'd tear up the tires and rims, but who's counting?"

Suddenly the familiar drone of the tractor engine choked to a stop, and the cockpit's floodlights dimmed. In the distance Rios heard someone shout, "What the fuck!" as the grassy bowl that fifteen minutes earlier had been awash in light and bustling with activity turned silent and black. "Carmen, hit the ground!" shouted Rios, shoving her into the dirt. Reaching into his sling for the .38, he handed it to her. "Take this."

Shaking, Carmen fumbled with the gun, uncertain what was happening.

"It's a five-shooter. Know how to use it?"

"Yes."

"Good, because it'll be your only protection for the two or three minutes that I'm gone." Patting along the ground, his injured shoulder suddenly throbbing, Rios pulled a white, angular rock out of the dirt and handed it to Carmen. "Memorize the shape of this rock. I'll lay it back down so the sharp edge points toward where I'm heading. Keep an eye on it. When you hear two horn blasts, look around to make sure they're coming from the same direction as the apex of the rock. And stay put," he added, looking around to get his bearings.

"Where are you going? What are you looking for?" asked Carmen, the .38 wavering in her hand.

"I'm going after a tire slasher and a truck. Here's hoping I can still do what I was trained to do in my youth." Kissing Carmen on the cheek, he said, "If the words *my old lady* don't follow soon after those horn blasts, be ready to shoot."

"But, Walker . . ."

"But nothing. Do what I said." Rios scanned the darkness, took the rock from Carmen's hand, and laid it down on the ground a few feet away.

"Okay."

"Start counting one, and two, and three, and . . . You should hear the horn blasts by the time you reach two hundred."

There was a brief rustle where Rios had been, and then, except for muffled, frantic voices down near the entry to the cockpit, everything around Carmen was quiet. Aware now why Rios had asked her to wear black, she continued counting. He had expected problems from the start. "Twenty, and one, and two . . ." she whispered, wondering what had tipped him off.

Suddenly she was a small girl again, dodging machinegun fire and hiding in the night, with Aunt Ket telling her to be quiet and, above all else, not to cry. "One hundred, and one, and two, and . . ." she said softly.

The distant crunch of a footfall on gravel sent a chill through her body, and there were the memories again: the swish of flamethrowers, and the smell of the tacky, misty, leaf-killing spray that made people die—sometimes years later. Breathing rapidly, she aimed the little revolver toward the noise, knowing that if she had to, she could squeeze the trigger in the blink of an eye. Pistol at the ready, she peered into the darkness. "One hundred sixty-three, and four and five . . ." she counted off as a truck engine started and a stream of light shot across the meadow twenty yards away. Moments later two horn blasts followed the sound of a second engine starting, and a new pair of headlights beamed out in front of her. The second beam moved slowly across the grassy bowl, bathing the cockpit below in a shower of light as two men, leaning over a tractor engine, fumbled to restart the motor and restore light.

"Gracias a Dios!" called out one of the men as Rios sped toward them in a one-ton flatbed truck, headlights blazing.

With her eyes glued to the truck, Carmen shook her head, wondering how the essentially one-armed Rios had had time to hot-wire not one but two trucks in near-total darkness. Smiling at his inventiveness and lowering the barrel of the Airweight, she watched Rios close in on the cockpit. The truck was twenty yards from the pit when three rifle shots in rapid succession shattered its windshield. Two more shots ripped through the truck's side windows seconds before a grenade exploded, plowing a three-foot-wide crater in the earth and knocking out a headlight.

Rios spun the truck toward the rifle fire and to a stop as light from the one operative headlamp streamed out into the darkened forest. Kicking his door open and jumping to the ground, he steadied the barrel of the shotgun he'd pulled from the rack behind the truck's seat, and squeezed off two twelve-gauge blasts. As he fumbled to reload the over-under double-barrel with the waxy shells he'd found in the door pocket, he heard three quick pops from a small-caliber handgun. Smiling, and thinking, *thata girl,* he snapped the shotgun's breech shut and squeezed off two more rounds.

As quickly as the exchange had started, it stopped, and except for the flatbed's idling engine, everything was quiet. The eerie silence was quickly filled with more sounds: men mumbling near the cockpit, and the shrieks of a man racing toward him shouting, "My truck!"

Abandoning the flatbed, Rios zigzagged his way toward Carmen, the barrel of the shotgun still trained on the dark thicket.

"You okay?" he asked, reaching her moments later, wrapping his injured arm loosely around her and wincing in pain.

"Yes," Carmen croaked. "Let's get out of here, Walker, please."

Feeling her shiver, he said, "In a sec."

The flatbed's owner was now circling his damaged truck. Arms extended skyward in frustration, he stepped into the beam from the headlight. "Motherfuck!" he screamed, racing toward Rios, stopping only when Rios stepped away from Carmen and jammed the shotgun's muzzle into his belly.

"Any idea who was shooting at us?" asked Rios, recognizing the man as one of the two who'd insulted Carmen earlier. When the man didn't answer, Rios gave the shotgun a nudge.

"No," said the man meekly, just as the generator kicked on, restoring power and flooding the area with light.

"Sorry about your truck," said Rios, trying his best to sound sincere as he realized that three men armed with baseball bats and tree limbs were headed his way.

The man didn't respond. Instead he smiled and watched the approach of his three friends. "You'll have to pay me, goddamn it."

"Of course," said Rios.

"And you'll also have to pay me for using my shotgun."

"That too," said Rios, nodding as he stepped back and swung the muzzle away from the man's stomach and toward his friends. "I really don't want to have to shoot you boys," he warned, his voice booming, "but if you insist on it . . ."

"So will I," said Carmen, aiming the .38 squarely at the truck owner's face, stopping the three men in their tracks.

Aware that he'd have to act quickly to maintain their advantage, Rios turned back to the truck's owner. "We're going to have to borrow your truck and your shotgun. Just think of it as a loan. But before we take off, I'm going to need some help loading a motorcycle on your flatbed."

"Fuck you," said the tallest of the truck owner's friends.

"No cursing, please," said Rios, singling him out with the shotgun muzzle. "There's a lady present." The man froze, along with both his companions. Rios pointed at the big yellow Indian. "It's right there. Let's move. You too," he said to the flatbed's owner; then he winked at Carmen as he herded the four men toward the motorcycle.

Carmen kept the little Airweight trained on the owner of the truck. When they reached the Indian, Rios assigned the tallest man the task of pushing the bike the twenty yards back to the flatbed. Then he set all four to hoisting the heavy machine onto the truck.

"Try not to scratch it," said Rios.

"It's too heavy," said a stringy-haired, puffy-faced man.

"No problem. Two of you up in the truck, two down here on the ground." Rios waved two of the men up onto the flatbed while the other two began lifting the front of the six-hundred-pound motorcycle. After a series of grunts and profanities, the motorcycle rolled onto the flatbed. Rios had the men ease it down on its side. "And make sure just the floorboards and handlebar touch wood, not the tanks—no scuffs on the bike, no scuffs on you. . . . Good. Now, back down on the ground," he said to the two men up top. When one of them frowned and hesitated, Rios said, "Hope you're not thinking I've only got one shell left—because she's got three. . . . Now, you, cinch it down," he said, tossing the stringy-haired one a tow strap from the cab.

With the bike secured, Rios said, "Now partner up. Two by two. Face to face. You know what I mean." As the men paired up, Rios nudged each of them with his gun barrel, "Closer, nose to nose." When he heard the clank of belt buckles, he smiled, glanced over at Carmen, and said, "Time to hop in the truck. And cover me while you do." Nodding at Carmen, who was leaning against the truck's open door, her .38 still trained on the men, he said, "You boys best remain kissin' cousins till we're gone." He slipped the shotgun across the seat to Carmen, then eased behind the wheel. "Fire it up!" he shouted.

Carmen reached over from her side, started the engine, and adjusted the shotgun in her lap. Jamming the truck into second gear, Rios floored it, spewing up a rooster-tail of gravel in their wake. Carmen, still clutching the .38, watched the four men fade into the darkness. Only when they reached the highway did she finally lay the .38 down on the transmission hump and breathe deeply.

Staring into the night through the shattered windshield, Rios released his grip on the steering wheel long enough to pat Carmen's hand. "You were great." When she didn't respond, he leaned over, kissed her on the cheek, and squeezed her hand tightly.

"What now?" she said, squeezing back weakly.

Rios leaned forward in the seat, straining to see as air rushed through the remains of the windshield and into his face. "Have you got spare tires for the Indian?"

"Yes."

"How fast can you change them?"

"Ten, twelve minutes apiece."

"Good. Then it's pit-stop time at your place first."

Carmen eased her hand out of Rios's. "Can't. The tires are at my aunt Ket's."

"Then we'll make a stop there."

"I . . . ah . . ."

"Do you want out of this mess or not?" said Rios, surprised at her reluctance.

"Well . . . ah . . . yes."

"Then we make a stop at your aunt Ket's."

"Okay," said Carmen meekly. They rode in silence for several minutes until Carmen finally asked, "Do you think it was Septian back there trying to kill us?"

"Probably. But he wasn't trying to kill us."

Still shivering intermittently, Carmen sat back in her seat. "What?"

"He was just sending a warning shot across our bow. Letting us know that he can kill us anytime he likes. The fact that we outmaneuvered him probably makes matters worse."

"Please tell me you're kidding, Walker."

"Afraid not."

"Then he's crazy."

"Right on the mark."

Carmen stared across the cab and realized for the first time that Rios didn't look the least bit shaken. "You're enjoying this, aren't you?"

"Not really."

"Then why are you so calm?"

"I'm not. I'm just busy trying to figure out how all the pieces of this crazy puzzle fit together."

"And once you've figured it out . . . ?"

"Once *we've* figured it out, you mean." He reached over and stroked her cheek. "Then I think we'll have the answer to something that's much larger than it appears right now. My guess at the moment is that Kimbrough and that goon of his, Septian, are searching for a mother lode of sorts. One that's somehow tied to Kimbrough's heat shock research and those old breeding and training records of Stone's. There's some kind of code hidden in those records. I'm certain of it. Stone's simply going to have to clue us in."

"Suppose he can't? Or won't?"

"Then we'll have to crack the code ourselves. Problem is, once we crack it, Septian won't have a reason to play games with us anymore. He'll want to kill us for sure."

Carmen looked down at the shotgun in her lap and wondered how she'd gotten herself into such a mess. She'd just held a gun to a man's head and threatened to use it, and fifteen minutes earlier she'd actually been willing to kill someone. She felt as guilty as she was afraid. Lost in thought and suddenly a prisoner to her conscience, she turned away from Rios and peered out into the darkness of Unaweep Canyon.

It was several minutes before she turned away from the black canyon walls. "My aunt Ket doesn't particularly like American men. Try and understand."

"It's just a pit stop," said Rios, his shoulder now throbbing from having to horse the badly damaged flatbed along.

Carmen shot Rios a wounded look. Aware that when it came to her aunt, he couldn't possibly understand, she whispered. "So was Vietnam."

CHAPTER
28

Rios felt something gently tickle his cheek. Ignoring it, he rolled onto his side, pulled the comforter Carmen had given him up over his injured shoulder, adjusted his six-foot-three-inch frame on the too-short futon, and drifted back to sleep.

By the time he and Carmen had reached her aunt Ket's place, amid the vineyards and fruit orchards of the village of Palisades, it was two A.M. They had unloaded the Indian in a remote corner of the property, using an old hand winch from the orchard tool shed. Since he didn't want Carmen involved if he got caught with a stolen truck, Rios had driven the flatbed back to the outskirts of Grand Junction and abandoned it on an isolated dirt road near the county line. After wiping the cab down for fingerprints, he'd called Sugar Cane Colby and wrangled a ride back to Palisades, informing Colby on the way back about what had occurred at the cockfight.

Carmen had reluctantly agreed to his staying at Ket's until daybreak, reasoning, in spite of her concern that she was violating her aunt's trust, that she'd have him off the property before Ket arose. Before settling into an old seasonal workers' cabin that was nestled among the peach, apple, and plum trees of the forty-acre orchard, Rios had given Carmen the .38, telling her to "shoot for the center" if anyone tried to come in. Before she headed back to the main house, she agreed to awaken him by five-thirty, an hour before her aunt usually got up. Then, Rios had planted himself on the lumpy futon and drifted off to uneasy sleep.

Suddenly the tickle was back, lingering this time and feeling strangely cold. Rios raised a hand to his cheek, and his knuckles brushed across something steely hard. Startled, he rose onto an elbow and opened his eyes to find the barrel of a twenty-gauge shotgun inches from his nose.

"What are you doing here?" said the pixie of a woman holding the shotgun. Her closely cropped jet-black hair framed a faintly lined oval porcelain-doll face. "I said, what are you doing here?" she repeated, her eyebrows pinching together in a squint.

"I'm a friend of Carmen's," said Rios.

"Who said you could sleep here?"

Aware of how steadily the gun barrel remained trained on his head, Rios said, "Carmen."

"This isn't her place."

"But she's here. She came in last night."

"Haven't seen her."

Easing the weight off his elbow, Rios felt the gun barrel nudge the end of his nose.

"Don't move again, you hear me?"

He nodded and froze.

"How do you know Carmen?"

"I'm one of her patients."

"Hah!"

"Honest."

"Hah!" The woman looked around the room, checking every nook and cranny as if she expected to find something missing. "I'm calling the police." She stepped back from Rios toward a telephone in the corner, keeping the shotgun muzzle squarely between his eyes. She was half a step from the telephone when the door to the shed swung open and Carmen stepped in.

"Ket!" screamed Carmen, loudly enough to finally cause the barrel of the shotgun to waver. "Put the gun down!" Looking confused, Ket Tran lowered the shotgun to her side. Still uncertain whether he should move, Rios stayed put, staring at Carmen, who was barefoot and clad only in a surgical scrub top and

cutoffs. Thinking that he'd never been rescued by a more capti-
vating apparition, Rios relaxed and sat up in bed.

"He says he's your friend." Ket continued to eye Rios suspiciously.

"He is. Now, would you please put that gun away?"

Ket reluctantly lowered the shotgun onto an unraveling
wicker table, her eyes never once straying from Rios.

"Your Aunt Ket?" Rios flashed Carmen a look of relief.

"Yes." Then, in a tone that sounded almost formal, Carmen
added, "Ket Tran, meet Walker Rios."

Her aunt hesitated, then moved forward to acknowledge Rios
with a brief nod.

"My pleasure," said Rios, embarrassed at having been am-
bushed in his sleep.

Ket turned back to Carmen, the look of betrayal evident on
her face. Then, without saying another word, she picked up the
shotgun, nodded once more, and, eyes to the floor, backed
slowly out of the cabin and closed the door.

"Damn!" Carmen said after making certain her aunt was out
of earshot.

Rios propped himself up on the futon. "You can say that again.
I thought she just might shoot me."

"She would have if you'd pushed her." Carmen let out a sigh.
"Maybe we'd both be better off if she had."

"What?"

Carmen shook her head and frowned. "This little caper we're
involved in is going to cost me, Walker. Plenty. My aunt's from
the old country, and I just broke a Pandora's box full of old-
country taboos. This orchard is as close to sacred ground as it
gets for her, and I brought a stranger onto it without permission.
A man. An American man, no less, who she finds sleeping in
one of her beds. Count on it—I've dug myself a hole I may never
be able to climb out of."

"She didn't seem that angry when she left."

"She wasn't. *Disappointed* is the word. And believe me, with her that carries a much higher tariff than anger. Besides, she'd never reveal her true emotions to a stranger. It's bad enough that she lost face having to put down that shotgun."

"What can I do to help?"

"Get out of here as fast as you can. Trust me—she'll be watching our every move."

"Can't you explain why I was here?"

"Perhaps, in time." Carmen checked her watch. "I overslept. It's six-fifteen. We need to be out of here in fifteen minutes. You can come to the hospital with me, check on Stone, talk to him about his birds, fill him in on nearly getting blown to bits last night—whatever. But right now, if I'm ever going to have a chance at mending fences with my aunt, we need to go."

"We'll need to stop by my place and pick up those breeding records of Stone's."

"Fine." Carmen turned to leave. "I'll be back in ten minutes. Stay put and don't set foot outside this room."

"Wouldn't dream of it," said Rios, watching Carmen move quickly out the door. Easing out of bed, he walked over to the cottage's only window and watched her stride quickly down a row of peach trees heavy with fruit. After she disappeared, he moved to the door, cracked it open, and inhaled the sweet fragrance of the orchard, feeling guilty for wishing that she had stayed and joined him on the futon.

A crisp seasonal chill hovered over the Grand Mesa. Roland Septian recognized the dry early-September coolness as a precursor to the 150 inches of snow that would blanket the mesa's Powderhorn ski area by year's end.

Septian, Emerson Walls, and Ariel Roundtree stood in a scenic byway pullout, looking north along aspen-covered slopes toward the Colorado River's Debeque Canyon and discussing the exit strategy that would take them safely off the mesa after they finished their mission. The salmon-colored canyon below them glistened, its rocky parapets seeming to waver in the sunlight.

"Magnificent!" said Walls, raising a hand to his forehead and squinting into the sun.

Agitated and in no mood for sightseeing, Septian cut Walls off. "Screw the splendor, Colonel. Have you got your equipment in place?"

Walls continued gazing at the canyon before answering, "Yes."

Septian turned to Roundtree, who seemed unconcerned with either of them. "Your men ready?" When Roundtree didn't answer, Septian gave him a nudge.

"Yeah," said Roundtree matter-of-factly. Feeling the need to have a question of his own answered, he said, "What about the rest of our money?"

"Don't worry. You'll get it," said Septian. Turning back to Walls as if Roundtree weren't there, he asked, "How'd you set up your cargo trailers?"

"Two trailers in the middle of the field. Just like we planned," said Walls, looking peeved.

"And their contents?" asked Septian. "Is everything packed in tight?"

"Everything's set. I already told you that," said Walls. "Why the third degree? Something got you spooked?"

"No," said Septian, forcing a smile.

"Seems like it to me. I've never seen you so jumpy."

"I just want everything to go right. No harm in that."

"No. But I'd cool my jets if I were you, before you burn 'em out."

"That's good advice, my friend," said Roundtree, chiming in. "What have you got to worry about anyway? You ain't riskin' your bacon." Roundtree slapped his own backside. "It's a bunch of Indian asses that'll be takin' all the risk out here. We're the ones lookin' at getting fried."

Septian shrugged, aware that Roundtree was right. He wouldn't be risking his life like Roundtree and the other Navajos. Septian would be miles away, marking time until he knew whether they survived. Staring at Roundtree, he wondered what made him and his little band of Navajo lowlifes tick—how they got their jollies. Given the empty look he'd gotten from Roundtree when he'd once been bold enough to ask, he doubted he'd ever know. Winging a rock out off the overlook, Septian said, "Run down your exit strategy for me one last time."

Roundtree frowned. "We move away from the fire zone in two vehicles. We head off the mesa with all my men still suited up. At the junction of the scenic byway and I-seventy you pick us up in the van. That clear enough?"

Septian nodded.

"Now here's a question for you," said Roundtree. "Why do you want us to stay locked up in those fire-retardant zoot suits for an extra twenty minutes? The damn things weigh sixty pounds and they're hotter'n hell. And why's the pickup zone so far away? There's plenty of places for us to get out of those things and hook up with the van within a mile or two of the fire."

Septian laughed. "First, my clever Indian friend, it's the fucking fire-protective suits that we're testing and not just your men's reactions to a fire. Second, the BLM manager we slipped twenty grand for a controlled-burn permit doesn't want us anywhere around if somebody starts snooping. It may not be illegal to burn down trees on the reservation, but it's damn sure a crime to torch a national forest."

Roundtree gritted back his anger and fingered the medal swinging from the gold chain around his neck. "You're pushing the wrong buttons, friend."

"Did you and your men take the ten grand each?" asked Septian.

Roundtree didn't answer, uncertain whether Septian knew that Walls had paid him not ten thousand dollars like the rest of his men, but twenty.

"Then follow the protocol and shut the fuck up."

Deciding that he had too much to lose if he decked Septian on the spot, Roundtree knotted both fists and walked away, crunching along the gravel path back to the trucks.

"Spooking Roundtree and his men won't help this mission," said Walls, realizing the need to calm Septian down. "You got some kind of problem?"

"No."

"Sounds like it to me, Lieutenant. I don't know what's got your balls in a knot, but you better tend to it. I've got my life tied up in this. It took me ten years to find someone like Kimbrough to buy what I was selling; I don't intend to spend another decade looking for somebody else."

"It won't come to that," said Septian, seething at being dressed down.

"Make sure it doesn't, Lieutenant. Now, let's finish our trial run and get off this mesa." Walls turned and started down the pathway toward their vehicle.

Septian stayed put, feeling strangely out of balance, knowing that he never performed well when he felt off kilter. It was Kimbrough's fault, he told himself. Kimbrough had him managing too many problems: a bunch of Indian fuck-ups, the half-breed bitch and Rios, and a dim-witted ex-colonel looking for a once-in-a-lifetime score.

He'd made a mistake last night by trying to warn off Rios and the woman instead of killing them outright, and that was what had him so edgy. He'd never been able to adjust to missing his prey—not as a child, not as a marine, and not now. He could remember moping around his father's farm, depressed for days after missing his bag limit of quail or finishing the season with an unfilled deer or elk tag. Thinking back on the failures, he'd end up cursing himself as he replayed a shot over and over until his head throbbed and his jaw hurt from clenching his teeth.

Rios had outmaneuvered him last night, tricking him with a shell game involving a couple of flatbed trucks. Embarrassed and dejected, he'd called Kimbrough to report his failure. "Finish the job," had been Kimbrough's terse reply.

He realized now the extent of Rios's cunning. But like most men, Rios had a weakness—a woman—making him as vulnerable a target as a doe with a new fawn. His thoughts had turned to stalking her as he'd tossed and turned in bed that morning, and he hadn't been able to think about much else the rest of the day. Smiling to himself, he turned to jog back to his big rig, knowing that everything would be back in balance just as soon as he bagged his prey.

CHAPTER
29

Stone was failing. He'd been moved to pulmonary ICU the night before, barely responsive. As specified in his written, notarized instructions, the cardboard box of belongings that he kept beneath his bed had been moved along with him. The nurse in charge of the unit had given the box to Carmen when she and Rios arrived to check on Stone. "Mr. Redstone left this for you," she'd said in a tone that sounded for all the world like a priest giving last rites.

Midmorning light now streamed through the window of Stone's room, where Carmen fidgeted in a folding chair at the foot of his bed, sifting through the contents of the cardboard box, recalling the departing sting of Aunt Ket's words as she'd left for St. Mary's. A hand-scrawled note that read, *For Dr. Carmen Nguyen Only*, rested on the stack of papers at her side. Rios stood at the head of the bed, looking sullen, listening to the hiss from Stone's respirator.

A sheet of paper bearing a notary's seal lay on the floor next to Carmen. Its single run-on paragraph of text stated simply that upon his death, Stone's body was to be cremated, and the contents of the cardboard box in his possession, his gamecocks, and a certain cabin and five-acre plot of land outside Grand Junction were to become the property of Dr. Carmen Nguyen. A quit-claim deed was paper-clipped to the document.

Fighting back tears, Carmen looked up at Stone. The respirator's mournful cadence brought to mind the all-too-frequent tragic downside of medicine. For a moment she considered giving Stone's box of valuables back to the duty nurse and separating herself once and for all from the dying old cock-fighter's problems. Briefly she thought about asking Rios to hold her. But before she could do either, Rios said, "What are his chances?"

Carmen looked up. "What chances?"

"Damn." Rios's lower lip stiffened as he wrapped an arm around her. Several minutes passed before he said softly, "Anything helpful in the box?"

"I don't know," said Carmen, sorting through what she suspected were the dearest artifacts of Luke Redstone's life: two pairs of hand-carved gaffs, along with a money clip that contained a fifty-dollar bill, a five-thousand-dollar certificate of deposit, and a torn strip of paper with the directions to his cabin. A roll of sepia-toned papers filled the rest of the box, along with odds and ends ranging from a bottle opener to a photograph of Stone, outfitted in an army parka during the Korean War. Moving the contents aside, Carmen lifted the roll of papers out. Brown with age, they crinkled in her hands as she unrolled them and read down the top sheet's detailed list of steroids, hormones, vitamins, stimulants, and coagulants.

Carefully she set the top page aside, unrolled the remaining six blank pages, and returned to examining a pair of old suspenders and a tightly rolled ten-foot leather tether with a spike attached to one end. A yellowed piece of paper was wrapped around the spike, held in place by a rubber band that broke as she slipped it off. The paper fragmented as she unrolled it, and long, arced scraps fell back down into the box until only a fragile half-sheet of paper remained in her hand. She held it up to the light, noticing that the paper's ragged top edge read, *Uravan, April 12, 1958.*

"Walker, come look at this," she said, laying the paper down and carefully flattening it with her hand until she could read several neatly printed columns of writing.

Bird/Hen	Cock	Grid	Training Time
Silver Queen	Thunder Head	#1	30 days
Velvet	Thunder Head	#1	30 days
Ruby	Pretty Boy	#3	30 days
Restless	Cajun King	#2	26 days
Sweetly	Dutchman	#3	25 days
Duchess	Rattler	#4	30 days

A note at the bottom of the page read, *Grid 1 birds superior, Thunder Head best. Tether exercising and vitamins are key. Think I know a way to win.*

"What do you think it means?" asked Carmen.

"I'm not sure. It sounds like some kind of exercising and nutritional regimen Stone cooked up for his birds."

"A training regimen, for making them stronger?"

"More than likely."

Carmen nodded and handed the paper to Rios before turning back to the box and searching through the rest of the contents. "There's nothing else related to raising birds in here. Just a bunch of spent shell casings and some rocks that have been painted silver and gold." Carmen flipped a couple of the rocks over and rearranged the box's contents. "What do we do next?"

Rios shrugged. "Since Stone can't clue us in, I guess we take a ride to Uravan."

"It's a ghost town, Walker. What good will that do?"

"Sometimes ghosts can talk. Besides, like I told you on the way over here, after last night this has turned into something real personal. I don't like people trying to kill me."

Realizing now that no matter what, Rios would play out the string, Carmen sighed and said, "We're not taking the Indian!"

"No. We'll take my truck. It's a lot safer."

"Think our friend from last night'll show up?"

"Maybe."

"You don't sound very concerned."

"Oh, I'm concerned—concerned enough to be prepared."

"Meaning . . . ?"

Rios looked pensive. "Ever use an M-sixteen before?"

Carmen surprised Rios with her answer. "Yes."

"Think you could use one again?"

"Yes," she said calmly, her gaze focused on Stone's respirator, her thoughts drifting back and forth between the sounds of war and what she was going to have to do to make amends to Aunt Ket.

For most of the truck ride down the Unaweep Tabequache scenic byway, Carmen remained silent, drinking in the beauty of the harshly eroded canyon land cut out by the Dolores and San Miguel Rivers. She gazed in wonderment at the dry granite cliffs and sandstone battlements, which had been cloaked in darkness during their motorcycle ride the previous evening. The sky was azure blue, and the air so dry that static sparks erupted every time she brushed against something metal.

Often before, in search of solace, she'd taken the Indian on the 133-mile loop across Colorado's lonely southwestern plateau country. This time, however, the freedom she'd always felt during those rides was missing, the rush of wind in her face and the roar of the Indian's engine replaced by the air whistling along the edge of her window—and somehow the noise seemed to reinforce the lingering sting of the words Ket had said to her before she'd left for the hospital this morning. Ket's six words, *"You've brought dishonor to my home,"* had been crushing. When Carmen had tried to explain the circumstances surrounding Rios's overnight stay, Ket had walked away. She had wanted to explain to Ket that twice in the past week someone had tried to kill her, but Ket had just blocked her out. Now the damage was done.

Although Ket had lived in America for more than thirty years, she remained a loner in her adopted homeland—a shrewd, reclusive businesswoman from a different time and place. A woman set in her ways, scarred by the horrors of war, and burdened with the task of forever proving both her own worth and that of her niece to a country of strangers.

Ket had mapped out Carmen's life for her, spearheading and cheerleading her rigorous education, establishing and then enforcing a harsh set of rules that demanded above all that she steer clear of entanglements with American men. Ket had been the one who insisted that she attend an out-of-state university steeped in conservative religious tradition rather than follow her friends to Boulder and the University of Colorado and run the risk of becoming poisoned by what Ket called Boulder's bohemian cesspool.

During Carmen's teenage years, Ket had kept her busy in the orchards, fostering wide-ranging interests in agriculture, chemistry, botany, and mechanics. During those years, Carmen learned to keep the orchard's tractors running, its smudge pots smoldering, the pruning schedule on track, and the conveyor belts on line. And years later, when she fled the University of Utah with her professional reputation barely intact, it had been Ket who used her influence with a member of the St. Mary's Hospital board to secure her niece an ER position.

Carmen wasn't a prude, and despite her aunt's overprotective zeal, she had had serious relationships with men. But they had always ended in fits of frustration that only seemed to reinforce Ket's mantra that American men were aligned with darkness and sorrow.

Turning in her seat and setting off a new charge of static, Carmen eyed Rios, thinking that no matter what spin she might like to put on it, he was more than likely just another bridge to darkness.

Rios turned to catch her staring and smiled. "You've been awfully quiet."

"I've been thinking."

"About what?"

"About following the guideposts in my life."

"Heavy," said Rios with a chuckle.

"Don't laugh. We all have them. Like my aunt Ket, for instance. She's been there for me whenever I've needed her. A true beacon."

"She seems mighty protective."

"She is. But when you come right down to it, she's pretty much made me what I am."

"She had help from you. Remember, water seeks its own level most of the time."

Carmen's tone turned defensive. "She came here with nothing, Walker. She picked fruit from sunup to sundown for five dollars a day, and she bought that land of hers without one ounce of help. And believe me, there were people who tried their best to keep her from buying it. She sent me to college and medical school while she went without."

"I'm sure she's wonderful, Carmen. No need to convince me. But so are you. Maybe it's time you started accepting the fact." Wincing, Rios eased his left arm out of the sling, draped three controlling fingers over the bottom of the steering wheel, and wrapped his other arm around Carmen. Feeling her relax into the crook of his arm, he said, "Let me tell you something my brother told me once when we were about to run a river down in Chile. It was class five, maybe six, and I was sure it was going to end up killing us both. We were into the run, with foam and walls of water shooting everywhere, when he screamed, 'Suck it up, bro. You can't live up to nobody but yourself.'"

"Was he right?" asked Carmen, peering through the windshield toward the classic 1950s Mobile gas sign coming into view.

"Pretty much." Rios eased off the highway, past the trademark sign of the flying horse, and pulled up to the second of two enamel-globed gas pumps flanking the barnlike structure that represented the last remaining vestige of the old mining town of Gateway. They sat silent and motionless until Rios lifted his arm, kissed Carmen softly on the cheek, and repeated, "Pretty much." Glancing toward the building, he said, "How about grabbing us a soda from inside while I fill up?"

"Sure thing," said Carmen, climbing out of the cab and smiling at Rios's two-word summary of life.

She went inside the former union hall and once bustling motel, now on its third life, as a struggling restaurant. A woman who looked to be in her mid-twenties stood behind the dime-store lunch counter. "Afternoon," she said, tossing her hair.

"Afternoon," said Carmen, glancing back outside at Rios through an uneven row of dusty windows. In his cocked Stetson, roper boots, and frayed chamois vest he looked every bit the lost cowboy. "Got any Cokes?"

The woman bent down and popped back up holding two bottles with a slurry of ice drizzling down their sides. "We keep our sodas on ice," she said with a grin, nodding down toward an old-fashioned soda tub. "Somehow they always seem to taste better. I'll pop the tops for you."

"What do I owe you?" Carmen asked.

"A buck."

Carmen laid a wrinkled bill on the counter. "How far's Uravan?"

"Thirty-one miles, to the inch."

"Anything there worth seeing?"

"Just a historical plaque and a bunch of settling ponds. The ponds and the town's original site are fenced off, but you can walk right up to the plaque."

"What are the ponds for?" asked Carmen, aware of the answer but hoping to gauge local sentiment.

"Radioactive cleanup. Putting the environment back in shape." The woman laughed. "When pigs fly, if you get my drift."

Carmen nodded understandingly. "And there's no way to get past the fence?"

"There is if you wanta risk going to jail or paying a ten-thousand-dollar fine. The place has been posted since I was a kid, and they enforce it."

"I see." Carmen took a sip of Coke. "You're right. It does taste better." Then, deciding to take a flier, she said, "Ever know a guy named Luke Redstone? He used to live around Uravan."

The woman looked puzzled. With a hint of suspicion in her tone, she said, "No, but there is an old man they say hangs around that Uravan site all the time. Never seen him, though. Could be this Redstone guy and him are one and the same."

"Could be," said Carmen.

The woman glanced up as Rios walked in. "Fifteen even," he said, strolling across the room.

"Regular or premium?" said the woman. "Gotta keep track of what I'm selling."

"Regular." Rios slapped the bill down on the counter.

"*Pour vous,*" said Carmen, resurrecting one of the languages of her childhood.

Rios laughed and took the frosted bottle. "*Merci beaucoup, ma cherie. Tu est tres gentille.*"

Carmen linked an arm through his. "Not bad. Where'd you get such a clean accent?"

"The marines, where else? It's part of their intelligence program's training package. You don't leave home without at least one foreign language." Rios glanced at the woman behind the counter, who was staring at them intently.

Sensing that he was about to say something to the woman in French, Carmen turned to her instead. "Thanks for the information. You've been a big help."

"You're welcome," said the woman, still staring.

Carmen nudged Rios toward the door. "What information?" he asked as they cleared the doorway.

"*L'information de Uravan,*" said Carmen.

"*Je comprends,*" said Rios. "*Quelle sort d'information est il exactement?*"

"I'll tell you once we're back on the road," said Carmen, laughing and dredging up her most mysterious voice.

Three miles down the highway, laughing and still conversing in French, Rios eased his truck out of a series of sharp curves and into a five-mile dead-straight stretch of road. When they were less than a mile into the straightaway, Roland Septian's truck swung into the same series of curves.

CHAPTER
30

Flora Jean Benson's rented security uniform fit as badly as any outfit she'd ever worn. The jacket sleeves were too short, the trousers pinched at the crotch, and a faint whiff of mothballs wafted up into her nostrils every time she moved. To make matters worse, her injured ear was throbbing. Rocking back and forth on her heels, she told herself that despite the odor and the fit, she'd have to live with the outfit a while longer if she expected to pass for a lower-downtown Denver rent-a-cop.

She'd been waiting for over an hour in a building alcove just beyond the alley entry that led to the back entrance to Felix Tangay's research lab, hoping to get a surveillance fix on Tangay. She wasn't sure why Rios wanted him shadowed, but he'd called that morning, and she was being paid handsomely for the effort. She tugged at the waistband of her trousers to loosen the seat and tried to ignore the pungent hope-chest smell tickling her nose.

She found it surprising that there were no telltale signs of her earlier break-in—no beefed-up security, no cops, not even a scrap of crime scene tape—and there'd been almost no activity since her arrival except for a truck driver who had attempted to make a delivery to Tangay's storage facility but had left, shaking his head, when there was no response to the half-dozen will-call rings he made at the delivery window.

Although she wasn't sure why Rios had her tracking Tangay, she had a hunch it involved a woman—especially after Darryl Gentry, the courier she'd used to deliver the stolen files to Rios, had returned from Grand Junction looking star-struck. When she'd asked him how things had gone, he had commented that Rios was all business and nice enough, and then volunteered, his face reddening, that Rios was working with an Amerasian doctor who was a knockout. Flora Jean shook her head knowingly when he went on to describe Carmen Nguyen, and she hoped that Rios hadn't once again gotten himself involved with a beauty queen without a drip of substance.

During the four years they had shared intelligence assignments, she had watched an Egyptian beauty dump Rios like a hot potato when she found a more secure American meal ticket. She'd heard that before Cleopatra there'd been a French intelligence officer who'd refused to leave her homeland for him, and finally, during Desert Storm, there had been a double-dealing, husky-voiced aristocratic British ice queen. Now Rios had an Amerasian war baby on his hands. *Figures*, thought Flora Jean, stretching her jacket's sleeves, trying not to feel self-conscious, and wondering why a good man like Rios attracted such a low caliber of women.

Deciding that it was time for a coffee break, she stepped from the alcove to head for a coffee shop in the next block, when a police cruiser turned into the alley. Uncertain whether the cruiser represented beefed-up post-break-in security or a routine patrol, she stepped back into the alcove.

She was still standing there twenty minutes later when a young deputy coroner she recognized from dealings he'd had with her boss pulled his city vehicle over to the curb and stopped a dozen yards down the alley from her. The appearance, in less than half an hour, of an additional squad car, a crime scene truck, and now a coroner told her that someone was dead. Champing at the bit to know what was going on, she stepped out of the alcove, adjusted her hat to make certain her hair covered her injured ear, and headed up the alley, reminding herself not to do anything that might get her busted.

Moving past the deputy coroner's black minivan, she racked her brain trying to remember the guy's name. A few feet from the ramp that led up to Tangay's lab, a baby-faced policeman with a fuzzy hint of a mustache held up his hand and stopped her in her tracks. "Crime scene. Better move on," he said, breathing the smell of garlic into her face.

"Just lookin'. I'm security from the building up the way." She nodded back toward the corner and flashed a solicitous smile.

"Good. Why don't you head back to your post?" said the cop, trying his best not to laugh at Flora Jean's ill-fitting garb.

She was about to try another ruse when the deputy coroner, eyes to the ground, hurried down the delivery ramp. "Dr. Thomas," she called out, recalling his name at the last second.

Startled, the coroner looked up, unable to place Flora Jean's face.

"Flora Jean Benson. I work for CJ Floyd." Pointing at the official-looking security company badge pinned to her jacket, she added, "I'm moonlightin' up the street."

"Ah . . . good to see you," said the coroner, still uncertain who she was.

The young cop stepped forward to move Flora Jean along, but the coroner waved him off. "She's okay—I know her boss." Then, looking at Flora Jean as if it were mandatory to offer her a bone because he'd forgotten who she was, he said, "Got a dead man inside. Name's Tangay. Know him?"

Flora Jean shrugged and shook her head. "Wrong side of the tracks for me, Doc."

"Strange. Someone broke in the other night. . . . Now this. Looks like they had unfinished business."

"Funky," said Flora Jean. Remembering the bandage on her ear, she turned away from the coroner. Then, figuring she'd pushed things as far as she dared, she added, "I'll tell CJ I saw you," and turned to leave.

"Do that," said the coroner, rushing past her for his car. "Good seeing you."

As she moved back up the alley, she realized that the cop who had stopped her was once again blocking her way. Giving her a look of distrust, he said, "You didn't see anything that might help us, did you?"

"Nope."

The cop pulled a dog-eared spiral notepad and the stub of a pencil from his shirt pocket. Flipping the pad open, he said, "Your name is . . . ?"

"Flora Jean Benson."

"Address and phone number?"

"Twenty-seven sixteen Hudson, five-five-five, one-nine-eight-four."

"Always good to know people in high places," said the cop, turning to watch the coroner fumble with something on the front seat of his van. "Gotta remember, though, coroners have their jobs and we've got ours. Sort of like separation of church and state," he said with a grin. "Bank on it—somebody from our side of the fence will be paying you a follow-up visit."

Flora Jean eased her way around him. "Fine by me." She smiled and walked away, aware that she needed to get in touch with Rios immediately, and secure in the knowledge that there wasn't a cop in Denver with the interrogation skills to get through her intelligence training.

Rios and Carmen were ready to give up. Nosing around the fenced-off moonscape that had once been the town of Uravan, they had kicked up two stray cats and a rattlesnake, and not much else. Even after trying vainly to see from their roadside historical-marker perch down onto the site of the once famous Joe Jr. uranium mine, they'd come up with nothing new to help them understand Stone's strange gamecock training regimen.

The historical marker paying homage to the original site of the dead mining town sat on a rocky hillside overlooking thousands of fenced-off acres. No-trespassing signs with the words U.S. GOVERNMENT and an official-looking seal embossed in blue were stapled twenty feet apart along the fence. Chickweed, stunted piñon pines, and gnarled sagebrush bordered the half-mile fence that separated the original mining site from the historical marker where Rios and Carmen now stood. The marker, its plat-style etchings of the original town of Uravan pockmarked from scores of shotgun blasts, offered visitors a one-paragraph summary of the site:

> From 1936 until its closure in 1984, the uranium plant that followed the original Joe Jr. mill, just to the west, mined over 42 million pounds of uranium. Over 800 people lived along the tree-lined streets of the vibrant town of Uravan, enjoying housing, schools, medical facilities, and even a town swimming pool and tennis courts. Since 1983 the 1,000-acre site in the nearby hills has been the subject of a $70-million reclamation project. . . .

Concerned that the only thing they'd seen of interest in their half-hour trek around the area had been a half-dozen evaporating ponds for processing uranium waste, Rios slipped off his Stetson, leaned against the marker, and reread its final two lines: *When the cleanup project is completed, you will see the surrounding canyon almost as it was before milling operations began.*

"My ass," he mumbled.

"What?" said Carmen, clutching the small leather folio of Stone's cockfighting records.

"Nothing. Just thinking out loud." Rios stepped away from the marker. "Wonder what the fine is for hopping a government fence."

Before Carmen could answer, a nasal voice pierced the air. "More than you got, son." Rios's eyes shot to the head of a bone-dry irrigation ditch a few feet away, which he and Carmen had explored several times during their earlier canvass. Without so much as a rustle from the surrounding grasses, a bearded man wearing a railroad engineer's cap and oil-stained coveralls and sporting a set of high-priced binoculars emerged from the ditch. "Been watchin' ya ever since you got here," he said, approaching Rios and Carmen guardedly. "You done a good job of can-

vassing the ground outside the fence. Real professional." The
man continued his uphill trek, walking with a noticeable limp.
In spite of the limp, he was within arm's length of Rios in four
quick strides. "Covered the ground almost like you'd done it
before," said the man, nodding at Rios, then smiling at Carmen.
"Will Grunamus," he said, flashing fluoride-stained teeth, raising his hand palm out and level with his head, in the traditional
Native-American greeting.

When Rios didn't respond, Grunamus laughed. "Guess sometimes you just gotta earn another man's trust." Locking eyes
with Rios, he said, "Keep your eyes on me while I'm talkin', and
don't look up. There's a man in a black Dodge pickup sittin' on
the hillside about a half-mile above us. My guess is, he's doggin'
your tail, 'cause he's been in and outta the truck with a set of
binocs trained on you and your lady friend ever since you pulled
in. While you was policin' the area he made one call from his
cell phone and took a couple of others. Biggest problem I'd say
he poses for ya, though, is the thirty-ought-six he's got in the
gun rack."

When Carmen started to glance up the hill, Grunamus barked,
"I said don't look. No need to telegraph to that ol' boy up there
what I'm sayin'. Keep your eyes either on me or the ground.

"When I was decidin' whether to cast my lot with you or the
fella up there in the truck, I said to myself, 'Will, maybe ain't no
need for you to jump in here. Could be this ain't nothin' more
than a lovers' spat, only with one woman and two men.' But
when I seen you and the lady here cover this unfenced patch of
dirt like you was surveyin' to build another Taj Mahal, I knew
wadn't no lover's triangle involved. Finally I says to myself,
'Will, this here's somethin' that could keep an old hermit like
you occupied for a while.' Told myself, screw the man up there
on the hillside—he's got a rifle, and his phone habits say he's
workin' for somebody else. Best I can see, the two down here
ain't got a gun or a phone. So, bein' the sucker I am for evenin'
odds, I decided to sign on down here with the two o' you."

"We appreciate that," said Rios, recalling Carmen's description of the reclusive man who was said to patrol the Uravan grounds.

Grunamus shot a quick glance toward the black pickup. "He's still there. I can shake him for you, but you gotta separate from your vehicle."

"No problem," said Rios.

"Just follow me and don't look back."

In half a dozen strides Grunamus disappeared back into the irrigation ditch. Carmen and Rios quickly dropped out of sight behind him. They followed the ditch for thirty yards as it skirted a stand of anemic-looking piñons before winding through a stand of aspen and finally snaking under the two mammoth corner posts of the government chain-link fence.

"Careful there," bellowed Grunamus, slowing and patting Carmen on her head. "You don't wanna touch your head to nothin' metal. There's enough juice runnin' through that fence above ya to fry ya to a crisp." Grunamus looked up. "This baby cooks an elk or two and half a dozen deer every year."

Rios nodded, slipping sideways through a tight two-and-a-half-foot opening before helping Carmen through. "Anyone else know about your trapdoor?"

Grunamus laughed. "Sure. The uranium cleanup boys, the Army Corps of Engineers, some BLM people, and I reckon a few other lazy-asses back in Washington."

"Why haven't they shut you down?"

"Two reasons, I expect: I'm better at scarin' people off than all their fancy no-trespassin' signs, and I don't cost 'em shit. Consider yourself special," said Grunamus with a smile. "You're gettin' a rare, once-in-a-lifetime, full-fledged tour."

Fifteen yards beyond the fence the irrigation ditch turned into a wide, six-foot-deep gully that trailed up a hill toward the site of the original town of Uravan.

"We got a uphill climb from here," said Grunamus, stopping and turning back to Rios. "Three-quarters of a mile or more. Good thing is, can't nobody see you inside this gully. You're just as safe as if you was in your mama's womb. The two of you up to it?"

Rios glanced at Carmen. "Game?"

Clasping her folio, Carmen smiled and said, "Let's do it."

Rios gave their companion a go-ahead nod.

"You two got names?" asked Grunamus.

"Walker Rios."

"Carmen Nguyen."

"Good to make your acquaintance," said Grunamus, shaking Rios's hand, then Carmen's. Staring at Rios's sling, he added, "A gift from the man in the truck?"

"No," said Rios, feeling a sudden pang of sadness. "Let me ask you something before we head off. Why do we qualify for your once-in-a-lifetime tour?"

Grunamus chuckled. "'Cause you didn't pull that gun you got stashed in your sling on me and start blazing away when I spooked you up by the marker, and because you and the lady walked off the ten acres up by the marker like folks that's done a little mine-sweepin' duty. Now, let me ask you somethin'." Grunamus nodded back toward the highway. "Your friend back there in the pickup—he's serious business. Didn't mention it earlier, but he's got a grenade belt strapped to his waist. You two FBI?"

"No," said Rios.

"Cops, then," said Grunamus.

This time Carmen answered, "No."

"Then you're either good Samaritans or CIA," said Grunamus, starting up the hill. "And if you're dumb enough to be the first, you need to get yourself a few grenades of your own."

Except for their labored breathing, the rest of their hike up the hillside and into the heart of the original Joe Jr. site went in silence. When Grunamus finally stopped at the tree-shrouded entrance to fifty acres of scarred earth, stunted vegetation, and jagged burnt-orange rocks, Carmen spoke up. "Looks like Mars."

"Might as well be," said Grunamus. "Believe it or not, you're standin' pretty close to the spot where the first yellow-cake for the Manhattan Project got itself discovered."

Carmen's expression told Grunamus that *yellow-cake* was a

familiar term. "Guess you know it's what us old-timers called *U*-ranium ore," he said.

"You're a man in the know," said Rios, surveying the landscape. "How come?"

Grunamus broke into a paternal smile. "'Cause I closed this puppy down back in 'eighty-four. Watched 'em dismantle the mill and truck it away piece by piece. Sorta sad. I spent twenty years bustin' my ass up on this hill. Started out as a rock loader and ended up mine superintendent. In a way, this rock pile of a graveyard's my home. Guess that's another reason they let me roam the place pretty much as I see fit."

"They?"

"The government. It's their land now."

"I see," said Rios. "Twenty years. That means you started working here in 'sixty-four."

"Right on the money."

"Ever know a man named Luke Redstone?"

Grunamus stroked his chin and thought for a moment. "Nope. He ever work here?"

"Yes."

"Then it was before my time. I can tell ya the name of every yellow-cake mucker that worked the hole in this hill during my beat. Never knew no Redstone. He the reason you're here?"

"Yes. We think he raised gamecocks around here somewhere. We're trying to pinpoint the spot."

Grunamus's bushy eyebrows arched in surprise. "Fightin' cocks. Now, ain't that a stretch! Wouldn'a been right here, though. This was all Vanadium Corporation property back then. Far as you can see. Woulda been off limits to your friend. Coulda been he raised his birds on the other side of the highway you come up, though. Lot of that land was in private hands back before nineteen sixty-one."

"We've got some of Redstone's records with us," said Rios. "Mind taking a look? Who knows? You might spot something that could help us."

Grunamus shrugged. "Why not?" he said before adding in a

more hesitant tone, "This Redstone character—he ain't on the wrong side of the law?"

"No."

"Good. I don't need nobody messin' up my program 'round here."

Rios looked at Carmen, who was leaning against the trunk of a dead chokecherry tree, still out of breath. "Got those training records of Stone's?"

"Right here." Carmen pulled Stone's spiral-bound training log from her folio, knelt, and spread it open on the ground. "We think Redstone trained his birds somewhere in the area," she said, looking up at Grunamus. "Can you tell anything from these records?" she asked, slowly flipping through the notebook page by page.

"Hold it. Go back a page," said Grunamus, a hint of recognition on his face as Carmen reached the notebook's halfway point. "Yeah, that one," he said, planting a stubby finger near the top of the page and running it slowly down Stone's neatly drawn columns.

Bird/Hen	Cock	Grid	Training Time
Silver Queen	Thunder Head	#1	30 days
Velvet	Thunder Head	#1	30 days
Ruby	Pretty Boy	#3	30 days
Restless	Cajun King	#2	26 days
Sweetly	Dutchman	#3	25 days
Duchess	Rattler	#4	30 days

"You know, raising fightin' cocks ain't legal," said Grunamus, smiling at Carmen. "But I been known to lay down a bet or two in my time." Continuing in a thoughtful tone, he said, "Names of your friend Stone's birds don't do nothin' for me. That trainin' time column of his don't mean much either. But that third column—the one labeled grid—now that could make sense. Strange as hell, mind ya, but it could make sense."

"How's that?" asked Carmen, focusing her attention on the column headed by the word *Grid*.

"Those numbers in the column, one to four, could be referrin' to the six uranium-tailing piles we once had here at Uravan. What we used to call grids. In fact, they was probably the country's very first radiation contamination heaps." Grunamus's eyes darted around the paper, finally locking on a date at the top. "Damn. Nineteen fifty-eight. They'da been the first ones, all right. Couldn'a been more than a hundred tons of tailings scattered around here back then. Even so, your friend Stone woulda had one hell of a time runnin' his fightin' chickens over them damn piles."

"Why?" asked Carmen.

"Two reasons. First off, he'da been runnin' his birds on a surface just about as rocky and uneven as the mountains that's surroundin' us. Second, he'da been runnin' 'em over the top of some pretty high-grade residual ore—radioactive leftovers that woulda barely been level, much less covered with rock and soil. Reclamation back then wasn't nothin' like it is today. Hell, he might as well been exercisin' those birds of his on yellow-cake itself. We didn't start hard-core uranium-tailin' management around here, coverin' the stuff with a overburden of rock and dirt, till a year or so after I come on board. That's seven years down the line from when your friend Stone started raisin' his birds. It's a wonder him and his birds all didn't glow."

Carmen looked up at Rios, her expression sullen. She was almost afraid to say what she was thinking. Stone's freak-show fighting cocks and his leukemia suddenly made sense. When she finally spoke, her tone was reflective. "I've got a feeling that without knowing it, Stone may have found a way of genetically altering his fighting cocks while slowly doing himself in at the same time. Couple that with data from the records Flora Jean dropped off, and the major players in this whole twisted mess are almost certainly radiation contamination and our monied friend Dr. Kimbrough's heat shock protein."

"I'm betting you're right on the dollar, Doc," said Rios, giving Carmen a peck on the cheek.

"You're a doctor?" Grunamus stared in awe at Carmen.

Carmen nodded.

"I'll be damned. Never would've thought it. Too good-lookin' for a sawbones. But since you are, mind translatin' what the two of ya just said?"

"Sure," said Carmen. "It's possible that Redstone altered the levels of a very special protein in his birds by training them for specific periods of time on a bed of radioactive uranium tailings. The protein seems to play a role in causing physical changes in the birds that not only protect them from injury but enhance their performance. Seems to make them sort of invincible."

"You mean your buddy Stone created hisself a bunch of super-chickens?" said Grunamus, shaking his head in disbelief.

"Super enough to have a man with a high-powered rifle and a pocket-full of grenades dogging our trail," said Rios.

"Sounds like your friend Redstone unlocked hisself a genie worth killin' for."

Rios swallowed hard and looked at Carmen as, in unison, they both said, "Yes."

Grunamus whistled loudly, rose, and eyed the surrounding landscape. "I always knew this place was magical. Just never knew how much. Uranium-fueled superchickens. Ain't that a kick! With a special protein inside 'em that makes 'em kick-ass tough. Who'da thought?" he said, slowly surveying the desolate Uravan landscape and shaking his head.

CHAPTER
31

Jack Kimbrough now understood the difference between ordering someone killed and doing it himself. He hadn't fathomed the difference until bludgeoning Felix Tangay to death with the angular ten-pound metal base of a microscope. He'd watched Tangay grab his fractured skull, eye him pleadingly, and then flop around like a pithed frog on the floor of his laboratory until he was dead.

Initially the murder hadn't bothered him. He had destroyed men before. But wresting a man's life and breath from him turned out to be very different from merely smothering someone financially or intellectually, and suddenly the psychological burden had started to take its toll.

To divert any suspicion, he'd done everything he could to make sure the murder dovetailed with the earlier break-in at Tangay's lab. He'd rifled Tangay's files, taken what remained of his research records, damaged some equipment, and even trashed Tangay's SUV. He'd policed the scene half a dozen times to make certain there wasn't any lingering physical evidence to link him to the crime, and then fled, a tangle of nervous energy, telling himself that Tangay deserved what he had gotten. He had mumbled as he sped away, "Nobody shakes me down."

Now it was twelve hours later, and he had been interviewed for more than an hour by a couple of police detectives who seemed more interested in a pending blockbuster Denver Broncos trade than in Tangay's death. Earlier he had consoled Tangay's grieving staff and made several calls to scientists he thought might be capable of taking over the dead biochemist's research.

Kimbrough sat behind his desk, staring out at the mountains and perspiring despite the air-conditioning. Duplicates of Tangay's heat shock protein data were safely tucked away in his own safe. He'd checked Tangay's liquid nitrogen storage tanks before leaving the murder scene, confirming that there was sufficient remaining tissue to complete future experiments, and late that afternoon he'd reread every one of Tangay's lab logs, research notes, and data printouts just to make sure he was up to speed on everything.

Rising from his chair, he walked across the room, reopened his safe, and checked to make certain all the documents were still in place, reminding himself once again that it was Tangay's own greed that had triggered his death.

He had plucked Tangay from nowhere, propped him up, and given him a cutting-edge research project to direct. He had paid him and stroked his ego, and what had he gotten in return? An ultimatum to cut the ingrate in as a partner, and a demand for more money.

Extortion was a nasty business. As a child Kimbrough had experienced it firsthand, when his father had feuded with a neighboring farmer over water rights. His father had then refused to pay the man to keep quiet about his midnight dumps of fertilizer, oil, and creosote into a Pecos River tributary, and the refusal had cost the family their farm, and his father his livelihood—everything. Chastened by his father's experience, Jack Kimbrough had always promised himself he would settle such things in a different way.

Although Tangay had been the one to entice the heat shock genie from its bottle, Kimbrough was now in charge. Now only one task remained: proving his hypothesis that heat shock protein could function as a protective development catalyst in humans. Kimbrough walked back to his desk, pulled a phone from a bottom drawer, and dialed Roland Septian. On the third ring Septian's voice boomed above a sea of background noise on the other end of the line.

"Where the hell are you?" said Kimbrough, shouting into the receiver.

"Game arcade in Grand Junction," said Septian, to the accompaniment of a crescendo of buzzers and whistles. Cupping his cell phone beneath his chin, he eyed his video target, a line of twelve samurai warriors, and steadied the virtual machinegun in his hand.

"Forget your fucking game for the moment, Septian. What about Rios and the woman?"

Septian squeezed off a burst of shots, dropping ten of the twelve samurai in their tracks. "Damn!"

"What?"

"Nothing. I missed something I was aiming at."

"Goddamn it, Septian. Drop whatever you're doing and answer my question."

Septian released his grip on the trigger, clenched his teeth, and adjusted the phone to his ear. Staring at platoon after platoon of samurai warriors advancing across the screen in front of him, he said, "I spent most of the day tracking Rios and the woman across the Uncompahgre Plateau. They eventually hooked up with some old derelict who appeared out of thin air in that dead mining town, Uravan."

"Uravan. That's the center of everything. If they're not onto us yet, they're damn sure getting hot. What did they do there?"

"They met the old geezer and then all three of them disappeared."

"How the hell did they do that?"

"Shit if I know. One second I had a bead on them; the next second they were gone. I couldn't risk running up their asses and blowing my cover, so I waited an hour or so for them to resurface. When they didn't, I headed back home."

"Any idea who the old man was?"

"No. But he seemed to warm right up to them." Septian squeezed off a battery of shots, dropping six samurai in a row.

"Anything else?" asked Kimbrough, rising from his chair.

"There was one other thing. Could be it's important, maybe not. The woman was hanging on to a little leather briefcase like it was the last raft on the *Titanic*. Whatever she was toting around in it must damn sure be important."

Kimbrough grimaced, his thoughts turning to Tangay's stolen research records. "Could be a problem. Someone broke into Tangay's lab and stole most of his research files the other night."

"Could be that's what she was lugging around. What does Tangay think?"

"He's not thinking anymore."

Septian looked up from his game. "You popped him? Son of a bitch!" he said, breaking into a smile.

Kimbrough swallowed hard, sidestepping the question. "You need to get back on their trail. I want to know what's in that leather folio."

A conga line of giggling teenagers swept past Septian's booth, the smell of stale beer following in their wake. "Done in there, mister?" said the last boy in the pack, peeking in at Septian's video screen.

"Get out of my face, son." Septian flashed the boy an icy stare that sent him scurrying. Returning to his conversation with Kimbrough, he said, "It shouldn't be a problem hooking back up with them. Sooner or later *Doctor* Nguyen has to swing past *Go*."

"What?" asked Kimbrough.

"Past *Go*! St. Mary's Hospital. It's where she works. Haven't you ever played Monopoly?"

The unending string of pops, clicks, and dings in the background reminded Kimbrough of the life-ending blow he'd landed to Tangay's skull. Suddenly shivering, he said, "Do what you have to."

"Done." Septian scooped up several quarters from a Styrofoam cup and dropped them into a slot above the video screen. Watching intently as a new group of samurai warriors danced across the screen, he smiled and licked the corner of his lip. "Where will you be?"

"Up on the mesa with Walls, holding his hand."

Sighting in on the warriors, Septian fingered the machine-gun's trigger until it felt just right. "Whatever," he said, squeezing the trigger and watching the line of swordsmen drop one by one.

"Get in touch with me when you're finished with the doctor and her friend."

"Will do." Septian snapped the cell phone shut and slipped it into his pocket. Then he took out another line of samurai and broke into a broad postcoital grin.

CHAPTER
32

After rallying from a malignancy that would have already killed most men, Stone was semialert and briefly off his respirator when Carmen and Rios returned from Uravan.

"Ain't never heard of no one named Grunamus," he told Carmen, coughing out a slur of words in response to her question.

"He thinks you may have trained your birds on uranium tailings."

"Then he's pretty smart," said Stone, flashing her an adolescent grin.

"So that's the secret to your cockfighting success?"

"Depends on how you look at it. The way I see it, what I got eatin' away at my insides now damn sure ain't no success."

"I didn't mean it that way," said Carmen, chagrined at how she'd phrased the question.

"Don't matter, Doc. Not one way or the next. Whatever successes I've had over the years gonna drift away on the wind. Just like pretty soon now all my worldly goods gonna end up bein' yours."

"I don't think that's . . ." Stone drifted back off to sleep before Carmen could protest. Fifteen minutes and several resuscitation attempts later, she and Rios left Stone semicomatose and once again on the respirator.

Carmen sat across the table from Rios in the hospital's cafeteria, feeling subdued, reflective, and obligated, drinking black coffee and asking herself why anyone would want to raise invincible gamecocks. Watching steam rise from her cup, she sat back in her chair and briefly closed her eyes.

"Penny for your thoughts," said Rios, reaching across the table and clasping one of her hands in his.

Carmen opened her eyes and smiled. "I was thinking about a research term I learned back when I was a resident—*outlier derivative*—and wondering why the term seems to pop up out of nowhere in life as well as in science."

Rios shook his head. "Mind running that by me once again in plain everyday English?"

Carmen smiled and squeezed his hand. "Easy. Let's use my motorcycle's two flat tires as an example. Ice-pick punctures notwithstanding, one of the reasons for my two flats the other night was because the Indian was outfitted with original equipment. Beautiful retro nineteen-fifties rubber, the true-blue thing. Tires with inner tubes, no less. And tires that were designed more to show off the Indian's streamlined form than to prevent punctures. In my zeal to remain true to the bike's original equipment, I let form override function. And in the end, an outlier derivative helped precipitate the two flats."

"Sounds convoluted."

"It's not. Think of it this way. In my zest to appease the original-equipment gods, I sacrificed fifty years' worth of evolution in tire technology that might have made our lives a lot simpler that evening. We could have been riding on self-sealing radials or even puncture-proof tires. Instead, an evolutionary glitch got in the way: my desire to remain true to the bike's original equipment. The bottom line is, evolution never stands still, whether you're talking about Goodyears, gamecocks, or human beings."

"So what you're saying is that over the course of fifty years Stone's gamecocks did the same thing. They evolved to the point of being damage-proof?"

Carmen shook her head. "Actually, no. I think they probably evolved to that point much more quickly. And I think Stone was aware of it. Those records of his certainly seem to support the notion."

"That still doesn't give us much to go on when it comes to Kimbrough and his crew. It only explains why Stone was able to earn an extra thousand bucks a night on the cockfighting circuit. It may be great bouncing-around-town money for a cockfighter, but it's certainly not enough money to account for Brandon DeVille's death, explain why someone tried to kill you, or fill in the blanks on why some nut out there with a belt full of grenades tried to blow us to kingdom come."

"You're right. That is, until we take a closer look at my outlier theory. This whole bizarre gamecock scenario is a lot easier to understand when you assume that, one, Stone stumbled onto a scientific outlier that he recognized right off, and, two, that *outlier* can be applied to not only gamecocks but human beings."

"Heat shock protein? You think that's the outlier here?"

"What else? It's common to both species, and it seems to be critically important to Kimbrough and his circus act down in Denver. And we already know that in the face of stressful living conditions, when heat shock protein ends up in short supply, animals, including humans, can develop a host of protective physical changes to accommodate to that stress in only a few generations."

"Ergo, Stone's superchickens?" said Rios, nodding and taking a sip of coffee.

"You got it. Can you think of any conditions more dire or stressful than that jungle of uranium tailings Stone's birds spent their days living and exercising on?"

Rios frowned and shook his head. "Sounds pretty far out."

"Maybe. But I'm going to see if I can't prove it by taking a little step back into the research world."

"That could take years."

Carmen laughed. "Not with the Internet and a medical library just down the hall. We're several years down the road from those crude wound-healing experiments that I was involved in at the University of Utah. I'm betting there's enough heat shock protein research data in the pipeline nowadays to fill a library."

"What do you expect to find?"

"I'm not sure. Maybe something that supports my theory that a cantankerous ex-uranium miner who spent a lifetime raising gamecocks on a sea of uranium tailings was half a century ahead of his time."

Rios slipped his hand out of Carmen's. "Suppose you find out you're wrong?"

"Then that's okay too. I've learned to expect to run into a few outliers when I'm dealing with science, and even more when I'm dealing with men." She flashed him a *gotcha* kind of smile.

"That's what I've always been told," said Rios with a wink. "When do you plan to start?"

"As soon as we finish up here." Carmen pushed her coffee cup aside.

"Good. While you're playing Einstein, I'll call Warren Anderson and fill him in on our trip to Uravan."

"Remember, Walker, he's a cop, and we were trespassing on an EPA Superfund site. Somehow I think the punishment for that's probably more than a simple tongue-lashing and a slap on the wrist."

"I'll be sure and skirt the trespassing issue." Rios rubbed his chin. "By the way, what was the name of Kimbrough's grenade-tossing friend?"

"Septian," said Carmen. "How could you forget?"

"I didn't. Just wanted to make sure you didn't either."

"The name's stamped into my brain. Meet back here in an hour and a half?" said Carmen, rising from her chair.

"It's a date," said Rios, scanning the room as intently as if he were back in the Kuwait desert, looking for grenade launchers and land mines.

The research article from the *Journal of Experimental Pathology* had been published two months earlier, but the article's acceptance date, a full ten months before publication, was printed in small type at the bottom of the title page. There was always a lag when it came to disseminating knowledge, Carmen told herself as she eyed the computer screen in front of her and scrolled down the text of the article's abstract. She'd already downloaded and read a half-dozen recent papers on heat shock protein, including two on the protein's ability to deactivate steroid receptor binding—a research interest of hers in the past.

Earlier she'd found a paper supporting the premise that radical protective genes, conserved by most species and held in check by HSP90, did indeed seem to be responsible for the adaptive genetic variations that enable a species to adjust to catastrophic events. When she'd stumbled across three research articles by Felix Tangay, and then an elegant paper by two former University of Utah colleagues delineating the role of HSP90 in the wound healing of postradiation therapy patients, she found herself suddenly questioning why she'd left academic medicine.

She was close to calling it a day when she finally ran across the twenty-two-page *Experimental Pathology* article. The paper's title, "HSP90 as a Stress-Sensitive Agent and Capacitor for Morphologic Evolution in White Mice," had stopped her in her tracks. Written by a Japanese scientist whose name she didn't recognize, the article had a compelling and frightening introductory abstract. In a few lines of type before the main body of the paper, the author reported:

> In addition to the usual cryptic anatomic variants seen in this heat shock protein study in mice, such as eye-color changes, muscle-mass increases, and connective-tissue thickening inside vital organs, more than half of the white mice evaluated in the study developed blood dyscrasias after multiple exposures to extreme temperatures—dyscrasias that bore a striking resemblance to certain human leukemias.

For the next twenty minutes, Carmen carefully read and re-read the paper, committing parts of it to memory. Each reading brought a better understanding of the gene-altering capacity of heat shock protein, but it was her final reading that caused a knot to rise in her throat. Just before the paper's conclusion, in a footnote that she'd somehow overlooked, the author reported that sixteen of the study's nonleukemic mice who were exposed not only to extreme temperatures but also to low levels of radiation developed multiple-organ-system failure as a result of vital organ fibrosis—a critical failure brought on by severe, irreversible scarring of the animal's vital organs.

Carmen sat back in her chair, almost afraid to believe what she'd read. The lump in her throat seemed to enlarge as she forced herself once again to consider the dark side of science. Suddenly all the reasons she'd left academic medicine flashed on the screen in front of her, and she broke into a cold sweat.

She'd found the outlier she'd been looking for—not in the two or three days she had expected, but in one brief sitting. An outlier that, at least in experimental mice, supported the concept that in the face of a reduction in the levels of heat shock protein, not only did rapid protective evolutionary changes occur, but some animals developed leukemia and organ scarring.

Staring at the computer screen, she found herself thinking first about Stone and then about Brandon DeVille. Stone was dying from leukemia, and the Mesa County coroner had reported that DeVille's organs had shown severe fibrosis and scarring. She knew now that there had to be some kind of heat shock protein–radiation exposure link between Stone and DeVille. But extrapolation of laboratory research findings from mice to human beings was clearly a stretch, and even if she made the assumption that both men's exposure to radiation had caused some kind of underlying heat shock protein protective mechanism to kick in, in both cases the protective mechanism had failed.

Stone and DeVille certainly hadn't knowingly exposed themselves to radiation as part of some heat shock protein experiment, but they'd each manifested one of the changes seen in the experimental mice. Carmen wondered whether any of Stone's gamecocks had ever shown similar responses. Suspecting that Jack Kimbrough and the research scientists at Trigenics probably already knew the answer, she suddenly found herself rooting for everything good about science. Maybe Kimbrough had a formula for wiping out leukemia, or a protocol for ending the fibrosis and lung scarring associated with chronic respiratory disease. Perhaps he had good reasons for keeping his findings to himself.

But each time she tried to justify Kimbrough's secrecy, the dark side of science—the side that had caused her to abandon her research career—reared its ugly head, and finally she found herself admitting that money, power, and fame were much likelier considerations. For the time being, she had no way of knowing which way Kimbrough's heat shock research was headed, but she did know one thing for certain: Her own scientific inquisitiveness was once again gnawing at her, pulling her back into a world she'd fled.

Determined to find the answers to Stone's bizarre heat shock puzzle, Carmen gathered up her papers and shut down the computer. She had the feeling that she was on track once again. It was a feeling she hadn't experienced in years, and it felt good.

Walker Rios dead-bolted the French doors to his library while listening to Carmen's explanation of her heat shock theory. He still felt as confused as he had two hours earlier, when they'd left the hospital. What he wasn't confused about was that with Septian on the loose, Carmen would be staying with him for the next few days. He'd insisted on it—demanded it, in fact—when Carmen claimed, on the drive from St. Mary's, that she could take care of herself. Only when he reminded her that a hand grenade did not care who was in the room, and that Septian probably had a cache of weapons capable of even worse destruction, had she reluctantly acquiesced.

They'd swung by Carmen's town house, where she checked her phone messages, hoping for some word from Ket. Finding none, she'd called Ket and listened to a series of endless rings as she pondered whether her aunt was screening her calls. Carmen had then dejectedly packed up enough clothes for three days away from home, telling Rios on their way out that sooner or later they would both have to make amends with Ket.

They had stopped by the Guadalajara Grill for Mexican takeout, taking with them, at Maria's insistence, enough food for six.

Once they reached Rios's place, he'd checked the split-rail fence surrounding his home as if it were a Star Wars shield, before they headed inside to polish off a fifty-dollar bottle of Chardonnay and far too many enchiladas and refried beans.

Feeling guilty about overeating, and a little lightheaded from too much wine, Carmen relaxed into an overstuffed chair in the library as Rios slipped a second dead bolt into place and checked the alarm keypad on the wall.

"Safety first?" she asked as he straddled the ottoman in front of her.

"You bet," he replied, slipping his injured arm from its sling.

"Looks like you're on the mend."

Rios flexed his left hand and raised his arm almost chest high. "I'm starting to get the feeling back in my hand. Like you said, it's only a matter of time."

For a while they sat looking at each other awkwardly, until Carmen broke the silence. "Do you think that Septian's still stalking us?"

"Yep. But I've got a little something for him if he shows up."

"What's that"

"Secret," said Rios, sliding the ottoman closer to Carmen.

"You're a strange bird, Walker Rios. Anyone ever tell you that?"

"All the time." He rose and kissed her softly on the lips.

Savoring the kiss, Carmen hesitantly pulled away. "My aunt would object."

"So would mine if I had one," said Rios, smiling as he gently pulled her from the chair.

Slowly she relaxed into his good right arm. They held each other, sharing kisses, dissolving into a tight embrace, until Carmen felt Rios wince. "Your shoulder," she said, stepping back and rubbing the tender musculature.

"It's okay." Rios shifted his weight, draping his good arm over Carmen's shoulder. "You sure?"

"As sure as I am that you're someone very special and that I'm real lucky you were sent my way."

She locked eyes with him. "Don't tease me, Walker. Relationships are just as serious to me as science. You need to know that I can be as determined about some things as my aunt."

"So can I." Rios pulled Carmen down with him into the overstuffed chair. "We all have our foibles," he said, smiling and nibbling at her ear. "We just have to learn to live with them." He ran his finger along the nape of her neck.

"I'm aware of that," said Carmen, relaxing as he pulled her tightly against him.

"Acutely," she added, meeting his lips with hers, feeling the rise and fall of his chest as she wedged herself even closer.

CHAPTER

33

Roland Septian was doing his best to control an urge to barge through the back door of Rios's house, spray the place with fifty rounds from his AK-47, and solve his problem once and for all. Frustrated from tagging after the Nguyen woman and Rios all day, spending too many hours behind the wheel of a pickup, and subsisting on a two-day diet of bitter coffee and stale peanuts, he was tired of doing things Jack Kimbrough's way. He could easily have taken Nguyen out while she was at the library, and dispensed with Rios later. But Kimbrough wanted them snuffed together, in what at first blush would look like an accident, and it always galled him to have to follow someone else's playbook.

He took a last drag on his cigarette, tossed it aside, and thought about torching Rios's house, knowing that if things turned messy, Kimbrough wouldn't like it. Brandon DeVille's murder had been picture perfect, and Larry Narine's just as sweet. But neither man had been expecting what he got. Unfortunately, Nguyen and Rios were on guard, and he knew he'd have to be especially careful—even inventive—to make these kills half as clean.

Eyeing the casement around a rear basement window, he set his binoculars aside, patted the xylene-filled flask in his shirt pocket, and checked to make certain that the highly flammable fatwood sticks he needed to sustain the initial blaze were still in his back pocket.

The lights inside the house had gone out half an hour ago, and he expected that by now Rios and Nguyen were busy screwing. As a boy he'd killed a bull elk during rut, severing the carotid artery with a perfect shot to the neck while the big bull was busy humping a cow. He'd then shot the startled cow elk. Smiling at the thought of taking out a man and woman in similar circumstances, he moved along the backyard fence perimeter, toward the house.

Davy Boy Lopez should have been finishing up his diversionary mission at the Powderhorn ski area, but he was drunk, as drunk as he had ever been. So drunk, in fact, that he was starting to see apparitions. All of a sudden, out of nowhere, there were angels and mountain spirits dancing in the foggy mountain mist, flooding him with light, shouting at him not to move.

"Don't move," said the taller of two apparitions, wavering back and forth in front of Lopez's startled eyes.

Lopez took a tentative step forward. The shorter apparition, the one beaming light from its hand, screamed, "Don't fucking move! Hands on your head and don't fucking move!"

Now he could see them clearly. They both had guns. Maybe instead of angels or mountain spirits they were cowboys, or tourists in disguise, he told himself, struggling to stand. It made sense. He was out in the middle of nowhere on a mountaintop in the wild, wild West. As the spirits moved toward him, he saw them more clearly. They weren't ghosts or spirits, or even tourists in disguise—just a couple of men standing in the headlights of a nearby Jeep.

The short man moved closer, the beam from his flashlight arcing along the ground. "What the hell are you doing out here under these ski towers? It's one A.M." All of a sudden the man was crowding him, breathing stale breath into his face, wheeling him around, slapping handcuffs on his wrists, and daring him to flinch.

"You homeless?" asked the taller man, who, Lopez could now see, was dressed in a uniform that matched his companion's.

"No."

"Drunk?" asked the taller man, stepping toward the ski lift towers.

"Nope."

"The hell you ain't," said his buddy.

"Shit!" screamed the tall man, stopping short of the tower's concrete base. His voice rose two octaves as he stared at something on the ground. "Shit!"

"What's up?" said his companion, squeezing Lopez's arm.

"Call the sheriff and tell him to get the bomb boys out here," said the tall man, moving away from the open duffel bag at his feet, shaking as he shone his flashlight onto the cache of dynamite inside. "Hurry up. I'll watch our friend."

The short man stepped forward, eyeing the duffel and handing Lopez off. "Holy shit!"

"Wilbur, hurry up!" Eyeing Lopez, the tall man said in a near-shout, "You must be some kind of fuckin' lunatic."

As the short man ran back across the meadow and into the headlight beam, Lopez got a good look at his clothes. He knew what the man was now, and he was clearly no ghost. The National Park Service Police insignia on his sleeve confirmed that he was just one of the white man's minions, there to keep order among the masses. All in all, Lopez wasn't surprised. The white man, after all, had always been able to materialize out of thin air.

The telephone's shrill ring aroused Rios from blissful slumber. Dragging the covers off Carmen as he sat up in bed and reached for the phone, he mumbled, "Rios," and yawned.

Carmen's left leg remained entwined around his, almost as tightly as when they'd made love. Lifting her head from the pillow, she looked at him quizzically and mouthed, "Who is it?"

Rios shrugged.

"You asleep? This is Warren," came the response on the other end of the line.

Rios shook his head, kissed Carmen on the forehead, and glanced at the clock on his nightstand. "What the hell do you think I'd be doing at three A.M.?" Rios said, mouthing, "It's the sheriff," to Carmen as she rolled on top of him.

"Beats me, but it sounds like you're having trouble breathing. You okay?"

"Yeah." He shifted Carmen's weight to one side. "You startled me, that's all. What can I do for you, Warren?"

"The question is, what can I do for you? Got a man over here in lockup who might interest you."

"His name wouldn't happen to be Septian, would it?"

"Nope. It's Lopez. David Lopez. Goes by the name Davy Boy, and he's Navajo."

"Never heard of him."

"He's a real sweetheart. We caught him snuggled up to one of the ski lift struts at Powderhorn."

"What was he doing? Loving it to death?"

"Nope. He was about to blow the damn thing up. Had enough explosives with him to take out the side of a mountain. But it turns out his nerve medicine got the better of him, and two park rangers caught him in the act."

"Drugs?"

"No. Whiskey. Little dipshit's full of Jim Beam."

"Sounds like you hit a home run. Mind telling me why I'm getting a call?"

"Because we found a phone number on him that links him to that big-shot research guy in Denver you told me about. Jack Kimbrough. I called the number and got a voice recording for the Trigenics laboratory, that research outfit of his. The phone number turned out to be for an in-house clinical facility where they draw blood."

Rios whispered, "Kimbrough" to Carmen, slipped from beneath her, and sat up in bed. "Sounds interesting," he said as Carmen struggled to listen in.

"It gets better. Turns out this Lopez character wasn't just trying to blow up the ski lift on a whim. He had a bunch of timers rigged to take the towers out at a specific time."

"Smart little bunny. Sounds like he had a plan."

"My thoughts exactly. One thing for certain, though: Lopez

isn't the mastermind here—just a worker bee. Kimbrough's the string puller. Got any idea what he's really up to?"

"I did a few hours ago. Now I'm not so sure. Lopez and his explosives put a whole new twist on things," said Rios, feeling Carmen flinch.

"You're not holding anything back on me, are you, Walker?"

"No."

"Good. Because with this explosives thing surfacing I had to call in the boys from the FBI. It's part of the new post-nine-eleven Homeland Security rules we have to abide by these days. And to the best of my recollection, no FBI types went to school with us at Grand Junction High. In other words, Walker, the federal boys don't give a rat's ass about the two of us being friends."

"I know their m. o., Warren. Let me ask you something, though, before J. Edgar's progeny start filling the deck."

"Shoot."

"That dead guy, DeVille, the one Luke Redstone found out in the desert—any more from the coroner on him? I'm wondering if he worked for Kimbrough."

"Not much. I did find out that one of DeVille's running buddies disappeared just recently. Guy named Larry Narine. His sister came in and filled out a missing persons report on him the other day. But so far we haven't found a trace."

"Narine. Don't know the name." Rios aimed his words at Carmen, who whispered, "Never heard of him."

"Any connection between Narine and Kimbrough?" asked Rios.

"None that I can tell. But Narine and DeVille match up pretty good when it comes to some other things. Navajos, both of 'em, and they were both about the same age."

"I see."

"I don't like the way you said that, Walker. Sounded sort of smug. I'm gonna ask you once again: Have you got some info I should have?"

"No."

"Good. Because your questions are starting to make me think you do."

"Just trying to think my way through the problem."

"Think all you want. Just remember what I told you about the Bureau."

"I'll do that. And you'll keep me posted?"

"Don't count on it. Right now my butt belongs to the feds. Never known those boys to want to share. Sweet dreams. And the same to Doc Nguyen—when you see her," said the sheriff, cradling the phone with an insightful chuckle.

Rios hung up and stared into space until he felt Carmen's soft, warm body snuggle tightly against his.

"You're not very good at charades," said Carmen, snaking her index finger slowly down his chest. "But I did make out the word *Kimbrough* while you were talking, and I couldn't miss the sheriff booming on about the FBI. Mind filling in the blanks?"

"They caught some Unabomber type up at Powderhorn. He was packing around a satchel full of explosives, and he had a phone number on him connecting him to Kimbrough."

"Explosives! That's a long way from heat shock protein or fighting chickens. What's the connection?"

"Don't know, but believe me, there is one. I just can't put my finger on it at the moment. Even worse, I can't figure out whether Warren stumbled onto the real thing with this explosives nut he's got locked up or if it's just some kind of operational diversion."

"What?"

Rios laughed. "Just military-speak," he said, running his hand through Carmen's hair. "Isn't Stone part Navajo?"

"Yes."

"Strange, this whole Navajo element. All of a sudden the sheriff's got one Navajo missing, a guy named Larry Narine. A Navajo's been murdered, Brandon DeVille. And we've got Stone, part Navajo, suffering with leukemia. My father used to say that there's never any coincidence to things that come in threes."

"You're talking in riddles, Walker. Mind clueing me in?"

"As soon as you run what you found during that library junket of yours past me one more time."

Carmen rose and shot Rios a look of surprise. "We covered that earlier. Heat shock protein, Stone's leukemia, DeVille's organ scarring—the whole nine yards. There's not much I can add."

"I know what we did. But that was before I knew anything about a Navajo connection."

"Can we do it in the morning?"

Rios glanced down at Carmen's sheet-draped figure, mesmerized by the rise and fall of her breasts. Pulling her against him until he could feel the fullness of her breasts, he said, "No, I think we can do *it* right now."

Before she could answer, Carmen felt the warmth of Rios's lips on hers. "I guess that other thing can wait," she said, locking a leg around him and pulling her body tightly into his.

Spent from lovemaking and a flicker away from dozing off, Rios told himself that the faint charcoal odor he was smelling couldn't possibly be for real. He was about to dismiss the scent when he noticed a hint of light creep along the bottom edge of a rear bedroom window. He was out of bed and on the floor so fast that he barely heard Carmen shout, "Walker!"

"Stay put," said Rios, duck-walking naked across the room. Reaching his dresser, he eased out the bottom drawer and extracted a .357 magnum revolver. "The thirty-eight's in my sling," he called back to Carmen, crawling out of the bedroom and down the hallway to the kitchen entrance before she could respond. When he reached the kitchen's cooktop island, the burglar alarm went off, and he dropped to one knee, aiming the .357 squarely at the room's bay window. As he steadied his aim on what appeared to be the outline of a man's torso, a burst of automatic fire peppered the back side of the house, shattering all the windows. Screaming, "Carmen! Don't move!" he crawled along the floor until he reached the TV stand in the corner. Grabbing the remote, he punched the On button, triggering a light outside and a grenade-caliber backyard explosion. He was about to set off another explosion when the smell of something burning caught his attention. Crawling back across the kitchen floor, he followed the odor toward the door to the basement. He swung back the door to a wave of smoke before scurrying back to a cabinet beneath the kitchen sink and grabbing a fire extinguisher.

Fighting his way down the stairs, choking on smoke, he reached the basement just as flames lapped their way up a back wall. Inching his way through the smoke and toward the flames, he triggered two lengthy blasts from the fire extinguisher. The fire subsided momentarily as he began frantically patting his way along a wall, muttering, "Where is it? Where is it?" Halfway down the wall he found the jutting valve he was looking for and frantically spun it a half turn. Almost instantly a mist of water showered down on him. It was another minute or two before the sprinkler system and several more blasts from his fire extinguisher brought the fire under control. Certain that he'd beaten the flames down, he turned and raced back up the basement steps, screaming, "Carmen! Carmen! Carmen!" streaking buck naked back to his bedroom, where he found her kneeling in the middle of the bed, the .38 Airweight firmly clutched in her right hand.

From behind a Dumpster, in the russet glow of a mountain sunrise, Roland Septian shivered in fury that Rios had outsmarted him once again. He watched the red-and-white pumper truck lumber away from Rios's house while a Grand Junction squad car and a Mesa County sheriff's cruiser remained parked out front. He had no idea how he had triggered Rios's alarm, set off a backyard explosion, or tripped the spotlight that had tipped Rios off in the first place. He suspected that his undoing was related to some sort of motion-detection system, probably strung along the fence and coupled to a sophisticated remote-control device, but he couldn't be certain. What he did know for sure was that he needed to hook up with Kimbrough and that, for the time being, he needed to disappear. As he slipped his cell phone from his pocket to call Kimbrough and let him know the score, he glanced back toward Rios's house and told himself that whether Kimbrough liked it or not, there was now a personal score to settle with Rios and his half-breed bitch.

CHAPTER
34

The foggy haze enveloping their two-hundred-acre burn site wasn't expected to lift until late morning, and nothing was better than nature's own camouflage when it came to troop movement, Emerson Walls kept reminding himself. Even in the wake of Jack Kimbrough's unexpected and disruptive arrival two hours earlier, things were still on schedule and going according to plan.

Just after daybreak Kimbrough, dressed in designer outback gear and driving an SUV, had popped out of the fog, shouting orders, intent on seeing the experiment he'd planned for a year unfold. Walls had walked Kimbrough through their firestorm plan, reviewed their exit strategy, and reminded him that with an operation as dependent as this one on time, temperature, humidity, and altitude, he didn't need any further surprises. Now, as they stood beside two recently painted olive-drab cargo containers in the middle of an alpine meadow that would soon become a raging inferno, Walls was hoping that Kimbrough's unexpected appearance would be the last of his surprises.

"They look innocent enough to me," said Kimbrough, stepping up to one of the containers.

"I wouldn't get any closer," said Walls. "In a sense, the container's already hot."

"I know the drill." Kimbrough glanced toward the other container, twenty yards away. "Trust me—there's no real risk until these babies catch fire."

"In the laboratory, maybe. Things can be very different out in the field."

Kimbrough laughed. "Don't be so timid," he said, unlatching the container's double doors and peering inside.

"I'd keep my nose out of there if I were you," said Walls, stepping back.

"I'll be done in a sec," said Kimbrough. Swinging the doors fully open, he stood face to face with a container full of twisted scrap-metal remains. "Is the other one packed just the same?"

"They're mirror images. Within fifty pounds of the same weight."

Kimbrough stepped back, closed the doors with a thud, and smiled. It had taken him two and a half years to get to this point, including nearly two years of laboratory tests, three months of arm-twisting a reluctant Walls, and a quarter-million-dollar cash outlay to convince Walls to become part of his plan.

But the most difficult part of planning for the day had had nothing to do with Walls, money, or even the intricacies of his heat shock protein research. The real difficulty had been rounding up just the right personnel to fight a superheated fire on a mountaintop. Luckily, he had had serendipity and an old uranium miner named Jimmy Turner to steer him in the right direction. He had Turner, a second-rate cock handler and ex-con, to thank for telling him, in a bar after a cockfight one night, after he'd watched Stone's birds destroy the competition, exactly how Stone had trained his birds back in the 1950s. After that, Kimbrough had pieced the heat shock puzzle together for himself. He had known all along that if his assessment turned out to be correct and Luke Redstone had actually stumbled onto an animal model for producing invincibility by reducing heat shock protein levels in his gamecocks and thereby speeding up their protective development genetics, he'd eventually have to field test his hypothesis in humans.

If the experiment worked, few would question his methods. He already had contacts in the Balkans and sub-Saharan Africa awaiting the results, not to mention his firm deal with the Central Asian consortium. If it didn't work, there would be time for more experiments. Besides, after fifty years, there were bound to be other Navajos with similar heat-shock-induced protective developments.

He'd thought about the risks involved with the experiment, and for months he'd brooded about getting caught. In the end, there had been two powerful reasons for moving ahead. First, Walls had assured him that they only needed a well-timed diversion, a dramatic Labor Day weekend counterevent to draw attention away from their routine controlled BLM underbrush burn, in order to keep the authorities off their backs. And second, the environmental and topographic conditions were almost a mirror image of the ones Stone had labored under during the 1950s, right down to the elevation, lay of the land, and the geology of the rocks. Stepping away from the cargo container, determination chiseled on his face, Kimbrough called out to Walls, "What time have you got?"

Walls checked his watch. "Nine thirty-seven."

"Still no word from that Indian Lopez?" asked Kimbrough.

"None. But he's not due to call until an hour before he sets everything off."

"What are the chances that someone nosing around up here will stumble across us, even with Lopez setting off the Powderhorn diversion?"

Walls thought for a moment and stroked his chin. "Slim. Our BLM burn permits are in order. The area's cordoned off. There's no wind, no clouds, and the humidity's just right. Perfect day for a controlled burn in my book."

"Then we'll have to take the chance. It's too long a path back to the beginning now. We go at noon."

"That's been my take all along."

"All your firefighters geared up and ready to go?"

"Yes," said Walls.

"And the respirators and fire-retardant gear that Septian delivered have all been passed out?"

"They've got everything," said Walls, irritated at being micromanaged.

"Don't take it personally," said Kimbrough. "We're running an experiment, not one of your fly-by-night military exercises. When it comes to science, things need to be triple checked."

Walls eyed the cargo containers and took a deep breath. "And if the experiment doesn't work?"

Kimbrough smiled. It was a sly, authoritative smile born of experience. "Then it's back to the drawing board. That's always the way with science," he added. Slipping a hunting knife and a baseball-sized object from his pocket, he knelt and ran the knife along the soft dirt that buttressed the container's metal edge. "And with science you never leave things to chance," he said, wedging a knot of heat-sensitive plastic explosive into the small cavern he'd made in the dirt.

CHAPTER
35

Rios's house had been transformed into a staging area for firefighters and cops, including three Grand Junction police officers who looked as if they'd stumbled into something way over their heads, two Mesa County sheriff's deputies intent on following Warren Anderson's every step, and a smug FBI agent, Everard Bolen, who acted as if he'd seen it all before. Bolen, a thick-bodied, no-nonsense G-man out of Texas with a forward-sloping crew cut, penetrating gray eyes, and grainy pale skin, had been busy questioning Rios for nearly twenty minutes, prefacing his queries by sucking air between his teeth.

"Now, run that timetable by me once again," said Bolen, smiling at Rios as if they were lifelong beer-drinking buddies.

Rios frowned at having to repeat himself. "Like I told you twice before, the whole thing took less than five minutes."

Bolen glanced across the room at Carmen, who looked embarrassed by his next question. "From the time you got out of bed and left Dr. Nguyen until you called Sheriff Anderson?"

"That's right."

"And you say the assailant was armed with an automatic weapon?"

"Three-oh-eight rounds—maybe an AK-forty-seven."

"You saw it?"

"Didn't have to. I know the sound of the report."

"How's that?"

Sheriff Anderson interrupted. "Rios spent six years in the marines."

Looking irritated, Bolen said, "Would you please let him answer the question himself, Sheriff?"

Anderson gritted his teeth, nodded, and walked across the room.

Tired of being grilled, Rios glanced at Carmen, then tore into Bolen: "Listen, buddy, someone just tried to kill me and burn down my house, and you're here pumping me like I was the shooter. If you want to know what kind of weapon the son of a bitch was packing, I suggest you ask him."

Bolen forced back a frown. "Let me remind you of something once again, Mr. Rios. Whether you like it or not, you're not the main attraction here; you're just a secondary event. I'm trying to tie a man we caught with a satchel full of explosives up at the Powderhorn ski area to what happened here only because you, Dr. Nguyen, and your friend the sheriff insist there's a connection. And so far I'm not convinced. If it turns out I wasted precious time holding your hand when I should've pointed my Powderhorn investigation in another direction, you'll have hell to pay, believe me. So there'd better somehow be a link."

"There's a link," said Rios, thinking, *Do I have to say this one more time?* "That heat shock protein I mentioned earlier, for one. And like I've said before, your shooter's a man named Septian who's taking his cues from a Denver businessman named Jack Kimbrough. Are those enough links?" When Bolen didn't answer, Rios added, "How the two of them are tied to your nut with the explosives is a problem you'll have to figure out yourself."

Bolen turned to Carmen, his face reddening. "Your boyfriend's turned into a broken record, Dr. Nguyen. Perhaps you can shed some light on the link between the man with the explosives and that protein the two of you seem so frantic about."

"I don't have anything more to add," said Carmen, her tone emphatic.

"Okay." Bolen rolled his eyes. "Then let me summarize. What you're telling me, according to this theory of yours, is that if the earth suddenly turns a hundred degrees hotter, instead of us all croaking from the heat, most of us will survive by virtue of this heat shock protein telling our bodies to develop a new kind of protective skin." Bolen snickered. "And if floods come later, maybe the protein will tell us to sprout webbed feet. Next thing you know, we'll all be growing tails."

"Close," said Carmen.

"And this knowledge is worth millions, you say?"

"To Kimbrough and your man with the explosives, probably a lot more."

"I don't think so. Our demolitions expert was just a Navajo drunk."

"A lot more to Kimbrough and this Septian character, then. Who cares?" said Carmen, reaching the point of complete exasperation.

Bolen brushed off Carmen's attitude with a smile. "And you say you stumbled onto this whole concept because a friend of yours perfected this heat shock protein mumbo jumbo in a gaggle of fighting chickens."

"Gamecocks," corrected Carmen.

"Gamecocks, chickens, tail-sprouting humans—it doesn't really matter, Doctor. You're talking science-fiction pie in the sky. Here's reality, in case you've missed it: I have a drunk Navajo bomber on my hands and some phone numbers scribbled on a paper towel scrap. Turns out one of the numbers is to a lab of Mr. Kimbrough's. I'll talk to Kimbrough because he's linked to my bomber. And I'd like to talk to this enforcer friend of his, Septian, because of what happened here. Nowhere in that mix do I see movement toward a new theory of relativity. Those are the facts as I see it. No postulates, no cockeyed theories, and no frogs with fur." Bolen eyed Carmen and Rios sternly. "I take both of you at your word when you say Kimbrough's trying to protect his heat shock genie. And maybe that's why someone tried to set fire to your house. But I need proof that Kimbrough's behind all this. Your claims that he is just aren't enough."

"If it's proof you need, then I'd try back up on the mesa," said Rios.

Glancing across the room at Sheriff Anderson, Bolen said,

"The sheriff has men combing every square foot of the mesa from Powderhorn back to Cedaredge. You don't need to tell us how to do our jobs."

"And the FBI?" asked Rios. "What exactly are you doing?"

"We don't give out that kind of information," said Bolen.

Carmen frowned. "Have you tried locating Kimbrough in Denver?"

"You heard the man. He can't tell us that," mocked Rios.

Bolen leveled an icy stare at Rios. "Don't try my patience, friend."

Rios shrugged. Walking over to Carmen and taking her hand, he said, "If you're done with us, we'd like to clean up a bit."

"Be my guest. Just stay out of the way of my evidence people, and don't set foot down in the basement until you're given an all-clear."

Rios nodded and led Carmen from the kitchen.

"Strange bird," said Bolen, looking toward the sheriff and shaking his head. When the sheriff didn't answer, he added, "You two friends?"

"From way back."

"I see," said Bolen, turning his suspicious gaze on the sheriff and sucking a lengthy stream of air between his teeth.

Bolen was gone when Carmen returned to the kitchen a half hour later. Only Rios, in his bedroom on the phone to Flora Jean, and Sheriff Anderson, seated at the cooktop island doing paperwork, and an arson investigator remained in the house. Surrounded by broken glass, bullet casings, and splintered wood, Anderson looked surprisingly relaxed. An empty glass and a half-full quart carton of orange juice sat in front of him.

"You look at home," said Carmen. Dressed in one of Rios's chambray shirts and loose-fitting jeans, she took a glass from a nearby cabinet, poured herself half a glass of orange juice, and took a seat across from the sheriff.

The sheriff stopped writing, looked up at Carmen, and nodded. "OJ always seems to calm my nerves."

"You and Walker go way back, don't you?"

"As far as two men can go, I expect."

"Has he always been a loner?"

"Except for hanging out with his brother, Danny, and tolerating me on occasion, I'd say the answer to your question is pretty much yes."

"Any reason for it?"

"Don't know. He's just always been that way. No reason for it, best I can tell. He never wanted for much, and he had real good folks. There is one hole in his life, though. His mom died just after he turned six. Rheumatic fever." The sheriff gave Carmen a pensive look. "You asking because you care, or because he might represent a real good experiment?"

"The former," said Carmen, looking hurt.

"Sorry. Just runnin' a few traps for a friend."

"Do you screen all his women for him?"

"No. But maybe I should. He's made mistakes."

"Perhaps that says more about him than them," said Carmen, taking a drink of orange juice and setting her glass aside.

"Could be. My take, though, is that he never takes the time to look deep enough. Gets himself too infatuated way too fast. You wouldn't think that a man who'd take the time to calculate the precise width of a river's path between two boulders would be so quick on the trigger. When it comes to women, though, it's as if Walker's always lookin' for something he missed."

"Maybe he'll look deeper the next time around."

"Hope so. He's a real decent man."

"I know that," said Carmen, turning to the sound of footsteps on the kitchen's hardwood floor.

"Private coffee klatch?" asked Rios, strolling across the room. "Or can anyone join in?"

"It's your house," said the sheriff, trying his best not to look self-conscious.

Rios took in the shattered glass, splintered window frames, fractured window moldings, and dozens of bullet holes peppering the walls. "What's left of it, anyway," he said, shaking his head. Then, as if to purge the bizarre scene from his mind, he said, "Where's Mr. All-World FBI?"

"Don't make fun, Walker. He's only doing his job," said the sheriff.

"He's an anal-retentive turd."

Sensing the need to mediate, Carmen stepped over to Rios and linked an arm in his. "What did Flora Jean have to say?"

"Not much. Just that Kimbrough's number one lab jockey, Felix Tangay, popped up dead."

"What happened?"

"Somebody smashed his skull with the base of a microscope."

"Hold on," said the sheriff. "Who's Tangay? And who's Flora Jean?"

"Tangay was Kimbrough's head research scut puppy. The guy who's been putting Kimbrough's heat shock theory to the test," said Rios.

"And Flora Jean's a *friend* of Walker's," said Carmen, making sure the sheriff caught her added emphasis.

"Looks like Tangay suddenly became expendable," said Rios. "And according to Flora Jean's timetable, I don't think it was Kimbrough's strong man, Septian, who did him in. He was too busy following us."

Warren Anderson frowned and rose from his stool. "Wait a minute. You two are talking in riddles. Now, start from the beginning of whatever it is you're jabbering about and bring me up to speed." He gave them both his best peace officer's glare. "And don't leave anything out."

Rios looked to Carmen and shrugged. "Okay, but I guarantee you'll find it hard to believe."

"Try me," said the sheriff. "I'm all ears."

Carmen was on her third cup of coffee by the time Rios finished explaining the entire heat shock protein scenario to the sheriff.

Shaking his head, the sheriff sat back in his chair and took a sip of orange juice. "Let's see . . . We've got at least two people murdered here, maybe three." Anderson counted off the toll on his fingers. "Kimbrough's lab jockey, Felix Tangay; Brandon DeVille; and my recent possible contribution to the kitty, a missing Navajo named Larry Narine. What a frickin' pot of stew."

"It's not that complex," said Carmen. "Especially if you assume that DeVille and Narine are the real keys."

"Why's that?"

"Because we know how Tangay died. We pretty much know what Kimbrough was trying to prove with his heat shock protein research, and we know very well what's killing Stone. What we don't know is a whole lot about Brandon DeVille or your missing-persons problem, Larry Narine."

"An *outlier* problem again?" said Rios.

The sheriff frowned. "A what?"

"Just listen to Carmen, Warren. You'll get the drift."

Carmen smiled, looked at the sheriff, and continued. "And an absolutely key outlier too, especially when you consider that both DeVille and Narine are Navajo. Toss in the fact that Stone is part Navajo too, and we're back to one of Walker's pet theories: Nothing's a coincidence that happens in threes."

Rios winked at Carmen and smiled. "What are you thinking, outlier-wise?"

"I'm thinking there's a link between every one of those people. Something about them that holds this whole thing Kimbrough has mapped out together like glue. And you know what? I think I know how to find it." Carmen stared into her nearly empty coffee cup and then looked back up at the sheriff. "Warren, do you know whether there are any blood samples left over from DeVille's autopsy that I can get my hands on?"

"Probably."

"Good. I'll also need a blood sample from Stone. I can probably round up one from hematology. They usually keep an extra frozen tube or two of a patient's blood around when they're treating a stem-cell malignancy like his."

"What are you searching for?" asked the sheriff.

"That outlier Walker brought up. That needle in the haystack that makes for exciting science."

"Sounds like a stretch," said the sheriff, "but we don't have much else. Assuming I can get the coroner to cooperate, I'll have some of DeVille's blood for you before I head back up onto the mesa to check on my crew."

"You're a sweetheart," said Carmen. "You too," she added, giving Rios a wink. "Can you drop me at St. Mary's? I've got a little research to do."

"And you're not saying what it is?" asked Rios.

"I'll tell you about it if I'm right. Now, while I'm playing scientist, what do you plan to do?"

"Check on a little outlier of my own," said Rios, downing the rest of his orange juice and returning Carmen's wink.

CHAPTER
36

There had to be more to the life of a man like Luke Redstone than the contents of a cardboard box, Rios kept telling himself as he made his way across the wildflower-covered meadow leading to Stone's cabin.

Halfway across the meadow, a sickening odor stopped him in his tracks. He cautiously moved toward the pungent smell, his hand on the butt of his .357, until the remains of a cow or steer came into view. The coyotes and buzzards had found it first, and now the maggots and scavenger beetles were cleaning up the rest. Walking around the carcass, Rios holstered the gun, nodded as if he'd suddenly discovered the answer to something that had been gnawing at him all day, and continued toward the cabin.

He wasn't wearing his sling, and although his left shoulder throbbed whenever he moved too quickly, and his hand still tingled from residual numbness, for the first time in a week and a half he had the sense that perhaps one day he'd be able to handle an oar boat again. He negotiated his way around Stone's hot-wired fence, aware that unless a sniper was on his trail or someone was waiting inside the cabin to take him out, he was pretty much home free.

Noting that the bird cages out back were empty and all the cabin's windows were shuttered, he paused, dropped to his belly, and began crawling toward the back door, following a set of recent footprints to the threshold. Motionless, inhaling the musty smell of the grainy high-country soil, he listened for movement inside the cabin. The squeak of a screen door opening, then slamming against the cabin sent him into a quick half crouch. In the blink of an eye, a baseball-bat-wielding Jimmy Turner was on top of him. Rios rolled onto his side as the business end of a Louisville Slugger slammed into the dirt inches from his head. A second blow caught him in the right buttock. Bat above his head, in preparation for a third John Henry–sized swing, Turner suddenly froze, looking into the four-inch barrel of a .357.

"Hollow points—blow your insides back into those chicken cages," said Rios, steadying his aim.

Turner gripped the bat. "Bullshit. That would be murder."

"Gotta do what makes sense."

"I'll take your head off with me."

"Swing, who knows? You might get lucky."

The bat wavered as Turner considered the odds. "You got that woman out there in the grass waiting to shoot me in the back."

"No. I'm the only one here that'll be doing any shooting. Now, drop the bat," said Rios, starting to feel the blow to his buttock.

"What the fuck you doin' here?" Turner surveyed the carpet of tall grass surrounding the cabin, still half expecting Carmen to pop up, before slowly lowering the bat.

"Same thing as you. Tying up loose ends. Now, drop it."

Turner tossed the bat aside and nervously watched Rios rise.

Grimacing in pain, Rios gingerly touched his hip. "If you broke anything, I'm going to return the favor."

"Ain't nothin' broke. Was, you wouldn't be standin'."

"Thanks for the reassurance, Turner. Now, move your endangered ass back inside that cabin." He motioned toward the open doorway. "Hope you don't have any weapons inside," he added, the muzzle of the .357 nudging the small of Turner's back.

Turner chuckled. "If I did I woulda already shot your ass."

"I figured that," said Rios, following Turner across the threshold and into a room in shambles. Broken glass, smashed plates and cups, shredded magazines, moldy food scraps, and dozens of food cans littered the floor. Bullet holes peppered every wall.

Splintered furniture, looking as if it had been beaten with a hammer, had been tossed helter-skelter around the room.

Rios shook his head. "You do this?"

"Nope. Found it like this."

"Looks like somebody let a pack of wild animals loose in here." Nodding toward the bullet-riddled remains of an over-stuffed chair, Rios motioned for Turner to take a seat. "Park it."

Turner sat down cautiously, his eyes trained on Rios.

"Whoever did this must be nuts. And if it wasn't you, then you must have one hell of a reason for pulling mop-up detail. Best spit it out."

"No problem. I ain't got nothin' to hide. Reason I'm here has to do with two things: chickens and money."

"Keep talking."

Turner laughed. "Stone ain't gonna have no use for 'em where he's headed. He's on his way out. And money. That old half-breed always kept a stash hidden 'round the house."

"How'd you know Stone was dying?"

"News travels fast in cockfightin' circles, friend. Heard it from a couple of Stone's Navajo buddies a little while back. You and that doctor lady ain't his only friends in the world."

"Those friends of Stone's got names?"

"Yeah, but I don't know none of 'em very well. Mostly just seen 'em around. Truth is, they ain't really friends of his—more like folk he just knew. One of 'em is a little snot of a con man named DeVille. Only other one I knew a name for, 'sides the cocker who told me Stone was on his last legs, is a tall, ponytail-wearin' Indian named Roundtree. Heard he was a hero from some war. Now, how about lowerin' that gun?"

Rios shook his head, squaring the revolver at Turner. "How many of these friends of Stone's would you say there were alto-gether? And by any chance were all of them Indian?"

"Ten, twelve at the most, and yeah, they was all Indians."

"Any of them have a connection to Stone outside the world of cockfighting?"

Turner scratched his head. "A few mucked uranium with him years ago. But most of 'em, like DeVille, was the kids of muckers. I even worked with a few of 'em myself. The daddies, mind ya, not the kids."

"Anything else I should know?"

Turner thought for a moment, never letting his eyes wander from the barrel of Rios's gun. "Don't think so. Except that most every one of them uranium miners' kids turned out to be losers in the end. Drunks, dopers, second-rate thieves. I think Stone and that Roundtree fella sorta kept 'em in line."

"Why would Stone do that?"

"Wouldn't know for certain. Maybe it was on account of them all sharin' Navajo blood. Maybe it was 'cause forty years ago them same kids tended Stone's chickens while he and their daddies was mucking yellow-cake in the mines."

"The kids of those miners took care of Stone's birds?"

"I don't stutter, I just told you that. And yeah, they tended 'em every day for years. Exercised the damn things, fed and watered 'em, even bedded 'em down at night for him."

"Where?"

"Over at that place of Stone's I told you about near Uravan. Them kids followed the same routine, eight, ten hours every day."

"Damn! And their fathers? What happened to them?"

"Most of 'em's dead."

"DeVille's father, too?"

"You got it. SOB died from cancer of the blood."

"Leukemia, you mean?"

"Yeah." Turner made a move to get up, but Rios motioned him back down in his seat. "I ain't likin' this," he mumbled, still staring at the gun. "'Sides, why you so interested in a bunch of fuckin' dead Navajos and their worthless-ass sons?"

"Because I think they might be the key to something a hell of a lot bigger and a whole lot riskier than either one of us can possibly imagine."

"What's that?"

"I'm not sure, but it's tied to Stone's knack for producing invincible gamecocks and the fact that someone's been trying to kill me for the past couple of days. That wouldn't be your buddy Septian, by any chance?

Turner broke into a grin. "Like I told you that night at the cockfight, sooner or later you'd get a taste of him. Now, if you'll lower that pea shooter of yours, I'll tell you somethin' else worth knowin'."

Rios eyed Turner cautiously, then lowered his gun. A look of relief spread across Turner's face. "You've got thirty seconds."

Turner said, "A couple of nights before I run into you at that cockfight, I took DeVille and Septian on a backwoods trip to where I knew Stone always stashed his birds in times of trouble."

Rios nodded. "Was it to the back side of Wild Horse Draw?"

"Yeah . . . How'd you know that?"

"Because a few days ago, just east of there, Stone found DeVille dead as a ham with a hole where his Adam's apple ought to be."

Turner suddenly looked concerned. "Shit. Think Septian did him in?"

"That would be my guess."

"Damn. DeVille musta pissed Septian off somethin' terrible." Turner rose from his seat and began pacing the floor.

"Why the sudden edginess?" asked Rios.

"Ain't got no concerns," said Turner, his voice cracking.

"Horseshit. All of a sudden you're out of your seat and dancing around the floor. Something's got you spooked."

Turner took a deep breath and stopped. "We snatched close to a dozen of Stone's birds that night."

"That's what's got you so confessional? The fact that you stole a bunch of Stone's birds?"

"No. It's the fact that DeVille turned up dead. Who knows, with Septian involved, I could be next."

"I don't think so. Seems as though everyone turning up dead around here happens to be Navajo."

"Maybe, but I ain't takin' no chances. I know a little too much.

On our way back from Wild Horse, DeVille told me that he and Septian was into something big. Threw it in my face. Fucker always was into boastin'."

"Did he tell you what it was?"

"Nope. But he did tell me one thing—said it like it was somethin' he needed to tell me to make hisself feel better."

"And that was . . . ?"

"That he was up for a big payday and so was a bunch of buddies of his who was bivouacked out in the Utah desert."

"Did you believe him?"

"Didn't have no reason not to," said Turner, inching toward the door.

Rios pointed at a telephone on an end table propped precariously on two badly smashed legs. "Get back over here."

Turner grudgingly obliged.

"Now dial 970-587-3551 and ask for Dr. Nguyen. When she answers, tell her you're calling for me and that I've got some new ideas about our heat shock problem."

"Your *what?*"

"Don't analyze it, Turner; just do what I said."

"Do it your own damn self," said Turner, his tone suddenly defiant.

Rios's eyes narrowed as he thumbed back the hammer on the .357. "Dial the number, Turner. Believe me, it's the smart thing to do."

CHAPTER
37

Carmen Nguyen walked briskly down the hallway of the newly remodeled clinical pathology laboratories at St. Mary's Hospital, clutching a test tube full of Stone's blood. She walked past the freshly painted microbiology lab and through a doorway with an overhead sign that read, ANALYTICAL MICROCHEMISTRY. Stopping a baby-faced med tech who was rushing from the lab, she asked, "Is Dr. Flamio in?"

"Over in the cubicle next to the eyewash station." The young woman slipped past her and through the doorway.

Carmen headed across the room, admiring the lab's fresh face. No longer dimly lit and cluttered, the place actually looked airy. The countertops were jammed with new equipment, and every-where she looked, there seemed to be another set of space-age bells and whistles. Strangely, the layout reminded her of her research days in Salt Lake City.

Rounding a work bench, she caught sight of Betty Flamio, director of the hospital's clinical chemistry labs. With less than a year until retirement, Dr. Flamio loved to boast that she was a short-timer, but Carmen knew otherwise. Flamio was the kind of driven person who would wither on the vine if she actually did retire.

"Betty," said Carmen, stooping to embrace Flamio, who was seated on a metal stool and busy racking test tubes.

"Carmen. I thought maybe you'd flown the coop. Haven't seen you in weeks."

"I've been busy doing my ER thing."

"So I've heard." Flamio eyed the test tube of blood Carmen was holding, relaxed back on her stool, and winked. "Also heard you've gotten pretty chummy with some hunk who nearly bought it in a swan dive over a cliff."

"Where'd you hear that?"

"I've got sources." Flamio shoved a rack of test tubes aside. "Remember, I've been here almost thirty years, and—"

"You're less than a year from retirement," Carmen chimed in.

"You've got it. Ten months and eleven days, to be exact. My ticket to the stars." Flamio beamed. "Enough about me, though. I can tell you're here on a mission. What can I do for you?"

Carmen hesitated before responding. "It's a pretty far-out request—one that probably belongs in a university research lab."

"Shoot," said Flamio, smiling and sweeping her arm out in front of her, ringmaster-style. "It's a new day around here, Doctor. We aim to please."

"Ever heard of heat shock protein?"

"Sure."

"Have you ever had any experience isolating it?"

"No. That *would* be ivory-tower university stuff."

A look of disappointment crossed Carmen's face.

"Don't slump off the earth, Carmen. I said isolating heat shock protein was ivory-tower stuff. Didn't say I couldn't do it. Probably could if I had to." Flamio looked around the lab. "With the renovations and all the new equipment the fairy godmothers here at St. Mary's have bestowed on me, this place has gone from being a backwater medical dungeon to pretty much state of the art. The real question, though, is, what would you need the heat shock protein isolated *from?*"

"Blood." Carmen held out the test tube.

"I see. Better than urine or bronchial washings. Not quite as good as fresh tissue, though. But I think I could get it done."

"There's another kicker. I need the results stat."

"How stat?"

"Three, four hours at the most."

Flamio stroked her chin. "I'd have to push it, but our new

chemi-luminance microarray robotic equipment might do the trick. Stuff cost an arm and a leg. Can't believe they plunked down that kind of cash on a virtual retiree." Flamio paused, then said, "In order to meet your timetable, someone would have to do the cell extracts."

"I'll do those," said Carmen.

"A little detour back to your research roots? I like it," said Flamio, one of the few people at St. Mary's who knew the full story behind Carmen's flight from academia.

"Guess you never forget how to ride a bike," said Carmen, scanning the lab and having the sudden sense that she was back home.

"Or know when you'll have to get back on one," Flamio said with a grin.

"Have you got a buffer around here capable of maintaining the protein's integrity while I extract it?"

"I've got high-salt-buffer C and a couple of those new detergent lysis buffers. Pick your poison."

"I'll use the salt. I'm used to it," said Carmen, looking around for the equipment she'd need. "I need a tabletop centrifuge, Eppendorf tubes, a refrigerated microcentrifuge, a cell pelletor, dry ice, and pipettes." Surprised at how fast her research instincts had resurfaced, she finished her inventory and turned to Flamio. "Mind showing me that new robotic protein-labeling equipment you mentioned?"

"Love to," said Flamio, rising from her stool. "You'll be amazed. The protein transfer stamps look just like bullets."

Carmen followed her toward a smaller, isolated lab. "Think we can really get this all done in three hours?" asked Carmen, hoping Sheriff Anderson had been able to prod someone from the coroner's office into delivering a blood sample from Brandon DeVille's autopsy to St. Mary's.

"If we can't, Popeye's a sissy," said Flamio, snickering as they headed into the room that housed the new protein-scanning equipment, unaware that a courier with a delivery from the coroner's office was just down the hall asking for directions to her lab.

*   *   *

It was a crude assay, but after two and a half hours of painstaking work, there could be no mistaking the results. The heat shock protein levels in the cell extracts from Stone's blood were twelve times higher than those from Brandon DeVille's. In fact, DeVille's HSP90 levels were barely detectable.

Carmen stepped back from where she'd been working and slipped a protein transfer stamp back into its well. Amazed that in less than three hours, with Betty Flamio's assistance, she had completed an experiment that a few years earlier would have taken several days, she felt a glow of satisfaction. "You've got a winner here, Betty," she said, patting the top of the robotic protein scanner. "Don't let it out of your sight."

"Told you," said Flamio. "But don't ever forget, my dear, it's just a machine. The proof of the pudding always rests with the cook. You were the chef here, Carmen."

"Food for thought," said Carmen, taking her cell phone from her pocket, remembering only then that when she'd started her experiment she'd turned the phone off. The words *You have one new message* danced across the display screen. "Uh-oh. I missed a call."

"Important?"

"I'm not sure," said Carmen, unable to recognize the call-back number. She punched in the number hesitantly, sighing in relief when Rios responded on the other end of the line.

"It's me," said Carmen. "I'm in one of the labs over at St. Mary's, and I've got something that'll knock your socks off."

Rios sounded drained. "You had me scared to death, Carmen. Where the hell have you been? I've been trying to get in touch with you for over an hour. Are you all right?"

"Yes. I've been here in the lab the whole time."

"Have you forgotten about Septian? We made a pact about keeping in touch."

"I know. I just got caught up in a little science."

"You *what?*"

"I'll explain it to you later."

"Good. Meet me at Sugar Cane's in fifteen minutes with your explanation!"

"Is that an order, Captain?"

"Sure is. And, Carmen, be careful."

"I'll be there in ten." She smiled and stowed her phone. When she looked up, she realized that Betty Flamio had been drinking in the conversation.

"Sounds like you've got a date," said Flamio, clearly embarrassed. "Your cliff-hanging friend?"

"Yes."

"Better go, then. Men are a lot like retirement. You never want to keep them waiting."

This time, Septian realized things were stacked in his favor. Before, Rios had always been there, shielding Nguyen, running interference for her. Now, as she walked across the hospital parking lot toward her motorcycle, he recognized for the first time since he'd been stalking her just how gracefully she moved, how dark her skin was, and how coal black her hair was as it blew lazily in the wind.

He had watched her enter the hospital three hours earlier and had waited patiently while she was inside. He'd even checked in with Kimbrough to let him know that soon she'd be dead. Kimbrough, caught up in his experiment and his fire, hadn't even seemed interested. Eventually he'd said to hell with Kimbrough, hung up, read a newspaper, flossed his teeth, had coffee and Danish, and even buffed his shoes while waiting for Nguyen. Now, as he watched her stride across the parking lot, he began to salivate. Double-checking the silencer, he snugged up his gloves and slumped down in the front seat of his truck, thinking, *One down, one to go.*

Twice he'd missed his chance to kill her, erring one time by toying with her, the other by employing unnecessary overkill. All he had to show for his efforts was a simmering rage and a reduction in his inventory of bullets, grenades, and fire accelerants. His only solace was that he'd managed to slip away after the two attempts without Nguyen or Rios knowing who he was.

He watched intently as she stepped up to her bike, unlocked the helmet from the frame, and glanced around the half-full parking lot. As she slipped on the helmet and straddled the bike, he slumped down twenty feet away, crouched in his seat with only the crown of his head visible above the truck's window ledge. Steadying the eight-inch barrel against the ledge, he sighted in on the top inner quadrant of Carmen's left breast. Knowing she had to turn the bike directly toward him to leave, he gnawed at his cheek and waited to squeeze off the shot.

The Indian's throaty roar erupted, and the bike's front tire swung in his direction. Steadying his grip on the trigger, he focused on his target and started to squeeze, when suddenly the stubby nose of an SUV blocked his view. Mumbling, "God-damn!" and gritting his teeth, he lowered the target pistol and inched up in his seat. A vehicle with the words ST. MARY'S HOSPITAL SECURITY emblazoned in red letters across the front door now blocked his view of Nguyen. A chunky man dressed in a faded powder-blue security jacket leaned across the vehicle's front seat and poked his head out the passenger window.

"The beast is soundin' good, Doc. Like it wants to run up the side of a mountain."

Carmen smiled and throttled back the engine. "She's had a rough week, Jim, but now she's running right."

"How's that?"

"Someone punctured my tires earlier this week."

"I'll be. Gettin' so nowadays ain't nothin' sacred. Didn't happen here, did it?"

"No."

"Good. Hate to think someone would try that stuff on my turf." Jim scanned the parking lot slowly, as if he half expected the culprit to appear. "Ride alongside me, Doc. I'll escort you out of the lot."

"There's no need for that, Jim."

"Heck if there ain't. Whoever popped your tires just might decide to come back."

"Okay," said Carmen, suspecting that the guard's concern was less for her than for her motorcycle.

Septian watched Carmen's head turn away from him as she swung the bike around. The rest of her body remained obscured by the SUV. "Shit," he mumbled. "Fucking shit!" he added, watching the vehicle move slowly toward the lot's exit, running unwitting interference for Nguyen and obscuring his view.

CHAPTER
38

Hot plate, hot plate!" Maria Colby placed a steaming bowl of chili in front of Rios and wagged her finger at him. "Wait for it to cool or you're gonna scald your tongue. And for once try not doctoring it up."

Carmen, seated across from Rios, watched him scoop two heaping spoonfuls of sugar onto the chili and quickly stir it in.

"Sure you don't want anything?" Maria said to Carmen, frowning at Rios's adulteration of the house specialty.

"No, my stomach's a little queasy."

"Okay. Just give me the high sign if you change your mind." Maria turned and headed back toward the kitchen, eyed Rios one last time, and shook her head.

"She knows you like a book," said Carmen. "And she's right about the sugar."

Rios shrugged, spooned up a generous helping of chili, and said, "What do you say we pass on my eating habits for the moment and compare our heat shock notes."

"Fine by me. You first."

"Here's what I've got. And it came straight from the mouth of our cockfighting friend Jimmy Turner. According to him, whatever Kimbrough's up to involves a bunch of Navajos bivouacked somewhere out in the Utah desert."

"How'd you find that out? And how'd you run across Jimmy Turner?"

"It's a long story."

"I'm listening."

"I ran into him on a side trip to Stone's cabin."

Sensing that for some reason Rios wasn't going to divulge much more about the encounter, Carmen said, "Okay. And the purpose of their Utah camping trip is . . . ?"

"I'm not sure. Turner claims the Navajos are the sons of uranium miners who once worked with Stone. Turns out one of them was that dead guy you and Stone stumbled across—Brandon DeVille."

"You're kidding!"

"'Fraid not. And it gets better. Seems as though when they were kids the Navajos spent a lot of time exercising Stone's chickens on uranium-tailing-contaminated ground over near Uravan. Ground that turned out to be no more than a toxic waste dump."

"Bizarre."

Rios nodded as he spooned up more chili. "That's pretty much what I dug up. Now, how about you? When you called from the lab you sounded as if you'd just discovered gold."

"Not gold, but something just as valuable. I ran heat shock protein assays on blood samples from Stone and Brandon DeVille. Turns out Stone's HSP90 levels were ten times normal. DeVille's, on the other hand, were practically nonexistent."

Rios set his spoon down, the look on his face pensive. "So what we've got is two dead men with heat shock protein levels at opposite ends of the spectrum, a gang of Navajos somewhere out in the desert who were probably exposed to high levels of radiation during their youth, a nut packing around a satchel full of explosives, and a man who's trying his best to kill us." Rios shook his head. "Maybe we should call the *National Enquirer.*"

"Not quite yet. This isn't a tale about baby-snatching aliens or film stars who claim to be able to communicate with the dead. There's plenty of scientific reality here, Walker. In fact, this whole heat shock scam of Kimbrough's pretty much hinges on hard, honest science. Ready for a scientific breakdown?"

"Sure. Something here needs to make sense."

Carmen nodded and leaned forward in her chair. "As bizarre as this might sound, I think we've stumbled onto some kind of in vivo experiment. What you found out from that character Turner makes me all the more certain."

Rios frowned. "You're spewing jargon, Carmen. Translate."

Carmen smiled. *"In vivo—in life.* A real-life experiment, as opposed to one that takes place in a test tube in the lab. What I think we've stumbled across here is the makings of a live field test designed to evaluate the protective development properties of heat shock protein. But instead of using gamecocks this time around, I think Kimbrough's using human beings. What's got me stumped, though, is why there'd be a need to blow up a ski tower in the process."

Rios thought for a moment before smiling. "If you look at it the right way, blowing up a ski tower makes perfect sense. I should have recognized it right off."

"What's that?"

"The whole Powderhorn ski tower explosive thing is a gambit. An outlier of sorts—an event designed to make everyone take their eyes off the real event."

"A ruse, in other words?"

"In military field operative parlance, it's called a diversion. Problem is, the guy in charge of pulling it off screwed up and got caught in the act. What did Warren Anderson say our bomber's name was again?"

"Davy Boy Lopez."

"Yeah. Well, instead of a diversion, what Lopez got for his efforts was a drop shipment of feds."

"Bolen."

"Exactly."

"Unfortunately, Bolen's just as big a problem for us. The way I see it, there's no way around Bolen or his FBI crew."

Rios leaned across the table and gave Carmen a peck on the cheek. "Oh, but there is. You see, my dear doctor, FBI types are a lot like military brass. They tend to spend a lot of time planning D-day exercises when guerrilla warfare will do."

"Meaning?"

"Meaning that if you've sized this whole thing up right, the one kernel of truth that we need to stay focused on is Kimbrough's in vivo experiment, not nutcases with explosives, Jimmy Turner, cockfights, or the world supply of superchickens. And what we need to find out first is where Kimbrough plans to conduct this real-life experiment."

"Utah?"

"I don't think so—too far away from the playpen. The Powderhorn diversion site, Stone's hideaway for his birds, and the original uranium tailing fields are all within fifty miles of one another. Besides, I don't think Kimbrough meant for his experiment to be played out in desert—too open. I'm betting he's planning on sticking a lot closer to home. The Grand Mesa maybe, Wild Horse Draw, some out-of-the-way site on the Uncompahgre Plateau. They all make more sense than the desert."

"That narrows it right down," said Carmen sarcastically. "You're talking about an area the size of New Jersey."

"I know. But I just might be able to do better with a little scientific help from my old lady."

"I'll do what I can," said Carmen.

"Good. First off, how many human guinea pigs do you think Kimbrough actually needs to pull this thing off?"

"I don't know."

"Come on, take a guess."

Carmen sat back in her chair, deep in thought. "He'd need several heat-shock-protein-deficient subjects and an equal number of heat-shock-protein-normal controls. A dozen men, maybe two. And his test subjects would all need some pivotal stress quotient to respond to in order to trigger a new heat-shock-protein-induced protective development response. Something equivalent to the radiation from the uranium tailings that kicked off the protective HSP response in Stone's birds. Something truly catastrophic for the men to react to so that Kimbrough can determine if the radioactively induced reduction in heat shock protein that occurred during their youth has afforded some of them a form of genetically induced protective development." Carmen paused and gave Rios a puzzled look. "Those explosives

Davy Boy Lopez was carrying around—maybe they were intended to be the stress trigger."

"I don't think so. Too far off the mark. Stone's chickens were primed to survive bruises, cuts, bleeding, and broken bones—not being blown to smithereens."

"What's the trigger, then?"

"I don't know. But if Kimbrough's angling for a product he believes will ultimately be marketable, his experiment can't include an event that's so catastrophic it wipes out his subjects. Guess I'll have to think about it for a while."

"You know what they say," said Carmen, smiling to ease the tension. "You think long, you think wrong."

Rios took another bite of chili and frowned. "I know. That's what has me worried."

The stoop-shouldered, sun-baked ball of a woman sitting in Sheriff Anderson's office wore a faded shawl that enveloped her from shoulders to knees. Her thick jet-black hair, pulled tightly back against her scalp, gave her the appearance of a half-finished bust sculpture. Her eyes were deep-set and moist, her skin badly wrinkled from too many years in the sun. Turning her attention from the stack of photographs resting in her lap, the woman swallowed hard and looked up into the sheriff's penetrating gaze.

"Let me see the most recent ones, Mrs. Cloud," said the sheriff, leaning forward from his perch on the edge of his desk and accepting one of the photos.

"That's him about a year ago. He's playing ball with my son."

The sheriff studied the photo of a smiling Larry Narine, squatting on a lawn with his arm wrapped tightly around a young boy of about eleven. A baseball glove rested in the boy's lap.

Dolores Cloud interrupted the sheriff's concentration with a heavy sigh. "A few months after that picture was taken, Larry began acting real strange. Quit coming by for Sunday dinner. Started spending all his time with his loser friends. Even stopped playing catch with my son."

The sheriff set the photo aside. "And you're convinced something's happened to him?"

"Yes. There's something wrong, Sheriff. I'm his sister. I know. It's been three weeks, and I haven't heard a word from him. I should've come to see you sooner instead of simply filling out a missing persons report. There's something terribly wrong."

Sheriff Anderson shifted his weight as Dolores Cloud inched deeper into her seat. "Those friends of his you mentioned—any reason to think he may have taken off with them?"

She shook her head. "Larry had more sense than that. Most of those friends of his were alcoholics and drifters. Some were out-and-out bums. They all had one thing in common, though: They stuck to Larry like glue. Any following that took place would have been the other way around—them following him. The only one of them with a lick of sense was a loner war hero—drifter named Ariel Roundtree."

"Any bad blood between Roundtree and your brother?"

"No. But I heard Roundtree's also been acting strange. Running around calling secret meetings, rounding up all his boyhood friends, even driving them across the state to Denver for regular medical checkups."

"You know this for certain?"

"Drunks tend to talk a lot, Sheriff."

"Maybe your brother's sick."

"I don't think so. According to my son, Richie, he's into something ritualistic."

"I see. How many of these friends of your brother's do you think might be involved?"

"A dozen or more. I'm pretty sure of that."

"And the medical checkups? What's the story there?"

"I don't know. I just heard Richie mention it."

"And your son's certain that these trips your brother took to Denver involved medical checkups?"

"The Navajo community around here's real small, Sheriff; you know that. And we've always been close-knit. Richie wasn't the only one who knew about Larry rounding up those other men, and he wasn't the only one who knew about their trips to Denver."

The sheriff rose slowly. The medical aspect of Larry Narine's disappearance suddenly had his full attention. "Let me ask you something. It may sound strange, but it could be significant. Did your brother ever work in the uranium mines?"

"No. He was way too young. But my father did—and it killed him."

"And the other men you mentioned—were their fathers uranium miners too?"

Dolores Cloud thought for a moment, eyeing the sheriff suspiciously before she finally responded, "Every one of them. What's going on here, Sheriff?"

"I'm not sure, to tell you the truth." The sheriff glanced out the window of his office at the pale, harsh-looking Book Cliffs and found himself wondering whether Rios and Carmen Nguyen had told him everything they knew about Jack Kimbrough. Turning back to Dolores Cloud, he said, "Is there anyone who might be able to tell me more about what's up with your brother?"

"Richie might be able to. He's beside himself over this."

"Can I talk to him?"

"Sure. I'll get him for you. He's waiting outside in the car. But before I do, Sheriff, tell me the truth. Do you think my brother's involved in something illegal?"

"Perhaps."

"Could it get him sent to prison?"

"Don't know."

Dolores Cloud's eyes glazed over as she fought back tears. "I guess it could be worse," she said, rising from her chair. "He could be involved in something that could get him killed."

CHAPTER
39

Rios stood at the vintage nickel-plated cash register that flanked the entrance to the Guadalajara Grill, jousting with Maria Colby over the breakfast tab he'd never received. Sugar Cane Colby stood next to him, feigning ignorance.

"I didn't get a check again, Cane."

Colby shrugged. "Must've got lost. Catch me next time."

"I could get hit by a bus before then."

"Then you'll always be one up on me."

Carmen watched the two longtime friends sparring, convinced that they could continue for hours. When Rios's cell phone interrupted the exchange, both men's faces slumped as if an umpire had suddenly stepped in to call their game.

"Give me a sec," said Rios, flashing Colby a smile that said, *This match ain't over*, before barking, "Rios here."

"Your shorts too tight?" said Warren Anderson, surprised by the intensity of Rios's response.

"Sorry. I've been sparring with Cane about a bill."

"Pay the man," the sheriff said, aware of Rios and Colby's game.

"Next time. What's up?"

"Plenty. I think I've got a line on what Kimbrough and his crew are up to. Got it from a ten-year-old kid, no less. Is Carmen there with you?"

"She sure is."

"Let me speak to her."

Rios shrugged and handed Carmen the phone. "It's Warren Anderson. He wants to talk to you."

"Hello," said Carmen, a hint of surprise in her voice.

"Warren here. I think I've got a lead on that heat shock protein problem you're chasing. But I need a few questions answered to see if I'm right."

"Shoot."

"I just finished talking with a ten-year-old Navajo kid whose uncle's in this heat shock thing up to his ears. The uncle's name is Larry Narine. A few weeks ago Narine let the kid in on a secret. Told the kid he couldn't tell anyone, not even his mother. Seems as though for the past three months, Narine's been practicing to become a firefighter, honing his skills somewhere out in the Utah desert." The sheriff drew a deep breath. "Here's my question. What's your take on Kimbrough starting some kind of fire in order to test his heat shock protein theory out on—I'm not sure I should even say this—human beings?"

"Strange you should ask. Walker and I were discussing a similar scenario just a little while ago. It's reasonable. But first he'd need a group of willing research subjects and a cadre of firefighters known to be heat shock protein deficient. And he'd probably need a bigger bang for his buck than a bonfire in the desert. If the heat shock protein protective development mechanism works the way I think it does, he'd need something for his firefighters to tackle that was potentially far more catastrophic than simply a fire in order to trigger it."

"Catastrophic or not, I think Kimbrough's got his group of research subjects. That kid I told you about said his uncle recruited a bunch of other Navajos to play firefighter with him. The kid's mother's been calling everyone she knows trying to find out just how many men her brother might have recruited. She's had some luck, but it's like pulling teeth. The men involved are either drunks, dropouts, or guys on the fringe, and they've done one hell of a job keeping whatever they're up to a secret. There is a kicker, though—one that makes everything more plausible. The mother knows several of the missing men. Grew up with them, in fact. Claims that when they were kids, at one time or another most of them spent time around Uravan babysitting your friend Redstone's chickens."

Carmen whistled, eyed Rios, and shook her head. "Sounds like fodder for some kind of twisted research protocol, all right. By confining his experiment to a handful of Navajos, Kimbrough would be able to keep the genetics clean. And if at one time or another all the subjects had exposure to Stone's uranium tailings, Kimbrough would have himself a truly unique sampling. But like I said before, fire alone wouldn't be enough of a stressor for Kimbrough to determine if he's stumbled across a group of heat-shock-protein-deficient, genetically altered, potentially armor-plated human beings. No matter how effective heat shock protein might be at conferring some kind of genetically derived protection on his research subjects, they'd simply burn up in a fire."

"Maybe not," said the sheriff. "Remember, Kimbrough's company manufactures fire protective gear. The men might have all the protection they need against a fire. Could be there's another more potent heat shock protein stressor out there—one that's capable of testing Kimbrough's protective development hypothesis in a single experimental trial. Anyway, I've got our FBI wonder boy Agent Bolen checking on it. He also ran a profile on Kimbrough and that character we think's been stalking you—Septian. Turned up a real interesting tidbit on him. Can you put Rios back on? I'd like to run what Bolen found out about Septian past him. And, Carmen, keep thinking about the stress quotient side of our heat shock protein problem. There's an answer out there somewhere; we just haven't pegged it yet."

"Sure will," said Carmen, handing Rios the phone.

"Yeah?" said Rios with a grunt.

"Didn't mean to ignore you, Walker, but I needed Carmen's scientific point of view on a matter first. She can fill you in. Bottom line is, I've got a scoop on that guy who's been trying to take you out."

"Septian?"

"Yeah. His first name's Roland. And he's a war buddy of yours. Pulled a tour of duty the same time you did during Desert Storm. Our FBI friend Bolen dredged up a page-and-a-half computer printout on him."

"Small world. What kind of duty did Septian pull?"

"Munitions expert."

"Bombs!" Rios stroked his chin. "Anything else?"

"Not much. He was a lieutenant, honorably discharged. Received a Purple Heart. That's it for the moment. Bolen's still checking. I'll let you know if we dig up anything else. In the meantime, you and Carmen need to keep a real low profile."

"Sure," said Rios sarcastically. "Someone tries to blow my head off with a grenade, kill Carmen, firebomb my house, and you tell me to keep my head down. Try another tack, Warren."

"Listen, Walker. This thing's escalating. The explosive angle forced my hand. In a few hours they'll have FBI boys, explosive experts, and maybe even the Eighty-second Airborne swarming all over the county. It's time to stay put. You should know that better than most. Friendly fire'll take you out as fast as the enemy's."

"I'll keep that in mind."

"Do that. And, Walker?"

"Yes?"

"Pay Sugar Cane's bill." The sheriff laughed and hung up.

"You look perplexed," said Carmen, watching Rios tuck away his cell phone. "What did Warren say?"

"Said to keep our heads down."

"Seems like good advice."

"It is if you're an ostrich. Come on, let's go."

"Where are we headed?"

"Home. To talk to Flora Jean," he said, linking his arm in Carmen's, slapping a twenty-dollar bill down on the counter, and moving toward the exit. "I need some intelligence information that's a cut above the sheriff's or the FBI's."

* * *

The SeaLand semi's weight had it mired in a slough-grass bog several yards from a small mountain spring. Ariel Roundtree had spent twenty minutes trying to free the rig, only to succeed in burying it in mud up to its axles. "We'll have to winch it out," Roundtree called out, getting out of his Jeep and beckoning to the three men who'd been helping him. "You shoulda never drove so close to that spring," said one of the men, a pudgy Navajo with an ugly scar that zigzagged across his forehead.

"I didn't see it," protested Roundtree. "Anyway, it's too late now. We're stuck. I'll go unhook the other tractor and we'll winch the damn thing out." Roundtree glanced across the meadow to where Jack Kimbrough was working, and broke into a trot. A few yards from the slough-grass bog, the meadow turned into a rutted field overrun with thistle, chickweed, and hounds-tongue. With each stride, a new cluster of hound's-tongue stuck to Roundtree's jeans, and by the time he reached Kimbrough, his pant legs were a mass of burrs.

Jack Kimbrough was down on one knee a few feet away from his Humvee, checking the two rows of respirators he'd laid out in the patchy grass and loose soil. "Still stuck?" he said, looking up.

"Yeah," said Roundtree, out of breath. "Gonna have to winch the fucker out."

Kimbrough stared past Roundtree toward a second eighteen-wheeler sitting in the middle of the two-hundred-acre meadow. Looking back and forth between the trailers, he said, "Remember, now, the containers inside have to be perfectly lined up side by side."

"I know."

"And you've got to make sure that the front and rear cables you've looped around them have at least two feet of slack up top."

"I know that, too." Roundtree rolled his eyes.

"Then you're set," said Kimbrough, sensing Roundtree's growing irritation.

"You're sure the choppers can lift both containers off the ground?"

"Didn't you practice the maneuver out in the desert?"

"Yeah. But not in the middle of a forest fire."

"Forest fire, my ass." Kimbrough laughed. "All you'll be doing is managing a controlled burn designed to clear off some thistle. No need to worry; everything will be fine."

"Hope so," said Roundtree, recalling a promise he'd made his girlfriend to take her to Vegas when the job was over. Life was going to be very different after payday. He was about to ask Kimbrough what time the first chopper was due when he noticed Emerson Walls approaching. By the time Walls reached them, Roundtree was behind the wheel. Starting the engine, he gunned the motor, popped the clutch, and lurched away.

Walls watched the cab-over tractor lumber off before turning his attention to Kimbrough. In a near-sigh he said, "Not one sign of that fuckin' Lopez. It's like he vanished into thin air."

The muscles in Kimbrough's forehead etched into a frown. "Fucking third-rate drunk. I don't know why you trusted him in the first place. He could send this whole operation south."

"In case you missed it, I only had ten men. I had to trust someone. I drove thirty miles back across the mesa looking for Lopez, and nothing. I didn't want to chance driving all the way back to Powderhorn, not this late in the show. So I turned around. Maybe he got cold feet."

"Or maybe he decided to talk to the police," said Kimbrough.

"I doubt that. They'd be all over the place by now."

"What do you think? Do we go ahead as planned?" asked Kimbrough, looking perplexed.

"Are you crazy? Of course. I've already ordered in the choppers. They're set to move the two containers out of here at four o'clock sharp. Trust me, there won't be a trace of anything but tire ruts around here once they've swooped in. Lopez or no Lopez, we go. I told you I never liked the idea of a diversion from the beginning. Next time maybe you'll leave maneuvers like this to people who know something about them," said

Walls, recalling Kimbrough's earlier disparaging comments about the military.

Kimbrough bristled. Checking his anger, he glanced across the meadow and watched Roundtree ease the second tractor up behind the bogged-down trailer. "Everything else in place?"

"Yes," said Walls as they watched Roundtree loop a cable around the trailer axle, return to the tractor, and bulldog the trailer out of the mud.

"What do your Navajos think is inside the containers?" asked Kimbrough.

"Exactly what's inside. Scrap metal."

"And the reason it's there . . . ?" asked Kimbrough, coaching Walls's response.

"To evaluate the meltdown rate of scrap metal in a fire. The same thing I've told every one of them but Roundtree from the beginning." Walls frowned. "Is this a test?"

"No."

"Then lighten up with the questions. My men know what they're doing."

Kimbrough nodded. "Hope so. One thing I'll give 'em, though—they sure as hell seem fearless."

"You'd be too if you were a drunk, a pothead, or a washed-up war hero looking at life's last chance." Walls turned away from Kimbrough and slowly scanned the landscape. They were two miles off the scenic byway and five hundred feet below a long-forgotten logging bed. He knew that for all intents and purposes they were lost to the world. "We set the whole thing off in an hour. Think my men have a fighting chance?"

"Of course," said Kimbrough. "This experiment isn't designed to kill anyone. It's set up to see how the men respond."

"Suppose they respond negatively?"

"Then I'll have to pursue other research avenues. For right now the road we're traveling looks to be the most promising. Is everything set up for their postburn medical evaluations and their monthly blood draws?" asked Kimbrough, surprised at Walls's concern for his men.

"Yes. I talked to Rebecca yesterday afternoon."

"Then we're set. By the way, where's our protective gear?"

"In my vehicle."

"Guess it's time we check it out," said Kimbrough.

Walls looked back across the meadow to where two cargo containers now sat perfectly aligned side by side. Roundtree and his men were milling around, smoking, playing grab-ass, or staring blankly into space. Nodding toward the men, Walls said, "I feel sort of bad about them not having the benefit of the same protective gear as us."

"You shouldn't," said Kimbrough. "They're being paid very well for their part in this trial. Besides, if all they were doing was simply putting out a fire, I wouldn't really have an experiment, would I? Everything and everybody has a purpose in life," said Kimbrough, his tone dismissive. "We have ours; they have theirs." Casting a final glance toward Roundtree and his men, he added, "Now, let's check on that gear."

CHAPTER
40

Your boy Septian's one hell of a chameleon," said Flora Jean to Rios, shouting to be heard on a phone line crackling with static. "Since leavin' the army, he's had his hands in more schemes than you can shake a stick at. Smugglin' stolen cars to Mexico, authenticatin' forged antiques, providin' muscle for the rich and infamous—the man does it all."

"Where'd you get your info?" asked Rios, pacing his basement floor and surveying the fire damage he was certain Septian had caused.

"A little birdy told me."

"No games, Flora Jean. This is drop-dead serious. I told you, the SOB tried to kill me and burn down my house."

"Okay. My source is golden. I called in a marker from Alden Grace."

"You're kidding! *General* Grace?" said Rios, surprised that Flora Jean had contacted their former commanding general.

"*Retired* General Grace. He lives in Bethesda, Maryland, now, right outside D.C. These days he's paid to keep an intelligence ear to the ground."

"CIA?"

"I'm not sayin', sugar, and neither's he."

"What's his tie to Septian?"

"None. But he had a Dumpster-full of dirt on a bigger fish. An army colonel named Emerson Walls. Another compatriot of ours during Desert Storm."

"What's his story?"

"Seems as though when Walls was a fast-track major buckin' to make colonel in the army tank corps, *Lieutenant* Roland Septian served as his exec."

"Tank corps boys. Now, that's a roughhouse crew," said Rios, staring at the cold embers of what had once been a built-in stereo system and the charred remains of watercolor sketches he'd painted of rivers around the world.

"Walls and Septian were more than that, accordin' to Alden. They were also a couple of thieves, although to this day no one's been able to prove it."

"What did they steal?"

"Tanks."

"Come on, Flora Jean."

"Kid you not, sugar. Alden wouldn't lie. But it's not what you think. The tanks they pilfered didn't even run. Seems as though your two choirboys were partial to incapacitated, burned-out Abrams hulks."

"Why?"

After a lengthy pause, Flora Jean spoke up. "You never heard this from me, Rios. Our friendship rests on it."

"Got you."

"Know much about depleted uranium?"

"Not much. Only that we were lobbing shells made out of the stuff directly at Saddam's army during most of Desert Storm."

"That's all I knew too, sugar, until Alden filled me in. Honey, that shit's nasty. They've even had Senate hearings about its use. According to Alden, the stuff's a by-product of the uranium enrichment process, depleted to about a third of its original radioactive content. And it's harder than shit. Just right for mixin' up with a bunch of other fancy metals if you wanta bake yourself up a projectile hard enough to penetrate a tank. How'd you like to have been one of Saddam's boys, trackin' around the desert in some armored Soviet coffin, and have a depleted-uranium shell come crashin' in on your ass?"

"I wouldn't."

"Well, believe me, it happened to some of ol' Saddam's troops. Problem is, it also happened to some of ours. Turns out that during our little skirmish in the desert, more than a few depleted-uranium shells missed their mark and took out some of our tanks instead of his. A dozen or so, all told, according to Alden. Turned every one of those bad boys into radioactive hulks. No Americans were killed, but more than a few got peppered with radioactive shrapnel and exposed to a lifetime's worth of radiation in the process. Alden says that in the face of those friendly-fire mishaps, everything from Gulf War Syndrome to hemorrhoids has been blamed on our use of depleted uranium shells during Desert Storm."

"Shit."

"I'd say. Now, here's the kicker. Guess who pulled cleanup duty on our little radioactive messes?"

"Walls?"

"You got it, sweetie. Along with your boy Septian. Word goin' around the intelligence community is that Walls understood the value of radioactive junk and decided to pack off a little for himself. How he scarfed the tank carcasses off the battlefield and smuggled 'em back home, no one knows. But word on the street is that he's been tryin' to peddle the stuff for years."

"To whom?"

"To anyone with the need for a low-grade uranium source. Nuts tryin' to make bombs, fools who wanta produce their own variety of tank-penetratin' shells, idiots hopin' to add somethin' radioactive to their military arsenal."

"Has he had any takers?"

"No one knows. But since the depleted shit's so low-grade, Alden thinks it's too tough a sell. Claims Walls will probably never find any takers."

Rios let out a lengthy sigh. "Unfortunately, I think the general's wrong. I believe Walls has already found his man."

"Who's that?"

"Our friend Jack Kimbrough from Trigenics."

"I thought he was busy experimentin' on some kind of protein. What the hell would he want with uranium-contaminated tank scraps?"

Rios stroked his chin. "To extrapolate from what he first learned on a bunch of chickens."

"What?"

"I'll explain it to you when I'm a little more sure myself."

"Better make it soon, Walker. I called in a hell of a marker on this. I wouldn't want what I've told you gettin' back to the general."

"It'll be soon. Count on it. By the way, how'd you get such a direct line to General Grace?"

Flora Jean snickered. "He and I go way back in the intelligence world, sugar. Further back than even you and me."

"You're not telling me everything," said Rios.

Flora Jean broke into an out-and-out laugh. "Some men prefer dark meat in their diet, sugar. Count your blessin's they do."

"Got you."

"Remember, none of this came from me."

"Who?"

"You've got the drift, sugar."

"You're the best, Flora Jean. I'll let you in on the rest of the story as soon as I know the ending."

"Watch your endgate."

"You know I always do." Rios hung up, frowning as he looked around his burned-out basement, then headed toward the steps, taking them two at a time, shouting, "Carmen! Carmen!"

When Rios called Warren Anderson to tell him what Flora Jean had dug up on Walls and Septian, the sheriff surprised Rios with a few new disturbing facts of his own. Facts that included what Larry Narine's nephew had told him about his uncle becoming a firefighter, and new insights that had the sheriff looking into every BLM and U.S. Forest Service controlled burn scheduled within a three-state region for the next two weeks. Three burns had popped up during his search: one in Utah, west of the Col-

orado state line and over 160 miles away; a second in the Para-
dox Valley, fifty miles southwest of Uravan; and a third on the
Grand Mesa, several miles east of an isolated knob known as
Chalk Mountain. In light of the new information, it disturbed
Rios that the sheriff was still busy investigating Davy Boy
Lopez's failed attempt to blow up the ski towers at Powderhorn.

"I'm telling you, Warren, the Powderhorn thing was meant to
be a red herring," said Rios, drumming his fingers on his living
room coffee table as he fidgeted nervously in his chair. "Drop the
Powderhorn investigation," he said, glancing at Carmen, who
sat facing him. "Kimbrough's experiment is the real issue here.
He could kill a dozen men, maybe two dozen, and contaminate
hundreds of thousands of acres of public land for decades."

Unconvinced, the sheriff said, "Not one of these three scheduled burns I turned up involves more than three hundred acres,
Walker. We're talking little more than brush fires here, when you
get right down to it. Weigh that against the fact that it's post-
nine-eleven and I've got a nut on my hands who was trying to
blow up a ski resort."

"I have."

"Good, because I'll let you in on a little secret: I'm not the one
calling the shots here. I've been told by the Bureau to concen-
trate my efforts on securing the Powderhorn ski area, policing it,
and keeping Labor Day traffic confined to the Cedaredge side of
the mesa and south of Powderhorn for the rest of the day."

Shaking his head, Rios said, "And you're doing exactly what
Kimbrough wants: You're buying him time. Carmen claims that
in order for Kimbrough's big-bang scheme to work, he'll have to
conduct his experiment under pretty much the same conditions
as Stone did almost a half century ago."

"Seems like that would be tough," said the sheriff.

"It will be. He'll need the same heat coefficients, the same kind
of terrain, a similar elevation, and a group of heat-shock-protein-
deficient human beings. The way I see it, his only choice out of
your three scheduled burn sites would have to be the Chalk
Mountain area up on the mesa. Carmen says that if Kimbrough

has assessed things right and he has stumbled onto a group of heat-shock-protein-deficient Navajos, then this experiment of his could go a long way toward identifying a cadre of human invincibles. Exposing his firefighters to a fire involving depleted uranium could be the ticket."

"Sounds like science fiction to me. What the hell would he do with them?"

"Who knows? Fight wars with their clones, fly them to the moon, send them diving after treasures sitting on the bottom of the sea. Maybe he'll sell his findings to some pharmaceutical giant or the next Genghis Khan. Hell, I don't know what's in his head. I'll tell you this, though: I'm siding with Carmen."

"Maybe you're right," said the sheriff. "Problem is, I've been told by the FBI where to place my chips. That Chalk Mountain area that you're so concerned about turns out to be a second-tier priority."

Exasperated, Rios said, "Guinea pigs fifty years ago, guinea pigs again."

"Who's that?" said the sheriff.

"Those Navajos. Just as expendable now as they were back in the mines."

"Walker, my hands are tied."

"I understand," said Rios, both of his eyes suddenly agleam. "But you can help me another way."

"Shoot."

"Is I-seventy access to the mesa blocked off yet?"

"It will be in about twenty minutes. You won't be able to get up on the mesa from either the Delta or the I-seventy side, even if you had a tank."

"And you've blocked off the mesa byway road at Powder-horn?"

"Yes. What are you getting at, Walker?"

"I'll tell you in a second," said Rios, aware from the sheriff's deployments that if Kimbrough and his crew were already at the Chalk Mountain site preparing to start a fire, they'd soon be boxed in.

"Don't even think about it, Walker."

"I'm not," said Rios.

"Walker!"

"Catch you later." Rios slammed down the phone. In one fluid motion he grabbed Carmen by the hand, pulled her from her seat, and started toward the door. "We're headed for the mesa."

"What did the sheriff say?" asked Carmen, struggling to keep up.

"Not much," he said, breaking out of her grasp, vaulting down his front steps, and racing for his pickup.

After leaving Grand Junction in a crawl of Labor Day traffic and following Rios along I-70 east for several miles, Roland Septian found himself several car lengths behind Rios's pickup, cruising along the ten-mile twist of Grand Mesa scenic byway that cut through Plateau Creek Canyon.

Helmeted, dressed in motorcycle racing gear, and hugging the frame of a Kawasaki crotch rocket, he locked his gaze on Rios's rear bumper as together they wove their way along the narrow canyon road. Low to the ground, nimble, and engineered for explosive acceleration, the bike was a perfect interceptor. Leaning into a curve, Septian smiled, thinking that ironically, it had been Nguyen who had given him the idea of using a motorcycle to finish the job.

Throttling back in order to keep from being seen, he ran through his plan. He'd intercept Rios at the canyon road's six-mile marker, where the road briefly paralleled Plateau Creek before making a sharp turn to the south to begin its ascent up the mesa. At that point, the road verged with a sheer forty-foot drop-off to the meandering creek below. Given the motorcycle's speed and maneuverability, it would be no problem to race past Rios's truck, riddle it with machinegun fire, and then continue east on an intersecting state highway to Colbran. The plan was simple, neat, and efficient. Even better, he'd had the good fortune to latch on to Rios when there was no other canyon traffic.

*   *   *

Rios frowned, realizing as he snaked his way along the canyon road that his truck was pulling badly to the right. "Damn."

"What's the matter?" asked Carmen.

"My front end's out of alignment. New tires all around, and now the thing won't track straight."

"Let me get this straight. Someone tries to burn down your house, machinegun us to bits, and blow us away with a grenade, and you're worried about your pickup not tracking straight?" Carmen shook her head. "I don't believe it."

"Okay. So it's not really that. Guess I'm actually concerned about whether we're chasing the right fire." Rios draped his hand over the top of the steering wheel and sat forward in his seat.

"You've been certain about a Chalk Mountain burn all along. Now's not the time to start second-guessing yourself."

"Suppose I'm wrong. Like Warren said, a bunch of lives are at stake. Not to mention the potential radiation contamination."

"Maybe not. I don't believe Kimbrough's experiment is designed to kill. I believe what he's really trying to do is gauge the human response to something catastrophic. In the end, I think he wants to learn whether exposure to a cache of superheated depleted uranium actually kicks in a genetically programmed protective heat shock protein response in his firefighters. I don't believe for one minute he wants to kill his experimental subjects. Quite the opposite, in fact. I think he wants his human guinea pigs to live to fight another day."

"And if his experiment works?"

"Then he'll have something to sell. An in vivo experimental model for turning on genes capable of speeding up the process of protective evolution. And he'll have proof that in certain HSP-deficient people, like his Navajos, random high-risk events, such as exposure to radiation as a child, can make them protectively adapt in no time at all to a second environmental hazard, like superheated depleted uranium."

"So you think that by exposing his firefighters to radiation for a second time in their lives, Kimbrough actually can reduce their

HSP90 levels enough to cause protective evolutionary changes in the men?"

"Not with one shot. But remember, it's the first pig at the trough that usually gets the most grain. Being first in line gives Kimbrough a leg up on the rest of the scientific world."

"Then let's hope I'm right about Chalk Mountain, because Kimbrough's one pig I'd like to shove back to the end of the line," said Rios, slowing his speed in preparation for the maze of curves ahead.

CHAPTER

41

It unnerved Warren Anderson to realize that he knew Rios so well he could predict his behavior. He grumbled to himself, pounding his cruiser's steering wheel in a fit of disgust, as he sped eastward on Interstate 70, hoping to beat Rios to the Plateau Creek access to the Grand Mesa.

By the time he reached the roadblock at the Plateau Creek off-ramp to the Grand Mesa byway, his temples were pounding. Screeching to a halt a few yards short of a string of blaze-orange barriers blocking the road, he had the sudden urge to urinate—an urge that always seemed to surface when tension overwhelmed him.

A female deputy with apple red cheeks and a hat that looked at least a size too small nodded at the sheriff and smiled as she paced the length of the sawhorse barriers, then turned and retraced her steps. Just beyond the barriers, the rooftop lights of three Mesa County patrol cars flashed amber and red.

"Afternoon, Sheriff," said the deputy, pausing momentarily, her tone almost lyrical. "The way you burned in here, I thought maybe you were doing a public service spot for the need to always keep a safe stopping distance."

The sheriff flashed a half smile that quickly faded. "How long you been deployed?" he said, glancing at the barriers.

"Fifteen minutes," said the deputy, her response suddenly all spit and polish.

"Any vehicles try to head up the canyon since you set up?"

"A half-dozen or so. We turned them all back."

"Who's sweeping the road up ahead?"

"Patterson and DeFreeze. They're chauffeuring a couple of FBI types."

"How heavily are they armed?"

"As far as I know, they're only carrying their service revolvers. Maybe some spare rounds in the trunk. As for the special agents, beats me."

Unconsciously biting his lower lip, the sheriff said, "Get me a jolly duck up here and have it fully loaded."

"Yes, sir." The deputy moved toward one of the cruisers, surprised that the sheriff was calling for a riot vehicle.

Walking briskly over to two other deputies, the sheriff said, "Any traffic go up the canyon before you closed the gates?"

"Nope, nothing at all," said one of the deputies.

Several feet away, a third deputy poked his head out of his patrol car. "I might have seen something. Can't say for sure, though. Could've simply been a reflection."

"What was that?" said the sheriff, approaching the car as the lanky deputy stepped out.

"A red streak. No, shorter than a streak. More like a zap. About twenty yards up the road before Patterson and DeFreeze started their sweep."

"Brake lights, maybe?"

"I don't think so. But if they were, I only saw one."

Warren Anderson looked puzzled, as if he were desperately trying to recall an answer that was on the tip of his tongue. Arching his eyebrows and shaking his head he said, "How big's their sweep?"

"The whole nine yards. Every barn and outhouse. The full twenty miles up to Powderhorn—side roads, pullouts, turnarounds, even roadside tables."

"Do they have a timetable?"

"I'll call them and see," said the deputy, reaching for his radio mike as the female deputy rushed up.

"We'll have a jolly duck up here within the hour," said the deputy, pausing to catch her breath.

The sheriff frowned. "Too long."

"That's as fast as they can get one up here, Sheriff, and that's running flat out."

Anderson pivoted slowly and looked back toward the canyon's narrow rock-walled entry. Suddenly he found himself thinking about football, high school, and lifelong friends. Turning back to the deputy, he said, "Call Patterson and DeFreeze. Tell them I'll be doing an end-around."

"By yourself?"

"That's what I said."

"I thought Agent Bolen said that except for sweeping the canyon, we should stay put here."

"He did. But then, he's not here, is he?" Focusing his attention on the mouth of the canyon, the sheriff said to the lanky deputy, "That light you saw—the zap—was there any sound associated with it?"

"Not that I recall."

"Hmm," said the sheriff, continuing his struggle to put a face on the mysterious light. "Strange. Real strange." Turning toward his cruiser, his brow wrinkled in thought, he said to the deputy, "No matter what happens, don't do anything stupid. Remember, I'll be up there running point ahead of Patterson and DeFreeze. If this all turns sour, I don't want you dropping any jolly-duck surprises on my head."

"Gotcha, Sheriff. And if Agent Bolen shows up, what do I tell him?"

The sheriff smiled as he crunched along the road's gravel shoulder back toward his car. "Tell him to go find a friend."

The taillight on Roland Septian's Kawasaki flashed bright red as, banking into the back side of a lengthy curve, he prepared to slingshot past Rios. Powering up, he rocketed out of the curve at just under seventy. Within seconds he was a car length behind Rios and closing fast at eighty-five.

Recognizing the high-pitched whine of a café racer, Carmen turned and glanced out the cab's back window to see the muzzle of a Mack-10 machine pistol. "Walker! Get down!" A spray of bullets riddled the cab as Carmen pulled Rios down in his seat and the motorcycle roared past. The pickup swerved out of control, into the oncoming lane and back across the double yellow line before angling into the canyon wall. Sparks filled the air as the truck scraped seventy feet along the rock face before coming to a stop. Thirty yards down the highway the motorcycle made a quick turn and headed back.

Rios and Carmen hugged the floor as a second barrage of automatic fire peppered the cab. "Carmen, out the door!" screamed Rios, as the motorcycle turned around for a third run. Carmen opened her door, banging it into the rock wall, and rolled out of the truck and down onto the ground as Rios struggled with the steering wheel, straining to angle the truck's front tires toward the highway. Wiggling over the transmission hump, he then reached back and floored the accelerator. As the truck lurched to straddle the highway, he rolled out the door and down onto Carmen. The screech of the motorcycle braking and the crunch of metal crashing into metal reminded him of the killing sounds of war.

A mushroom of flames rose twenty feet into the air as the Kawasaki's fuel tank exploded, sending Septian careening head over heels across the highway and down the rocky forty-foot cliff. A second explosion erupted as Rios lifted his weight off Carmen. Moving around the cab in a half crouch, with Carmen desperately clutching his belt, he circled the truck's front bumper and duck-walked his way to the highway's edge, toward a plume of black smoke rising from the creek bed below.

Carmen shaded her eyes as she and Rios peered over the edge of the highway and down at the mangled remains of a Kawasaki café racer, its front tire sunk several feet into a sandbar. The nauseating smell of gasoline and burning rubber penetrated the air. Still in a crouch, Rios wrapped an arm around Carmen, pulled her to him, and scanned the wreckage, looking for signs of life. After several minutes they realized, as they hugged one another, that there would be none.

*   *   *

Jack Kimbrough enjoyed the crackle and pop of underbrush and the enticing aroma coming from his high-mesa blaze. The fire, which had begun as a series of perfectly timed hot spots, was not a broad circle of flames.

"That smell—isn't it tantalizing?" said Kimbrough, glancing at Emerson Walls before lowering his binoculars.

Walls responded with a grunt. They were twenty yards beyond the ring of fire, protected from it by a wide bog. "It won't be for very long. Another forty acres catches, and trust me, you'll be glad you're standing over here on the sidelines. Ever been in a fire before?" asked Walls, expecting Kimbrough's answer to be no.

"Yes. When I was a kid. My grandmother's house burned to the ground." Kimbrough paused, his voice barely a whisper. "Her braids went up in flames as she carried me from the house. She suffered third-degree burns to most of her face, but other than that, she barely had a scratch. After the burns healed, she looked like a mummy. I always hated the way she smelled after that."

"Then you know the power of fire."

"Very well, since I was the one who started it."

Trying his best not to look shocked, Walls turned his attention to the two cargo containers in the center of the meadow, watching through binoculars as the fire snaked its way toward them. He watched as Ariel Roundtree and his men, outfitted in Trigenics firefighting gear, separated into two groups of five along opposite sides of the trailers and prepared for their assault on the blaze.

"When will Roundtree and his men make their move?" asked Kimbrough.

"They've been trained not to lift a finger against the fire until they're totally surrounded by it," said Walls.

"Then what?"

"They'll control it as it fills in the circle."

"Before it reaches the trailers, you mean?"

Walls shot Kimbrough a look of surprise. "Yes. Have you forgotten the drill?"

"And the choppers?" said Kimbrough.

Walls checked his watch. "They'll be here in precisely twenty-five minutes. What's with all the questions, Jack? I'm carrying out your frickin' orders."

"Just checking," said Kimbrough, wondering how long it would be before the thermal-sensitive plastic explosive he'd had Rebecca Ellerby pay Ariel Roundtree to cache beneath the lips of the cargo containers exploded, spiraling depleted-uranium-contaminated shrapnel everywhere. The explosive he'd placed himself was added insurance that there would be a shrapnel bath for everyone.

Forcing back a smile, he considered the long-term implications of his plan. If all went well and none of his firefighters was killed, he'd have nearly a dozen new research subjects peppered with the contaminated shrapnel. He'd also have a cadre of Navajos with just the right prior stress exposure and genetic makeup to afford him the chance to institute a long-term study of the evolutionary effects of heat shock protein on humans. In six months, maybe even less, he'd have enough in vivo research data to bring not only Central Asian strongmen but world powers as well knocking at his door. In the end, his experiment would speak to the very essence of human protective development, and perhaps even launch the first serious contemplation of human invincibility. Armies, governments, and mercenaries, not to mention the broader world of science, would camp on his doorstep.

All he needed to do now was demonstrate that his theory worked in practice. He had only to prove that a few unsuspecting Indians who'd had the youthful misfortune of exercising gamecocks on discarded uranium tailings could end up decades later blessed with a heat-shock-protein-induced protective development mechanism capable of shielding them against the truly catastrophic. Everything was about to fall into place.

Turning his attention from the fire back to Walls, Kimbrough checked his watch. "When do we move out of harm's way?"

"Just before the fire engulfs the containers. Roundtree will signal me. The choppers will swoop in, remove the containers, and we'll get our asses down the hill. You've always claimed the Navajos only need a thirty-minute exposure to the superheated uranium for the experiment to work, Jack. Hope you're right."

"And if something goes wrong?" asked Kimbrough, thinking about the explosives he and Roundtree had planted, second-guessing himself for keeping Walls in the dark.

"Nothing will. Roundtree and his men could do this in their sleep."

"But if something does?" said Kimbrough, his tone insistent.

"Then we're out of here in nothing flat. The men all know the drill."

"Sounds good enough."

Walls nodded, eyeing Kimbrough suspiciously. "Why so jumpy, Jack? Maybe you should've stayed at home."

"Guess it's the price you pay for unraveling one of nature's great mysteries."

"Whatever," said Walls, watching Roundtree's men continue to beat back the fire. "A half-hour from now there won't be anything to show we were here but a burned-out meadow. And believe it or not, next summer everything will come back green."

Kimbrough eyed his watch nervously, aware that in less than twenty minutes the catastrophic explosion he needed to test his heat shock theory would go off as planned. He'd never fully understood why the Navajos believed they were simply testing the ability of Trigenics fire-retardant gear to withstand a superheated fire. All he knew was that Roundtree had sold them on the idea. Weeks earlier he had calculated how far away from the blast he'd need to be in order to avoid flying shrapnel. Now he planned to double the distance. Suppressing a smile, he watched as the Navajos became hemmed in by the circle of fire. "Less than twenty minutes," he said, tapping the face of his watch and glancing skyward.

"Exactly. Just like we planned," said Walls, convinced that at this late stage of the game nothing was likely to go wrong.

CHAPTER
42

Warren Anderson pulled his cruiser to a stop several yards from where Carmen and Rios stood staring down a craggy embankment toward Plateau Creek. Dazed and trembling, Carmen watched spits of flame and black smoke rise in the air.

"Are you all right?" asked the sheriff, racing up to her as she shivered in Rios's protective grasp.

"Yes," said Carmen, her answer weak and hollow.

"What happened?"

"I don't know—it happened so fast—he had a machinegun."

Rios nodded as he walked Carmen away from the edge of the drop-off. "Septian?" asked the sheriff, staring down at the motorcycle's twisted remains.

"Probably," said Rios.

"There's probably not much left of him," said the sheriff, staring at the black smoke. "I'll call an ambulance."

"No rush." Rios glanced back over the drop-off, at what looked to be either a charred tree limb or a severed arm poking from beneath the frame of the motorcycle, and pulled Carmen tightly to him.

Minutes later, Carmen sat quietly in the backseat of the sheriff's cruiser with a blanket draped over her shoulders and a bottle of water clutched in one hand. After drinking a half pint of tepid orange juice from the sheriff's emergency medical kit, she had mostly recovered from the adrenaline rush that still had her a little rattled. The *rat-a-tat-tat* of Septian's weapon had brought back childhood memories—fragmented images, fragmented bodies, the death and destruction too much the same.

The sheriff had called Mesa County dispatch for a mountain rescue team, but he'd been told that it would be at least an hour before they could get there. Wiggling a pinkie around in one of the dozens of bullet holes in the rear quarter panel of Rios's truck, the sheriff shook his head. "You've got nine lives—I'd swear to it, Walker."

"Or a guardian angel." Rios inspected the bullet holes. "Different gun than the one back at my house."

The sheriff nodded in agreement. "Nasty."

"The son of a bitch was probably packing grenades, too. It's a wonder he didn't blow himself up."

"Sounds like he was looking to start a war."

"Could be he's already part of one." Rios eyed the sheriff quizically. "Ever heard of depleted uranium?"

The sheriff's eyebrows almost touched. "As a matter of fact, I have. Heard it discussed at an antiterrorism conference a few months back. The military uses it to harden shell casings. What's the connection to Septian?"

"I think—"

Carmen bolted from the cruiser's backseat, her right arm jutting skyward. "Walker! Walker!" she yelled, pointing toward a plume of smoke in the distance.

"I'll be damned," said Rios. "I was right."

"Kimbrough?" said the sheriff, gazing at the smoke rising from the vicinity of Chalk Mountain.

"I'd bet money on it."

The sheriff jumped in his cruiser and grabbed the radio mike. "Mesa One, Anderson here; come up, come up."

"Mesa One," came the staticky response. "That you, Sheriff? I can barely hear you."

"Yeah. The reception's terrible in this canyon. Got a fire and probable armed suspects up at Chalk Mountain. I'm on my way there. Requesting fire dispatch and backup."

Only the words "on my way" were audible to the deputy on the other end.

"You and Carmen will have to stay here, Walker," said the sheriff, cradling the mike and realizing that Rios had slid into the backseat next to Carmen.

"No way," said Rios.

"No civilians, Walker. It's procedure."

Rios leaned forward, elbows on the seat back. "So we get to stay here and wait for Septian to come back?"

"He's dead."

"You're certain of that?"

Looking at Carmen and then back into the eyes of his closest friend, the sheriff said, "Damn it, Walker, I can't break my own rules."

"Then bend 'em."

The sheriff glanced toward the plume of smoke rising in the distance. "Shit! Damn you, Walker Rios." Starting the engine, he reached beneath the seat and retrieved a stockless Mossberg shotgun. Placing the shotgun on the front seat, he then grabbed his police mike and barked over the airwaves, "Mesa County One, I'm rolling."

The response on the other end was suddenly crystal clear. "Gotcha, Sheriff. Backup's on the way."

"Out," said the sheriff, flooring the accelerator and flinging gravel against Rios's bullet-riddled pickup, slamming Rios and Carmen back into their seats.

Ariel Roundtree felt disoriented and listless. He was running on empty. Things seemed almost the same as they had during their practice runs in the desert, but somehow there was a subtle difference. The twin cargo containers next to the trailers in the middle of the fire zone were identical; he was certain of that. And the encroaching fire was nothing new. Even his shiny silver fire-retardant suit was a perfect match, right down to the adjustment toggle on the right sleeve that controlled the air filter in his headgear. But there was a difference. He could feel it in his bones.

At first he suspected the difference had something to do with the mesa's swirling winds, but after watching the fire burn for a while, he realized that wasn't it. Then he'd thought that maybe his uneasiness had something to do with the fact that the surrounding forest made everything seem closer and darker than in the desert. But then, that wasn't the problem either. Struggling to cope with his edginess, he barked an order to Ricky Little Dove on his two-way. "You're lagging behind, Ricky. Move your men!" he shouted into the mike, waving frantically as if he expected Little Dove to be able to see him through the dense curtain of smoke, and questioning himself for putting someone like Ricky in charge. "Gotcha," came the reply. The word, a tag-line from his youth, stopped Roundtree cold. It was a playful word that reminded him of the endless games of hide-and-seek he'd played as a boy, and it suddenly had him terrified.

"Ricky, hold off a second."

"Okay, but why?"

"Just stay put." Roundtree stared across the field and away from the fire in an effort to locate Kimbrough and Walls. Stashing his mike, he slipped a pair of binoculars from the safety of his fireproof jacket and scanned the entire field. Finally concentrating his search on the patch of slough grass where he'd last seen Kimbrough and Walls, Roundtree lowered the binoculars and mumbled, "Shit, they're gone! Ricky, something's not right here! I want you to back your men off," Roundtree shouted into his radio mike.

"What's the problem?" said Little Dove.

"Screw that for now. Just move your men back. I'm ordering my line back too."

"If you say so."

"I say so," said Roundtree, staring into the smoky haze and hoping, for the sake of his men and everything they'd been through for the past four months, that what he was thinking was wrong. As he barked the orders that sent his men scurrying away from the two cargo containers, he wished he'd never had the misfortune of knowing Emerson Walls or of having served under him during Desert Storm.

The nose of Emerson Walls's Humvee broke out of the smoke, its two-and-a-half-ton mass directed straight at Sheriff Anderson's cruiser. The sheriff jammed on his brakes and swerved to avoid a collision, sending the cruiser slamming into the wall of the canyon. With sparks and windshield glass flying, the cruiser came to a stop a few feet from a boulder twice its size.

Anderson grabbed his radio mike and screamed, "Patterson, DeFreeze, come in, come in! Anderson here, come in."

Rios shouted, "There were two of them, Warren. I got a good look."

A wave of garble erupted from the police radio. "Patter . . . here . . . Sheriff . . ."

"Son of a bitch!" the sheriff grumbled. Tapping the mike sharply against his palm before speaking into it, he bellowed, "Patterson, you've got a Humvee with two men in it headed down your way! Stop the damn vehicle!"

"Pat . . . Sheriff . . . I . . ."

"Patterson, just stop the damn thing!" he said, slamming down the mike and turning his attention to the backseat. "Everybody okay back there?"

"Yeah," said Rios.

"I'm in one piece," said Carmen.

"Good." Then, eyeing the smoke in the distance, he tipped his hat back on his head and said, "This time we wait for backup."

"Fine by me," said Rios as the heavy thump of helicopter rotors sounded in the distance.

"Damn!" said the sheriff, looking skyward.

"Yours or theirs?" said Rios, shading his eyes.

"Don't know. And I can't call anybody to find out."

"They're getting closer," said Rios.

"And lower," said Carmen, recalling the horrifying sounds of her youth.

"Gunships?" asked the sheriff.

"Too big," said Carmen. "But there're two of them. I'm sure of that. I used to count them in my sleep. They're lower now and hovering."

"Right on the mark," said Rios, nodding in agreement.

"You're sure?" asked the sheriff.

"Yes."

The sheriff slapped the radio mike again and barked, "Patterson, over," to the sound of white noise.

Ariel Roundtree kept telling himself that he should have been gone by now, but he wasn't. He should have been headed off the mountain and on his way to collect the final five thousand dollars in blood money he'd been promised by the Ellerby woman for setting up his Navajo buddies.

But instead of tooling down easy street, he was busy directing the hookup of a cargo container to a giant, twin-rotored helicopter, aware that somewhere along the line he'd let Navajo blood ties and sentiment for his friends get the better of him. Still questioning his recent string of decisions and wondering who the woman who had promised him twenty-five thousand dollars actually worked for, Roundtree watched Ricky Little Dove complete the first cable hookup and then jump from the top of the first cargo container to the second one, only seconds before the first container lifted skyward. Fifty feet above the ground the chopper seemed to stall, then drifted off to the west in a thumping drone.

When Roundtree turned to check out the second cargo container, he realized that Little Dove was struggling with the cable hookup. "There's not enough slack in the cable," Little Dove screamed down to him from his smoky perch atop the container. "The chopper's grapples are gonna be too fuckin' big."

"It's the same setup we've used all along!" shouted Roundtree, glancing back toward the approaching fire.

"Then something's wrong!" Little Dove shouted. "Check the cable out from down there."

Roundtree rushed to check the first of the two three-inch braided cables looped around the container. The first cable looked fine. Running his asbestos-gloved hand down the cable from eye level toward the ground, he could feel plenty of slack. Feeling woozy, he moved to the second cable as the raging fire moved to within ten feet of the containers. If Little Dove stayed on top of the cargo container much longer, the soles of his shoes would melt. "Shit!" Roundtree mumbled, realizing that several feet of the second cable had been pinched beneath the lip of the massive container.

"I've gotta get off this thing before I fry," screamed Little Dove. "Did you find out what's wrong?"

"The cable's wedged beneath the bottom of the container!" shouted Roundtree, staring at the cable and the knot of the plastic explosive he'd placed there earlier. "We'll never get the cable out in time. Wave the chopper off."

Frantically Little Dove waved his arms back and forth above his head. The lumbering Chinook rose and banked slowly off to the east, seconds before Little Dove jumped to the ground.

"Let's get the hell out of here," screamed Roundtree. Fumbling with the doughy plastique, he removed it along with the two explosive balls Kimbrough had secretly cached next to it. Slipping the mysterious additional knots of explosive into his pocket, he shouted into his two-way radio, "Everybody head for the bog." The two columns of men ran toward safety, Roundtree between them, racing toward a narrow window in the ring of smoke and fire. He couldn't help thinking about the plastique and the grenade he'd brought along for good measure. Somewhere along the way, they would surely explode. Jamming his hand into a pocket in his fire-retardant jacket and fingering the grenade, he stopped and waved the other men past him, watching as they struggled to run in their cumbersome suits, knowing that as their leader, he'd made the right decision.

CHAPTER
43

After twenty years in law enforcement, very few things still surprised Warren Anderson. But the sight of ten men dressed like astronauts, clambering over one another in a race toward safety while fire nipped at their heels, was a definite first.

"Hold your fire!" he shouted into a bullhorn to two of his deputies and a startled-looking Everard Bolen. All three men stood, guns at the ready, calf-deep in frigid bog mud. "Stop right where you are," Anderson commanded the fleeing men. "This is the Mesa County sheriff." When the men kept running, his warning shot into the air finally brought them to a halt.

"Hands behind your heads and down on your knees!" bellowed the sheriff, as one of the men turned back toward the fiery haze. "You, off to the left: hands behind your head and down on the ground."

Ignoring the sheriff, Ariel Roundtree continued sidestepping back toward the fire, telling himself with each step that there was no way he could go back to scrounging aluminum cans and mopping floors.

"Out of the smoke and down on the ground!" bellowed the sheriff, his weapon aimed squarely at Roundtree. "Now!"

Roundtree looked at the sheriff and then back toward the remaining cargo container, now completely engulfed in flames. Through the haze he could hear the container's metal pop and see the supporting framework buckle. Glancing back toward the sheriff, he saw his men down on their knees in the mud with their hands behind their heads. "Okay," he said. Snapping the pin from his grenade, he dropped on it, hugging it tightly to his chest. Counting to himself, *one, one thousand, two, one thousand, three, one thousand,* he smiled and inhaled the smell of charred earth, knowing that he would never have to mop floors again.

Emerson Walls could barely keep the Humvee on the road. "We can't go any faster," he said, responding to Kimbrough's demand for more speed. "Unless you want to end up over the side of this road and down in a creek. Hell, we're lucky we didn't smash head-on into that cop car."

Ignoring Walls's comments, Kimbrough said, "Something's wrong. Both choppers should've passed overhead by now. There's only been one."

"I can count," said Walls, his eyes glued to the winding road. "Things are probably just a little off schedule. They're still less than six minutes behind the clock."

"Don't think so," said Kimbrough, aware that by now his explosives, as well as Roundtree's, should have gone off. "We need to get off this mountain. Speed it up."

"Can't. The road gets worse after this straightaway. Nothing but switchbacks the rest of the way."

"What's that?" said Kimbrough, peering through the windshield, inching forward in his seat. "There's something up ahead."

"A wrecked truck, that's all," said Walls, swerving to miss Rios's disabled pickup. "Calm down; don't piss your pants." Walls downshifted, preparing for the upcoming curves. Halfway into the first curve, he saw something straddling the highway. Seconds later he realized he was speeding toward a fifteen-ton police riot vehicle.

"Dodge it!" screamed Kimbrough.

"Are you crazy? That thing's outfitted with enough artillery to blow us to the moon. Besides, there's not enough room to squeeze around it."

Kimbrough slipped across the seat and jammed his foot onto the accelerator. "What the fuck!" screamed Walls as the vehicle lurched to the left and Kimbrough grabbed the steering wheel.

"Idiot!" Walls bellowed. Locking his left hand on the steering wheel, he cocked his right arm and slammed an elbow into Kimbrough's temple. Kimbrough groaned, listed to the right, and slumped over in his seat as the Humvee continued speeding toward the riot vehicle. Realizing that the accelerator was stuck, Walls slammed on his brakes and wrestled with the steering wheel as the Humvee fishtailed toward the riot vehicle and a sea of flashing lights. He held his breath as it zigzagged to a stop less than thirty feet from the jolly duck. Shaking his head, he glanced over at Kimbrough, who was holding his head and moaning.

"It's important to know when you're outnumbered," said Walls to his dazed boss. "It's a cardinal military rule," he added as someone shouted through a bullhorn, "Stay seated and keep your hands on the damn wheel!"

There was nothing Carmen could do for Ariel Roundtree. In fact, there was little to find. She said, "He had to be aware of what he was doing." Stone-faced, she looked up at Rios and the sheriff. "Must have held the grenade right next to his heart."

A rush of fiery pops and crackles filled the air, escalating as Agent Bolen interrupted the on-site postmortem. "A radiation decontamination team is on the way from Grand Junction," said Bolen, glancing down at Roundtree's body. "Why the samurai act?"

"Don't know," said the sheriff. "And we probably won't until we interrogate the rest of the men. One thing for certain, though: He didn't want to talk to us." The sheriff turned to where two of his deputies stood with their riot guns trained on a group of nine men handcuffed together in a circle. "They're Navajos to a man," said the sheriff. "Tight-lipped, as a rule. We may never know what happened."

A sudden gust of wind darted across the meadow, kicking up sparks, fiery knots of sagebrush, and smoldering pine straw. Starved for oxygen and dying from a lack of fuel, the ring of fire around the remaining cargo container slowly subsided.

Carmen watched the flames fade. "I think maybe we should move upwind," she said. "That container out there's probably more than a tad radioactive."

"Let's move back uphill," said the sheriff, motioning for his two deputies to move the handcuffed men. "You, too, Walker," he added, watching as Rios, down on one knee, examined the gold chain still looped around what remained of Ariel Round-tree's neck.

When Rios didn't budge, Carmen interrupted: "Is there a water source nearby?"

"Not really," said the sheriff. "Why?"

"Detox for those firefighters. They need it."

"I told you, there's a decontamination team on the way," said Bolen.

"Too little too late. They need a first-stage detox right now. They've been fighting what amounts to a low-level radioactive fire. They need to get out of that gear they're in and into water right now."

The sheriff stroked his chin. "There is one water source: that jolly duck I called in. The thing's got a hundred-and-fifty-gallon water tank and a high-pressure hose hookup on board. Patterson," the sheriff called out, "find out where that jolly duck is and see if we can't get it up here right now."

The deputy snapped his radio mike off his shoulder and barked the sheriff's request into it.

"Now," said the sheriff, looking around at everyone, "like the good doctor said, let's all move upwind."

Carmen took a step back toward Rios as he slipped the gold chain from around Roundtree's neck. "Bag this, will you, Warren?" said Rios.

"It's probably contaminated," said Carmen, holding her hand up in protest.

"I'll chance it," said Rios, handing the chain to the sheriff and watching as Anderson slipped it into a plastic bag.

"Why such an interest in that chain?" asked Carmen as they trudged upwind from the fire.

"It wasn't the chain that interested me. It was what was left of the medal dangling from it."

"Special?" asked Carmen.

"You bet."

"What was it?"

"Silver Star. Right up there next to the Congressional Medal."

"Guess he was a man who'd seen his share of firefights," said Carmen.

"None like this, I'd bet," said Rios, glancing toward the grassy bog and noticing a sheriff's deputy running their way. "But the medal may explain his connection to Walls and help to explain why he blew himself up."

"Jolly duck's on the way, Sheriff," said the out-of-breath deputy.

"Great."

"And there's good news from down below," said the deputy. "They've got two men in custody six miles down the road. Can you believe they were stupid enough to try and ram your jolly duck? Real dumb-shits. Do the names Kimbrough and Walls mean anything to you?"

"Sure do," said the sheriff, winking at Rios.

"Any news from down there on a man named Septian?" asked Rios.

"No," said the deputy. "Just those two names I gave the sheriff. . . . Who?"

"A ghost from Christmas past," said Rios, picking up the pace, squeezing Carmen's hand and squinting into the setting sun as they continued moving upwind.

CHAPTER

44

It was midnight by the time Carmen and Rios finished their FBI debriefings. Except for thirty minutes of downtime, most of it spent with two EPA agents responsible for their decontamination, they'd undergone nonstop questioning. Although their radiation levels were found to be within normal limits, a third, more intimidating EPA agent had read them both a legal-sounding directive, made them sign it, and hovered around as they showered, ultimately confiscating their clothes.

Now, dressed in blaze-orange prisoners' garb and county-jail-issued sneakers, they sat in Warren Anderson's office undergoing a final debriefing.

The sheriff, dressed in his own decontamination outfit, a heavy Air Force Academy sweatsuit and red 1950s-retro high-top Converse All-Stars, looked up from the legal pad he'd been writing on, adjusted his reading glasses, and ran a hand across his brow. "Seems hot in here," he said.

"Not in these tents we're wearing." Rios snapped one of the sleeves of his oversized smock. "Your problem is you're dressed for winter."

Ignoring Rios, the sheriff pushed the sleeves of his sweatshirt up above his elbows and sat back in his chair. "Where was I? Oh, yeah, what made you suspect that Kimbrough was trucking around radioactive material?"

Rios let out a half-sigh. "Warren, we've been through all that with Bolen. You know as well as we do that we didn't know this had anything to do with stolen radioactive material until you told us about Walls's cleanup responsibilities after Desert Storm."

"Simmer down, Walker." The sheriff shoved his papers aside. "I'm just doing my job."

"Well, it's not *our* job," said Rios, the annoyance creeping into his voice. "Bolen had us here under lock and key, grilling us for hours. We've been asked the same damn questions fifty different ways."

The sheriff peered over his reading glasses. "And you'll be asked again. This isn't about a couple of kids out joyriding, or an assault case, or even your run-of-the-mill homicide. We're talking multiple murders here, Walker. And a possible breach of national security. You were an intelligence officer—you know the score."

The look on Rios's face suddenly turned reflective as he found himself thinking about the yellow cyanide capsules he and Flora Jean had packed around during Desert Storm. "Guess I do," he said, the words barely audible.

Sensing Walker's frustration, Carmen chimed in. "What's the story on Kimbrough? Who's interrogating him?"

"Can't say. Other than that he's in custody along with that arms agent of his, Emerson Walls."

"Arms agent!" Walker's eyes ballooned.

"That's what I said. The FBI boys aren't excluding espionage."

"And you're glomming onto the brainwaves of those nitwits. Warren, come on—espionage?" Rios laughed. "What you've got here are a couple of egos out of control and the potential for someone to rake in lots of money. And maybe on top of those two things, Walls and Kimbrough got their jollies from killing off Native Americans, or simply wielding power. But espionage? No way!"

"Walker's right," said Carmen. "This whole thing's been about machismo and greenbacks from the start. Remember, it started out with cockfighting. What's more macho than that?"

"Or more godlike, when you consider what the bottom line

was with Kimbrough's experiment," said Rios. "The SOB probably really does believe he can redirect the way humans evolve."

The sheriff frowned. "There's more than a couple of egos and a deity complex at stake here. Sure, Kimbrough may have needed his ego stroked, but I'm betting that what Walls, those Navajos I've got locked up, and the three or four dead people strung out along the way were really looking forward to was a big fat payday."

"Any of the firefighters talking?" asked Rios.

"Nope. Kimbrough and Walls are stonewalling, still waiting for their lawyers. And the Navajos have been about as cooperative as clams." The sheriff shrugged and looked at Carmen. "You're the doctor here. Think you can give me a bottom line on what this heat shock thing was really all about?"

"I've got one that speaks to the science," said Carmen. "As to why the people involved did what they did, sorry, Sheriff, you're on your own."

"Run your scientific angle by me. At least it's a start."

"Simple. Kimbrough was trying to produce the human equivalent of Luke Redstone's invincible birds by superheating a low-grade radiation contaminant that would trigger a latent heat shock protective development response. In order to do it, he chose a group of men who'd been primed for the response since childhood. When you come right down to it, Kimbrough's premise isn't really new. What's new is that he tried it out on a group of previously sensitized humans. By further reducing the heat shock protein levels in a group of men who had experienced HSP90 depletions as children, Kimbrough expected to end up with a cadre of human guinea pigs he could experiment on for years. All he had to do to succeed was subject his guinea pigs to a new HSP-reducing catastrophic event."

"Walls's depleted-uranium scraps," said the sheriff.

"You got it. Who knows? Over time he may have seen dramatic increases in muscle mass or watched a new protective coating develop in their skin. In the long run he may have had some very interesting human protective development alterations to sell."

"Or he could have eventually gone into the mercenary business or espionage game, touting invincible gladiators for hire," said Anderson.

"Come on, Warren. You're starting to sound like you're CIA or FBI," said Carmen.

"You don't understand yet, do you, Doc?" said the sheriff, looking to Rios for support. "Sooner or later you're going to have to clue her in, Walker."

"I will," said Rios, keenly aware that there was more than a kernel of truth in what the sheriff was saying.

Anderson looked up and rustled his papers. "Well, anyway, Kimbrough's out of the invincibility business now."

"Everything's settled, then?" said Rios, waiting to hear the words *You're free to go.* "Kimbrough was on a money-grabbing ego trip. Walls was out to make a bundle peddling his depleted-uranium wares. And our Navajo firefighters were looking for a new lease on life and a pocket-full of cash. Only one question remains: What about Septian?"

"Muscle," said the sheriff. "Plain and simple."

Rios shook his head. "I'm not referring to his job assignment, Warren. I'm talking about his persistence. He locked on to Carmen and me like a heat-seeking missile."

"His ticket's been punched, Walker."

"You got a body?"

"No. But our mountain rescue boys found a couple of fingertips and more splattered blood than one person could afford to lose. When the sun comes up, they'll find the rest of him."

"Would you two quit one-upping each other?" said Carmen.

"Sorry," said the sheriff.

"Are we done?" she asked, looking washed out and weary.

"For today."

"Good." Carmen rose from her chair and turned to Rios. "I've had enough. I called Ket and told her what happened. I think I scared her half to death. She's expecting us."

"Us! At one A.M.?"

"Yes. It may be my only fence-mending opportunity for years."

"We're dressed like convicts," said Rios. "Besides, she doesn't like American men, remember?"

Expressionless, Carmen said, "There's something involved here that neither of you can possibly understand. Something as old as Vietnamese culture. Ket sees our brush with death as an omen—one that offers her an opportunity to save face and me a chance to restore my reputation. She'll behave differently when we drop by this time, Walker. You can count on it." Carmen paused and took a deep breath. "I'm going to see her with or without you. Please come."

Rios tugged at the sleeve of his smock and shook his head. "Are we free to leave?"

The sheriff shrugged. "Yes, but you'll hear from me tomorrow. And early."

"We'll cherish the thought." Rios followed Carmen toward the door. Catching a glimpse of himself in one of the room's two-way interrogation mirrors, he considered the fact that his jail-house garb probably wouldn't win him any brownie points with Ket Tran.

CHAPTER
45

Maybe I should stay here," said Rios, fidgeting uncomfortably in the front seat of Warren Anderson's borrowed car, fumbling with the seat adjustment as he peered past Carmen into the night, toward Ket Tran's house, trying his best to forget about the fact that in less than twenty-four hours he'd come close to losing his home, totaled his truck, and almost been killed twice.

"You can't," said Carmen. "That would make you a coward in her eyes. This has to be on her terms. There's no other way."

"Okay," said Rios, feeling the muscles in his face tighten, unable to understand why he was finding it so difficult to confront a diminutive Vietnamese woman old enough to be his mother.

"And, Walker, let me do the talking."

Rios nodded, scanning the darkness. On his previous visit he remembered seeing a cobblestone walkway curve its way up to the house; now there was only blackness. An overhead light flashed on inside the car as he swung the door open. Almost magically, the walkway appeared. An owl hooted in the distance, in sync with their footsteps crunching across the graveled drive. Taking Rios's hand and smiling, Carmen said, "Just follow my lead, and whatever you do, act as though you're here at her request."

It wasn't until they reached the wraparound screened-in porch that Rios realized that lights were on inside the house. The screen door opened with a creak as Carmen pulled it back. Moving toward the ornately carved russet-colored front door, she slipped off her shoes, nodding for Rios to do the same.

Rios was down on one knee unlacing a shoe when Carmen shook him by the shoulder. "Walker, get up. I hear her coming." Kicking off his left shoe and then his right, he sprang erect just as Ket Tran partially opened the door.

Dressed in an aquamarine silk cheongsam with braided gold threads that interlinked across the front to form perfect diamonds, Ket appeared to Rios as if she belonged in an imperial palace. Her elegantly styled salt-and-pepper hair framed the perfectly oval face with smooth, delicate features. She looked taller than he remembered, but her eyes were just as penetrating.

"I'd like to reintroduce you to my friend, Walker Rios," said Carmen, bowing gracefully and watching as Rios did the same.

"Mr. Rios. I'm pleased to meet you once again," said Ket, ignoring the bright orange outfits and Rios's sling.

"The pleasure's mine," he replied awkwardly.

"Please come in," said Ket. Swinging the door back all the way, she turned and walked down a hallway that led to a dimly lit living room filled with East Asian and Polynesian antiques and California-mission-style furniture.

"Please have a seat," said Ket, motioning for Rios to sit down. "I've brewed some spiced tea. You like tea, don't you, Mr. Rios?"

"Yes." Rios glanced at Carmen, hoping he'd said the right thing.

"Carmen, please get the tea service. It's in the kitchen."

Carmen swallowed hard, marveling at how efficiently Ket was separating her from Rios. Custom wouldn't allow her to go to the kitchen and return to interrupt what by then would clearly be a private conversation. She'd have to wait for Ket's invitation to reenter the room. She eyed Rios nervously as she moved toward the kitchen, thinking, *Please, Walker, don't say the wrong thing.*

When she was certain Carmen was out of earshot, Ket took a seat in an uncomfortable-looking high-backed wooden chair. "I understand that you and Carmen had a brush with death this afternoon," she said, adjusting herself in the seat, her tone surprisingly matter-of-fact.

"We did."

"And you thwarted it?"

"Yes."

"You are aware, of course, that Carmen has faced death before?"

"She's told me about your escape from Vietnam."

"I see. Unfortunately, Mr. Rios, that's not the encounter I mean."

Rios looked puzzled. "She's never mentioned anything else."

"It would be too painful." Barely a muscle moved as Ket sat forward in her chair. "You are familiar with My Lai?"

Rios's face stiffened as he nodded that he was.

"Then you can understand her pain."

"Yes," he said, thinking back to the first time he'd ever heard the words *My Lai*. He had been a five-year-old, fascinated by airplanes and moon rockets. Photos of the second U.S. moon landing had filled newspaper front pages when news about the American military's slaughter of Vietnamese civilians at My Lai had broken in late 1969. He didn't know why he remembered the words. Perhaps it had something to do with their pleasing sound. But the words had stuck with him, just as certain other words from his childhood had, and when they resurfaced during a junior-year college course in Asian studies, he realized that *My Lai* represented the antithesis of anything pleasing.

Later, during his tour in the Persian Gulf War, when he realized that because of an intelligence breakdown he had temporarily placed Iraqi civilians in harm's way, he wondered whether a similar error had also contributed to the 1968 massacre of somewhere between two hundred and four hundred Vietnamese men, women, and children at My Lai. During Desert Storm the horror of My Lai was never repeated, as far as he knew, but the possibility that it could have been remained imprinted in his subconscious during most of his tour.

"You look wounded," said Ket, noticing Rios's pale face.

"You were both there?" he asked after a lengthy pause.

Ket Tran nodded. "Running, screaming, clawing in the dirt to escape your army's cruelties."

"I'm sorry."

"It has branded Carmen's life. She lost her mother there. I lost a sister."

"What about her father?" said Rios, regretting the question the instant he'd uttered it.

"He deserted her. After all, she was *my den*," said Ket, realizing by the look on Rios's face that he understood the term. "In my country, being *my den* means you're less than half of nothing, Mr. Rios."

"This isn't Vietnam. Carmen has nothing to prove."

Ket gave Rios a sad, knowing smile. "Only that she's worthy, Mr. Rios, only that."

"She's worthy to me."

Ket shot Rios a stare that told him he'd once again said the wrong thing, just as Carmen reentered the room. "Spiced tea for everyone," said Carmen dutifully, hoping that she'd somehow be able to make amends later for interrupting. "It's . . ."

The look on Ket's face told Carmen she'd returned at an awkward moment. Maintaining her composure, Carmen set three delicate teacups and their fragile saucers down on an antique teak-inlaid table. Filling one cup with tea, she handed it to Rios. "Solve the world's problems?" she said boldly.

"No," said Rios, trying not to look self-conscious.

"Mr. Rios and I were discussing Vietnam."

Carmen moved to serve Ket without responding. Pouring the tea, she looked Ket squarely in the eye. "Have you told Walker about the Vietnamese tradition of second chances?"

"No, I haven't." Caught off guard by Carmen's assertiveness, Ket relaxed back in her seat and took a sip of tea.

"Would you, please?" asked Carmen, taking a seat in the chair next to Rios.

Ket looked across the coffee table at Rios, drinking in his features, studying the way he occupied his seat as well as the way he seemed almost to guard the cup and saucer he was holding. Watching how his eyes moved back and forth from her to Carmen, she said, "Carmen's talking about another place, another world."

"*La tante Ket, s'il vous plaît,*" pleaded Carmen in the language of her youth. "Share the fable of second chances with Walker."

"*Oui, s'il vous plaît,*" said Rios, hoping he wasn't overstepping his bounds. "*Je voudrais bien entendre.*"

Startled, Ket said, "*Vous parlez français?*"

"He does," said Carmen, her words erupting in a rush. "And very well."

Ket eyed Rios guardedly. For her, French represented the bridge in her life between good times and bad, Vietnam before it was divided into North and South. She had attended French-run schools, adopted French customs, even loved a Frenchman and watched him die. No American could ever appreciate what she'd once had. But Carmen's brush with death that afternoon had raised the second-chance issue, and in their stand-off over customs, by asking Carmen to drop by, she'd been the one to blink. Perhaps, she told herself, the tall, muscular American with his arm in the sling—a man who spoke a language as precious to her as young love—could appreciate her fable.

"Please," said Carmen in a final, high-pitched plea.

"*Et vous,* Mr. Rios?"

"*J'aimerais bien entendre l'histoire.*"

Ket hesitated, eyeing Carmen and then Rios, knowing that the tale of exoneration she was about to recite was designed to pardon the moral transgressions of those to whom the story was told.

Carmen edged forward in her seat, her eyes fixed on her aunt.

Ket began slowly. *Il y a longtemps en provence de Son Ha, un tigre et un singe . . .*"

Tears welled up in Carmen's eyes as she began softly translating her aunt's words from French to English, the same way she had done in her effort to master English as a child.

Long Ago in Son Ha Province

A tiger stalked a monkey
till he had him in his grasp.
But the glib, resourceful monkey
took his captor to task.

Pleading for his life, the monkey said to his foil,
"I'm blessed with knowledge of your future toil.
Free me and gain favors you'll desperately need.
Kill me and be cursed for failing to take heed."

"Why should I believe you," said the tiger so bold.
"I roam as I please; this land's mine forever to hold.
My future, silly monkey, is all up to me.
No tales of future darkness will make me set you free."

"It's not as you see it, be certain of that.
Your future is much bleaker, o powerful cat.
Free me and linger for years on this plain.
Eat me and toil for others in vain."

Cajoled into a decision he expected he'd regret,
the tiger released the monkey and started to fret.
"Don't worry, o tiger, your decision was sound,"
screamed the monkey as he scurried away on the ground.

Years passed, and the tiger grew slow and quite old,
until he was captured and caged to be sold.
As he languished behind bars and thought of his youth,
a monkey appeared who claimed to see truth.

"Freedom is yours, o tiger of yore."
With those words he opened the cage's door.
The tiger retreated with nary a backward glance.
Under cover of the monkey's chatter, he'd won a second chance.

Except for the faint ticking of an ornate, two-hundred-year-old Vietnamese clock sitting on a table near the kitchen, the room fell silent. Smiling broadly, Carmen moved across the room to pour Ket more tea. She'd heard Ket recite the fable hundreds of times, and she was aware that as the fable built slowly toward its imperative, in the eyes of her aunt, she and Rios had already been forgiven.

CHAPTER
46

The teapot was empty by the time Rios finished telling Ket the details of their bizarre heat shock adventure.

"You'll stay here tonight, then?" Rios whispered to Carmen, surprised that Ket, busy refilling the teapot in the kitchen, had left them alone.

Carmen flashed a smile. "I have to. It's part of the whole second-chance scenario. I have to spend the night under my aunt's roof to seal the bargain. I'll give you a nod when it's time for you to leave."

"Okay," said Rios, directing his attention to Ket as she returned to the room with a fresh pot of tea and a tray of Vietnamese-style ginger cookies. "You're quite a storyteller," he said, helping her with the tray.

"As are you. How do you say it again, *heat shock protein*?"

"That's right. A genetic building block capable of making humans invincible."

"A modern and quite unthinkable fable," said Ket as she took a seat. "Please, take one," she added, watching Rios expectantly eye the cookies.

He took one of the delicate cookies from a stenciled white doily, leaving a star-shaped spot of grease behind. He bit off a piece, savoring its spiciness. "Delicious," he said, smiling as Carmen took a cookie and held it in her hand as if it were a jewel.

"Now I have a second story for you," said Ket. "Another of Carmen's favorites."

They both sat munching on cookies as Ket recited a tale of

budding love. When Ket stood at the fable's end to remove the dessert tray, Carmen signaled Rios with a quick nod.

"Think I had one too many cookies," said Rios, on cue. "I should probably leave before I make a glutton of myself. Thank you for your hospitality," he said, standing and bowing to Ket.

"I'll walk you to the door," said Carmen.

Before Rios could take a step to leave, Ket said, "My Carmen likes you, Mr. Rios. Please remember, however, that I have no third-chance fables."

"I will," said Rios, realizing he'd just been put on notice.

Recognizing his dilemma, Carmen smiled, clasped one arm in his, and began walking him to the door. "I'll tell you more about Ket's rules tomorrow," she said. Grasping the front door's wrought-iron handle, she swung the door back to the flash of headlights and three reports from a rifle. She screamed as the wind rushed out of her and all of Rios's protective weight crushed her into the floor.

"You okay?" said Rios, his tone a mix of concern and raging anger.

"Yes," Carmen whispered as a second trio of shots splintered the partially open door.

Rolling away from Carmen, Rios nudged the door shut. "Get back into the house!" He watched Carmen crawl to safety as machinegun fire peppered the front of the house.

"Septian!" screamed Carmen in disbelief.

"Who else?"

"How'd he survive?"

"Nine lives, I guess."

His heart pounding, Rios began inching his way back toward Carmen when suddenly the house went dark. Seconds later, he felt a tug at his ankle. Cocking his leg to deliver a punishing kick, he looked back to see Ket Tran down on all fours. Her ankle-length kimono was pulled above her knees, and the flame from a Zippo lighter flickered in her hand. Before he could say anything, she slid an army-issue Colt .45 across the floor. As he grabbed for the .45, he realized that the sawed-off shotgun he had once awakened to rested in front of Ket.

"The phone lines are dead," said Ket.

"Septian, the man we told you about—looks like he's back."

Ket nodded.

"My cell phone's in the car," said Carmen, exasperated.

"We can head out the back. Follow me," said Ket, pivoting on one knee.

"No. Wait . . ." Rios grabbed Ket by her sleeve. "He's probably expecting that."

"We can't stay in here, Walker. He's crazy. Sooner or later he'll start tossing firebombs and grenades," said Carmen.

"The root-cellar exit," said Ket. "He can't possibly know about that. The door's camouflaged by a summer's worth of ground cover at this time of year. What do you think, Carmen?"

Carmen confirmed the choice with a tentative nod. "We'll have to chance it. It's our only way out."

"You and Ket take that exit. I'll go out the back," said Rios.

"Walker, no!"

Rios slipped the clip out of the .45, eyed it, and slammed it back in place. "Full."

"Walker, you'll be a sitting duck."

"Go with Ket," Rios said authoritatively.

"Walker, you can't."

"Carmen, move."

Hugging the floor, Carmen began crawling behind Ket. When she reached the steps that led to the root cellar, she looked back for Rios, but he was gone.

Septian checked the blood clots at the tips of three of his left fingers. The wounds were mushy and still oozing, but the codeine tabs he'd taken had dulled the pain. A bloody softball-sized divot in the back of his right thigh puckered along the margins of a crusty second-degree burn. Ignoring the pain, Septian checked the four grenades on his belt and limped toward his prey.

Following his motorcycle crash, he'd soaked his injured hand and badly burned leg in the icy waters of Plateau Creek for nearly an hour. He'd watched a riot vehicle head up the canyon, dodged a mountain rescue team, and lingered in the canyon's darkness, hidden among the rocks, until the rescuers had given up their search for the night. He'd climbed out of hiding just as Rios and Carmen were being whisked off the mesa in the protective custody of the sheriff. Instead of fleeing, he'd stolen a mountain rescue truck and followed the sheriff to his office in Grand Junction, hoping for a final chance to settle his score with Rios and Nguyen. Racked with pain, he'd waited for them to leave the office, knowing that before the night was over, he'd have the pleasure of killing them both.

Wincing as his injured fingers brushed against the truck, he was finally ready to put the contest to rest. Swaddled in the darkness of the forty-acre orchard, he moved to the front of the truck, reached in through a window, and flicked on the rack of mobile floodlights mounted on the truck's roof. Instantly the small farmhouse was awash in light. Watching for movement inside the house, he decided to wait a moment before tossing one of his grenades. There was no need to rush things. If Rios and Nguyen survived the explosion, he'd pick them off one by one as they ran from the house.

The sudden rush of floodlights had Rios spread-eagled on the floor and mumbling, "Shit!" as he moved to cover Carmen and Ket's exit. Reaching the back door, he swung it open, inched beneath the arc of light flooding the porch, and worked his way down the steps until he heard a muffled thud. Suspecting that the sound was the thump of the root-cellar door swinging back against the dirt, he froze, concerned that it had also been audible to Septian. When the floodlights rotated from the porch steps to the side of the house, he knew he was right.

Rising to one knee, he squeezed off three shots toward the light before rolling into a flower bed and onto his injured shoulder. Seconds later a new beacon of light blazed down on him. As he stood to run, a grenade exploded, demolishing the back porch and sending him flying.

Miraculously, he had taken no shrapnel. By the time he picked himself up, he was surrounded by light, and he could hear the roar of a big-block truck engine rapidly closing on him.

Searching for cover, he broke out of the light and raced toward a row of peach trees. The light followed him until the truck's engine stopped revving. When he glanced back to see the barrel of a rifle jutting from a truck window, he swallowed hard and kept running.

The tree line was less than ten yards away when a rifle shot rang out. He stumbled to one knee as the bullet slammed into the dirt inches from his leg. He continued crawling and scratching his way toward the trees as a swath of light followed him. With his injured arm throbbing and the trees so close he could smell the ripeness of their fruit, a second errant shot rang out. Expecting a third to follow, he spun to return fire, but instead of a rifle's retort, the unmistakable sound of a shotgun blast filled the air.

Staring back into the light, he saw a rifle lying on the ground next to the truck's cab. Above the rifle, a head and torso dangled out of the driver's-side window. Within seconds, Carmen and Ket moved into the light. Rising to his feet, Rios ran toward them, .45 at the ready. A few feet from the truck's front bumper, he stopped and aimed the Colt point-blank at Septian's head. Waving Rios off, Carmen said, "He's dead."

Rios lowered the gun, noticing only then that Ket stood less than five feet away, clutching her shotgun. Looping his good arm around Carmen's waist and draping the injured one over Ket's shoulder, he pulled them to him slowly.

Ket's eyes remained fixed on Septian. "Second chances, yes," she whispered, staring at the barely recognizable remains of Roland Septian's face. "But never a third."

EPILOGUE

Walker Rios flexed his injured shoulder and watched a blanket of autumn leaves drift downstream into a cut bank of the Colorado River. Enjoying the unseasonable warmth of early October, in a sleeveless T-shirt and faded khaki shorts, he made the final preparations to launch his new twelve-foot self-bailing inflatable raft.

"Sure you're up for this?" asked Warren Anderson, helping Carmen into the raft as Rios untied the moorings from a big cottonwood.

"Gotta get back on the bike when you fall off," said Rios, steadying the bow. "Figured I'd start with a tricycle and work my way up. I expect it'll take me the better part of a month."

The sheriff studied Rios's and Carmen's midsummer attire and shook his head. "Hope you both get yourself new outfits before then. You can be sure that a month from now T-shirts and shorts'll be things of the past. You'll more than likely need mukluks around here by then."

"I'll make sure I stock up," said Carmen, smiling as she adjusted their fishing gear lengthwise in the raft. "Who knows? By then we may actually be in the middle of a trial."

The sheriff laughed. "Don't bet money on it. Unlike medicine, the law trudges along pretty slow."

"You'd think they'd want to move faster on people like Kimbrough and Walls," said Carmen. "After all, they were engaged in the unthinkable: illegal and potentially catastrophic human experimentation. Not to mention the dicey little radiation con-tamination problem they caused."

"I'm afraid their lawyers see it differently. Word on the street has it they'll argue that Kimbrough was only trying to further the cause of science, and that those Navajo firefighters of his were not only aware of what he was doing, they were paid handsomely and knew about the risks. From what I've seen of how courts operate these days, the strategy could work. Espe-cially since the government's not sayin' very much about Kim-brough, his depleted uranium, or the radiation contamination problem he caused. Makes you suspect some folks in Washing-ton would like to keep a few of Kimbrough's research secrets tucked away for a rainy day. They've confiscated all his records, you know, and offered immunity to Rebecca Ellerby, that research tech of his. Could be the fix is in."

"Let's hope you're wrong," said Carmen, so agitated she began twisting in her seat.

"Easy," said Rios, now in the water and grasping a pontoon with one hand. "It may feel like summer, but you don't want to swim."

"Sorry. I just can't believe what Warren's saying. There's no way the government would let Kimbrough off scott-free."

"At least they're behind bars," Rios said with a shrug.

"Only because of charges that they attempted to explode a nuclear device," said the sheriff. "There's no bond for crimes like that. You can be sure they'd be walking the streets right now if all they'd done was set a forest fire and torch a few unsuspecting Indians."

"But Kimbrough killed a man—that research associate of his, Tangay," Carmen said, shaking her head in disbelief.

"From what I hear, the homicide boys in Denver are having a tough time proving that," said the sheriff. "Their best witness against Kimbrough is Walker's friend, Flora Jean, and so far everything she's delivered linking Kimbrough to the crime falls into the realm of what the law calls 'circumstantial.'"

"I don't believe it," said Carmen, pounding the rubber pontoon with her fist.

"Don't worry. In the end, Flora Jean's testimony will nail him," said Rios, barely causing a ripple as he slipped into the boat. Grasping the oars, he planted them in the rocky river bottom and steadied the raft.

"How?" said Carmen.

"Motive, opportunity, and the knowledge that the base of a microscope can be one hell of a lethal weapon. If Flora Jean can't place him at the murder site, she'll cloak him in enough suspicion to get a jury to convict. She was an intelligence operative, remember?"

"I hope so," said Carmen. "And what about Walls?"

"He'll fare worse. The government doesn't take kindly to military types stealing classified materials. Trust me, he'll never see the light of day. Ready?"

"Yes."

Pushing out from the shallows, Rios called out to the sheriff, "Catch you downstream at the takeout." The boat moved quickly into the river's main current.

"You're pretty good," said Carmen, giving the sheriff one last wave.

"We'll see. It's four and a half miles to takeout. Far enough to test my arm." He rotated the oars in and out of the water, establishing a rhythm, taking deep breaths. All the while, Carmen eyed the long scar running across his shoulder and down his forearm.

"How's the arm?"

"Feels good."

"Let me know if it starts to hurt."

"Sure thing, Doc. But right now it's not my arm I'm worried about."

Carmen frowned, sensing what was coming. "Walker, please, it's in the past. You can't bring the boy back."

"I keep telling myself that, but something inside my head

keeps resisting. Funny how our heat shock odyssey served to mask the guilt."

"Wounds take time to heal," said Carmen, leaning forward and rubbing Rios's arm. "Sometimes the ones we can't see take even longer."

"I know," said Rios, reminding himself that Carmen had psychological scars of her own. His expression turned pensive as he tried to imagine a terrified five-year-old caught in the chaos of My Lai. "Guess some scars remain forever."

"You learn to deal with them," said Carmen, watching his T-shirt sink into a divot in the deltoid muscle, just below his shoulder blade, each time he began a stroke.

"Guess so," said Rios, raising the oars and letting the current take over. "Speaking of coping, what about Ket? Any lingering problems from what happened with Septian?"

"None that I can see. Even if there were, she'd never admit to it. She's always been able to insulate herself that way."

"And you?"

Carmen shook her head. "I've told you before, I'm tougher than I look."

"Tough enough to leave emergency medicine behind and get back into oncology where you belong?"

"Tough enough to take over Betty Flamio's research lab when she retires in six months. I'll be leaving my ER position in three weeks. Maybe this time around I'll find a cure for leukemia." Carmen's expression saddened. "You know, Stone's been dead now for almost a month."

Rios didn't answer. Instead he snapped a crisp salute skyward and smiled. After a moment of silence, he said, "You've been holding out on me. You never mentioned taking over Flamio's lab. And in six months, no less. Sounds like she's really pushed her retirement up. Question is, what do you plan to do until then?"

"Don't know for sure. Help Ket with the orchard. Spruce up Stone's place. Testify in court . . ." Carmen's voice trailed off. "Look for my father . . ."

"Your father?" said Rios, slipping forward in his seat.

"He's here in the States," she said with a slight hint of guilt.

"The way you've always talked about him, I thought he'd been killed during the war."

"No. Just sort of erased."

Rios dragged the right oar, easing them around a boulder, then looked Carmen in the eye. "Where is he?"

"It's something to discuss later, Walker. Right now, the immediate man problem in my life happens to be you."

Rios shook his head in protest. "I'm easy enough to keep on the straight and narrow."

"That's not what I've been told by Flora Jean. We've talked a lot, you know."

"Sometimes she gets confused," said Rios, wondering just how candid Flora Jean had been.

Carmen laughed. "Don't worry, she's in your corner, and surprisingly, in a way she's a lot like Ket."

"How's that?"

"She claims that sometimes it's tragedy that affords us our second chances in life."

"I think she's right," said Rios, surprising Carmen by slipping both oars back into the boat. Aware that he'd caught her off guard, he pulled her toward him and kissed her speechless.

"We'll drift off course," she protested at last.

"No way. We're on automatic pilot," said Rios as the boat continued drifting in the lazy current, bearing them slowly downstream, ever closer to home.